I0731837

THE PROTECTOR'S VICTORY

BOOK SEVEN OF THE TALES OF CALEDONIA

PETER WACHT

The Protector's Victory
By Peter Wacht

Book 7 of The Tales of Caledonia

This book is a work of fiction. Names, characters, places, and incidents are the product of the author's imagination or are used fictitiously. Any resemblance to actual events, locales, or persons, living or dead, is coincidental.

Copyright 2023 © by Peter Wacht

Cover design by Ebooklaunch.com

All rights reserved. In accordance with the U.S. Copyright Act of 1976, the scanning, uploading, and electronic sharing of any part of this book without the permission of the publisher constitute unlawful piracy and theft of the author's intellectual property.

Published in the United States by Kestrel Media Group LLC.

ISBN: 978-1-950236-31-2

eBook ISBN: 978-1-950236-30-5

Library of Congress Control Number: 2022917276

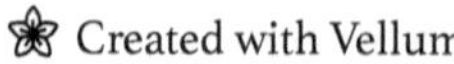 Created with Vellum

ALSO BY PETER WACHT

THE REALMS OF THE TALENT AND THE CURSE

THE TALES OF CALEDONIA

Blood on the White Sand (short story)*

The Diamond Thief (short story)*

The Protector

The Protector's Quest

The Protector's Vengeance

The Protector's Sacrifice

The Protector's Reckoning

The Protector's Resolve

The Protector's Victory

THE TALES OF THE TERRITORIES

Stalking the Blood Ruby (short story)*

A Fate Worse Than Death (short story)*

Death on the Burnt Ocean (Forthcoming 2023)

Monsters in the Mist (Forthcoming 2023)

The Dance of the Daggers (Forthcoming 2023)

Bloody Hunt for Freedom (Forthcoming 2024)

THE SYLVAN CHRONICLES

(Complete 9-Book Series available at Amazon)

The Legend of the Kestrel

The Call of the Sylvana

The Raptor of the Highlands

The Makings of a Warrior

The Lord of the Highlands

The Lost Kestrel Found

The Claiming of the Highlands

The Fight Against the Dark

The Defender of the Light

THE RISE OF THE SYLVAN WARRIORS

*Through the Knife's Edge (short story)**

* Free short stories can be downloaded from my author website at PeterWachtBooks.com.

YOUR FREE SHORT STORY IS WAITING

THE DIAMOND THIEF

This short story is a prelude to the events in my series *The Tales of Caledonia* and is free to readers who receive my newsletter.

Join Peter's newsletter and get your FREE short story.
PeterWachtBooks.com

SETTING THE STAGE

The Protector's Victory, Book 7 of *The Tales of Caledonia*, is set more than one thousand years before the events that occur in *The Sylvan Chronicles* and takes place in a separate land of *The Realms of the Talent and the Curse*. Caledonia, though a monarchy, functions more like a loose confederation of Duchies, even more so now that the King of Caledonia, Marden Beleron, has met his end in the Pit at the hands of the Volkun.

During this time some of the more adventurous and grasping members of the Caledonian nobility accepted King Corinthus Beleron's territorial grants and begin to colonize the Territories far to the west on the other side of the Burnt Ocean. These Territories will eventually become the Kingdoms of *The Sylvan Chronicles*.

In Caledonia, as in the other realms, the ability to use the Talent sets apart the person gifted with this unique skill. But being able to use the Talent is only part of the dynamic. For if a Magus chooses to follow a darker path, the Talent becomes the Curse.

1

TIRING OF THE GAME

Bryen stepped to the side just in time, pivoting away, the blackened steel of the Ghoule's spear sliding through the space he'd been standing in just an instant before. He slipped to the side again, avoiding another lunge, staying on his toes, always moving. Then one more time, bending backward so that the Ghoule's spear stabbed just short of his face, Bryen gaining a much too close view of the sharpened tip.

Tiring of the game, knowing that allowing the Ghoule to control the rhythm of the combat would only hurt him in the end, Bryen infused the double blades of the Spear of the Magii with the Talent as he spun away from the beast one more time. Sensing what his opponent was going to do next, he jabbed backward with a short thrust, hearing a pleasing grunt of pain, the sound telling him that he had hit his mark, the spear dipping in his hands as the beast began to droop toward the ground, his life counted in seconds.

Ripping the blazing steel out of the Ghoule's gut, the nauseating yet satisfying stench of burning meat hitting his nostrils, Bryen ducked, a large claw passing over his head. The lethal swing missed him by no more than a hair, one daggerlike finger actually cutting neatly across the side of his brow. Ignoring the trickle of blood that flowed down the side of his face, Bryen jumped over the spear the frustrated Ghoule swung at his knees.

The massive Ghoule – the beast was well over eight feet tall – was fast. Really fast. Almost as fast as Bryen was. Even so, speed rarely compensated for bad decisions.

By allowing his uncontrollable drive to kill Bryen to rule his thoughts, giving little consideration to the need to defend against a counterstroke, the beast had overextended, never believing that he might miss. Bryen was more than happy to show him the error of his ways.

With the Ghoule off balance, Bryen, with an economy of motion, only really having to flick his wrists, slashed swiftly with his Spear, the top blade cutting right through the beast's wrist, a spurt of blood erupting from the wound as the blazing steel sliced through flesh and bone. The sword, claw still holding the hilt, clattered to the stone.

Before the badly wounded Ghoule could even scream, Bryen finished the beast, continuing his initial motion and bringing the lower blade up and then across the Ghoule's throat, the beast's head falling not too far from the severed claw, the body crumpling to the smooth grey rock, a thick black blood bubbling out from the clean cut across his neck.

"You do not belong here, Protector," hissed a voice from just above him. "This is the center of my power. I rule here!"

Bryen stepped back then, finally having a few seconds to get a better look at his surroundings. He hadn't had the chance to do so before.

How he had gotten there was a mystery to him. As soon as he opened his eyes, the massive Ghoule attacked him, the speed of the assault so swift that he gave little thought to where he was or what he was doing, allowing his instincts to govern his decisions as he defended himself.

What was this place?

He had been asleep in a borrowed bedroll behind a tent that had been erected next to one of the snowdrifts lining the Winter Pass.

How had he gotten here, wherever here was?

Had he somehow made use of the Talent while he slept?

Now that he had a brief moment to think, he began to understand. It was all making a strange kind of sense.

It had to be the Seventh Stone. The artifact had done this to him before, seeking to help him learn about the challenges he would need to overcome in reconstructing the Weir by actually taking him to the Sanctuary in his dreams.

But was this a dream or was it something more?

Bryen stood at the very edge of a large square space, what he realized was actually the top of a truncated pyramid. Roughly crafted, worn and chipped steps ran down the four sides to the bottom, which was several hundred feet below. Beyond that, he couldn't see much at all. A wispy grey haze blocked his gaze, though every so often he glimpsed through the swirling mist a sprawling city just beyond the massive plaza that surrounded the ancient structure.

Looking back across the top of the pyramid, a large stone slab sat perfectly centered on the dull grey stone. Carved columns, pitted and worn, stood like silent sentinels around the outside of the summit, a large dome with a hole in the very center that aligned with the stone slab set on top of them.

Right in front of the altar stood three very large Ghoules, much like the two he had just dispatched. Although the beasts held their spears at the ready, strangely, the Ghoules looked at him more with a hint of curiosity than hunger, which was a rare occurrence. Bryen could only assume that these Ghoules had yet to face a human who could match their own martial skills, so he had captured their interest, the beasts likely trying to determine how he had eliminated two of their brethren at the cost of only a scratch.

Behind the Ghoules, twisting in and out of the ancient columns, was a billowing black cloud that seemed to have a mind of its own, the mist failing to obey the demands of the wind that blew steadily across the top of the pyramid from west to east.

He knew where he was now. There was no other answer.

The Temple of the Ghoules.

He had never been here before. Even so, he knew that he was right. This was, indeed, the center of Ghoule power. The fortress of the Ghoule Overlord and, perhaps more important, the source of the Lost Land's Dark Magic.

That could only mean that the swirling black fog was the Curse, the power once contained in the black diamond, the power that had corrupted the people who had once lived in this land and become the Ghoules, the twisted power that had set the beasts on a path of conquest and slaughter.

It seemed so long ago, yet it was only just yesterday that Bryen had defeated the Ghoule Overlord in the Sanctuary, eliminating the Curse's host. Bryen had realized then that even with all the power that the Master of the Lost Land exercised north of the Shattered Peaks, that's all that the Ghoule Overlord was. A physical manifestation of the Curse. A container, a puppet, for the Dark Magic of the Lost Land.

Still, that didn't reduce the peril that he and Caledonia faced in any way.

Bryen had come to understand that even though he had killed the Ghoule Overlord, destroying the Dark Magic's vessel, he had not destroyed the Curse itself. Doing that, removing this corrupt evil from the Lost Land, was the only way that he could ensure the safety of Caledonia.

So he had no choice. His task was not yet complete.

He had to destroy the Curse.

Even with the rebuilt Weir that he had constructed with the help and guidance of the Ten Magii, the Curse could not be contained. If he did not do what was required, the Curse would contaminate Caledonia just as it did the inhabitants of the Lost Land. Bryen was certain of that.

It was inescapable. Because just like its Ghoules, the Curse was insatiable. Its thirst for power, for control, unquenchable and always driving it forward.

"You will die here, Protector," hissed the voice just above Bryen, the black mist punching in and out of the pillars, teasing him, taunting him, coaxing him, "and in your death I will be reborn. I will kill everyone you love. I will take Caledonia and make it mine, and then from there I will take the world. But first I will take you. I will make you mine, what I need you to be." The mist twisted through the columns faster and faster, appearing agitated, angry, unfulfilled, as if its patience was being tested. "You do not have the power to stop me, Protector. Even with the Seventh Stone, you cannot defeat me. In the end, you will have no choice. You will serve me."

Bryen heard the truth in the Curse's words, chilling him to his core, and understanding the grim reality of what would happen if the Curse consumed him.

He thought that he had saved Caledonia. He thought that he had won.

He hadn't.

He had only delayed the inevitable.

So many of his friends, so many gladiators in the Blood Company, so many soldiers in the various Guards, had died for him.

Sirius had died for him.

Yet the true threat, the more dangerous threat, to Caledonia remained.

Bryen had failed them.

That thought almost crushed his spirit, filling him with an angst that threatened to freeze him in place.

He had done what was needed. He had accomplished what was supposed to be impossible.

He had rebuilt the Weir.

Still, it wasn't enough. More was required of him, because he was likely the only one who could challenge the Curse. The only one likely to have any chance at all of destroying the Curse.

Bryen was pulled from his debilitating thoughts when the black mist surged out from between the columns, hovering right above the stone slab. The fog began to take shape, Bryen's eyes widening in disbelief.

Floating above the altar wasn't the Ghoule Overlord as he thought would be the case.

No, it was something far worse.

A terrifying image.

It was him.

A confirmation of what Bryen feared the most. A confirmation of a niggling suspicion that had teased him since he left the Sanctuary.

The Curse wanted him as its next host.

Bryen closed his eyes for just a moment, taking a deep breath, seeking to control his growing fury at this new fate.

He couldn't let it happen. He wouldn't let it happen.

Feeling the need to strike out, his rage mimicking the white-hot energy of the Talent, Bryen drew on the power of the Seventh Stone, the blades of the Spear of the Magii glowing brighter than a bolt of lightning. Two streams of power shot straight at the Curse.

At the image of himself.

At what the Curse wanted to make of him.

He needed to destroy the Dark Magic. He needed to destroy himself.

Before he could determine the result of his efforts, in a flash of blinding light, the Temple of the Ghoules vanished and with it the Curse. Yet right before the dream that wasn't a dream disappeared, Bryen caught a glimpse of his image laughing at him. Mocking him for his naivete, for him believing that he could actually do something about the destiny in store for him.

"You need to be careful, Bryen," said a voice right at his side. "Even with the Seventh Stone, the Ghoule Overlord holds the advantage over you in the Lost Land. Whether you are there in body or spirit, it doesn't matter."

Bryen blinked a few times, clearing the spots from his eyes. He was back on more familiar ground. The Sanctuary. The carved out hollow in which six of the Seven Stones rested on their pedestals, streams of unwavering power shooting from each one -- emerald, ruby, black opal, white pearl, sapphire, jade -- into the air, the kaleidoscope of energy forming the Weir.

"The Ghoule Overlord isn't really the Ghoule Overlord," said Bryen, understanding finally what he was truly up against.

He turned to face the shimmering figure who was just as tall as he was and had a very similar frame, lean, muscular. The only real difference between them was the hair, Bryen's white with a few flecks of brown mixed in, the spirit's a light brown. That and the scars that marred Bryen's cheek and neck.

Bryen lifted his hand to his brow. The trickle of blood had slowed, though still had not come to a stop. Reaching for a thin stream of the Talent, Bryen applied the natural magic of the world to the slash, the flow of blood ending as the wound healed, leaving behind nothing more than a thin scar that would only be visible when the light hit it a certain way. Just another mark on his body to add to all the others.

Courtesy of a dream that was more than a dream.

"He is and he isn't," corrected Viktor Keldragan. "In that you're right."

"Now you sound like Sirius," said Bryen, immediately regretting what he had said as soon as the words left his mouth, a feeling of loss and a pang of guilt surging through him. He could only imagine what Viktor must be feeling. Sirius had been a complicated man, but a good man, and he was Viktor's brother. He had been Bryen's grandfather, although he had never really known him as such. If not for Sirius' sacrifice, Bryen and the Ten Magii never would have succeeded in rebuilding the Weir. "I'm sorry. I shouldn't have said that."

"It's all right," replied Viktor, placing a misty hand on Bryen's arm. "You're absolutely right, nephew. It's exactly something that Sirius would say."

Bryen nodded, silent, thankful for Viktor's understanding.

"It's just unfortunate that he's not here to tease anymore," continued Viktor. "He was always so serious, it was so easy to get him going."

Bryen smiled then. "It was, wasn't it? Sometimes you could set him off with just a look."

Viktor chuckled at that, remembering several instances of that occurring when he and his brother were growing up. "Indeed, you're right. You didn't have to be doing something wrong to raise his ire. He simply had to think that you were doing it." He allowed those pleasant memories to wash over him for a few seconds more. Then his expression turned serious. "Don't feel guilty for his death. It was not your fault."

"Easier said than done," replied Bryen softly.

"Sirius died doing what he knew was necessary. He died doing what he believed was right. He died doing what he wanted to do. In fact, I can't think of a better way for him to go to the other side than to do so in a combat against the Ghoule Overlord. It was his choice. It was his right. Don't take that away from him."

"I'll try," promised Bryen, nodding. He understood what Viktor was telling him. And, in truth, a small part of him agreed with his uncle. Still, his guilt and grief made it difficult for him to believe and accept what his uncle told him.

Knowing that it would take his nephew time to adopt a more honest perspective on what had occurred during the rebuilding of the Weir, one not colored by remorse, Viktor moved back to the topic that had brought them together in the Sanctuary.

"As I was saying, the Ghoule Overlord is the Ghoule Overlord, but the Curse is much more than the Ghoule Overlord. It is not restricted to the Natural World. Boundaries hold no meaning for that scourge. It runs rampant where it chooses."

"How so?"

"Just as you are the Seventh Stone and the Seventh Stone is you, the Ghoule Overlord is the Curse and the Curse is the Ghoule Overlord. It's easiest to think of the Curse as an essence that's alive, an evil miasma with a sentience all its own, regardless of whether it is constrained by the flesh of the Ghoule Overlord or it is running free. The Curse is the Talent in its worst possible form. No matter how much we hate it, we can't ignore the fact that it's a part of our world. It will always be a part of our world. Though we may be able to restrict the Curse's power, the Curse will always seek a way around whatever barriers we try to place around it, and more often than not it will succeed. It is inevitable."

Bryen thought about what Viktor had said for a moment, watching with a great deal of pleasure as the energy contained within the Seven Stones flowed without a flicker or flash in sight into the barricade that would keep Caledonia safe from the creatures of the Lost Land.

But that wasn't entirely true, was it?

Based on what Viktor was saying, the Weir could keep the Ghoules from Caledonia, but not the Curse. The Curse would find a way past the Weir. It already had in the form of Tetric and the other incidents of Dark Magic that blackened the history of the Kingdom, the several times that the members of the Order of the Magii needed to combat those peers who had chosen a darker path.

The Curse would find a way to take Caledonia, whether through the Ghoules or in some other manner. That meant it would find a way to take him.

"So my work isn't done," Bryen concluded, having already figured it out but needing to say it to confirm it in his own mind.

"Unfortunately not," agreed Viktor, "assuming, of course, that you would want to take on this additional challenge."

"You say it as if I have a choice."

"My apologies," chuckled Viktor. "I was simply trying to soften the blow."

Bryen nodded, accepting his uncle's apology. "So the only way to ensure the safety of Caledonia is to destroy the Curse."

"That's correct."

"Can that even be done?" asked Bryen. "If the Curse is like the Talent, how can you destroy something so powerful? Something so omnipresent? It doesn't seem possible."

Viktor thought about Bryen's question for a time, clearly in no rush to answer, because he wasn't really certain himself. All he could do was offer a mix of fact and conjecture, and even then it was weighted more toward the side of the latter.

"With the Seventh Stone, theoretically, yes. It can be done. You can destroy the Curse."

"Theoretically?" asked Bryen. He really did feel as if he was engaging in a conversation with Sirius, though he kept that belief to himself this time.

Viktor shrugged his shoulders, an apologetic look on his face. "I will speak more with the other Magii. Unfortunately, that's the best answer I can give you at present."

"What about practically? Theory means little when it comes to challenging the Curse."

"I just don't know," sighed Viktor. "I will talk with Mikayla and the others. Perhaps they will be able to share more than I can."

Bryen nodded, thanking him for that. He felt as if he was right back where he had started when Sirius and Rafia had begun badgering him to take responsibility for reconstructing the Weir. An almost impossible task with no clear outcome, other than the likelihood of his own death.

So much had changed in the last few days. Then again, so much hadn't.

Destroying the Curse couldn't be easier than rebuilding the Weir. In fact, based on what he had just experienced at the Temple of the Ghoules, he had no doubt that it was several magnitudes more difficult with the expected outcome much the same and much more certain.

Just as always happened when Bryen was faced with a difficult choice, a choice that wasn't really a choice actually, Declan's words played through his mind. Words that now were beginning to gnaw at him.

"You must do what you must do."

Bryen shook his head in resignation, feeling slightly sorry for himself.

Why was he always the one who needed to do the doing?

Embarrassed, he crushed that emotion immediately. As always, regardless of how he felt, the truth in Declan's words couldn't be denied.

The Ghoule Overlord had wanted him. The Ghoule Overlord had wanted the Seventh Stone so that he could destroy the Weir.

But now as Bryen thought about it, his mind opening to the broader possibilities, the image of himself that the Curse had formed above the altar stuck in his head, he realized that the Curse actually had wanted him for another reason altogether.

Bryen would be the perfect host. Combining the power of

the Seventh Stone with the Dark Magic of the Lost Land, the Curse embodied within him would be unstoppable.

But it wouldn't be him.

He would be the Curse, and the Curse would be him. They would be one.

The Curse would rule him. He would be a slave once more.

So just as always Bryen really didn't have any choice at all.

As Viktor and the Sanctuary began to fade away and Bryen slipped back into his fitful slumber, he realized that he was really getting tired of Declan's sayings. And he was really getting tired of these dreams that were more than dreams.

2

MANIFESTATION OF THE CURSE

"Do you have any proof?" asked Aislinn. "Any real evidence? Anything tangible?"

"Nothing substantial. No more than just a belief. Just what I saw and heard in the Sanctuary after I killed the Ghoule Overlord, or rather destroyed his body. And then just what I saw in my dreams."

"In your dreams?" she asked, her tone suggesting a faint hint of disbelief.

"Yes, in my dreams."

"Why would you have faith in your dreams?"

"Because dreams aren't always dreams. Sometimes there's little difference between what's real and what's a dream."

He touched the thin black scar that ran through the larger scars marring his cheek and his neck to make his point, those wider marks a constant reminder of what happened if you allowed your concentration to lapse, even for just a few seconds. A lesson that he had taken to heart in the Pit and beyond.

Aislinn nodded, really not in a position to argue with him. When Bryen finally had told her how he had gotten that burn that never faded, she had believed him. It had made too much sense. Nevertheless, she had been curious, so she had asked Rafia about it.

The Magus had confirmed what Bryen had said, noting that it was a rare skill, to be awake in a dream. A dangerous one as well. Because if you brought so much of yourself into a dream, what happened in the dream would have the same effect as if it was occurring in real life.

You could die in the Spirit World just as if you were in the Natural World. Something that Bryen had escaped by the skin of his cheek when he faced off against the Ghoule Overlord for the first time.

Aislinn and Bryen had just emerged from the medical tents that had been set up for the wounded, finding some rocks off to the side that allowed them to sit for the first time since the sun had risen and rest for a few minutes. They had spent most of the day there, both catching only a few hours of sleep during the early morning. Although Aislinn doubted Bryen had slept much at all the night before if he had entered more fully than he should have the world of dreams.

They were both exhausted, and it showed. They had come straight from the Sanctuary, having no time to recover. Before that they had no rest because of the chase through the tunnel and then across the floor of the Trench to the sandstone pillar upon which the Sanctuary was built. From there they jumped right into the fight in the Winter Pass after flying across the continent on the backs of their Griffons, joining their fellow Magii in their efforts to eliminate the Elder Ghoules from the battlefield.

When that task was complete, they had then turned their attention to the Ghoules. The beasts had held for a time, retreating slowly back up the Winter Pass, only fleeing to the north once they realized that they had lost the only defense they had that could protect them from the Magii's unwavering ferocity.

Then, for most of the late afternoon and well into the night, Bryen and Aislinn had joined the many other Magii with skill in healing to help as many of the soldiers wounded in the battle as they could. This addition of several dozen physicks versed in the Talent to the ranks of the Caledonian Army had proven fortuitous.

The Caledonians had won the battle, and a great many lives also were saved, thanks to the timely arrival of the Griffons and the Magii.

Even so, the victory came at a great cost. It had been a bloody encounter, and unfortunately there was little that the Magii could do for some of the soldiers struck by the Curse. It seemed that only Bryen and Rafia had any real ability to heal the worst of the wounds caused by the Elders' Dark Magic, and even that proved to be a struggle for them depending on how far the Curse had progressed.

"Let's think this through," continued Aislinn. "You watched his body turn to ash, yet you think that he may have survived somehow, correct?"

"I'm not sure," Bryen replied, a touch of uncertainty in his voice.

"You're not sure? You're not sure that you killed the Ghoule Overlord?"

"I did kill the Ghoule Overlord, but it's not that simple. There's more to this story than just flesh and blood."

"So what you're saying is that there is the living Ghoule Overlord and then there's the living Curse."

"Yes, that's a good way to put it."

"What do you mean specifically by that?" asked Aislinn, thinking through the ramifications of what Bryen was saying, about what the consequences would be if there was a separation between the two. "If I'm understanding correctly, you're implying that the Curse isn't just a power, a corrupt power, it's also an entity all on its own. Some kind of sentient being."

Bryen raised his hands, asking for patience. It had been a long last few days and nights. He knew that they were both tired and easily irritated. So to avoid the last, he decided to start fresh, hoping that what he said provided the clarity that was required.

"Yes, you're explaining it all better than I am. As you're suggesting, I believe that there is more to the Ghoule Overlord than just his flesh. There is the body and the spirit, and the two can be one or they can be distinct because the body is just a shell for the Curse, just as Tetric became a shell for the Ghoule Overlord during the uprising. The true essence, the true power, of the Ghoule Overlord is the spirit. Even so, the spirit of the Ghoule Overlord isn't the Ghoule Overlord. The spirit of the Ghoule Overlord, the power that drives his thoughts, decisions, and actions, is the Curse. The Ghoule Overlord is simply a physical manifestation of the Curse. A tool to be used, nothing more."

"That's quite a lot to take in and doesn't bode well for us," said Aislinn, her sharp mind working through what her Protector had just told her.

"I know."

"So in the Sanctuary you killed the Ghoule Overlord. The host for the Curse."

"I know I did. I watched it happen with my own eyes."

"But the spirit of the Ghoule Overlord – the source of power, the Curse itself – survived."

"Yes, after I killed the Ghoule Overlord, or rather destroyed the vessel the Curse was using to achieve its objectives, the Curse escaped when the black diamond dissolved."

"Diamonds just don't dissolve," murmured Aislinn, more for herself than Bryen, trying to wrap her brain around what Bryen was explaining to her.

"This one did, just as the Seventh Stone did when it merged with me. Twice."

Aislinn took a moment to think about what Bryen was saying. There was a certain kind of logic to it all, though she really wished they had some kind of proof. She preferred confirmable fact to speculation, but with the Talent and the Curse there was little to be had with either.

Having no choice but to acknowledge that truth, who was she to say what was and wasn't possible? It would be foolish after all that she had seen and experienced in just the last year.

"I want to make sure that I understand. Tell me again what you saw."

"During the combat with the Ghoule Overlord, I broke his staff," explained Bryen. "The black diamond slipped from the top of the black ash and shattered on top of the pedestal."

"Right, but that ..."

"But that doesn't mean anything, I know. What happened next does. When I killed the Ghoule Overlord, or rather when I destroyed his body, or what was actually the Curse's shell, the broken pieces of the diamond transformed into a black mist that blasted through the Weir and back into the Lost Land, probably back to the Temple of the Ghoules."

"The Temple of the Ghoules?" asked Aislinn. What happened with the black diamond certainly was possible -- again, she wasn't in a position to say what could and could not happen, especially not after her Protector's experience with the Seventh Stone -- but she had no knowledge of the Temple of the Ghoules.

"Yes, it's the source of the Curse in the Lost Land. Or it could just be where it resides. I'm not sure entirely. I need to find out more about the Curse before I can say for certain."

Bryen answered with such confidence. She wanted to believe him. Yet, how could he know where the Curse came from? And how could he know about such a place as the

Temple of the Ghoules? No one had ever survived a trip into the Lost Land? No one but …

Aislinn lifted her head, her eyes widening as she began to understand from where Bryen might be getting his insights. Bryen had said that his conclusion was based not only on what he had seen, but also on what he had heard.

"Bryen, who did you speak with in the Sanctuary when you were crafting the Weir?"

"Viktor Keldragan," replied Bryen, saying it as if it was the most natural thing in the world to speak with a Magus who had died more than a thousand years before.

A small part of Aislinn's mind found it difficult to comprehend what Bryen was suggesting. She ignored it, knowing that she needed a much broader perspective when it came to discussing the Talent and the Curse.

Bryen had explained briefly how the Ten Magii had aided him in rebuilding the Weir, and Rafia hadn't batted an eyelash after he had explained it all. So if the Keeper of Haven believed what her Protector had said, she could try to do so as well.

"What did he say?"

"We were discussing the power that the Ghoule Overlord exercised," said Bryen. "I'll never forget what he said. 'Even with the power he can manipulate, the Ghoule Overlord has lived a long time because of that power, but I expect that he has forgotten that the power that he controls is also controlling him. He is not a master of the Curse. The Curse is the master of him. Just as you are a host for the Seventh Stone, he is a host for the Curse, and right now the Seventh Stone is the stronger master.'"

Aislinn thought about that. There was a symmetry to the statement that her analytical mind appreciated. "What did he mean by host for the Curse?"

"My guess?"

"Yes, your best guess."

"That the Ghoule Overlord is the Curse and the Curse is the Ghoule Overlord. As I said, I believe he is a physical manifestation of the Dark Magic of the Lost Land. However, the Curse itself, the spirit, is distinct from the flesh. The Ghoule Overlord is simply a means for the Curse to achieve its objectives in the Lost Land. The Ghoules don't obey the Ghoule Overlord. They obey the Curse. They just don't know it. Or if they do, they don't care. Or they can't do anything about it."

Aislinn nodded as she mulled his answer. It made sense, too much sense, and it was the direction that her mind had been going as well that led her to one inevitable and frightening conclusion. "The Curse survived and remains a threat to Caledonia."

"Yes, it does. I think that the Curse that was contained within the black diamond and gave the Ghoule Overlord his power returned to the Temple of the Ghoules when I destroyed the body that it had been using for the last however many centuries."

"So the black diamond, which is an artifact of the Curse, did what the Seventh Stone can do. It merged with a Ghoule to create the Ghoule Overlord, essentially an embodiment of the Curse as you explain it, just as the Seventh Stone merged with you."

"Yes, that's the theory that I'm working from right now. It's the only explanation that looking at all the various puzzle pieces gives us a chance to craft a larger whole and understand what has occurred and what could occur."

The more she thought about it, the more what Bryen was telling her made a frightening kind of sense. Then her musings returned to something that Bryen had said that had stuck in the back of her mind. "Wait a second. The Temple of the Ghoules. You said that it was ..."

"It's the seat of power for the Ghoule Overlord in the Lost

Land. It's also the bastion of the Curse. The Dark Magic of the Lost Land is centered there, comes from there."

"How do you even know about the Temple of the Ghoules? I've never even heard of it. I doubt anyone has ever heard of it. Rafia and Sirius certainly never mentioned it."

"There's a good reason for that."

"What would that be?" Aislinn asked, even though she believed that she already knew the answer. All her doubts and concerns were slowly fading away as she, too, began to fit together all the pieces.

"Because only one person has ever seen the Temple of the Ghoules," replied Bryen. "Only one person has even been there."

"Viktor Keldragan," Aislinn murmured, her confidence in Bryen's theory growing.

"Yes, my uncle went there to retrieve the Seventh Stone and steal the black diamond so that the Ten Magii could construct the Weir the first time."

"He told you about all this?"

"In part," Bryen confirmed. "He showed me a good bit of it. He shared some of his memories with me since his essence and those of the other nine Magii remain within the Seventh Stone. Remain within me now. He showed me how he navigated the Lost Land -- the route that he took and its many dangers, escaped with his prizes, and what happened when the Ten Magii built the original Weir."

"So you can retrieve those memories whenever you want?"

"No."

"Why not?"

"Viktor and the spirits of the other Magii will share information with me if they choose. If they believe it's necessary. They don't obey me. We just work together when the need arises."

"And this is all that you're going on?" asked Aislinn, who

struggled to keep the unease that remained within her from breaking free.

What Bryen was telling her made too much sense, and that's what worried her. Just because you didn't understand something didn't mean that it wasn't real. However, her hesitation came from another more personal source. Her concern for Bryen. Because if he was correct, she understood what the next step would be.

Bryen smiled. He knew that Aislinn was reaching the same conclusions that he had already. She just needed more time to digest everything and to get past her fears. But there was no reason not to be entirely honest and perhaps give her a gentle, final push over the edge. "There is something else."

"What would that be?" A tinge of trepidation tainted her voice.

The stresses and strains of the last few days, added to her growing concerns regarding what Bryen was telling her, were beginning to wear on Aislinn. She needed some sleep. This probably wasn't the best time to have this conversation. Nevertheless, it was too important not to have it now. So she took a few deep breaths, trying to control her very short temper, realizing that giving in to it now wouldn't be helpful.

"As I said, I had a dream. Two actually. One on the way here. The other early this morning. Both were very similar."

"About me?" she teased, wanting desperately to feel, if only for a moment, that she was in a normal relationship instead of one that was always colored by death and destruction.

Aislinn's comment made Bryen smile and earned her a wink. "Well, if you want to know about those dreams …"

"No. No." Aislinn waved her hands in front of her, stopping him before he could embarrass them both, her irritation gone, now replaced by resignation. "Tell me about the other dream."

Bryen took a moment to gather his thoughts. At first, he had thought that it was just a nightmare. He had dozed off while

Banshee flew to the east, away from the Sanctuary after he had reestablished the Weir and the Blood Company had defeated the Ghoules.

He had hoped that the Ghoule Overlord truly was dead. He wanted to believe that he had killed the beast, but Bryen was having a hard time convincing himself of that. The fact that one of Sirius' comments – "Hoping doesn't make it real" – kept playing through his mind didn't help matters.

"Let me do one better," Bryen replied, realizing that giving Aislinn the chance to see it for herself was much better than an incomplete recitation. "Let me show it to you."

Bryen reached for the Talent, then using the trick that he had learned from Viktor, he connected with Aislinn so that she could experience the dream just as he did.

Instantly Aislinn was transported to the Temple of the Ghoules, the stench of sulfur infusing the air, observing everything through Bryen's eyes.

He stood on top of the massive, truncated pyramid that rose several hundred feet into the air, the steps worn and pitted, running down to the expansive square surrounding the structure.

Aislinn was amazed by the clarity of it all as she took in this strange, new environment. The large slab of raised stone in the center. The dome held by soaring pillars covering the summit of the pyramid. The circular hole in the dome.

From where Bryen stood, he stared down at a city of arches and rectangles that stretched on for miles. There were no tall buildings, most appearing to be long communal structures that were separated by dry, winding canals with dozens of bridges spanning the gaps that were no longer needed. By the bridges closest to the pyramid, there were large, dark holes that dropped into the ground reminiscent of the nests of the black dragons that littered the base of the Trench.

Who knew what resided in those burrows, and Aislinn

could tell that Bryen had little desire to find out, gazing upon those shadowy enclaves making her feel distinctly uncomfortable. The temple was kept apart from the rest of the city by a huge square that must have been at least a quarter mile wide and could easily hold a hundred Ghoule Legions if not more.

Scanning beyond the outskirts of the city, the Ghoule metropolis sat in the dormant hollow of a towering volcano, which in turn rose out of a lake, the water of which appeared to steam and boil as it flowed off toward the horizon in all directions, the far shore just a distant smudge. Along the cusp of the crater, a dozen waterfalls fell off the mile-high rim.

Aislinn was taken by surprise when the Ghoule Overlord made an appearance. She almost reached for the Talent, catching herself just in time. She had to remind herself that this was Bryen's dream. She was simply observing, experiencing what he did.

"I see you, Protector," said the Ghoule Overlord. The beast revealed himself atop the pyramid just on the other side of the altar, stepping out from between the pillars. "Again. No matter what I do I can't seem to get rid of you."

"I wouldn't think that you'd want to get rid of me. I thought you wanted the Seventh Stone. You can't take the Seventh Stone until you kill me."

The Ghoule Overlord offered an evil grin, revealing his sharp teeth, his black eyes blazing with the power of the Curse. "You're right, Protector. But you're also wrong." The Ghoule Overlord leaned in closer, his shadow extending across the slab of stone. "I do want you. When the time is right, when I am done with you, I will eat your flesh. I will gnaw on your bones. All your efforts will have been for naught. I will use the Seventh Stone to destroy the Weir you constructed and open the path to Caledonia for my Legions. My Ghoules will hunt and your humans will suffer."

The certainty with which the Ghoule Overlord spoke sent a

shiver of fear through Aislinn. Even though Bryen had defeated this beast, in his dream, it appeared to have never happened at all. It was as if the Ghoule Overlord didn't know that Bryen had killed him or refused to accept that reality.

"That will be difficult for you to do now that you're dead," Bryen said.

The huge beast laughed, a horrible, teeth-rattling sound that drifted out over the dead city. "You didn't kill me, Protector. You can't kill me. You took my flesh, yes, but you did not kill me. You can't kill the Curse."

Aislinn played the monster's words over and over in her mind. All the while, Bryen stared at the Ghoule Overlord, studying the creature, fixing his gaze on the carving of the black diamond in his forehead. She hated the conclusion that she reached, what it truly meant. Nevertheless, she was certain that she was correct, having reached the same conclusion as Bryen did, his words confirming it for her.

"You're not a Ghoule. You use the Ghoules. Tools to be employed and no more than that."

The Ghoule Overlord laughed again, nodding his head. "Correct, Protector. You are smarter than I thought. I am strongest in my flesh form, although I do not need flesh to survive. I am the Curse. I am the Dark Magic that exists in all the realms of this world, more strongly in some than others. And here I am very strong. I made the Lost Land what it is. I made the Ghoules what they are. And when I am done, the human lands to the south of the Shattered Peaks will be mine as well. From there I will expand my rule, spread my Dark Magic, because that is my true purpose. To make all the realms of the world, Natural and Spirit, mine. The Curse can be defeated, though even that is rare. It can never be destroyed."

"And you need me to do that," offered Bryen. "You need to become me to do that. You need the power that only I can give you."

"Perceptive, Protector," said the Ghoule Overlord, nodding his head in agreement once more. "Yes, that's why I need you. You will be my tool for spreading the Curse. The Seventh Stone will make my work much easier. In fact, I can feel it in you right now. It's restless, the Dark Magic within you. You've done a clever job of suppressing it. Still, you won't be able to control it forever. The Curse is chaos. It cannot be restrained. It will find a way to break free. It will find a way to run wild. It always does. That's what it is. That's what it does. That's what I am."

"I've defeated you once," challenged Bryen. "What makes you think you can beat me now? You said it yourself. You're weaker when you don't have your host. You need to be flesh to access your full power. I destroyed your body. I will destroy you in your current form."

The Ghoule Overlord's black orbs flashed in anger, his clawed hand gripping the twisted black staff with the black diamond wrapped within its top just a bit tighter than usual as he struggled to control his building rage.

"You didn't defeat me, Protector. I let you win the combat. Consider it a test of sorts. To find your weaknesses."

Bryen smiled at that, sensing the lie. "And what did you discover? What are my failings?"

The Ghoule Overlord grinned evilly then, his eyes now sparkling with delight. "That you care, Protector. About your people. About your land." The Ghoule Overlord shrugged his shoulders, as if what he had just revealed actually was all too obvious. "I don't care. That's the difference between us, and that's what will lead to your death. What will lead you to me. You care about the humans fighting for you. I care nothing for my Ghoules. They are tools just as you said. They serve a purpose. They can be discarded as needed. Not so your precious humans."

"Compassion isn't a weakness," countered Bryen.

"It is the ultimate weakness!" roared the Ghoule Overlord.

"Your compassion will lead to your undoing. It is what in the end will give you to me."

With barely a flick of his staff, a stream of Dark Magic shot from the black diamond straight toward Bryen, who opened himself to the Seventh Stone and crafted a shield of energy to his front that resembled the scuta his gladiators used so effectively against the Ghoules.

Just in time. The blazing white energy deflected the threads of darkness.

Aislinn cringed within herself as the Dark Magic sped toward Bryen, sped toward her. She shouldn't have worried. The Dark Magic flailed uselessly against Bryen's shield, unable to penetrate his barrier.

She realized as well what the Ghoule Overlord was doing. The monster wasn't trying to kill Bryen. Not yet. The beast simply stood in place, studying him, satisfied to keep him pinned where he was for a few moments more.

"That is quite impressive, Protector. But it is not good enough."

The stream of Dark Magic continued to flow toward Bryen, and with another flick of his wrist the Ghoule Overlord adjusted the tainted energy's form, the Curse becoming an inky cloud that descended upon Bryen, covering him entirely so that he could see nothing but pitch black.

Bryen responded instantly by shifting the shape of his defense to a protective dome, the Talent preventing the Curse from touching him. Even in a dream, Aislinn realized that Bryen needed to avoid coming into contact with the corrupt power. Because this dream wasn't just a dream. It was much more than that.

Every so often, a sliver of evil reached out from the surrounding murk toward Bryen's shield, the two distinct energies flashing brightly whenever they came into contact, and then just as quickly the misty black drifted away.

Aislinn saw immediately what the monster was doing. The Ghoule Overlord wasn't trying to break through Bryen's barrier. The beast was trying to determine how strong he was. The Curse was attempting to determine what he needed to do to kill him.

No. Aislinn realized in an instant that she was wrong. The Curse didn't want to kill him. The Curse was trying to determine what would be needed to take ...

Aislinn felt a debilitating pain burn through Bryen, starting in his gut and working its way out to his extremities, the shock of the assault almost making Bryen drop his shield. He suffered through the torment for several agonizing seconds, barely able to hold onto the Talent. She could sense him losing control. The power was slipping through his fingers, until thankfully he was able to lock away most of his suffering just as he did the Curse within him. Bryen was thinking clearly again.

With a shiver of fear, Aislinn realized that the pain Bryen had just experienced wasn't the Ghoule Overlord attacking him. It was the Curse within him, the Dark Magic contained by the Seventh Stone choosing that moment to try to break free and rejoin its Master. How he had managed so much of that blighted evil, she didn't know.

Aislinn felt the Dark Magic slam against the barrier that Bryen had created within himself to protect against the corruption of the Curse. She marveled at his control as the Dark Magic pounded with a fast and regular rhythm against the thin barricade, desperate to gain its freedom, to break free, to claim Bryen for its own.

"As I said, Protector. I am the Curse. I am the Dark Magic of this world. You can challenge the Ghoule Overlord. But you can't challenge me. You cannot fight against the Curse, because I am already a part of you. No matter how much you might deny it, no matter what you might do to prevent it, it's too late. You already belong to me. You just don't know it yet."

Aislinn sensed the pull of the Curse intensify within Bryen, with even greater force the Dark Magic slamming faster and faster against Bryen's defenses much like a blacksmith crafting a new blade.

Aislinn experienced Bryen's rising fear, sensing how close he was to losing this terrible fight. Then she noticed a subtle shift in Bryen, his racing heart slowing, reason returning to battle the fear.

As the seconds passed everything around him, everything within him, faded away, until there was only his heartbeat. It was the only sound that Aislinn heard. An incredible ability, she believed, Bryen able to concentrate so acutely.

Once he regained control over himself, he took the next logical step. He focused on the Seventh Stone, allowing the power of the artifact free rein within him, reveling as the overwhelming amount of the Talent residing within the jewel crushed the Dark Magic, the barrier protecting him from the Curse knitting itself back together and solidifying before its prisoner could do as it wished.

When Bryen opened his eyes once again, Aislinn saw that the Ghoule Overlord had not moved, the stone slab still separating them. The beast was still as a statue, except for the slow shake of his head. His adversary's rapacious grin suggested that he had just discovered exactly what he wanted to know.

"An enjoyable diversion, Protector," rasped the Ghoule Overlord. "But I have what I need. We can continue this at a later time."

"You seem very sure of that," said Bryen. "That we will meet again."

"We will, Protector. Much sooner than you might think. You know my words are true. You can't deny them. It is getting harder for you to control the Curse. I just confirmed that. And as time goes by, it will only become more difficult for you. You want to know why, Protector?"

Bryen didn't bother to respond, simply staring at the Ghoule Overlord. Aislinn knew why, coming to that horrible realization in the blink of an eye. She already comprehended the truth, just as Bryen did. He was just reluctant to admit it to himself.

"Because you can't control me, Protector. Listen to my words, for they are the truth. I am the Curse. I am chaos. I will come for you again, and when I do you will not be able to deny me. You will be mine. You will serve me."

In a flash, Aislinn was ripped from the dream, the action disorienting, making her feel slightly ill.

"After that, the dream faded," Bryen said, locking eyes with Aislinn as he released his hold on the Talent and severed the connection between them.

"That was all of it?" asked Aislinn. "You didn't leave anything out."

"I showed you everything that happened."

"What's the city surrounding the Temple of the Ghoules called?"

"Viktor named it Mertvey Gorod, which he translated as the Dead City. The crater itself and the lake around it are known as the Cauldron."

"Show me the second dream, the one from this morning with your uncle. I want to hear what he said."

Bryen complied, using the Talent to share the memory with Aislinn so that she could listen to his conversation with Viktor. When that was complete, Aislinn reached up to his brow, running her fingers gently over his newest and most likely not his last scar.

"These dreams that are more than dreams certainly support your theory that the Ghoule Overlord is a manifestation of the Curse. That the Curse has a consciousness of its own."

"The black diamond and the Curse are no different than the

Seventh Stone and the Talent. I believe that Rafia would agree with me on that."

"She probably would," admitted Aislinn. "Your dreams are so real, terrifyingly so. But what if you're wrong? What if they were just dreams?"

"Then I'm wrong. Regardless, we still need to find a way to remove the Ghoule Legions from the Winter Pass."

"And if you're right?"

"Then we're not done. The Weir is in place. The Ghoules can't get through. But ..."

"The Ghoule Overlord can. Or rather the Curse. The Ghoule Overlord and the Curse are one and the same. And the Curse already has demonstrated that it can bypass the Weir and work its evil in Caledonia."

"Yes, the Curse, or rather the Ghoule Overlord can since he is the physical representation of the Curse. He will continue to hunt me. He will not rest until he has the Seventh Stone and he can use me as he wishes. Then he will do exactly as he said he would. He'll destroy the Weir and release the Ghoules on Caledonia."

"So if the Curse makes it back through the Weir," said Aislinn, "we don't stand much of a chance."

"Unfortunately ... correct."

"What's correct?" asked Declan, who approached with Lycia and Davin, Rafia stepping out from the medical tent just a few seconds afterwards and coming to stand behind the twins to listen.

Bryen spent the next few minutes explaining what he and Aislinn had been talking about, as well as the conclusions they had reached because of his dreams and his conversations with Viktor Keldragan.

"So let me just get this straight," cut in Davin. "You don't believe that the Ghoule Overlord is just a Ghoule. You believe that he's the corporeal representation of the Curse. A vessel for the Dark Magic of the Lost Land, nothing more. You also believe that the Curse made the Lost Land what it is, made the Ghoules what they are today. When the body of the Ghoule Overlord dies, the spirit of the Curse simply returns to the Lost Land and takes a new host. A new Ghoule is selected to become the Ghoule Overlord so that the Curse can continue its efforts to spread across the realms. Because of that, we can't stop the Ghoules unless we destroy the Dark Magic of the Lost Land. And we can't do that unless we destroy the spirit of the Ghoule Overlord, or rather we destroy the Curse itself, since those are one and the same."

"Yes," Bryen replied, shrugging his shoulders as if to say that it was just a small matter in the larger scheme of things. "That about sums it up."

Davin nodded his head a few times, letting everything that he had just said percolate in his mind.

"Great, the fun never ends," he finally replied with a wink and a nod. "But seriously, can't this monster just die?"

"You trust what you learned in your dream?" asked Declan. He had no cause not to believe Bryen, even though the rational part of his brain found it difficult to lend a great deal of credence to something that was constructed more of belief than reality. "I mean it could have been just a couple of bad dreams, lad. No more than that."

"It was too real for that, Declan," Bryen replied softly, understanding Declan's hesitation. "I've had dreams like these before. Dreams that aren't really dreams. I think they're connected to the Talent ... and also to the Curse." He admitted that last reluctantly. "I don't think I'd have them otherwise. I don't think they're dreams so much as conversations taking place in a different space. That's the best I can describe it. I'm there, and I'm not there. The Ghoule Overlord is there, but he's not there."

"And you believe this is real?" Declan asked again.

Bryen pointed to the thin, black scar on his cheek just above the other scars that ran down to his neck.

"I got this scar from the Ghoule Overlord. We fought in the Sanctuary. That happened almost a year before we actually made it to the Sanctuary to repair the Weir. I talked with him and fought with him in my dream, just as I did last night. I confirmed it all with Viktor."

"Viktor Keldragan?"

"Yes."

"How did you confirm it with the spirit of a dead Magus. That's ..." Declan looked at Bryen, taking in his serious expression, realizing that there was no point in questioning him. He just needed to get used to the fact that strange things always seemed to happen around Bryen, in large part because of the Seventh Stone and the power he facilitated. "Never mind. I don't need to know. I don't want to know."

"How will you know where to go?" asked Lycia.

She appreciated Bryen trying to explain everything to them, but she knew him too well. She understood that this conversation was more for their benefit and not his. Bryen had already decided what he was going to do, and there was no point in trying to dissuade him.

"I just know. I saw it all when I was speaking with the Ghoule Overlord. I've never been to the Lost Land, but thanks to Viktor sharing his memories with me, in my mind I can see the route he took to steal the diamonds. All of it. I know where I need to go. I know how to get there. I can navigate the Lost Land like I can navigate the Colosseum. With my eyes closed."

Declan nodded, willing to accept Bryen's reasoning. "You can't do this on your own, lad. You need help."

"I'll be going with him," said Aislinn, her tone daring anyone to challenge her.

Declan nodded again, considering. "That's a good thing. A Magus and a warrior. Two Magii, I should say, assuming you can escape your father," and before Aislinn could protest that she could do as she pleased, he raised a hand to placate her, then turned his attention back to Bryen. "The Lady of the Southern Marches is a good start, but you'll still need more help. That's why these two are here."

"Davin and Lycia?" Bryen valued what his friends brought to the table, their skills as warriors unmatched. Even so, he didn't want to put them at even greater risk than they already were. Nevertheless, he realized upon looking at his friends that they had already decided. Despite his misgivings, there was no point in trying to get them to reconsider.

"I guess having the best fighters in the Pit with me couldn't hurt. Might even help."

"Thanks for the vote of confidence," said Davin, his sarcasm apparent.

"Then it will be the four of us," Bryen said.

"Five," interrupted Rafia. "I'll be coming with you."

With the stormy look on the Magus' face, not even Declan was going to try to stop her.

3

HOPING DOESN'T MAKE IT REAL

"The question that I've been mulling is what we can reasonably expect to achieve with the resources available to us now," said Noorsin. "The arrival of several dozen Magii has changed the equation dramatically, at least for a time. We need to make use of that advantage now and for as long as we can. Although I fear it might be for a much briefer period than we would like."

She pushed her unfinished meal to the side, having invited the Blademaster, Tarin Tentillin, and Declan to join her and Kevan for dinner. They were seated across from one another at a round table set in the middle of a small pavilion that had been erected just a quarter mile from the front lines.

After the Magii had made their dramatic appearance on the backs of Griffons, decimating the Elders and forcing what was left of the Ghoule Legions back toward the Weir, Noorsin had moved their forces several leagues farther north. After so many days of desperate fighting, the Caledonian Army took a great deal of pleasure in harrying the beasts to a point where the Winter Pass tightened even more severely, which would aid their efforts to slow the Ghoule counterattack.

No one disagreed with Noorsin's assessment. Because everyone around the table knew that another attack was coming. Even with Bryen having killed the Ghoule Overlord, the Ghoule Legions that had made it into the Kingdom before the Weir took shape had only one direction to go. South, toward the Breakwater Plateau and the fertile lands of Caledonia just beyond.

Yesterday's much-deserved triumph had bolstered the spirit of the army. It was a good victory and well earned. Nevertheless, it was only one victory, and, even with the fortuitous arrival of the Magii, it still came at great cost, hundreds of soldiers losing their lives.

Their success was to be savored, though it also needed to be tempered by the fact that more Ghoule Legions even now were marching down the Pass. Based on reports from the Magii tasked with searching the Winter Pass and the Shattered Peaks to ensure that they were not taken by surprise on their flanks, the first Legion was only a few hours away and with them came several dozen more Elders.

"Quite right," agreed Tarin. "You've gone right to the heart of the matter, General Stelekel. How much longer we can hold."

"Exactly so," confirmed Noorsin.

"We've done well so far," replied Kevan, "though it hasn't been easy, and even with the Magii it will only get harder. Our soldiers are tired, and we've already lost too many to the beasts."

Jurgen Klines nodded his agreement. "The Ghoules have pushed us. Still, we've made it as difficult for them as we could. The beasts are still a good distance from the entrance to the Winter Pass now that we've advanced farther north."

"So there's a good chance that we can keep them from reaching the Breakwater Plateau if circumstances play out in our favor," continued Kevan. "There are no guarantees, I think we can all agree on that, but we can hope that more

Duchy soldiers and Magii will join us in time to bolster our forces."

"We do know thanks to Duchess Stelekel's eyes and ears that more troops are on the way ..."

"Magii as well," interjected Noorsin.

"Yes, but we also all must remember one of Sirius' favorite sayings," said Tarin, "something that he said quite frequently when he was in the Southern Marches and which I think is directly applicable to what we are discussing now."

Referencing the deceased Magus who sacrificed his life so that Bryen would have the time that he needed to resurrect the Weir brought an abrupt stop to the conversation, an uncomfortable silence settling between them. They were all saddened by the loss of the Magus.

Yet none of them could focus on that right now, not when more immediate issues needed to be addressed. Not when so many other Caledonians had given their lives during the last few weeks and so many more would in the weeks to come. At the right time Sirius would be mourned.

"Hoping doesn't make it real," replied Noorsin quietly after a few minutes had passed, her eyes watering as she said it. "Tarin is correct. I can't deny that. Hope can only take us so far. But right now all we have is hope. Hope that the Protector can accomplish the impossible task that he's set for himself. Hope that we can hold long enough for the reinforcements to reach us in time. Hope that we won't be overrun by the Ghoules. Right now, I'd rather focus on hope, because our reality is quite grim."

"Fair enough," replied Tarin.

"And do you believe in what the Volkun has told us?" asked Klines. "Why he believes he needs to do this? Any rational person would view his argument with a healthy dose of skepticism."

"I have no reason to disbelieve him," said Declan.

"Nor do I," replied Tarin. "The Protector has been right so far about a great many things. Besides, Magus Rafia clearly supports what he wants to do." Tarin shrugged his shoulders as if to say they really had no choice in the matter. They had no way to stop the Protector from doing what he believed was necessary. "He has done everything that's been demanded of him, even when the likely result was his own death. He has not been wrong yet. He has not failed yet. So I'd rather place my hope in him as well. Perhaps if we give him our hope, he can create a new reality for us."

"That would be an excellent consequence of the Protector's efforts, although I won't be holding my breath," said Kevan. "Besides, regardless of whether the Protector is right or not, we have Ghoules here that need to be stopped, Curse or no."

"Nor should you," agreed Noorsin. "We can hope that Bryen achieves the goal he has set for himself. While he's doing that, we need to concentrate on what we need to accomplish here."

"I agree. If we're going to succeed in our current endeavors, we must control the environment," added Kevan. "Like Tarin did when fighting the Ghoule packs in the Southern Marches. Like we've been trying to do here. It's the only way to buy the time that we need."

Tarin used the opening provided by the Duke of the Southern Marches to offer his suggested approach for preventing the Ghoule Legions from pushing farther south, focusing in particular on the formations and tactics that had proven most effective against the Ghoules in the past and a few that he believed would work in the current landscape. He knew that what he was proposing would only work for so long. Even with the additional Magii, even with the additional soldiers coming their way, they couldn't stop the Ghoules entirely. Not with the strength the beasts were bringing to bear. Rather, they could only hope to slow the Ghoules down, which at the moment was a reasonable objective.

"We've already implemented several of these approaches," concluded Tarin. "They've proven their value, and they've stood the test of time."

"This is the Protector again?" asked the Blademaster.

"Yes, it's his strategy that we continue to refine," answered Tarin. "The Ghoules have been adjusting their approach in response to our tactics, so we adjust as well. We need to stay one step ahead of them."

"A quite competent young man," murmured the Blademaster.

"Dangerously competent," agreed Tarin, "and the best fighter that I've ever seen."

"We still need to deal with the Elder Ghoules," said Declan. "What Tarin is suggesting can work for a time, but we need a way to defend against the Elders. Without that, we won't stand a chance."

"We'll assign a Magus to each company," replied Noorsin.

"Do we have enough Magii to do that?" asked Klines.

"For now, we should," said Noorsin. "Of course, there are no guarantees as to how long that will last."

They had already lost several members of the Order of the Magii fighting the Elders, the beasts not only skilled in the use of the Curse, but also benefiting from more experience in applying their tainted energy for deadly purposes. Many of the Magii had not done so for centuries, some never having been called upon to employ the Talent in a lethal manner.

"A suggestion?" asked the Blademaster.

"Of course," nodded Noorsin.

"There seems to be no lack of Elders. All of them trained to use their Dark Magic for a singular purpose."

"An unfortunate piece of our current reality," agreed Noorsin.

"I'd like to propose that we try to mitigate that advantage. Form the Magii with the most experience using the Talent against the Curse into a single squad or squads if we have enough of them. The other Magii should be able to keep the Elders from harming our soldiers with their Dark Magic, but this squad ..."

"I like how you mind works, Jurgen," said Declan with an evil grin, having already worked out where the Blademaster was going with his suggestion.

"Will have just one goal," Klines continued. "Kill the Elders."

"I agree with Declan," said Kevan. "That's a smart approach."

"Do you think we have enough Magii to do that?" asked Tarin.

"I'm sure we can make it work," replied Noorsin, clearly pleased with the twist the Blademaster offered, although she'd need to work closely with the other Magii to identify those best suited to the task and to ensure that each company still gained some protection against the Curse.

As her precise mind worked through how to implement the suggestion, she realized that this would be an excellent opportunity to enhance the ability of those Magii not used to employing the Talent effectively in a fight to do just that. She could rotate Magii needing experience through this squad, giving them a chance to learn from their peers, and then return to their companies better prepared to take on the Elders.

"This is all a good start, but we also need to consider the Ghoule packs protecting the flanks of the Legions," said Kevan. "Our scouts and Magii during their searches of the surrounding terrain are finding more and more of the beasts in the mountains on both sides of us."

"Yes, they've gotten bolder," murmured the Blademaster. "They know if they get behind us, we don't stand a chance."

"Perhaps they won't come too close to us now that we have

Magii watching our flanks who can warn of any impending threat," suggested Noorsin.

"We can hope, but we can't trust our success to that," said Kevan. "Not after the beasts almost turned our flank thanks to that hidden trail."

"No, you're right," replied Noorsin, the glimmer in her eye a familiar one to Kevan. This was the look that she got when she had already puzzled out a problem before anyone else had. "I was just thinking that perhaps we can convince them to stay where they are for a bit longer."

"How are we going to do that?"

With a broad smile, Noorsin turned her gaze to Declan and Tarin. "I know you two have been discussing this challenge."

"We have," they both replied in unison.

"Do you believe that you can make it seem like we have several companies in the peaks on each side of the Winter Pass that are working their way through the surrounding mountains so that they can come at the Ghoule Legions from behind?"

"We can create that illusion, yes," the Blademaster confirmed. "Although it won't take much for the Ghoules to discover the ruse."

"And if I give you both a few Magii who can use the Talent to strengthen the deception?"

"That certainly won't hurt," replied Tarin.

"That will give us a few more options to consider," confirmed Declan, a rare, devilish smile breaking out on his usually serious countenance, "and it will buy us more time."

"That's all I ask. Because at the moment, time is really the only commodity that matters."

4

NECESSARY CONVERSATION

Even though the sun had yet to color the eastern horizon, the Caledonian camp was already a buzz of activity. Smoke from hundreds of cookfires drifted into the sky. Shouts floated through the canyon as Sergeants and Corporals prepared their soldiers for battle. Whinnying and neighing horses stomped through their corrals, absorbing the anticipation the soldiers radiated. Yet what was most striking and least surprising was the unmistakable scratchy hiss of thousands of whetstones sliding across steel.

The Caledonians assumed that the Ghoules would attack within the next few hours. The scouts placed the beasts three leagues to the north, and they were coming fast. An hour away, no more.

The soldiers would be ready, as would Declan. He just wanted to do one thing first.

The Sergeant of the Blood Company had climbed partway up the side of the Winter Pass, using the stakes the scouts had driven into the side of the wall to reach the narrow trail fifty feet up from the canyon floor that meandered along the top of the gorge before disappearing between the peaks. He understood what needed to be done with respect to the Ghoule Legions, and specifically what would be demanded of the Blood Company, the additional challenge that it would entail. It was a difficult assignment, yes, but it was one that he felt his gladiators could manage quite well.

They had faced death every time they walked out onto the white sand. This would be no different.

Still, he wanted to get a better view of where he and his soldiers would be fighting, not wanting his decisions to be restricted solely to what the scouts and the Magii told him. With what was being required of his gladiators, he needed a broader picture of the battlefield. He needed to view it with his own eyes and make his own judgments.

From where he stood on the rim of the canyon, he could see for leagues down the gorge in each direction, although he was primarily interested in the terrain that ran along the western side of the mountains and how the Winter Pass broadened the farther north the gorge traveled through the Shattered Peaks.

This was where he and the Blood Company had been stationed. This was where he and his gladiators would take responsibility for a single, critical task. Clear the trails of Ghoules, and if they could kill a few Elders along the way, even better.

At the very edge of his vision, where the snowcapped mountains became a blur, Declan caught a faint glimmer that grew in brilliance as the sun slowly began to rise above the peaks. It was at least ten leagues away. Even so, it was unmistakable, the shining intensity exactly the same here as it had been when he and his gladiators were fighting in the Sanctuary.

The Weir.

He smiled at the sight. He was incredibly proud of Bryen. How the lad had done it, he didn't know. It was truly a remarkable achievement, and Declan hoped that it was something that Bryen was himself proud of.

Yet just as he assumed he would, the lad had taken only a moment to enjoy his success and then had moved on to the next challenge that he had set for himself. Hunting and then destroying the source of the Curse in the Lost Land. Declan smiled at that. He certainly couldn't fault Bryen for dreaming too small, because this challenge was even more difficult than his last.

In fact, what Bryen proposed to do was an insane effort in the minds of some. Then again, no one had expected a barely trained Magus to accomplish a charge that initially had required the strongest ten Magii of a thousand years past to achieve. So who was he to say what the Protector could and could not do? Who would want to even try?

Bryen had a habit of proving people wrong. Something that Declan had quite enjoyed watching while they were in the Pit. Something that he enjoyed even more now. So though he was worried for the young man he had raised in the shadow of the Colosseum, he was confident of his success.

A few flashes of movement in the Winter Pass pulled Declan's eyes away from the Weir. It was too far for him to say for certain what it was. Ghoule scouts most likely. If so, that meant that the Legions weren't far behind, arriving sooner than they expected.

Initially, based on the scouting reports, he had assumed they had two hours before the battle began. Now it was probably closer to one.

That was all right with him. He and the Blood Company were ready. His gladiators had acquitted themselves well at the Sanctuary. He had no doubt that they would do the same here.

"Are you certain that it's safe here?"

Declan turned at the voice, not smiling, though his eyes widened just a touch as he saw Rafia pull herself up the steep incline, using the large rocks on both sides of the trail to aid her efforts. Declan offered the Magus his hand, helping her the last few feet until she stood next to him. They both took in the vista as the sun slowly crested the mountain peaks, Declan certain that Rafia also had caught the movement now just a league to the north in the Winter Pass.

"I checked with some of your Magii before I came up here. There are no Ghoule scouts for leagues on either side of the Winter Pass. They have all pulled back for now." He nodded to the north. "They all seem to be in the gap instead, preparing the way for the Legions."

"And if there were Ghoule scouts here, you could probably manage them just fine," Rafia said with a slight grin.

"Maybe," Declan admitted. The Sergeant of the Blood Company wasn't one to brag. Of course, after his experiences on the white sand, Ghoules didn't bother him, so long as there weren't too many to fight at one time.

Rafia shifted her gaze from the rising sun, staring at him now. She could usually read people quite easily, identifying their primary attributes and personality traits with just a quick glance.

Not so with Declan. He was just like Bryen. He came across as quietly competent, also intimidating and slightly frightening. Beyond that everything else was a mystery, only to be revealed by his actions or if he chose to, and Declan rarely chose to share anything with anyone.

Feeling the press of time, Rafia turned back toward the gorge, reaching for the Talent and searching around them for several leagues, wanting to confirm for herself. The other Magii were correct. There were no Ghoules for half a dozen leagues or more along the sides of the Winter Pass, all of the beasts currently working their way through the canyon.

Even so, that could change quickly, and she suspected that it would. It was because of that expectation that there were several scouting parties from the Blood Company on this side of the gap, just as many from the Battersea Guard led by Tarin on the eastern side.

Rafia nodded knowingly upon making her discovery. "I can see why you're not worried."

Declan only offered her a nod himself as a response. She should have guessed as much. He was always planning. Always looking at all the angles, which was probably why he was here now, having his gladiators get the lay of the land, preparing for every eventuality, knowing that circumstances would change as soon as the battle began and that it wouldn't be long before they were drawn into the fighting.

She could only imagine what he had in mind for the Ghoules, because she was certain just as he was that the beasts wouldn't limit their activities to the floor of the Winter Pass. Not after the success they had enjoyed sneaking around the Caledonian flank before the Magii joined the fight yesterday.

"Are you worried?" she asked.

Declan assumed that she was referring to the approaching Ghoule Legions. "Any sane man would be."

"I don't take you as entirely sane." Rafia said it matter of factly and without the hint of an insult, judgment, or humor.

"There's probably some truth to that," Declan admitted, finally allowing himself a small smile. "And no, I'm not worried, although I probably should be. More resigned if anything. We know what we're facing. It'll be no harder than fighting in the Pit."

Rafia caught flashes of the memories floating in the back of the Master of the Gladiators' eyes. "Do you miss it?"

Declan took almost a minute before responding, apparently having to think about the question. "No. No, I don't miss the pain and the sorrow. I do miss the good moments that were interspersed throughout that dehumanizing experience. Teaching Bryen. Laughing with Davin. Calming down Lycia. Training the gladiators who have become the Blood Company. The Colosseum was a terrible place. It does horrible things to you. Yet, weirdly, even with all that, I still have good memories of my time there."

She could understand that. She could say the same about some of her own experiences. "And now?"

"Now," said Declan, taking some time again before responding, "I'd like to make a few more good memories if possible, although how events play out during the next few weeks likely will determine whether I will get that chance."

"You're worried."

Just then, Declan caught sight of some of the gladiators coming back along the trail they had disappeared down an hour before. The men and women were talking animatedly, apparently excited by what they had discovered. Of course, Majdi, who led the squad, was as quiet as he ever was. The large man nodded to Declan and Rafia as he passed.

"Did you find what you were looking for?" asked Declan.

"We did," Majdi rumbled with some satisfaction.

"It will work for you?"

"Most definitely," agreed Majdi, his broad grin lighting up his scarred face. "We just need to work out a few more details."

Once the gladiators had continued farther down the trail, circling back to the north as they made their way up the switchback, Declan returned his focus to Rafia.

"I'm always worried," he admitted. "Although not for me or the Blood Company."

The Magus nodded in understanding. He was anxious about Bryen. Davin and Lycia as well, as the twins would be joining the Protector on his latest quest.

Declan spent a moment studying the Magus. Since Sirius' passing, they'd spoken a few times. He liked to think that they were becoming friends. Whether that perception was real or simply a temporary result of the Magus' grief and her need to speak with someone there was no way to tell.

"When do you begin your latest assignment?" Rafia asked.

"As soon as we're done talking," Declan replied.

"I'd like to spend more time with you when we return," said Rafia tentatively, rushing out her next words as if she was worried that if she waited too long she wouldn't say them at all. "I'd like to talk with you about a few things that have been going through my mind. Things that relate to you and me."

Declan didn't respond immediately, observing her. She found it difficult to be under such close scrutiny and not break the silence, although Rafia forced herself to wait patiently, having come to learn that Declan did things in his own way and in his own time. He could not be pushed and he could not be rushed. To expect anything different from him would be folly.

"I'd welcome the chance," Declan finally replied, his smile widening just a tad as he saw that the Magus was tapping her fingers together, a sign of her nerves.

Rafia nodded, letting out the breath that she had been holding, pleased by his response, initially fearful about how he was going to reply, her inability to get a sense as to what he was thinking intensifying her fears. "You know why I'm doing this? It's not that I don't want to be ..."

"I know, Rafia," Declan replied softly, seeing how difficult it was for the Magus to express her feelings. "Do what you must do. I will do what I must do. I will be here when you return. We can talk more then."

Rafia smiled broadly at that, glad that Declan understood that this was the only way to gain closure for Sirius' death. Then she nodded, her eyes softening as she stepped forward quickly and gave him a soft kiss on the cheek.

The Magus then turned on her heel and headed back down the trail toward the ladder that would take her to the main camp, leaving the Sergeant of the Blood Company standing there on the ledge, a faint smile cracking his usually grim expression.

Rafia hoped that Declan would be here when she returned. Assuming, of course, that she returned. Only one person had ever entered the Lost Land and returned alive. Viktor Keldragan. The Magus had barely made it out, the Ghoule Overlord and his beasts right on his heels.

Bryen had intimate knowledge of that journey thanks to his connection to his forebear through the Seventh Stone. It would prove essential to their efforts. But a millennium was a long time. She had no doubt that the Lost Land that Viktor had snuck into was not the Lost Land of today.

5

THE LOST LAND

Bryen climbed the stakes hammered into the canyon wall. He placed his feet carefully, realizing that if he fell, he'd be taking Aislinn, Davin, and Lycia down with him. When he reached the top, he knelt and offered a hand to the others, helping them step onto the trail that Declan had surveyed earlier that morning.

Rafia waited for them there, nodding a quiet greeting. She had returned as soon as Declan had moved farther into the mountains, wanting to concentrate on where she was going rather than on where she had been. Her face was a mask, betraying no emotion.

Whether that was a good or bad thing, Bryen couldn't tell. He'd find out soon enough. The Magus appeared to have shifted her focus to the task they had set for themselves, which he hoped helped to push to the side the pain that Bryen was certain that she was feeling with the loss of Sirius.

He knew why she felt the need to accompany them. He respected that. Still, he was worried about her.

"Any changes?" he asked.

"Nothing worth noting," replied Rafia with an indifferent shrug. "Other than the fact that the next battle is about to begin."

Bryen smiled at the dry comment, appreciating the humor in a time of so much stress. Then he took hold of the Talent, wanting to check for himself.

There were still no Ghoule scouts close to them on this side of the Winter Pass, although he did sense a few packs coming this way along the edge of the mountains, probably hoping that they could take the soldiers below by surprise as they did yesterday. They weren't an immediate concern. They wouldn't get here for several hours.

Besides, preparations had already been made for them. The beasts were in for a few surprises of their own with Declan and the Blood Company haunting the route the beasts would be taking.

He then searched farther down the Winter Pass. Declan had been right when he spoke with him earlier that morning. Several Ghoule Legions were advancing down the middle of the canyon, the beasts maintaining a pace that made it difficult to get a good count of their numbers.

The Ghoules were no more than a league to the north, which meant they would arrive within the hour. For just a second, his overdeveloped sense of responsibility tugged at him, questioning why he was leaving his gladiators and his friends to their fates while he went off on a quest where the odds of success likely were lower than what he faced when he went in search of the Sanctuary.

Bryen ruthlessly crushed that niggling worry. Today's fight wasn't his concern. Duchess Stelekel and all the others with her were more than capable of putting up a strong resistance. Yet none of them could do what needed to be done. What only he could do.

He needed to focus on what he believed was most important. Killing the spirit of the Ghoule Overlord. Destroying the Curse. Because if he failed to do that, the men and women fighting today and in the days to follow, the men and women who would die today and in the days to follow in defense of their Kingdom, would have sacrificed themselves for nothing.

He couldn't allow that to happen. He needed to do all that he could to ensure that their sacrifice meant something, that it contributed to a success and not a devastating failure.

"Then let's get moving," he said. "Our friends are waiting for us."

He and the others continued along the trail, the switchbacks of the narrow path taking them farther up the almost sheer side of the mountain until they reached a fork. Rather than continuing higher up the peak to the north, Bryen turned to the west, that section of the trail winding between two mountains that had grown one on top of the other so that the only path through was a narrow gulley that took them to an ancient copse. From there it was just a short walk beneath the trees before they emerged into a large clearing.

Hearing a welcoming squawk, Bryen grinned and walked over to Banshee, the Griffon standing patiently in the long grass with four of her brethren.

"Hello, my friend," said Bryen with the Talent. *"It's good to see you."*

Banshee rubbed her head against Bryen's chest, the Protector's scratching in between the feathers of her neck eliciting a loud purr of contentment.

Rafia walked over to a Griffon that was almost as big as Banshee, offering her hand to allow the animal to get her scent again before she tried to rub the Griffon's feathers and soft fur. Aislinn, Davin, and Lycia did the same, following Bryen's instructions for greeting the animals. They had ridden the majestic creatures just the other day. Still, it took time to build a bond of trust.

As the Griffons became acclimated to the humans once again, Bryen took a few minutes to think about their next steps. The night before Bryen had used the Seventh Stone to speak with Viktor Keldragan.

Viktor had shared what he remembered about the Lost Land. His knowledge wasn't complete, as the Magus could only provide information on the route that he had taken, that piece of the Lost Land that he had seen with his own eyes.

It would have to do. It certainly was more than what Bryen would have had if he had not enjoyed the additional help provided by his uncle.

Of course, Viktor tempered everything that he shared with the warning that a thousand years had passed since he had last been there. He was certain that some aspects of the environment likely had changed since then, particularly because of the landscape's volcanic nature.

A valid concern, but it wasn't enough to dissuade Bryen from the course that he had decided upon. The course that he had to take, Viktor not missing the similarities between them as his nephew prepared for a journey much like his own.

Bryen's first thought had been to take the easiest and fastest recourse open to him. To use the Talent to craft a portal and simply appear at the Temple of the Ghoules, which he believed to be his final destination. Although Viktor couldn't say with any certainty since no human really knew much about Ghoule practices, he too believed that based on the information that he had pieced together before he had made his own sojourn into the Lost Land that Bryen was correct. The dreams that Bryen had experienced only confirming it in both their minds.

When Viktor had stolen the artifacts, he had found what he was looking for at the Temple of the Ghoules, and as he snuck through the dead city surrounding the Temple, he had sensed the overpowering essence of the Curse, the corruption pervading the sprawling metropolis, that stomach-churning power centered around the altar set atop the pyramid that rose several hundred feet into the sky. It was the only place that Viktor could think that a ceremony such as what was required for the Curse to occupy another Ghoule host would occur.

In response to Bryen's initial proposal, Viktor had told him that he could do just that. He could open a portal near the Temple. But he advised against it. Bryen needed to weigh the dangers involved against the simplicity and speed of the approach.

The Magus argued that it was best not to use a portal to travel a long distance if you'd never been to where you wanted to go, especially when you had little experience in crafting a portal of the size needed to bring five Griffons with you. You could lose yourself too easily, lose control of the power you were trying to manipulate, the magical gateway unstable no matter how clear a picture you might have of the location in your mind, no matter how confident you might be in your abilities.

What you thought it would look like, even if based on the memory of another, or based on a dream, couldn't compare to the certainty offered if you'd actually set foot in the place first before attempting such an undertaking with the Talent. So the easiest approach, yes, but in his opinion also the riskiest.

He also suggested that even if Bryen succeeded in creating a portal that allowed them to step out onto the top of the Temple of the Ghoules, he had no way of knowing what might be waiting for them. You couldn't search through a portal with the Talent. The only way to know what was on the other side was to go through. The altar could be deserted, which would be a welcome discovery, or it could be teeming with a Ghoule Legion, and five against one thousand of those monstrous beasts, even when three of the five were Magii and one of those Magii was the Seventh Stone, was not a recipe for success.

Viktor then focused on the specifics of actually crafting a portal, a skill that few Magii had ever acquired. To bring the Griffons through to the Lost Land would require building a very large gateway, something that had never been done before, not even by the Ten Magii. From his perspective, it was better not to travel too far when you didn't have much experience in crafting a large portal. A few steps at a time before you took such a giant leap.

As Bryen listened to his uncle's reasoning, although he had little desire to delay, he found it difficult to challenge his logic. Moreover, he couldn't help but think of Sirius, the brothers clearly of a similar mind and temperament, as he and Viktor worked through the various options.

After considering every detail of Viktor's argument, Bryen decided to take his uncle's advice. By crafting a portal that opened just on the other side of the Weir, they would have a farther distance to travel to their destination, but that's why the Griffons were there. They would help them make up some of the time they would lose by not using a portal to travel farther north.

The approach also would give them more of a chance to get their bearings in the Lost Land. Bryen had no illusions that he and the others were intruders in the Ghoule homeland, and since they had no firsthand experience on which to rely, he preferred a more cautious approach for what no doubt would be an exceedingly risky mission.

After Bryen scratched Banshee's beak a few more times, he pulled himself up onto her back, his friends following his lead and doing the same with their Griffons. Lycia, Rafia, and Aislinn all appeared excited about the flight. Strangely, Davin, who was always up for a new adventure, less so. He seemed to be a little green around the gills when he finally lifted himself up onto his Griffon's back, the large animal easily distinguished from his peers because of the streak of auburn feathers and fur that ran down the back of his head all the way to his front paws.

Usually, the Crimson Giant was more than game to try something new, the riskier the better, in fact. But he hadn't enjoyed his ride from the Sanctuary to the Winter Pass, spending most of his time hunched over and trying not to spill his guts. He consoled himself with the fact that there was nothing for it now. He'd simply have to suffer for a time, because the Griffons played a critical part in their strategy.

"You all right, Davin?" Bryen asked. "You look a little off."

"We're not even in the air yet but it still appears like you're about to puke," chuckled Lycia, clearly more amused than sympathetic to her brother's plight.

"I'll live," grumbled Davin. "I've done this before, and I can do it again. The more I do it, the easier it will be."

"Let's hope so," offered Lycia. "For both your sake and that of your Griffon."

"That's the spirit," said Aislinn, trying to provide some support to the obviously uncomfortable gladiator after his sister's less than charitable comment.

Bryen smiled at that. Davin would do what was needed. He always did.

Then the Protector's expression hardened. He was all business now as they faced two immediate pressures.

The first was the need to move quickly because of the Ghoule Legions coming down the Winter Pass. The second was the fact that they would be traveling through an environment that was foreign to them, which meant that any mistake they made, no matter how small, could have deadly consequences for all of them.

Bryen was about to reach for the Talent when Davin cut him off.

"So let me get this straight, just so I understand, we understand," said Davin, motioning with his hand toward those assembled around him. He could tell that Bryen was about to get started, but he needed a little more time.

He still couldn't decide if he was going to be sick to his stomach even with Fuerza still on the ground. For just a moment, he chided himself. He should have guessed that this would happen after his last and only ride on the back of a Griffon. If he had been thinking more clearly that morning, he wouldn't have had such a large breakfast. But there was nothing to do about that now, and the eggs, bacon, coffee, and toast had been quite good.

"You create a magical gateway larger than you've ever crafted before, and you think that you can do this because you learned how by watching the Ghoule Overlord do it," continued Davin. "Once you're done with that, we and the Griffons use the magical gateway to enter the Lost Land, a place that a human hasn't entered and exited alive in I don't know how many centuries."

"More than a thousand," Aislinn clarified, understanding that the conversation was helping to get Davin in the right frame of mind.

"A thousand years," Davin repeated, nodding his thanks to the Lady of the Southern Marches. "That doesn't really make me feel any better, but it is what it is."

"The story of our lives," interjected Lycia. "You must do what you must do."

"Now even you are quoting Declan," accused Davin, the red-headed gladiator shaking his head in mock disgust. "Bryen doing it all the time was bad enough."

"Can we get back to the topic at hand?" asked Bryen.

The conversation seemed to be making Davin a little more comfortable, the green tint to his skin lessening. But Bryen really wanted to get moving. He didn't know how long the Caledonian Army could stand against the Ghoule Legions, so the sooner they started the better.

"Sorry," said Davin. "Once we're in the Lost Land, we fly to the edge of some forest that could be hiding we don't know what, then we leave the Griffons, who are all excellent fighters and would be quite useful if we got into a pickle, and cross the Caldera on our own, which I assume based on the name and description you gave it is just as dangerous as it sounds."

"Probably more dangerous," said Lycia. "You know how Bryen tends to understate the threats and dangers we face because nothing ever seems to faze him."

"True," said Davin, agreeing with his sister. "So probably the most dangerous place in the world. Once through the Caldera, we find some way to cross an inland sea in order to reach the Cauldron. Although we're not sure how to do that, the name, the Boiling Lake, suggests that we might face some additional challenges as we take on that endeavor."

"If I remember correctly from last night," Lycia offered, continuing to egg her brother on, in part because it was fun, and also in part because it seemed to be helping to shift his focus away from the ride he was about to take, "Bryen said that the water in the Boiling Lake was acidic and that it would burn through flesh to the bone in just seconds and then through the bone itself in only a few minutes."

"Not very helpful, Lycia, but thank you anyway," grumbled Davin, who shook his head in irritation. "So no baths in the Boiling Lake and assuming we make it across the water that's really more acid, we need to find some way to the top of the Cauldron since the cliffs are at least a mile high. Once we scale the heights, and I'm giving us the benefit of the doubt that we will indeed reach the top of the Cauldron, we sneak into the ancient metropolis of the Ghoules, also known as the Dead City, the name not really filling me with a great deal of confidence or a warm feeling, and make our way to the Temple of the Ghoules."

"Assuming, of course, that Mertvey Gorod isn't filled with Ghoules who are just waiting for a taste of human flesh," said Lycia.

"I didn't think that even needed to be mentioned," said Davin nonchalantly, his usual smile finally coming back as his color continued to improve. "Once we find the Temple, Bryen kills the spirit of the Ghoule Overlord, or the Curse I guess, since they are one and the same, before that evil can inhabit another Ghoule. And if we're too late, he kills the flesh and then the spirit, or the spirit and then the flesh. I guess it really doesn't matter so long as he destroys the Curse in the Lost Land, which is the only way to ensure the future safety of Caledonia. Once that's done, the Griffons appear again with almost perfect timing, and we make our way back to Caledonia through another gateway constructed of the Talent."

"Yes, that's about right," said Bryen with a strained grin, really wanting to get moving. "Although since Lycia mentioned that I tend to ignore certain dangers, I just want to make sure that everyone understands that all along the way we'll need to worry about Ghoule packs and who knows what other kinds of creatures, because even with the information Viktor was able to provide, we don't really know what might be waiting for us now."

"Got it," said Davin with a smile. "Should be a piece of cake."

"Piece of cake?" murmured Rafia. "Do all gladiators have a death wish?"

"Most of us, yes," answered Davin. "You should have figured that out as soon as you met Bryen."

"You're right about that," agreed Rafia. "Every time I think he doesn't, he does something to prove me wrong."

"It's one of his stronger and more irritating qualities,"

agreed Aislinn, having heard too frequently of some of Bryen's more audacious exploits that any sane person would think twice about before engaging in, but that Bryen seemed to jump at with barely a thought or concern.

"Before this conversation heads off on a tangent from which it never returns, are there any other questions about what we'll be doing before we get started?" asked Bryen, not wanting to relive all his past decisions that Aislinn had defined as foolish or bad or both.

"The Ghoule Overlord," said Lycia.

"What about him?" asked Rafia.

"Bryen explained that the Ghoule Overlord is just a host for the spirit of the Curse in the Lost Land. He needs to destroy the spirit, which returned to the Lost Land when Bryen killed the host in the Sanctuary. He also said that the Curse will select a new host, create a new Ghoule Overlord, and then come again for the Seventh Stone."

"Come for me, you mean," clarified Bryen.

"Yes, come for you. We've been dancing around this issue since you told us that you needed to do this, Bryen, but do you really think it's a good idea for you to enter the Lost Land? You're the Seventh Stone. You are what the Ghoule Overlord wants. If he kills you and takes the Seventh Stone, we've just made things easier for him."

"A valid concern," agreed Bryen. "Although slightly misdirected. I don't think the Curse wants to kill me."

"Why would you say that?" asked Lycia, Rafia staring intently at Bryen, realizing now that he had been holding something back from her. "That's been one of the primary concerns since all this began."

"Your dreams," said Aislinn, understanding.

"Yes," Bryen confirmed. "My dreams."

"What dreams?" demanded Lycia, irritated that she was only hearing of this now.

"We don't have time for me to take you through everything," said Bryen, who raised his hands in a placating gesture to cut off the sharp comment that was on the tip of Lycia's tongue. "I will tell everyone everything, answer any questions you have, I promise. Just not now."

"At least explain to everyone why you believe the Ghoule Overlord doesn't want to kill you," urged Aislinn. "They deserve to know."

"The Ghoule Overlord said that he wanted to make me his new host."

"He what?" asked Davin, unable to mask his shock.

Before Bryen could reply, Rafia cut in. "That would make sense, wouldn't it?" she murmured, as she mulled the consequences of that statement. "With you being the Seventh Stone, merging that with the Curse itself, you would be ..."

"Invincible," said Lycia softly. "And not in a good way."

Bryen nodded, his expression grim. "You know what this means?" he asked, directing his question to Rafia.

She nodded in turn. Her fears that it would come to this had lessened over time as Bryen demonstrated his skill with the Talent and his ability to contain the Curse. Now all of those concerns came crashing back on her tenfold.

"If it becomes necessary, I'll do what's necessary."

"What are you two talking about?" asked Lycia.

"If it appears that the Curse is going to take Bryen, or has taken Bryen, Rafia will kill him," explained Aislinn.

"She'll what?"

"It's necessary," explained Bryen. "If the Curse takes me, then Caledonia is doomed."

"But that's ..."

"No buts, Lycia," interrupted Bryen. "I ask all of you now to make the same promise, that if it becomes necessary, you do what needs to be done."

Bryen ran his gaze over each of his friends, locking eyes

with them, not releasing them until they'd acceded to his demand with a nod, Lycia taking the longest of them all before finally agreeing.

"Thank you," said Bryen. "With that out of the way, let's get back to why we are here."

"Yes, despite these new concerns," said Rafia, "the risk still needs to be taken. And this might be the best time to avoid the additional threat Bryen just revealed to us. The Curse is weakest when it does not have a host. This will be the best time to try to destroy it. It will be weaker than it would be once it regains its flesh, so even though the risk to Bryen is great, it's a risk worth taking. Bryen is the only person capable of killing the Ghoule Overlord and the only one with even the slightest chance of destroying the Curse, so if he is going to attempt this, he has to try now. If not now, it will likely be too late in the future. He won't get another chance."

"Do you know how to kill it?" asked Davin. "Not the body, or the shell, or whatever it is. I know you can do that. I mean the spirit. Do you know how to destroy the Curse?"

"I have a good idea," replied Bryen, who rubbed his hand along Banshee's feathers, the Griffon starting to get restless. Bryen had explained what was needed of her and her brethren, and the Griffons had agreed readily. Now she was just as anxious to get started as he was.

"But you're not certain that your idea will work?"

"No."

Davin nodded after giving Bryen's response a few seconds' thought. "That's good enough for me."

"Good enough for you?" asked Lycia, though she wasn't surprised. Her brother was known for his impetuousness. In fact, it was something at which he excelled.

"That's good enough for me," Davin repeated.

"Figures," said Lycia. She shook her head and then shrugged. "We've been through worse. And what Bryen just told us doesn't really change anything. We need to get this done so are we going now? I'd like to get a move on."

"We are," Bryen replied.

Doing as Bryen requested as he communicated with her through the Talent, Banshee turned her body so that she was facing away from the other Griffons, the rest of the large glade spreading out before her. Because Bryen had to expand the size of the gateway, he decided that he needed to adjust his approach from that of what he had done before when forming a portal just for himself.

Pulling in more of the Talent, Bryen crafted a small portal of white mist that spun just a dozen feet in front of Banshee. It was too small, obviously. Only he could fit through it. But it was a good start because he knew that he could manage this quite well. The next part would be trickier.

To enlarge the gateway, he used the Spear of the Magii, which he held in one hand across his thighs, the blades on both ends glowing brightly as he called upon the power of the Seventh Stone. With the Giant-crafted spear serving as his focal point, it was a simple thing to draw on the necessary additional power to expand the size of the gateway until it was large enough for two Griffons to walk through side by side.

Taking a few seconds to study his work, just to make sure that all was as it should be, he nodded to himself, satisfied.

"Are you ready, Banshee?" Bryen asked.

With a shriek of excitement, she walked through the portal at a stately pace, her head swinging from the left to the right and then up and behind her when she reached the other side, looking for any signs of danger. Nothing that she saw worried her. At least not yet.

Even so, the other Griffons following after Banshee did the same as she did, the animals focusing their attention on different directions so that they could identify any threats that might come their way. With the Griffons on guard, Bryen gained a moment to take a look around after he severed the connection to the Seventh Stone, the portal winking out.

At his back he knew the Weir rose no more than a few leagues to the south. He could sense the energy in the barrier, the power calling to him, or rather calling to the Seventh Stone. Unlike before, however, the Seventh Stone wasn't upsetting the balance between the two competing powers, the stream remaining strong and undisturbed. Bryen's efforts in partnership with the Ten Magii to meld the two distinct flows had been so successful that he had created a new form of energy, the Talent and the Curse plaited together so seamlessly that they had merged into a new substance.

That was a good sign, Bryen thought as he turned back around to get a sense of what lay before him. Although the looks of surprise were quite evident from his friends, what he saw was what he had expected to see. Grasslands stretching off to the horizon, the wood that they would be seeking more than a hundred leagues away and not yet even visible.

With them being so close to the Shattered Peaks, the Lost Land was really no different from Caledonia. The environment wouldn't begin to change until they went farther north and reached the edge of the Great Forest that ran from east to west through the Ghoules' homeland. Once they traveled beyond that, they'd have to navigate the Caldera.

But that was a worry for later. Bryen was feeling confident. He had crafted the portal, and they were alone. No Ghoules were in sight, making for good start. And even though he'd never been here before, thanks to Viktor's assistance and the mental map that he had shared that Bryen now had in his head, he knew exactly where he was.

The northwest corner of the Shattered Peaks, the Trench only a few leagues to the west, the Sanctuary behind him almost on a straight line. From here, there was only one direction to go. Straight to the north, over the Great Forest, and then on to the Cauldron and the Temple of the Ghoules.

Rafia was the last to walk her Griffon through the portal, having watched intently as Bryen worked with the Talent to create the gateway to the Lost Land, concentrating on his efforts so that she could learn to do it herself, though reluctantly admitting that she might need some help to master the skill since the weave was so complicated. After taking a few minutes to gaze upon the domain of the Ghoules, she nudged her Griffon up next to Banshee.

"Well done, Bryen," said Rafia, a broad smile brightening her face for the first time since Sirius died. "Very impressive. I'm hoping you can show me how you did that."

"I can."

"Good. It's a useful skill, and I love learning new things."

Bryen reached over and placed his hand on top of Rafia's free hand, her other gripping her Griffon's feathers tightly. When he looked at the usually intimidating Magus, he recognized a surprising vulnerability there that he had never seen before. "Are you certain you should be doing this? I know that Sirius was ... important to you."

Rafia turned her sad eyes to Bryen. "Have I told you how much I like you?"

"Frequently," Bryen replied with a soft chuckle.

"Just remember that I'll keep my promise. If I need to kill you, I will."

"I'm counting on it."

In response, Rafia laughed deeply, finally feeling some of her grief transition into something else, and something just as powerful. Purpose. "It's because Sirius was important to me that I need to do this."

Bryen gave Rafia's hand a squeeze and tried to let go. Rafia wouldn't let him, holding onto his callused hand with a strong grip. They sat together like that for several seconds before Bryen looked at Rafia again, the Magus nodding.

"Then let's make this count," he said.

The two gladiators, two Magii, and one Protector allowed their Griffons to put some space between themselves, then with Banshee in the lead, the animals that were several times larger than a draft horse launched themselves into the air, their powerful wings pulling them higher into the sky, taking them to the north and deeper into the Lost Land.

6
____

QUESTIONING HER OWN AUTHORITY

Maps covered the table that took up more than half of the small pavilion that Noorsin Stelekel was using as her headquarters. She had been staring at them for more than an hour, not moving, barely seeing what she was looking at now.

She had memorized every single feature on each of the maps carefully positioned on the surface, some with more detail than others, some scribbled hastily just minutes before by her scouts or the Magii, visualizing it all in her mind, her own scouting trips into the surrounding terrain helping to complete her picture of this section of the Winter Pass that she sought to defend.

She had been up since before the break of dawn, scouts and messengers coming in and out, providing the latest information. Noorsin believed that they were ready. Or at least as ready as they could be. Kevan, the Blademaster, Tarin, and so many others were seeing to that. Which was a good thing, because from all reports the Ghoule Legions would be there shortly and in greater numbers than they originally had expected.

She told herself that she needed to stop worrying. There

was no time to make any changes. Now all she could do was hope that their strategy worked.

It was a good one. It gave them a good chance for victory, which to her way of thinking was ensuring that the Ghoules didn't break through their defensive line.

Nevertheless, she couldn't stop herself. She felt the weight of every decision she had made since entering the Winter Pass pressing down on her shoulders.

"I still don't understand why you suggested that I lead the Caledonian Army," protested Noorsin, a hint of humor in her voice. She understood all too well the cost that they would pay if they failed to keep the Ghoule Legions in the Winter Pass, the responsibility for preventing that from happening primarily hers. "I thought you cared for me."

Why Kevan had put her forward for command, she still didn't understand. Why not himself? Even though she had slipped into the role with a grace and intelligence that no one else could match, she still felt uncomfortable. She was used to making decisions for the Duchy of Murcia, not for the entire Kingdom of Caledonia.

"I do care for you. You know that. But I care about Caledonia as well, and you're the best person for ensuring that Caledonia still exists when we're done here."

Noorsin was about to respond, feeling the need to challenge him. Kevan didn't allow her.

"There are several reasons, in fact," said Kevan. "Lately I've been questioning my own judgment, what with what happened with the Protector and keeping Aislinn at the Broken Citadel for longer than I should have and putting you in danger as a result." He didn't feel the need to regurgitate all that had occurred when Tetric had visited the Southern Marches.

"Yes, but ..." Noorsin tried to interject.

"And while I was being held captive in Tintagel, you set the groundwork for saving me and Aislinn."

"I think Bryen and the Blademaster played larger roles in that than I did," corrected Noorsin.

"Perhaps, but they would not have succeeded if you didn't take the initiative and seek allies, bringing Cornelius and Wencel here and moving others in this direction, and most importantly the Magii."

"Anyone could have ..."

"No, not anyone. You. Only you could have done this. I'm a fighter, Noorsin. You're a leader. Allow me to fight for you."

She smiled at Kevan's request with a knowing grin, the first time she had smiled since she had received reports of the Ghoule Legions coming south again. "You don't have to fight for me. You already have me."

"You are truly a difficult woman, you know that," replied Kevan, trying to sound irritated by Noorsin's distracting comment and failing miserably in his attempt as he couldn't stop himself from laughing.

Before he could say anything else, Noorsin pulled him to her and gave him a soft kiss, just strong enough to remind him of her mettle. "That's what you love about me."

"One of the things I love about you," he murmured softly.

"Then I accept you service, Duke Winborne. You will fight for me and I will fight for you. And we will fight for each other, for Caledonia."

Just then Tarin Tentillin poked his head through the tent flaps. "General Stelekel, the Ghoules have arrived on the field."

7

A NEW HOST

The Curse soared above the Cauldron, then cut down toward and sped across the rooftops of Mertvey Gorod, loose shingles and bricks falling away from the low-slung buildings, ripped free by the speed of the monster's passage. The roiling streak of black resembling a comet burst out across the massive plaza that separated the city from the Temple of the Ghoules, covering the distance in barely a breath before surging up the hundreds of steps that had been worn down by centuries of use.

When it reached the top of the truncated pyramid, the Curse twisted around the more than one hundred columns set around the edge that supported the dome, taking on the appearance of a sinuous snake seeking to bite its own tail. Round and round the monster went, driven on by its rage, by memories of its failure, until finally it came to a stop, emerging from the pillars and hovering above the large stone altar that sat beneath the center of the dome, its swirling, pitch-black mass blocking the weak sunlight that shone through the circle cut out of the stone.

Unable to control itself, the Curse released a shriek of frenzied rage that blasted out across the city. There was no answering response. Only silence emanated from the Dead City of the Ghoules.

It had been so close. The Seventh Stone had been within its grasp, there for the taking.

The Curse screamed again in fury, the ear-splitting sound dying over Mertvey Gorod.

The Protector had escaped. At the very last moment. Again.

A third scream reverberated off the columns, the black mist twisting and turning, needing to do something to release the rage that tortured it, that distracted it from its larger objective. The objective that it had just failed to accomplish despite its best-laid plans that had served it so well for centuries.

Finally gaining control of itself, the Curse settled a second time in the center of the Temple, drifting above the stone slab that was set right under the center of the dome.

The corrupted spirit of the Lost Land stared up through the hole cut in the center of the dome for several seconds. It had failed, that could not be denied. What it had strived for had not come to pass.

Even so, a path still lay open to it. The Curse could still achieve its goal. It would just require more work than it had anticipated.

It should be used to that by now. It seemed to be a fairly common occurrence when challenging the human who had become the Seventh Stone. The Protector had a unique ability to complicate its plans and stall its victory and that of its Ghoules.

No matter. What was done was done, and it could not be undone. A new approach was needed. And perhaps that would provide the Curse with an even greater opportunity. One that it had not considered until just recently.

The Curse would do what was necessary.

It would take what belonged to it.

It would take the Protector.

The Curse would become the Protector.

Then nothing could stand in its way.

But to do that would require a patience that grated on the Curse. Having reached that frustrating but inevitable conclusion, the Curse assumed the form of the Ghoule Overlord, the misty darkness holding the shape of the massive beast. In a flash, it dissolved, then reformed again, shifting from shape to shadow every time the monster allowed its focus to drift, its anger still diverting it from what it needed to do next.

The Curse still couldn't understand how the Protector had learned to use the Seventh Stone so quickly. The monster still couldn't believe that the Protector defeated the power it had used against him.

It should have been impossible. Yet that term didn't seem to apply to the Protector.

The Protector must have gotten lucky. It was the only answer. To think otherwise was something that the Curse did not want to do. Because if the Protector had, in fact, discovered how to master the Seventh Stone, that presented a problem for which the Curse did not yet have a solution. It might not ever have a solution, and that was a conclusion that the Curse could not contemplate.

Still, the essence of the Curse believed that the situation could be salvaged. In fact, the situation could be turned in its favor.

A good number of Ghoule Legions had broken through the Weir and into the human lands during the fight in the Sanctuary. The Ghoules in the Winter Pass would buy the Curse the time that it needed to take a new host.

Once the essence of the Curse had joined itself with the flesh of a new Ghoule, its power would be enhanced, and it could hunt the Protector a final time.

When next they met, the Curse would take the Protector and through him the Seventh Stone.

The Protector would serve the Curse.

The Protector would be the Curse and the Curse would be the Protector.

One and the same.

The Curse the Master, the Protector the slave.

From there, the rest of the world awaited.

Satisfied that it could still achieve the victory that it craved, the Curse turned away from the slab and studied the handful of Ghoules who stood ramrod straight at the top of the steps that led up the truncated pyramid, the beasts staring at some spot far off in the distance.

As the sun drifted across the sky, its rays moving slowly across and heating the top of the slab until wisps of heat could be seen drifting off it, the Curse closely examined the Ghoules, all of whom stood at least eight feet tall. They were all perfect specimens.

The Curse had not needed to take a new body for more than ten centuries. Even so, the practice remained within the Ghoule culture, the beasts waiting before the Curse bred for the specific purpose of serving as its host.

These Ghoules had been raised in the Temple. They had been trained to fight. All had demonstrated an incredibly high intelligence. Most important, the Elders had worked with these Ghoules to ensure that they had the capacity to manage the overwhelming power of the Curse, because it would reside within them, become them. In short, these handpicked Ghoules were the best vessels for what the Curse required.

After more than an hour of studying its options, finally the Curse moved, drifting from the left to the right, then back to the left, examining the possible hosts, searching for strengths and weaknesses, the intangibles that it needed, sending out tendrils of its power to test each Ghoule against a set of standards to which only it was privy.

The Curse determined that all were of excellent quality. Nevertheless, the Curse decided that one of the Ghoules was better qualified than the others, stronger both physically and mentally.

With the selection made, the Ghoules who were not picked took up positions at each corner of the slab, facing outward, spears in hand. The chosen Ghoule strode purposefully to the steaming slab. Seemingly impervious to the searing heat, the Ghoule lay down on the carved rock, the four straps made of Dark Magic, one attached to each corner, snaking up the stone at a flick of the ephemeral Ghoule Overlord's claw, fastening onto the beast's arms and legs and leaving the Ghoule spread-eagled, unable to move.

Once the host was in place, the Curse didn't waste any time. A thread of Dark Magic drifted out from the misty figure, expanding when it reached the slab so that it became large enough to cover the Ghoule, a thin blanket hovering just above the beast.

Once the black shawl was large enough, the Dark Magic floated down and wrapped itself around the host, forming a pitch-black cocoon that quickly hardened into a shell. Pleased with its work, the Curse took a position several feet above the bound Ghoule, staying connected to the chrysalis the entire time with its slim strand of Dark Magic.

Slowly, the Curse began to infuse itself within the Ghoule. Once the evil essence was certain that all was proceeding as it should, it broadened the stream of Dark Magic until the link between the Curse and its host was as wide as the haft of a Ghoule spear and pulsed a black deeper than the night. As each day passed, more of the spirit of the Curse would enter the beast, merge with it, make the Ghoule its own.

But it was a delicate process. It could not be rushed.

It would take time because it was not an easy transition for a creature made of flesh. Yet as more of the Curse joined with its new host, the chosen Ghoule would become stronger, more able to manage the energy gifted to it. In turn, the weaker the spinning cloud of evil would become, the mist diminishing until it was no more, becoming fully a part of the Ghoule.

Then a new Ghoule Overlord would rise, ruled by the Curse. The beast would be the source of Dark Magic in the Lost Land, yet it would answer to the master within it. Until that happened, the Curse needed to remain where it was, and as it flowed into its host, it would be vulnerable, thus the four Ghoules assigned to protect it.

Yet despite its current limitations, that didn't mean the Curse couldn't continue with its work. It would just need its servants to manage events while it was tied here to the Temple of the Ghoules.

Just then, a portal of swirling Dark Magic opened on the top of the truncated pyramid. The four Ghoules eyed the gateway warily, spears pointing in that direction. The Ghoules returned to their poses when Nibli strode out of the portal, ignoring the Elder when he kneeled in front of the stone slab.

"Rise, Nibli, we don't have time to waste," hissed the Curse.

The Elder pushed himself to his clawed feet, taking a moment to study the process his Master had begun that would allow it to rejuvenate and claim a new body. He knew in an instant that the power and skill required were well beyond his abilities, something that his Master knew as well.

"How many before the Weir took its place again?"

The Ghoule Overlord had charged Nibli with taking command of the Legions and pushing as many as possible through the Weir into Caledonia. They were then to advance to the south for the Breakwater Plateau. To complicate matters, the Elder only had a few weeks to do this before the weather turned and the Winter Pass became impassable again.

"Twelve Legions, Master." Nibli grinned, running his tongue along his sharp teeth, having exceeded his promise by two Legions, giving his Master two thousand more Ghoules to work with against the Caledonians.

The Elder was not only glad but also relieved that he could give that answer, knowing that if he hadn't his Master's temper, never good to begin with, might cost him his life. There were always other Elders who could take his place.

With that thought guiding him, Nibli decided to keep the details of how that work had gone to himself, not wanting to reveal the great loss of life that coincided with the taxing effort to get that many Ghoules into Caledonia. He and his Elders had forced a half dozen Legions through the Weir, but for every Ghoule who made it another Ghoule had died, caught in the magical barrier that had demonstrated a lethal unpredictability. Still, the Elders persevered, unfazed, demonstrating a remarkable courage, because for every ten Ghoules who made it through, an Elder gave his life, caught by the Talent within the unstable Weir.

Then Nibli had gotten lucky, having positioned as many Ghoule Legions as close to the Weir as he could during their work so that the Elders could speed it along. When the Weir collapsed for just a few minutes, after getting over his shock at his good fortune, he had been ready to take advantage of the unexpected gift. Another six Legions crossed through the space that had become a graveyard for the Ghoules.

Nibli had just made it across himself right before the power of the new Weir slammed back in place, claiming several hundred Ghoules caught within the energy of the strengthened barrier and dooming the beasts to a slow and painful death. Since then, the Elders had tried to create gateways through this new Weir, which clearly was different from the last.

All had failed miserably. Every Elder who tried had died, any attempt on their part to connect to the barrier met with an immediate, deadly response, a bolt of energy snaking out from the Weir and incinerating the Ghoule, leaving nothing but ashes where the Elder once stood.

After seeing that happen time after time, Nibli realized that the Weir was too strong and the Elders too weak. Until the Ghoule Overlord destroyed the Weir, only those Ghoules who had made it into the lands of the humans could do the bidding of their Master.

"Where are they now?" hissed the Curse.

"Moving down the Winter Pass," Nibli replied. "We should make contact with the Caledonians within the hour."

The misty Ghoule Overlord was silent for a time, the pulsing of the black thread distracting the Elder. His Master's words refocused him.

"You have enough Ghoules to complete the task I have set for you. Push for the tip of the Winter Pass as hard as you can. I will join you when I am done here. When I come our victory will be assured and you and your Ghoules will run rampant in the lands of men."

"And the Weir?" asked Nibli, worried for just a moment that he might have overstepped by questioning his Master, the swirling black losing the shape of the Ghoule Overlord for just a moment before swiftly recapturing it.

"Kill the humans in the Winter Pass first. Once done, I will focus on the Weir. I will make the Protector mine, and then nothing will be able to stop me after that."

8

PLAYING FOR TIME

The Ghoules who sprinted south down the Winter Pass and onto the battlefield early that morning believed that they were going to have an easy time of it. The Elders had told them that there weren't that many humans standing against them, no more than ten thousand.

The Elders assured them that the humans would run if given the slightest chance. The humans were weak. They were cowards. No more than cattle to be slaughtered. The Ghoules would only need to pressure the humans for a short time, make them see the impossibility of trying to fight so many Legions, and then they would break.

When that happened, the hunt would begin. It wouldn't be a battle. It would be a massacre.

But the weak humans hadn't fled as soon as the Ghoules attacked as the Elders suggested that they would. They had stood their ground, and they continued to do so, making the Ghoules pay in blood for every foot they pushed the humans closer to the southern entrance to the Winter Pass. These cattle frustrated them in a way that the Ghoules hadn't thought possible.

The Ghoules' shrieks of anger and roars of hunger that echoed through the gorge didn't seem to faze the humans in the least. Nor did charge after charge against the humans' shield walls. The soldiers held their ground, calm, composed, no matter how viciously the Ghoules attacked. They stayed in their dreaded square formations. The long spears jabbed at them just over the top of the shields that formed the front rank. A constant threat that couldn't be ignored, too many of their brethren falling victim to the humans' sharp steel as the beasts' desire to earn a bone knife all too often outweighed their commonsense.

Breaking into the human formations proved to be much more difficult than any of the beasts imagined. To add to the Ghoules' challenge, and now much too frequently to their misery, they faced a new and deadlier threat. Mounted soldiers thundered through the spaces between the squares, the humans using their heavier and powerful war horses to do their fighting for them.

The Ghoules had learned how to counter the soldiers' tactics by leaping over the first line of animals and oftentimes pulling the humans from their saddles. Once they had the humans on the ground, isolated, alone, their prey could do little to defend themselves. But the humans had recognized that danger and adjusted their tactics as well, shortening the distance between their charging ranks and adding two more lines of cavalry behind the usual two.

Now even if the Ghoules succeeded in jumping over the first line of mounted soldiers, they didn't have the time to evade the second, third, or fourth. So they had only two choices. Either stand against the charge, not the best option in their opinion, or escape.

Most of the Ghoules wisely decided on the latter, seeing no reason to be mangled by the large animals against which they had few options to defend themselves. Yet, that obvious solution created a different problem.

Even when they evaded the cavalry, the angles of the humans' charges pushed the Ghoules together right in front of the squares of soldiers, the rapidity and frequency of the attacks forcing the Ghoules to stay there to avoid getting trampled. That allowed the humans, staying safe within their squares, to use the tight space in which the Ghoules had been maneuvered against them, pushing the Ghoules back step by step, as they spent more time jostling with one another in an attempt to gain some room to move than they did attacking the humans.

The Ghoules had no choice but to admit that their prey was more determined and more skilled than the Elders gave them credit for. Still cattle to be slaughtered. Nevertheless, these cattle had horns.

Even so, that didn't stop the Ghoules from giving in to their vicious nature. Though the humans put up a good defense, the Ghoules attacked, time after time, refusing to give ground, refusing to disengage, seeking only to spill blood.

Whether that blood was theirs or the humans didn't matter to them.

Noorsin Stelekel, who remained near the center of the Caledonian line in the middle of a square composed of the Murcian Guard, appreciated the simplicity and effectiveness of the Ghoules' approach.

Attack.

There was nothing more to the beasts' strategy than that. The Ghoules paid little attention to organization or coordination, allowing their bloodlust to reign.

Three Ghoule Legions had begun the assault just hours

after the sun had risen, and three more Ghoule Legions were less than a half-day away from joining the fight, more Ghoule Legions following just behind those.

Not good odds for her and her soldiers. She acknowledged that. But there was little that she could do to change the odds. She could only deal in their current reality. Not the reality she wanted.

The beasts were aggressive to begin with, so why would the Elders do anything to restrict that? Simply allow the beasts' natural instincts to be used to their full advantage, the Elders realizing that even if the Caledonians held back these first few Legions, more would be joining the fight in short order. Any initial Ghoule losses would be replaced almost immediately.

There was really no more to it than that, the beasts believing that eventually they would wear down the Caledonians and put them to rout. Noorsin hoped that didn't prove to be the case, and so far her hopes were strongly founded in reality.

Noorsin, Kevan, and the Blademaster had been incredibly thorough with their preparations -- the formations employed preventing the beasts from attacking on a straight line, instead forcing them to weave so they couldn't build up the momentum needed for an effective charge; ballistae and other weapons of war slowing down any attack; archers protected by squads of spears located on the snowdrifts on each side of the Pass so that they could complicate the Ghoules' efforts and possibly even narrow the battlefield; with a few surprises yet to be revealed -- so the Caledonians were enjoying some success. Yet there were two uncomfortable and undeniable truths that her troops simply could not escape.

There were more Elders than Magii, and the beasts were using their greater numbers in that regard to good advantage, forcing the practitioners of the Talent to spend most of their time defending against the Elders' attacks with the Curse rather than attacking the Elders themselves. Without the direct assistance of the Magii, the Ghoules were incredibly difficult creatures to kill, inevitably the soldiers of Caledonia falling in greater numbers than the beasts from the Lost Land.

The challenge of fighting the Ghoules was made readily apparent when Duke Stennivere led a charge down the center of the gorge. The Three Rivers' cavalry split into two columns, coming around the squares and driving into the Ghoules. This time, however, rather than trying to evade the mounted soldiers, the Ghoules stood their ground, the Elders forcing them to hold.

The Caledonians enjoyed an excellent beginning, the first few rows of beasts trampled beneath their war horses' hooves. But then the massed ranks of Ghoules behind the fallen beasts quickly bogged down the assault, the Ghoules leaping over the front rank of soldiers and onto the men and women crammed together behind them.

In minutes what had started as a well-organized attack devolved into a free-for-all in which the Ghoules' greater strength and agility played havoc with the soldiers who had been pressed together tightly in an already crowded space, often unable to maneuver their horses, the Ghoules swarming around the soldiers from the Three Rivers looking for easy kills, the Duke fighting desperately as the beasts tried to pull him and his soldiers from their saddles.

"Fight for your homes and families!" roared Duke Stennivere as he swung his sword with a deadly precision, slicing across claws and arms, yet all with little effect as he and his troops were unable to break free from the mass of fighters, Ghoules and soldiers locked together in life and death struggles, most of those individual combats won by the Ghoules.

The soldiers from the Three Rivers responded with a cry of their own to that of their Duke, putting up a valiant resistance, understanding the cost of failure. Unfortunately their defiance wasn't something that could be sustained for long.

Unable to maneuver with the Ghoules pressuring them so intensely, the Caledonians lost the advantage given to them by their war horses, their mounts actually becoming an impediment and leaving them perfectly placed to be plucked off their saddles by the Ghoules. If circumstances didn't change quickly, several companies of soldiers would be lost in just minutes.

With that fear guiding his decisions, the Blademaster sought to remedy the situation by attacking from the left flank. Recognizing that he couldn't charge into the jumbled mix of men and monsters with cavalry, as he would kill and wound just as many if not more soldiers than he did Ghoules, he took a different tack instead, ordering his Royal Guard companies to dismount and form into a testudo, the formation that he had come to appreciate and value after employing it so effectively during the last few months against the Ghoules.

"Soldiers of the Royal Guard!" the Blademaster called in a booming voice. "We advance now!"

The impact of the shield wall against the milling mass was felt immediately, the scuta bearers pushing into the fight, the spears stabbing into the distracted Ghoules from behind, catching them by surprise. The beasts were so focused on the mounted soldiers, the bulk of the beasts unaware that they were even under attack, that the Caledonians drove several dozen yards into their ranks before any of the Ghoules turned to face this new threat.

The spears followed the shields, targeting the neck, chest, and guts of the beasts. The swords focused on cutting free the cavalry, eliminating any of the wounded Ghoules who still might be able to rise, littering the ground with bodies.

For a short time what had become a trap that favored the Ghoules in the blink of an eye turned against the beasts. Now the Ghoules, seeking to regain the momentum, found it increasingly difficult to break free, caught between the Blademaster's steadily advancing shield wall and the compressed cavalry from the Three Rivers, Duke Stennivere having managed to reform his troops into an uneven, makeshift line that step by step pressed against the beasts from the other direction.

"My thanks to you, Blademaster," called Duke Stennivere when he met the Captain of the Royal Guard in the center of the mass of fighting soldiers, the two forces finally joining together. Thanks to the Blademaster's initiative, the Caledonians had eliminated almost all of the Ghoules that just moments before had threatened to annihilate the fighters from the Three Rivers. All that was left now was for the spears and swords to finish their bloody work.

Jurgen Klines simply nodded, not having the time to reply. He had already shifted his focus to pulling back his troops so that they could move farther along the Caledonian line and seek to address the next challenge. Using the Talent, Duchess Stelekel had sent him a warning that to the west Duke Roosarian had been placed in much the same situation from which he and his soldiers had just extricated Duke Stennivere. The Blademaster and the Royal Guard needed to relieve the pressure before the Ghoules crushed the soldiers from Roo's Nest.

The Blademaster wanted to assist. He just wasn't certain that he would make it to that section of the field in time, if at all. Another Ghoule Legion was sprinting down the Winter Pass from the north and about to join the fight.

No doubt Duke Roosarian needed assistance, but Klines needed to focus on his own soldiers first. This new Legion was coming right at him, the beasts howling and roaring, brandishing their spears and swords as they glided across the rough ground, eager to join the battle and test their mettle.

"Royal Guard!" Klines shouted, lifting his sword into the air, the steel flashing in the sunlight that barely made it over the surrounding mountains. "Form square!"

The shift in formation took longer than the Blademaster would have liked. Even so, he had to give his soldiers credit. They performed the maneuver with a precision beyond compare in a difficult situation, stepping over the bodies of dead soldiers and slaughtered Ghoules, knowing the deadly threat that was charging toward them, still managing to lock their shields in place right before the next wave of Ghoules slammed into them.

Using the Talent to identify the new threat facing the Blademaster, Noorsin realized that another solution was needed on the other flank, if there was to be any chance of saving Duke Roosarian and his troops, and that solution needed to be now. Because if they didn't prevent the Ghoules from breaking through the Caledonian line, the beasts would sweep into their rear from the west. And then their defense would end before it really even had begun. So she sent an urgent message to Kevan, who responded as quickly as he could, pulling several cavalry companies from an already weakened reserve to try to stem the shifting tide.

Fortunately, even with the pressure being applied by the Ghoules, Duke Roosarian had kept his soldiers in good order. The cavalry from Roo's Nest made sure that their lines held strong, the Ghoules, who were attacking from all sides, unable to get in with his troops.

The archers, who had taken positions atop the snowdrift just a few hundred feet to the right of the Roo's Nest Guard, aided in that effort. Flights of arrows flew through the air with increasing regularity as they quickly found the range, the steel-tipped shafts slamming into the beasts with a frightening and effective regularity. The barbs piercing Ghoule flesh forced the beasts to pay more attention to the men and women shooting at them from above than to the mounted soldiers they so desperately wanted to feast upon.

That lethal diversion helped Duke Roosarian's efforts to break free from the encircling Ghoules. Even so, the Duke knew that it wouldn't be enough to give them their freedom. Although the archers helped to relieve the pressure, they were too few in number to cut the noose. The Ghoules were too many and in little danger of losing their position around his soldiers without an additional incentive.

That final nudge to unlock the trap came from Duke Winborne. Dividing his companies into two columns, one swept from the east along one side of the swarm of Ghoules and the other from the west in a thunderous charge that set the ground shaking, trampling the beasts too slow to get out of the way on the first pass and cutting away at the Ghoule edges. When the two columns passed each other at the apex of the circle, the soldiers from the Southern Marches -- Dani leading one column, Kevan the other -- lowered their spears to come at the disoriented and wavering beasts from the other direction.

The Battersea Guard's second run through the Ghoules, which finally broke the Ghoule encirclement, allowed Duke Roosarian to get most of his soldiers back to the Caledonian line, Duke Winborne waiting until the last of his cavalry completed their attack and turned to the south before heading back himself for the safety of the squares. As soon as he did, he sensed the danger coming at him from his back.

Urging his war horse to a gallop, Kevan glanced over his shoulder. He caught the blur of mottled green streaks at the very edge of his vision, several packs of battered and angry Ghoules who had survived the charge of the Battersea Guard in pursuit.

Kevan gave his horse his head, realizing that he might have delayed too long his own escape, the Ghoules matching the speed of his galloping horse, inching ever closer, Kevan imagining that he could smell the beasts' rancid breath on the back of his neck. Recognizing that the safety of the Caledonian line was still several hundred yards away, and his soldiers were well ahead of him just as they should be, he feared that he might have to turn and fight.

He understood the likely result if he did so, having no chance on his own against so many Ghoules. Even so, better that than a claw in his back. His horse sensing the threat behind them, the destrier lengthened its stride and its pace, just as anxious as its rider to escape their pursuers.

Despite the gallant effort of his mount, Kevan knew that it wasn't going to be enough. The Ghoules were too fast, still closing the distance, now only a few dozen yards and coming hard. He gripped the hilt of his sword tightly, preparing to face off against the beasts. At least then he'd have an opportunity, slim though it may be, to take a few of them with him.

But then he caught a glimpse of the last line of his escaping cavalry just a hundred feet in front of him leaping over a furrow in the ground. That action filled him with a brief surge of hope, as he realized that thanks to Noorsin's creativity he might just have a chance if he timed it right.

Urging his war horse on, just before he reached the wide groove in the ground, he nudged his horse in the ribs and pulled back on the reins just a tiny bit, the well-trained destrier knowing exactly what to do. Kevan held on tightly, grabbing the pommel with his other hand, as his horse leapt through the air for a dozen yards before landing deftly on the muddy ground and without breaking stride galloping toward the safety of the soldiers who were already forming up to meet this latest Ghoule attack.

The angry Ghoules' blood was up as they chased after the fleeing human, recognizing him as the one who had led the attack to break their hold on the mounted soldiers. With no other soldiers near him, he was an easy target, and they wanted vengeance for their many brethren who had been killed in the surprise attack.

Fixated on the lone soldier who was fleeing, they missed the furrow in the ground. That singlemindedness, so useful in the battle so far, in an instant became a liability that cost the pursuing Ghoules dearly, the ground beneath them giving way. Several dozen of the beasts fell through the carefully hidden netting that the Caledonians had covered with a thin layer of dirt and mud, the beasts impaling themselves on hundreds of steel spears that had been lodged in the bottom of the ditch.

Before the few Ghoules who somehow had avoided the spears could climb out of the ditch, Cinjin and his team of Magii were there. Charged with killing Elders, they were more than happy to concentrate their efforts on the Ghoules for a time, going to it with a will.

Suzane, her grey hair wisping around her round cheeks that made her look like a kindly grandmother, revealed once again that there was nothing kindly about her in the least when it came to fighting the creatures of the Lost Land. She sent a stream of energy sizzling through the pit, catching several of the beasts trying to pull themselves out of the ditch while burning through the beasts impaled on the stakes, several of them only with puncture wounds in a leg or arm and trying to extricate themselves from the steel. Telly, a bit scattered though always smiling, even in the midst of a battle, did the same from the other side. In seconds, nothing alive remained within the trap.

The two Magii immediately turned their attention to the handful of Elders who had climbed to the top of a snowdrift that ran along the side of the canyon wall. The beasts had wanted a better view of how events were playing out on the battlefield when their new Ghoule Legions charged down the gap.

They didn't give that decision enough thought, however,

because their desire for a better perspective also gave Cinjin a better view of them. And he was more than ready.

Doing as he had done when aiding the Blademaster against the Ghoules leaping down from the goat trail, the tall Magus sent streaks of white-hot energy into the base of the snowbank, the hard-packed snow melting in a flash, turning to slush and water, the beasts losing their footing and falling or sliding down toward the canyon floor.

Before the Elders could get their clawed feet back under them, Usil attacked with an unsurpassed hatred. A kinetic energy seemed to radiate from the Magus in waves. He was always moving, always doing something. He didn't like to, in fact he couldn't, sit still, and that aided him now as he glided across the rocky ground with a remarkable grace, his stout frame dancing in front of the Elders as he sent bolt after bolt at the beasts.

Usil had fought the Ghoules before in the Shattered Peaks, the scar peeking out from his collar that started at his shoulder and then cut diagonally down to his abdomen proving it. A Ghoule had tried to gut him and had failed to finish the job. The beast never had a chance to regret it, just as the Elders who had so foolishly climbed to the top of the now melted snowbank had no chance to regret that decision, as any of the beasts who escaped Usil instead met their end at the hands of Suzane or Telly.

With a satisfied smirk, Cinjin nodded to his peers and then toward the east. Done here, he and the Magii with him moved farther down the Caledonian line in search of more Elders to kill.

Noorsin used the Talent to watch it all, benefiting from the birds-eye view of the battle that she crafted for herself. The perspective she gained allowed her to more easily adapt to rapid changes on the battlefield, just as she had done to help the soldiers from Roo's Nest and the Three Rivers. She was impressed by how well their strategy was working, although she readily admitted that was really because of the skill and experience of the soldiers putting that strategy into play.

The Caledonians were holding their own. For now. She understood that could change in an instant. And if it did, she would adapt as needed. Because they had no choice but to continue the fight no matter how difficult their circumstances. They couldn't allow the Ghoule Legions to flood the Kingdom.

A tall task, she knew, though not as difficult as the one taken on by the Protector.

No one had said it when Bryen had explained his plans, but she had understood exactly what he was trying to do. He wasn't just trying to ensure that the Ghoule Overlord was well and truly dead. He was also trying to destroy the Curse. He was attempting to achieve the impossible.

But the same had been said of his repairing the Weir. So who knew. When it came to the Protector, hope and reality often appeared to be the same.

9

LEADING THE FIGHT

"How far?"

The Sergeant of the Blood Company kept his head on a swivel, eyes never staying in the same place for more than a second as he looked for the first sign of movement. When there was space for the Ghoules to move unhindered, it was always a blurred mottled green, so you needed to know what to look for.

The Ghoules sprinted so fast that they were difficult to track with the naked eye. Here on the side of a mountain that bordered the Winter Pass the beasts would need to be more cautious. If they weren't, with a single misstep on the narrow trail that snaked along the top of the gorge, they would risk a fall of several hundred feet to the canyon floor below.

"A couple hundred yards. No more than that."

Declan grunted in acknowledgement. Looking to the far northern end of the path finally he caught a few flashes of movement among the rocks. The Ghoules were moving much slower than usual, so they were hard to miss.

"Are you ready, Maria?" asked Declan.

"Yes," the Magus replied, having used the Talent to search

around them one more time just to make sure that she hadn't missed anything. She nodded to herself. She hadn't. Two packs of Ghoules were coming their way accompanied by only one Elder. That should play right into her hands. "Are your soldiers in place?"

Declan turned his gaze toward the Magus, the Ghoules still coming toward them and demonstrating little concern, which satisfied him that the beasts hadn't sniffed them out. Maria stared right back at him, making Declan think of a hawk preparing to swoop down on its prey.

After spending a few days with her, he had learned that she had a unique intuitiveness, having the ability to read someone like a book in just seconds. He could understand how that would be useful. You could learn a lot, gain a lot, if you could decipher a person's true though hidden intentions. But that skill was of little use on him or his fighters.

The soldiers of the Blood Company were more straightforward than most. After having spent time on the white sand they had little use or, more importantly, time to waste on trying to figure out meanings or insinuations. They preferred directness, which was why Maria fit in so well with them.

Just like the gladiators, she wasn't one for small talk, the Magus wanting to get to the point as quickly as possible. So he tried to do that every time he spoke with her. What he liked most about her, however, was her aggressiveness. In his opinion, she would have done well in the Pit.

"We are."

Declan glanced to his left and right quickly, just to confirm that his fighters were prepared. There was no need for him to do so. Of course they were. His gladiators were well hidden among the rocks that had settled just thirty feet above the narrow trail. The men and women fighting for him had locked onto the beasts as soon as they came into view, the Ghoules now advancing even more cautiously across the loose rock.

It was just as Maria had said. Two Ghoule packs, which his fighters could handle, and the one Elder. That was why Maria was there.

Duchess Stelekel had attached several Magii to the Blood Company, which was responsible for preventing the Ghoules from sneaking around the Caledonian Army's western flank on the trails that snaked through the mountains on that side of the Winter Pass. A smart move on her part after what had happened just a few days before when a large party of Ghoules had almost overrun their left flank by using a trail similar to the one that ran just below Declan.

Using hand signals, Declan issued his final orders. He knew it really wasn't necessary. It was habit more than anything else. His gladiators knew what to do, although they did grip the hilts and the hafts of their weapons just a little more tightly as they prepared to launch their attack.

Declan grunted in amusement, this time nodding his head in appreciation. He was impressed. Majdi and Jenus, the two largest men he had ever trained in the Pit, somehow were keeping their bulk hidden behind the boulders, the Ghoules unaware of their presence. Quite an achievement for two gladiators who were only a head shorter than the beasts and almost as broad.

The Ghoules began to make their way in front of the Blood Company, stepping carefully along the trail, every so often a loose rock skittering over the edge to fall into the gorge. A surge of adrenaline shot through Declan. Almost time. He checked his gladiators once more just to make sure.

His fighters were balanced on their toes, kneeling down, ready to emerge from their hiding places. Most soldiers placed in the situation of having to wait before they could attack, seeing their adversaries calmly walking by them, would be antsy, finding it difficult to control their nerves, to wait, wanting to get on with it.

Not so with his gladiators. They had spent too much time in the Pit to display openly any nerves. If anything, before a fight his gladiators became calmer, their minds achieving an acute level of concentration, their movements more controlled and subtle, almost fluid.

They had spilled a great deal of blood during their time on the white sand, much of it their own. So they didn't mind waiting just a little bit longer before attacking if that delay enhanced their odds of success.

The gladiators only had to bide their time a few seconds more before Maria shot a bolt of energy toward the Elder that slammed into the ground right at the clawed feet of the beast.

For just a heartbeat, the Elder grinned maliciously, staring up at the incompetent Magus who had attacked him and missed, thinking that he had escaped the strike. But he hadn't.

Maria had struck exactly where she wanted, not needing to engage the Elder directly as long as her aim was true, and it was. In a screech of sliding stone, the Elder disappeared, the section of the trail the beast had been standing on crumbling off the side of the mountain and taking the Elder with it to his doom.

Before the Ghoules could fully comprehend what had happened to their leader, the Blood Company struck, Majdi and Jenus leading the charge. Declan had issued only one rule for the gladiators for this fight. Don't let the Ghoules get behind them, a requirement they agreed with readily, because if they failed they would face the challenge of having to fight the beasts with their back to the Winter Pass, and that didn't appeal to any of them.

None of the gladiators had anything to worry about in that regard. Their surprise was so complete and the attack so fast that half the Ghoules died in just the first few seconds of the skirmish, most pushed off the trail and falling to their deaths on the rocks far below when instinctively they sought to avoid the long spears thrust at them.

It took a bit longer to finish the other half. That didn't bother Declan in the least. With their overwhelming numbers, better for his gladiators to be careful. Better to be safe and sure rather than risking a bad wound or even death because of a rash decision.

Maria being there helped to make that possible. She sent several more bolts of energy into the trail itself, the strength of her strikes shattering the rock face and creating small landslides that swept away many of the beasts.

The shock and power of the Magus' attack allowed the gladiators to finish off the rest of the beasts with a few well-placed lunges of spear or slashes of sword. Majdi and Jenus both chose a more direct approach, slamming into their opponents with their shields and knocking them over the edge.

Declan quickly analyzed the results of the skirmish, a wicked grin cracking his usually taciturn countenance. It was a well-planned attack that went off without a hitch. No one died. No one was badly hurt but for a few scrapes that Maria could manage. And they had killed all the Ghoules in just a few minutes in addition to one Elder.

This time, he was careful to note to himself. Most clashes wouldn't play out like this one. Usually, something would go wrong, whether it would be the Ghoules discovering them before they attacked or one of the beasts getting behind his gladiators or Maria missing the mark with the Talent or Majdi slipping before he crashed into a Ghoule.

It could be anything, but there was usually something that complicated sound tactics and strategy. So this was a rare and welcome occurrence and a victory to be savored.

For a few minutes only, however, because their work was far from done. They had eliminated two Ghoule packs so far, but

Maria had reported that there were several more coming this way. There was little time to waste.

Declan sought to move farther north along the trail, closer to the oncoming Ghoules, so that there wouldn't be any evidence of the fight that had occurred here. Wanting to take a similar approach in the next fight, he saw no reason to give away a strategy that had worked so well for them.

It probably wouldn't go as smoothly as this skirmish, but the tactics certainly were sound, and he believed that they would continue to be effective unless the Ghoules became aware of their presence. It was that concern that played through his mind as he waited for his gladiators to finish pushing the last few dead Ghoules over the side before the Blood Company went on its way.

"What are you thinking?" asked Maria, the Magus just as pleased as Declan was by the result of their latest clash with the Ghoules. "I can tell that the wheels are turning."

Declan waited a moment before answering, thinking for just a few seconds more about the idea that came to mind, seeking to poke any holes in it, before he decided to move forward with it. Satisfied that nothing had slipped by him, he turned to Maria with a devilish spark in his eyes.

"Can I ask you something about your skill in the Talent?"

10

INTO THE LOST LAND

Bryen stood in a small glade near the northern border of the Great Forest. He was worried, although he tried not to show it. He didn't want the Griffons to get riled up, and Banshee had an innate ability to sense his emotions through the link that they shared.

While flying from the Shattered Peaks north into the Lost Land, the Griffons had stayed near the clouds so that they could disappear into the mist if there was any concern about being spotted from the ground. Bryen, Aislinn, and Rafia also were ready to use the Talent to blend them into the sky, or at least try to, as it was incredibly difficult to manipulate the Talent in such a way when you were moving, even if you were just gliding a thousand or more feet above the ground.

Thankfully, going to that extreme never proved necessary. The entire time they traveled toward the expansive wood the Magii had found nothing of concern, the monotony of the massive steppe below becoming mind-numbing at times.

They all had assumed that the Lost Land would be teeming with Ghoules. But they had yet to find any. Perhaps most of the

Ghoules were in the Shattered Peaks, seeking to invade the Kingdom.

Their panorama only changed when they were flying over the Great Forest that stretched for as far as the eye could see to the east and west, plumes of steam rising into the air far to the north that offered them something different from the constant stream of yellowish green that streaked below them. The sulfurous smell, at first just a distracting hint, and then an over-powering stench that took up residence in the back of their throats, warned that they were almost to the limit of how far the Griffons could safely take them.

They had flown from just below the Shattered Peaks for several days. No Ghoules. No game. They only caught sight of a few small animals when they settled in for the night, eating the rations they brought with them, the Griffons doing their best to find a meal, often having to settle for a rabbit or two and little more than that. Perhaps that explained the absence of the beasts in their homeland. If the Ghoules didn't have anything to hunt, there was no reason for the beasts to be on the plain.

Not running into any Ghoules while they crossed the steppe was certainly a welcome development. However, here, on the southern edge of the Caldera, signs of Ghoule activity were everywhere. To stay safe, one Magus used the Talent at all times to ensure that they didn't get too close to any of the beasts.

At the moment maintaining that continual search was Bryen's responsibility. He was tracking a dozen Ghoule packs. Maybe more because he kept having to expand and narrow his search based on how certain packs moved through the Caldera. None of the packs presented an immediate danger. Some had changed course, moving in their direction for a time, yet those packs always turned away.

Nevertheless, all the packs were within a few leagues, which meant it wouldn't take them long to find them if Bryen and his party gave themselves away. To maintain the calm that he needed to do his work, he rubbed his hands along Banshee's feathers and then down into her fur, the Griffon purring contentedly and every so often rubbing her head against his chest.

He stayed with Banshee until nightfall, which hadn't been too far off when they landed. He stepped back when he noticed that the other Griffons were getting restless. With a quiet squawk, Banshee launched herself into the air, the other Griffons following.

The Griffons would fly back the way they had come in search of food, the small animals of the grassland more active during the night. Banshee and the others knew that they would have to make do with what they could find. The deer, elk, moose, and caribou so common to the Breakwater Plateau and the Shattered Peaks were nowhere to be found in the Lost Land.

It was surprising, but then again perhaps not. Bryen guessed that the lack of big game was another reason why the Ghoules were so desperate to invade Caledonia. Their primary food supply, if it hadn't already, was disappearing rapidly. They needed larger quarry to live. To find that, whether animal or human, they needed to expand their territory, something that the Weir prevented.

With the Griffons gone for at least the next few hours, Bryen walked back to their campsite, which was set among the trees, waving to Davin as he passed by. The gladiator was on guard for a little while longer, walking slowly around the perimeter based more on habit than need since Bryen, Aislinn, and Rafia were sharing the duty of ensuring that they traced all Ghoule movements. When Bryen stepped from between the trees and into the small hollow, he saw that Aislinn and Lycia had their heads together, deep in conversation, Rafia sitting about twenty feet away, clearly caught up in her own thoughts once again.

Rafia had been like this every night since they had entered the Lost Land, the Magus keeping to herself, lost in her memories and her mistakes. Bryen understood that she continued to struggle with Sirius' death. He didn't blame her. She had known the old Magus for a very long time. They had been close. He wished that he could help her, but he didn't know how.

He had approached her a few times, checking cautiously to see if she wanted to talk. It had been wasted effort, the Magus not yet ready to discuss Sirius and what he had meant to her. Respecting the fact that she wanted to grieve in her own way, he left her alone.

And based on the animated conversation that was taking place on the other side of the campsite, their hands flashing through the air as they spoke, it appeared as if Aislinn and Lycia were getting along. Bryen didn't know if that was a positive development or he should be worried. The pointed looks they directed toward him when they caught him glancing their way suggested the latter.

Rather than join them, he decided it was better to steer clear, finding a place among the trees that was a good distance away from the three women. To while away his time, he split the Spear of the Magii in two and began to run a sharpening stone along the blades.

It really wasn't necessary. Weapons crafted by the Giants of the Rime never needed sharpening. The steel always retained its edge, never degrading over time, no matter how it was used.

Even so, the exercise he had practiced so often in the Colosseum served as a calming influence for Bryen. Whether he felt the need to do it because of the Ghoules who he continued to track or the fact that Aislinn and Lycia were getting along better than he thought they would, he wasn't sure. If he was honest with himself, both reasons were probably the cause.

He focused on the stone running across the steel, allowing his mind to wander, doing his best to ignore the soft laughter that every so often drifted over from the other side of the campsite.

"I should have told you earlier," said Lycia, "for what you did in the Sanctuary. Thank you." Davin and several other gladiators had told her about how Aislinn had stood over her after the Ghoule Overlord wounded her, refusing to move no matter the foe she faced, whether Elder or Ghoule, until Bryen had finished his work with the Seven Stones and had come to heal her. "I'm sorry about waiting to do that."

"You're welcome." Aislinn shrugged off the need for an apology, slightly embarrassed. Then she looked at Lycia with a sly grin. "Am I allowed to call you sister as well?"

Lycia grumbled for just a second, remembering she had used that honorific while she was laying on the shimmering stone of the sandstone pillar's summit, the Ghoule Overlord's Dark Magic burning through her, stealing who she was. "I was waiting for when you were going to ask me about that." She shook her head in amused resignation. "You may. Just don't do it too often. In the Pit, the term was only used in serious circumstances. That's how it should remain. If you use it too much or to make fun of me, I'll stab you."

"I'll keep that in mind," said Aislinn, pleased by Lycia's response, "sister." She couldn't resist, at least just this one time, her eyes sparkling with delight.

"You know, you really can be aggravating," said Lycia, even though a small smile slipped through her usually unforgiving expression, "which makes it hard to like you all the time. But you're a good fighter, so I'll forgive your poor attempt at humor."

"Thank you for the praise and the criticism both," replied Aislinn, her broad grin tempering the seriousness of her tone.

Lycia nodded, thinking about how strange life was. When she had first heard of the Lady of the Southern Marches and then had the misfortune to meet her, she had hated Aislinn Winborne with a vengeance, wanting nothing more than to slide a dagger into her gut, viewing her as the cause for everything bad that happened to Bryen. But Lycia had learned after spending more time with the Lady Winborne that her perception was more than just a bit skewed, based more on her emotions than on reality.

"Don't let it go to your head."

"Of course not," Aislinn replied. "My instructors would be displeased if I did."

Lycia nodded, thinking of the two men who had helped to craft Aislinn into the warrior she was now. The Volkun and the Blademaster. Probably two of the most dangerous fighters in the Kingdom. Their efforts certainly testified to the quality of her pedigree. "You know, you're almost as good as me with a blade."

Aislinn laughed softly. She was thankful for the additional praise, though she assumed there was a reason for it. She had learned early in life that nothing was ever given for free, even kind words. "I would hope so. Otherwise, Bryen would probably be disappointed after having spent so much time training with me."

"He probably would be," agreed Lycia, who glanced quickly over toward the scarred gladiator, who didn't appear to be listening. He was focused on sharpening his blades, every so often his head perking up for a few seconds, then lowering again, probably because of his searching around them with the Talent. "I don't blame you, by the way."

"Blame me?" Aislinn had a feeling that she knew to what

Lycia referred. Still, she didn't want to make a mistake by jumping to the wrong conclusion. Especially at this moment.

"I don't blame you for what happened to Bryen," clarified Lycia with a sigh. "At least not anymore." Why she had chosen this moment to raise this issue, she didn't know. It just kind of popped out of her mouth before she could stop herself. Now out of the barn, it was too late to wrangle it back in. "He explained to me what occurred in the Southern Marches. About how your father was to blame, not you. That you didn't want to accept the Protector's collar but that you didn't have a choice. It was too late for you to do anything about it. And then how you helped him. Time and again."

"I was still responsible," Aislinn murmured, a slight touch of shame coloring her cheeks as she remembered the experience of having Bryen as her Protector. As her slave. "He was linked to me. I was the reason my father bought him."

"Yes, but he said that once you two had reached some kind of agreement, you got along a lot better. Bryen said that you treated him well. That you treated him like a person, not as another tool to be used. Not how your father treated him."

Aislinn didn't reply. She didn't know what to say.

"And I don't blame you for the fact that he's more interested in you than he is in me," continued Lycia, who couldn't look Aislinn in the eyes when she said the words, barely speaking loudly enough for her to hear. Making that admission was mortifying, though cleansing as well. It was as if she was letting go of a massive boulder that she had been carrying on her back.

Aislinn stayed quiet. What was she supposed to say to that? She realized that as the silence built between them, all she could do was be honest with Lycia just as Lycia was being honest with her.

"I'm sorry. I didn't expect to ..." I didn't think that I would fall in love with my Protector, she was thinking. Yet she couldn't speak the words that she wanted to say. She didn't have Lycia's courage.

"I know," said Lycia. "That's why I don't blame you. It just happened. That's how it is sometimes. I understand that. I don't like it, but that's irrelevant. I don't have to like it. I just have to deal with it now."

Aislinn could see the pain on Lycia's face. A deep sadness struck her. She knew that there was little that she could say that would take it away. "I'm sorry. I'm sorry for how I feel. I love him. There's nothing that I can do about it."

Lycia nodded, even giving Aislinn a small smile. "Don't feel that way. Please. I'm a big girl. I can handle it." She lifted her head to the sky and looked at the stars for a moment before letting out a deep breath. "Life is messy, and we have no choice but to deal with it." Lycia turned her gaze back to Aislinn, hoping that the angst that she still felt was no longer visible. "Have you spoken to Bryen about it yet? About how you feel about him?"

"No, not really," Aislinn said quietly, having a hard enough time just talking to herself about it. "Not in any depth. I haven't had the courage."

"It looks like we're both cowards then."

Aislinn and Lycia laughed at that, allowing some of the stress woven into their discussion to dissipate.

"We aren't the only cowards. Bryen is too. He owes you the truth, Lycia. I don't think he's treated you as he should."

Lycia nodded, grateful for the comment. "I'm sure Bryen and I will deal with it when the time is right, whether he wants to or not."

"Finally the truth comes out," Rafia grumbled after listening with half an ear to their conversation. "Finally you both have admitted that you have feelings for the same slightly oblivious young man who most of the time struggles to find his own feelings. I hope you both understand now that you have more in common than you don't. Strong women. Fighters. Yet both in love with a man constantly playing with a death wish." Rafia tried to say the last with humor, although it failed to come out that way.

Aislinn and Lycia just stared at each other, not expecting Rafia to speak so bluntly what neither of them had yet come to grips with themselves.

"If nothing else, I hope this exercise has shown you that it's not worth dancing around the edges of things," continued Rafia. "Life is short. Way too short. You don't want to waste the time that you have. So just admit the truth and move on regardless of how it plays out."

"Admit what?" asked Lycia tentatively, her nerves almost getting the better of her.

"Admit that you know the truth of what you've both been trying to avoid since the fight in the Sanctuary. Bryen loves you both, though he hasn't said it. The difference is that Bryen loves Lycia in a way that she wished he didn't, and he loves Aislinn in the way that she wants, but Lycia is still struggling with the fact that Bryen doesn't love her like she loves him, and Aislinn doesn't have the courage to tell Bryen how she feels about him and she's worried that speaking honestly will upset you, Lycia."

Aislinn and Lycia could only stare at the Magus. First, because it took them some time to work their way through what she had just explained to them. And second, because the Magus seemed to be right on the mark with her assessment, which unsettled them.

"Tell who about who she feels about who?" asked Bryen, lifting his head from the work he was doing on his blades, finally paying attention in large part because of Rafia's raised voice.

Aislinn and Lycia just glared at him, their eyes sharpening to the points of daggers. Clearly, he wasn't invited to join this conversation, Bryen's eyes widening slightly as he began to feel incredibly uncomfortable. Not knowing what to say or do, he was rescued when Davin walked into the small camp.

"Your turn, ladies," he said, completely unaware of the tension in the hollow. "Is there any dried beef left? I didn't really like it at first, but the taste has grown on me the more I've eaten it."

After he walked over to one of the supply bags and began to rummage through it, he realized that his arrival had been met with silence, which he found unusual. Aislinn usually had a kind word, Lycia perhaps a cutting stab. When he turned around with his dinner wrapped in waxed paper, he surveyed everyone at the campsite. The women stared at him intently. Bryen shrugged his shoulders as if to say that he didn't know what was going on. "Did I interrupt something?"

"No," Lycia replied hastily, pushing herself up off the ground and offering a hand to Aislinn as she made to rise from her seat against the tree. Neither felt ready to continue the conversation in that moment, as neither felt ready to deal with what Rafia had referenced. At least not yet. And certainly not with Davin as an audience.

"Tell who about how she feels about who?" asked Bryen again as the two women walked off into the darkness to check the surrounding wood, focusing his attention on the Keeper of Haven, hoping that she might be willing to enlighten him.

"You'll find out when you're ready," Rafia said, shaking her head in disgust, "and not before. It's not your story to tell."

"That doesn't help much," Bryen replied.

"It wasn't meant to be helpful."

"Clearly," he said.

Rafia smiled, though there was little kindness in it. "It's a good thing that I like you, young man. You'll understand this better than most based on what you've had to deal with in your life, but allow me to give you some advice. It's the same advice that I gave the young ladies. I don't know if they'll pay attention to it. I can only hope that you will."

Bryen nodded that he was ready for the knowledge that she was about to share with him.

"Don't wait."

Bryen was quiet for a time as he considered what she had said. Then his eyebrows rose. "Don't wait for what?" he asked.

Rafia shook her head again, this time in irritation. "Don't wait," she repeated. Then she pushed herself up and walked off among the trees.

Bryen looked at Davin, who hadn't said a word, his red hair more disheveled than usual as he stuffed several pieces of dried meat into his mouth.

"Do you understand what she means?"

Davin just looked at his friend as he chewed, his teeth working on the stringy, tough meat. He appeared uncertain at first, but then he smiled. "It seemed like pretty simple advice actually."

"Don't wait," Bryen said skeptically.

"Yes, don't wait. Don't wait for anything. If you want something, go after it. If you want to do something, do it. If you want someone, don't wait to tell them." Then Davin turned away from his friend and started digging into their supplies again, looking for a few more pieces of dried beef.

Bryen stared at Davin in surprise. He had been expecting a joke rather than words of wisdom from his friend, who usually preferred not to think too deeply on a topic. Then again, perhaps that's why Davin deciphered Rafia's advice so easily.

11

─────────

HUNTED BY A SHADOW

"I don't like this," said Lycia. "This is worse than fighting that giant scorpion in the Pit."

She crept carefully among the daggerlike rocks that stuck up out of the ground and were just as sharp as her blades. The spearlike barbs that broadened toward the base were strangely all about five feet in height and would tear her to shreds if she wasn't careful where she stepped. Every few seconds her eyes flicked up to the gentle slope that would lead them out of the depression, looking forward to reaching the higher ground, the slow progress grating on her already stretched nerves.

Not rocks, she realized, cautiously reaching out every so often to use the keen projections to maintain her balance, always careful where she placed her hands. Her brother had already garnered a nasty slice across his palm that wouldn't stop bleeding until Bryen healed it for him.

A petrified forest that resembled the stalagmites you would see deep in a cave, although thinner and keener, as if they had been whittled down over time by the wind and rain of the Lost Land, the ossified remnants of the forest pockmarked, rough, yet still incredibly dangerous.

It appeared as if some massive creature had swiped through the grove with its claw exactly at chest height, leaving razor-sharp stone spikes in its wake. She would have been curious about how the unique and distinctly unsettling forest had been created if she wasn't traversing it herself with the threat of Ghoules coming their way hanging over her head.

"The fact that we're moving through a petrified wood where the slightest misstep means a nasty wound or is there something else that you don't like?" asked Davin, who had pushed his usual impetuousness to the side and was taking his time now as he followed his sister out of the hollow and up to a plateau shrouded in a grey mist that stretched off into the distance. Ominous, he thought, but he preferred the fog to what he was calling in his own mind the Garden of Spears.

Bryen, Aislinn, and Rafia waited for them, all of the Magii staring intently at what lay ahead. They were more than a day beyond the Great Forest, yet it seemed like they had barely made any progress, and from what Bryen had told them of the Lost Land they still had a good distance to travel before they reached the heart of the Caldera.

"We're too exposed," clarified Lycia, glad to finally be free of the depression as she scrambled out of the hollow, Bryen giving her a hand, relieved to leave the petrified forest and its needle-sharp spikes behind her.

"It does send a shiver up your spine, doesn't it?" asked Davin, although that fact seemed to enliven the gladiator. He fed off the energy of being in danger, needing that charge to feel fully alive. "Although ever since we've left the Great Forest, I've felt just as you said. Exposed."

"Like we're not meant to be here," suggested Lycia.

"Correct," said Davin, whose eyes whipped from side to side as they started walking across the steppe, the twins leading the way. He soon discovered the rocky plain wasn't like the Breakwater Plateau with its endless grass waving in the wind. Rather, it actually was a land of gullies and fissures hidden by a wispy, fetid fog that spit out from the many vents and cavities that blemished the ground. "I know there aren't any Ghoules near us. Still, it feels like we're being watched."

"You feel that as well?"

"I do," Davin grumbled, "and I hate it."

"Then as Declan would say …" Lycia began.

"Eyes sharp," finished Davin.

As they began their journey through a landscape that they had never encountered before and never knew could exist, Bryen and the others sought to travel near the top of the small ravines, though they were careful to stay off the crests as much as possible so as not to reveal themselves to anything that might be watching for them.

They also kept out of the trenches unless they had no choice but to hike through the defiles. Those shadowy, ragged gashes in the land worried them. They screamed ambush.

They loathed the stench released by the silky mist that billowed out of the flues, the odor often taking their breath away as they continued north through the Lost Land, unable to get used to the terrible smell. No matter what they tried, spitting, washing out their mouths with water, breathing through a piece of cloth, the stench still burned the back of their throats. Although they viewed it as a small sacrifice to make if the path through this noxious landscape kept them clear of the Ghoules and whatever other beasts they had yet to identify that might be hunting them.

In front of the many slits in the ground, too often they glimpsed the sun-bleached bones of several large animals. Though no animal they were familiar with because all of the bones were shattered, crushed, or gnawed down.

Those discoveries didn't worry them too much, the kills obviously having occurred well in the past. It was the handful of carcasses that they came across where there were still some strips of flesh hanging off the skeletons that worried them.

The skeletal remains didn't give them a clue as to what might have been eaten. They did reveal what had done the eating.

A large creature, bigger than a Ghoule, with teeth sharp enough to crunch through bone. What they found strange and just a bit worrisome were the unique swirls in the dirt. Definitely not the clawed feet of what they viewed as their greatest threat. But even Rafia, with her broad knowledge of the creatures created by the Ghoule Overlord, had no idea what could have made the marks and slaughtered these beasts.

"It might have been better if the Lost Land had remained lost," grumbled Lycia.

"You're just being a sourpuss," challenged Davin. "Where's your sense of adventure? We're in the Lost Land! No one but a long-dead Magus has even made it this far into a place that's more myth than reality in the minds of Caledonians."

"I'm being realistic," argued Lycia, motioning to the skeletons down below them. "We don't even know what killed whatever those animals were. Those bones might actually be Ghoules, but there's no way to tell because whatever ate them was too thorough. I don't mind dealing with threats. I'd just prefer to know more about the dangers we face. I like to be prepared. Here it's just one surprise after another."

"But that's what makes what we're doing so interesting," countered Davin. "So much fun. We're explorers! We're doing something that no one else will ever have the opportunity to do. How could that not be exciting?"

"There's a fine line, which I'd prefer not to cross, between doing something that's exciting and doing something that's foolhardy."

"Maybe so," Davin admitted reluctantly, "but Aislinn is using the Talent right now to keep an eye on what's around us.

Nothing can take us by surprise, so we have nothing to fear. And we have three Magii with us to boot. We should be able to kill with little trouble anything that comes at us."

"I'm sorry, I just don't share your confidence." Lycia reached out a hand to balance herself, the loose shale beneath her feet giving way and sliding down to the base of the trench where another fairly recent carcass was visible along the side of the defile. Thankfully, she didn't follow the tumbling rocks and pebbles, her brother grasping her hand just in time. "There's just something about this place that feels wrong."

"Could be the smell," suggested Davin, thinking he was being helpful but really only succeeding in irritating his sister, Lycia not believing that he was taking her concerns seriously. So she decided to try to impress upon Davin the need for caution, a conversation they had engaged in many times before, usually with few useful results.

Bryen let his friends' discussion drift over him, not really paying attention, knowing from experience that the argument would continue between the twins until someone else put a stop to it. He didn't have the heart or the energy to do it. As Davin had said, Aislinn was using the Talent to search around them for any unseen perils, and the banter between the two seemed to be taking their minds off the intimidating environment they were navigating.

In fact, as they made their way above the crevices that darkened the rocky floor of the gulley, he had been thinking about Banshee and the other Griffons waiting for them in the Great Forest. Had he made the right decision to ask them to stay there? He wasn't certain. With the Griffons, they could have avoided the petrified forest and this noxious environment of fumes and trenches and whatever came after as they moved across the Caldera.

He was certain that with all the Ghoule packs wandering around them as they made their way toward the Cauldron and the Temple of the Ghoules that they would have been spotted eventually. Any of the Elders leading those packs that were moving through the Caldera as if they were searching for something would have found them out.

Even so, was the surprise they were seeking to achieve worth the additional time and risk required to get to the center of the Ghoule Overlord's power?

When they stopped for the night, Bryen always reached out to Banshee to find out how she and the other Griffons were doing. Perhaps he should ask them to find a spot farther north than the Great Forest where they could remain concealed but be closer if there was a need for their assistance.

"Lost in thought?" asked Rafia, the Magus walking behind Bryen and bringing up the rear, Aislinn right in front of him, the twins slowly extending their lead.

"Rethinking my decision to not bring Banshee and the other Griffons this far into the Lost Land," replied Bryen.

"It was the right decision," said Rafia, the certainty in her voice helping to reduce his doubt. "We would have been spotted if we had flown directly to the Cauldron. And if that had happened, then the Ghoule Overlord, or rather the Curse, would have been aware of our presence. Who knows what we would have faced when we arrived?"

"Still, a Ghoule Legion might have been preferable to this," suggested Bryen. "At least we'd know what we were up against."

"True, we would have that," agreed Rafia, "and I'm certain that you and the other gladiators would do just fine against the beasts. But at least now we have a chance at surprising that monster, and surprise is never a bad thing when you're fighting in an environment that's foreign to you. When you're fighting against something that requires more than just destroying its flesh to kill it."

"Good point," said Bryen. "I just can't get what Lycia said out of my mind, that we don't belong here."

"Lycia is quite correct," confirmed Rafia. "We don't belong here. I don't think the Ghoules belong here either. I think they're stuck here. Of course, that's their problem, not ours. Once we do what needs to be done, we can put the Lost Land behind us once and for all."

Bryen grunted his agreement, then turned his attention to Aislinn for a moment. "Anything to worry about?"

"Nothing right now," replied Aislinn, "and I'm extending the Talent into the crevices in the gullies below us just to be safe. Empty so far. I'll let you know if that changes. The Ghoules don't appear to be entering this outer rim of the Cauldron, preferring to do their scouting around the edge."

"What do you mean?" Bryen asked, curious about that revelation.

"I've tracked several Ghoule packs to the border of the petrified forest, as if they may have found our trail. None of them have ventured out of that ossified wood, though, staying well clear of this maze of trenches and vents."

"Any idea why?" asked Bryen.

"Nothing that I can tell with the Talent," replied Aislinn. "One strange thing did happen, however, and it continues to worry me."

"What was that?"

"One Ghoule pack did come up through the petrified forest and began to walk in among the fissures no more than a league to the west of where we did. For a time, that pack concerned me, because they were coming in our direction, so I kept a close eye."

"But you're not worried anymore?"

"No, not as much as I was."

"They turned back?" asked Bryen.

"No, not exactly," replied Aislinn, continuing to scan around them with the Talent as she conversed with Bryen. "They disappeared. That's why the whole thing still bothers me."

"What do you mean they disappeared? You lost track of them?" Bryen's most immediate concern was that there was a Ghoule pack following them that they couldn't identify. His concern shifted in a different direction when Aislinn explained.

"One minute, the Ghoule pack was there. The next, it was gone. I searched the area thoroughly, and even with the fog and the fumes, I didn't see anything to suggest that the beasts were still following us. I assumed that they turned back, but I never found them again after I lost them. If they didn't turn back, then what happened to them?"

"Was there an Elder with them?"

"There was."

Bryen thought about that for a few seconds. "When you realized the Ghoules had disappeared and you couldn't find them, did you search for the Dark Magic of the Elder?"

"I did. I couldn't find it. The Curse affiliated with that Elder simply disappeared. There one moment, gone the next."

"Thanks," said Bryen, knowing that Aislinn was always exceedingly thorough in her work. "If you sense anything else that seems off, let me know."

"Have no doubt of that." Aislinn, who had been slightly distracted when speaking with Bryen since she was tracking more than a dozen Ghoule packs at present, looked back at him with a questioning eye. "Are you thinking what I'm thinking?"

"That the Ghoule pack didn't turn around? That it disappeared for another reason? Yes."

"You think something made the beasts disappear," interjected Rafia.

"The only way to lose the taint of the Curse that identifies an Elder is for that Elder to die. As soon as that happens, the Curse within it slips away, returning to its original source. It's gone. If the Elder moved in a different direction, Aislinn should be able to find the beast again."

Aislinn thought about what Bryen had just said, then began

searching with greater diligence around them. "If what you're suggesting is correct, what could kill an Elder and a pack of Ghoules in their own homeland?"

"I don't think we want to find out the answer to that question," replied Rafia.

"I certainly don't," agreed Bryen. "Aislinn, let me know if you find anything out of place with the Talent. Anything that doesn't fit."

"You're not being very specific."

"I'm being as specific as I can be. This is a strange place, so it's the best that I can do. We expect to find Ghoules here. If you identify anything else that gives you even the slightest cause for concern, let me know."

She nodded and returned to her task, redoubling her efforts with the Talent. If Bryen was right, they had bigger concerns than the Ghoule packs that were always circling on their periphery.

Bryen then added his efforts to hers, using the Talent to search around them, paying particular attention to the crevices that lined the base of the trench they were walking above.

"Find anything?" asked Rafia.

"No, I didn't. Nothing but the Ghoule packs that Aislinn is tracking."

He should have taken that as good news. He didn't, however, his worry only increasing. Not after hearing from Aislinn that an Elder and a Ghoule pack had vanished. He was becoming increasingly uneasy. Even more uneasy than he had been when they had made their way through the petrified wood. That anxiety building within him with every step he took deeper into the Lost Land.

Bryen's senses gained greater clarity as he scanned around them, using the Talent to see what they couldn't see. Not looking for Ghoules. Not really looking for anything. Just looking at the world in a different way.

It was quiet. Eerily so. There was no movement but for a few small rocks skittering down the side of the gulley, unavoidably knocked free by their boots. And there was no breeze now, so the fog had settled over them rather than swirling about, making it difficult to see more than a dozen feet in any direction. The noxious odor that hung in the air mixed with the unaccustomed warmth from the steam spouting out of the many vents and crevices peppering the landscape didn't help either, making him feel slightly queasy.

"You're still worried," said Rafia.

"I can't help it," he replied. "I don't like not knowing what I don't know." Just a heartbeat later he realized that his concern was justified, the skin on the back of his neck prickling. He was certain now. They were being tracked.

But why did he feel this way? There was no good cause to give credence to the warning.

Aislinn hadn't found anything that should give them concern, and neither had he. Could it be the uniqueness of their circumstances that was playing on his fears? He didn't think so. So he continued to search around them with both his eyes and the Talent, trying to see what he couldn't see, wondering if whatever was hunting them could hide just like he could with the Talent.

Rafia chuckled at that. "One of Noorsin's favorite sayings."

"It seems particularly appropriate for what we're dealing with now, Ghoule packs and Elders disappearing, a landscape that's hiding secrets that we can't discover even with the Talent."

"There's more to it than that," nudged Rafia. She had gotten to know Bryen quite well since first meeting him on the Haven dock what seemed like years but was only months ago.

After a time, Bryen nodded reluctantly. "You are all here because of me, and we're facing some dangers that we can't even identify. I don't like putting others at risk if I can avoid it. If there's a threat that needs to be faced, I'd prefer to be the one to do it."

"That's the curse of being a good leader," said Rafia, "worrying about the people you are responsible for. I'd ask that you keep in mind that we're not just here because of you, though that's a part of it. We're here because we need to be. You can't succeed without us. You need us, it's as simple as that."

"You know, that really doesn't help."

"Nor should it," said Rafia. "If it did, I would be worried about you."

"We wouldn't want that," said Bryen, his sarcasm plain.

"No, we wouldn't," confirmed Rafia with a soft chuckle. "Since Aislinn is doing such an excellent job of keeping an eye out for any danger, even with the anomaly of a Ghoule pack and Elder having gone missing, perhaps we could talk about something else that you need to be aware of."

"What would that be?"

"The Order of the Magii."

Rafia's response almost made him stop short, as he hadn't been expecting that. "What about it?"

"With Sirius gone," said Rafia, saying that truth out loud making her eyes water, "the responsibility for leading the Order has fallen to me, and there are some things that you need to know."

"I'm all ears," replied Bryen, pleased to have something to talk about that would sidetrack him at least temporarily from his current concerns. Even so, he continued to add his efforts to Aislinn's, searching around them with the Talent, trying to see what he couldn't see, each time finding nothing that would explain his current disquiet, which only served to frustrate him all the more.

As they continued along near the top of the trench, Rafia provided a brief history of the Order of the Magii in Caledonia, the role it had played historically, even touching upon the fear that those with the Talent engendered. She didn't feel the need to discuss the Order's responsibility with respect to protecting against the Curse and the Ghoules, Bryen already quite knowledgeable in that regard. What Bryen found most interesting was when Rafia discussed how the Order had played a role in the politics of the Kingdom since before the First Ghoule War, achieving mixed results at best.

"So that's the primary tension, then," said Bryen, "and it's likely helped to mold how people view Magii to this day. How the Order has used people without any real concern for them, trying to attain some larger goal that the Magii believed was worthy of the effort yet more often than not failing to achieve the desired objective or gaining a result that only made the situation worse."

"Just so," confirmed Rafia. "It's been going on since the Order was first formed, openly and surreptitiously depending on the need and who was leading the Order at the time."

"Obviously it hasn't worked out very well over the years."

"Not as well as we would have liked," admitted Rafia, unafraid to speak bluntly with Bryen. "The Order's attempts to guide events in Caledonia were all carried out in the name of peace and prosperity and always in the name of the greater good."

"The greater good wasn't always good for the people ensnared, though, was it?" asked Bryen.

"Unfortunately not," confirmed Rafia. "Besides, it's arrogant to think that every variable can be controlled or managed. Even the best-laid plans can be thrown awry by the smallest miscalculation. One need only look at the Belerons."

"How so?" Rafia had piqued his curiosity, already guessing at what she might reveal to him.

"Centuries ago the Order helped to engineer the rise of the Belerons. It worked well for a time, Caledonia strong and stable, but as you know from personal experience that lineage proved rotten in the end. Thankfully you cut if off before it could fester even more."

"It's like that saying about a butterfly," said Bryen. "That the movement of a butterfly's wings can be the beginning of a tsunami that strikes on the other side of an ocean. That one event, one decision, can lead in a variety of unknown directions that in turn create multiple possible conclusions, most of which were never considered or desired. The Order of the Magii couldn't account for all the possible pathways down which any decision might take them."

"True," said Rafia, recalling the analogy herself. "The reality is that when you try to control events, control the future, it never works out the way you expect. Fixing one thing often creates a problem somewhere else. So all you do is spend your time trying to fix your mistakes, mistakes that wouldn't need fixing to begin with if you'd left well enough alone."

"That's not a position I would want to be in."

"Neither would I."

"That's why you left for Haven, isn't it?" said Bryen, understanding dawning within him. "Not just because of the other issue."

"Yes, in part," Rafia admitted. "As you know, the main reason was because of Sirius. But it was also because when Sirius became Master of the Magii, he tried his hand at managing events in the larger world. No matter how well intentioned, I didn't like how the Order was playing with people's lives all with the goal of trying to craft a better world. As you learned through your own experience with Sirius' plans, nothing ever works out in the way that you expect or want."

"And now that you're the Master of the Magii?" asked Bryen. "What's your take on the role the Order should play in the world?"

"Now that I'm the Master?" Rafia took her time before responding. Both she and Bryen needed to watch their footing as the steepness of the path forced them down a slope of loose shale toward the base of the gulley, no other options for crossing this part of the Caldera open to them. "Now that I'm the Master, the Order will advise, not guide. If we can help, we will. And if we are ignored, we will still try to help. But we are not what we used to be, nor should we be, so we should not try to play at what we have done in the past. It's time for a fresh start."

"And I'm assuming that this history lesson applies to me since I'm one of those anomalies that you didn't expect to find at the end of the path."

"Exactly so," admitted Rafia.

"So once this is over, if I survive, if we achieve our objective, the Order will leave me be? I can choose my own path for going forward? I won't be just another piece to be played?"

"Yes. Some of the Magii likely won't like that. They'll view you as too valuable, even possibly as a threat, what with the Seventh Stone joining with you. But that isn't important. What's important is that you lead the life you want. As I said, it's time for a fresh start, for all of us."

"I couldn't agree with you more, and thank you," said Bryen, although he didn't reveal that his comment related to more than what Rafia had in mind for the Order of the Magii. He shoved those thoughts to the side as a more immediate and dangerous concern became top of mind. "We're being hunted. I'm sure of it now."

Bryen's words brought everyone to a stop. They had reached the bottom of a gulley, the path that would take them back to the crest and away from the crevices that littered the ground just a few dozen feet in front of them. Yet in that moment it seemed like a very long way to go.

"How do you know?" asked Aislinn. "I haven't located anything with the Talent that should give us reason to worry."

"Neither have I," said Rafia, "and I've been using the Talent to search around us every so often just as Aislinn has been doing."

"It's just a feeling. No more than that. When I get this sensation, I tend to listen to it."

"That's good enough for me," said Davin, spear held lightly in his hands, ready to bring the weapon to bear. He looked around them warily, his eyes drawn inescapably to the several dark crevices in the ground that could be hiding almost anything.

"His premonitions do tend to be right," admitted Lycia, both swords in hand, who like her brother was also searching for any movement that might reveal an unseen threat.

"I also checked around us with the Talent," Bryen said. "I didn't find anything, but this feeling is never wrong. It kept me alive in the Pit."

"Then by all means listen to it," said Davin.

"What is it, Bryen?" asked Aislinn.

"I don't know what it is," he replied. "I can't pinpoint it. It feels like a disturbance, barely there. But it is there. I'm sure of it. I just can't identify it. At first, I thought it was just because we were in the Lost Land. Not anymore. There's more to it than that. I think this disturbance, whatever it is, is stalking us, and has been ever since we left the petrified forest."

"Do you think it might have something to do with the Ghoule pack that disappeared?"

"I wouldn't be surprised," said Bryen. The warning had turned his gaze toward a point just a dozen paces to his right, his eyes narrowing as if he could see something that no one else could.

Aislinn and Rafia both reached for the Talent again, using the natural magic of the world to search around them.

"I still can't find anything," said Rafia, Aislinn nodding reluctantly in agreement. None of the Ghoule packs that they had been tracking were anywhere near them, and they could sense nothing else that should give them any cause for concern.

"It's flitting about, not staying in one place long enough to identify it," said Bryen. "It's there, then it's not. Close, then far, then close again. Sometimes no more than a few feet away. It's testing us. It wants to know if we can find it. It wants to see what we're going to do."

"Could it be more than one?" asked Aislinn.

"That's certainly possible," admitted Bryen.

"The Talent won't give us more than what we're getting now," said Rafia, "and that's certainly not enough. Perhaps, Bryen, you could search for whatever it is in a way that might give you more information than Aislinn or I can acquire?"

Bryen nodded. He understood what she was asking him to do. Months before, he might have hesitated. Not now. Maintaining his control over the Talent, he opened himself to the Seventh Stone. When the artifact had first joined with him and he had learned that a large quantity of the Curse resided within him, Bryen had been terrified. Because he had learned how to protect himself against the taint of the Curse, he was only mildly concerned now, and more out of a residual fear that had no basis in reality.

Now he hoped the Curse would aid him in what he was about to do. He had learned over time that there was a benefit attached to the Dark Magic lurking within him. It sought out other Dark Magic, trying to connect with it.

With that thought in mind, Bryen allowed that urge, that desire for the Curse locked away within him to connect with any Dark Magic close to him, to take hold for just a few seconds.

In an instant, he had it. He locked away the Curse at the exact same moment that he locked onto what was hunting them. At first, he thought it was a shadow. Then he realized immediately that it was much more than just that. It was all too real.

Bryen glided forward a few feet and slashed down with his spear, then spun around faster than a black dragon, lunging backward with a thrust before he whipped back around with another slice that if it had struck a Ghoule would have taken the beast's head from his neck. He then began to twirl the Spear of the Magii in front of him, the blades sparking with the Talent, as he walked toward one of the crevices, forcing whatever it was he fought away from everyone else.

Once he had gained the distance that he judged would keep Aislinn and the others relatively safe, Bryen slashed and cut again, moving in a blur from side to side, trying to keep the shadow that only he could see thanks to the power of the Seventh Stone from getting past him, and that's all that mattered to him in that moment.

Bryen thought that he could make out a dim outline of the creature, though even with the energy of the artifact guiding his movements, a good look at the beast eluded him. The creature was still just a dim shape that twisted and turned in front of him, though it was enough for Bryen to fight with some confidence.

Davin and Lycia wanted to offer the aid of their steel, Aislinn and Rafia the Talent, but unable to see what Bryen was combating, they held back, fearing they would only get in his way or distract him at the worst possible time. They had no idea what kind of beast was opposing him no matter how hard they looked.

Then they saw a spark, Bryen's steel cutting across some kind of invisible armor. Then another spark. And a third as the flashes of contact became a more frequent occurrence, Bryen demonstrating the speed and agility that he had come to be known for in the Pit.

Growls and hisses soon followed every time Bryen's blazing

steel struck true. Whatever Bryen was fighting clearly was not pleased with how the combat had turned, the creature giving up the advantage of stealth and giving in to its anger. Wanting to build on his success, the Protector continued to attack at a furious pace, slashing and slicing with a ferocious speed, flecks of pitch-black blood now flying through the air.

Then, after more than a dozen flashes in just a few seconds, a high-pitched screech of rage ripped through the narrow trench. Bryen stepped back, holding the Spear of the Magii in front of him, watching as the shadow slipped into the crevice that was right in front of him, slinking away from the combat.

Silence fell again in what was usually a silent land. When Bryen turned back around, his black leather armor hid the creature's blood. His arms and legs didn't. By all accounts, the gladiator had done well against the creature based on the splatter covering his body.

"What was it?" asked Davin.

"I think it was an Echidna," Bryen replied.

"A what?" asked Lycia, never having heard the term.

"An Echidna," Bryen repeated. "I couldn't see it very clearly even with the power of the Seventh Stone, which only gave me an outline of the beast's body and a few flashes of color whenever I scored a hit. Viktor Keldragan told me of some of the beasts that he came across when he entered the Lost Land, and this was one of them. An Echidna stands taller than a Ghoule, although that's a relative term because the lower body is that of a serpent. It's incredibly fast with a sinuous, snakelike movement. They also have fangs instead of teeth, and from what I remember from what Viktor said, the fangs release a toxic agent in the bloodstream that paralyzes their prey so they can take their time eating."

"That sounds thoroughly unpleasant," murmured Aislinn.

"We couldn't even see what it was," protested Lycia.

"An Echidna isn't invisible, but it is almost perfectly camouflaged. The Dark Magic within it allows it to blend into its surroundings like we can with the Talent, but the beast does it naturally."

"I don't like the sound of that at all," said Rafia.

"Neither do I," agreed Bryen. "We need to figure out how to fight it. That one escaped, but we have several more following us. They travel in packs of no fewer than six."

"Well, that's just wonderful," Lycia offered with a heavy dose of sarcasm. "Our time in the Lost Land is just getting better and better."

12

BAIT AND SWITCH

Jerad slashed down with his sword, his timing perfect as the sharp blade cut off the claw of the Ghoule who had been reaching for him over the boulder. The beast screamed in shocked agony just as the Sergeant of the Battersea Guard's steel sparked against the stone, the Ghoule rearing back as black blood spurted from the stump.

He didn't have time to savor that small victory, bringing his sword back up to knock away another Ghoule's spear right before it punched through the chest of the soldier fighting next to him. Jerad's blow was strong enough to push the beast's lunge off target, giving the soldier the opportunity to slice across the overextended beast's neck with his sword, the Ghoule falling away from the clash, losing his footing as he tried uselessly with his claws to stop the river of blood pouring from his neck.

Jerad wasn't done, far from it. He shifted quickly down the line to his left, cutting across another Ghoule's forearm, the beast having hooked one of the Battersea Guard in the arm with his spear. The Ghoule was attempting to pull the woman over the boulders, and she was losing that battle, the beast too strong and too determined. The soldier's eyes filled with terror, understanding that if the Ghoule succeeded, when the fight was done she would be his next meal.

The unsuspecting Ghoule, so focused on taking his prize, hissed in pain, then fell backward, dropping his spear when Jerad drove his sword between the beast's ribs and then gave the steel a sharp twist for good measure before tearing it free. With a hard tug that brought a cry of anguish from the wounded soldier, Jerad freed her from the blackened steel, then claiming the weapon as his own he moved her behind him.

"Back over the crest!" he shouted at the soldier. He could tell that her wound was painful. It wasn't incapacitating. "And take as many of the wounded with you as you can. You have two minutes!"

The soldier nodded in understanding. Cradling her arm, she started to help the handful of other soldiers who had been wounded in the skirmish back toward the trees behind them. Once the wounded soldier was free from the fight, Jerad hefted the spear in his left hand a few times, then threw it back over the boulders.

Although his aim wasn't as good as he would have liked, the sharp steel point still sliced across the bicep of another Ghoule who was reaching over the boulders, drawing the beast's attention before he could attack one of Jerad's soldiers who was already fighting for his life against an even larger Ghoule. The beast appeared to have only one desire, and that was to pound the Caledonian into the ground with either his sword or his claws, which one didn't seem to matter.

Realizing that the one throw wouldn't be enough to save the struggling soldier, Jerad swung his sword over the boulders in a deadly arc, aiming for the Ghoule who was having some difficulty holding onto his spear, his clawed fingers refusing to work because of the gash across his arm, Jared's steel cutting to the bone. The Sergeant took advantage of the beast's moment of indecision, the Ghoule trying to decide whether to drop the spear and just use his claws, which were more than capable of shredding leather armor and flesh. Those few seconds of hesitation were all that Jerad needed to make the decision for the Ghoule, slicing down with his blade through the wrist and removing the beast's claw that was still grasping the haft of the spear.

Ignoring the Ghoule's anguished cry, Jerad cursed himself for a fool as he surveyed the clash swirling around him. He should have followed the plan. Instead, he had decided to make use of the opportunity he had been given when the Ghoules didn't try to climb over the boulders right at the start of the fight.

He had gotten greedy. Now several of his soldiers were dead, a few even pulled over the large rocks so that the Ghoules could feast on them later, and his wounded were struggling back the way that they had come. Hopefully they would get over the hill in time.

Jerad gripped his sword with both hands, parrying a swing by another Ghoule he had just wounded, blocking the clawed strike right before it dug into his chest. Then, with a quick flick of his wrists, he sliced right between the beast's clawed fingers and into the Ghoule's left hand.

Not done with his bloody work, with a vicious twist, he ripped his sword free and with his steel came two of the Ghoule's needle-sharp fingers. The howl that Jerad earned from the Ghoule gave him some small satisfaction, although not enough to absolve him of his mistake.

He was only supposed to lead one charge against the Ghoules, not try to dig them out of their makeshift fortification, the beasts having rolled several large boulders across the path that snaked between the mountains to prevent the soldiers of the Battersea Guard from moving farther north along the boundary of the Winter Pass. He just couldn't help himself. It was too tempting a target.

After the success of that first charge, his soldiers killing two Ghoules with no losses of his own, Jerad had pressed the attack rather than disengaging and moving on to the next step in their plan. He believed that he could reduce the beasts' numbers by a few more before pulling back.

He was certain that the Ghoules' natural aggressiveness would kick in, the beasts unwilling to stay behind the boulders for very long. Because of the additional losses he would inflict on the beasts, the Ghoules would be even more motivated to follow him, unable to resist the chance to gain some revenge on the humans who had embarrassed them.

He had also assumed that having one company of the Battersea Guard with him would be more than enough to press the beasts. He was mistaken in that regard as well. The Ghoules recovered faster than he thought was possible from their initial setback and now were fighting so murderously that Jerad had no good way to disengage without putting even more of his soldiers at risk.

He was still surprised that the beasts demonstrated the discipline to fight from a defensive position, never having seen them do so before. It seemed to go against everything they had learned about the Ghoules, their ingrained belligerence always before guiding their decisions. So he could only hope that their self-control would falter when it was most needed.

Jerad had sensed the possibility of that happening during the fight, many of the Ghoules desperate to leave their makeshift breastwork, often getting a leg over the rocks before being called back. But the damn Elder kept shouting at the beasts in that guttural language of theirs, keeping them in place, the beasts too afraid of the servant of the Ghoule Overlord to do anything other than remain behind their fortification.

Cursing himself for his mistake one more time, he swung for the neck of the Ghoule who stood across from him, then twisted his grip so that the steel skidded across the stone and sliced into the beast's side instead, the Ghoule unable to compensate for the speed of the maneuver. Jerad pulled his blade back with a hard tug, the steel pulling free and bringing with it a large splash of the Ghoule's thick black blood.

Recognizing the seriousness of the wound, Jerad stepped back a few feet from the barrier, the Ghoule clutching at his ribs, stumbling back, then disappearing behind the rock. The beast had either fallen to his knees or the ground. Jerad didn't care. It just meant one less Ghoule to have to fight.

With the few seconds of breathing space that followed, Jerad realized that it was time to implement the larger strategy that he had formulated with Dani and the Magus before he had gone off plan. With his charge stalled, Jerad and his soldiers had no chance of getting past the beasts, and he had no way to break free from them either. At least not without some help.

And that's what he needed now, because as soon as his soldiers turned their backs, he doubted that the Elder would be able to exercise much control over the Ghoules; in fact, he was counting on that. His soldiers would be too enticing to the beasts, the Ghoules unable to resist a hunt.

Dani had suggested that there would come a time that he would need to think like his friend, the Volkun. Sometimes the straightforward approach that he preferred when leading the Battersea Guard wasn't always the best. She was right about that.

Now was when he needed to think like the Wolf. He needed to focus on being fast, smart, and cunning, because brute strength wasn't going to win this fight. It rarely did when fighting Ghoules on foot.

"Maria!" shouted Jerad. "When you're ready!"

"Give me just a moment," replied the Magus, sending just a

few more spikes of energy over the boulders that blocked the path so that the Elder leading the Ghoules had no choice but to focus on her rather than the soldiers from the Southern Marches.

The beast ducked below the makeshift barrier to avoid the first few shots, then attempted to show his disdain for her attack by forming a shield of spinning black mist. He quickly gave up his bravado, diving back down as she sent several shards of power toward the boulders rather than at him, the rapid-fire explosions that followed filling the air with thousands of stone splinters that cut into flesh just as easily as a blade.

Satisfied that the Elder would be keeping his head down for at least the next few seconds, Maria did exactly as they discussed before they had engaged with these Ghoules.

"Take cover!" Maria shouted in a voice loud enough for every soldier to hear.

She then employed the skill that she had learned from her mentor, Rafia. Stretching out her arms so that they were parallel to the ground, she whipped her hands down to her sides. At that same instant, a series of lightning bolts slammed into the dirt right in front of the Ghoules' stone barricade.

The power of the strikes shattered two of the boulders, blasting thousands more splinters of rock back toward the beasts, ripping into their flesh. Two of the Ghoules died instantly, one with a stone shard piercing his eye and lodging in his brain, the other asphyxiating as a small piece of rock shot through the air and crushed his windpipe.

A heavy silence fell over the battlefield that was soon interrupted as the Ghoules coughed and gagged, breathing in the dirt and the pulverized rock. Ignoring their brethren who had died in the Magus' attack, the beasts waited expectantly for the humans to continue their assault, assuming that the use of the Talent presaged another attack, their quarry advancing toward them again once the cloud of detritus cleared.

When it finally did, the Ghoules stared dumbstruck, never expecting that the humans would flee. The soldiers were already well beyond the sparse thicket that they had first emerged from when they attacked and were racing for the crest of the gradually ascending hill that was behind the wood, the humans who had been wounded just then making it over the top and disappearing from view.

Why the humans thought that they could escape, the Ghoules didn't know. In fact, they found the effort almost amusing, even more so intoxicating. There was nowhere for their prey to run. Nowhere to hide.

Behind the hill there was only a gentle slope that led down to a small plateau that was nestled between the two peaks that towered into the sky on each side. The humans weren't running to their freedom. The humans were running to their doom. They were falling into a trap of their own making.

The Ghoules' natural instinct to pursue was too strong to be ignored this time, the sight of their fleeing prey setting their blood pulsing through their veins. Many of the beasts were desperate to earn their bone knives, and this was their best chance to do that.

They were also hungry, not having had a decent meal since they had forced their way through the Weir. Once they caught up to the humans, they could feast on the fools who had thought that they could stand across from them on the battle-field as equals and then those Ghoules yet to craft the symbol that marked them as warriors in their society could do so.

Despite the harsh admonitions from the Elder to stay in place, who was only now pushing himself up off the ground and dusting himself off, the Ghoules vaulted over the boulders and gave chase. Screaming in both anger and frustration at his loss of control, the Elder had no choice but to follow his

Ghoules. If he didn't they would risk fighting the Magus on their own, and though they were accomplished warriors, they had no effective defense against the Talent.

As the Elder loped through the trees and then up the grassy slope just behind his Ghoules, his clawed feet tearing great tufts of turf from the hill, despite his fighters' disobedience, he was actually pleased that he and his Ghoules were taking the initiative. Fighting from a defensive fortification did not sit well with him. It was not the way of the Ghoules.

Even worse, it made him feel weak, and the Elder hated that feeling. Besides, he really wanted to kill that Magus who had been such a thorn in his side, the woman who had the temerity to challenge him. Once he killed her, he would fracture her bones and drink the marrow within.

Then again, maybe he would begin while she was still alive. He could start with an arm or a leg. That would be more fun. That would keep her alive longer. It would serve her right for her lack of respect.

The Elder followed right after his Ghoules when they raced over the cap of the hill. He was confused when their howls of pleasure shifted to grunts of pain, dismay, and even fear.

Even more so when he realized that the humans had stopped running.

JERAD HAD MADE it through the small gap in the shield wall that closed as soon as he sprinted between the soldiers, Dani standing right behind the spears with the swords, all of the fighters ready for the Ghoules to attack. She had selected this position carefully, spreading two full companies of the Battersea Guard just twenty feet below the crest of the hill. The Ghoules couldn't see them, and she doubted that if they chased after Jerad and his soldiers with their usual speed and fervor that they would be able to halt their progress in time.

That certainly proved to be the case for most of the beasts, their black eyes widening when they hurtled over the crown and saw what was waiting for them, the frustratingly familiar shield wall and long spears sticking out over the top of the steel scuta beckoning to them.

A handful of the beasts, knowing that they had no chance of slowing their momentum, simply continued their attack, thinking that with the speed they attained coming down the slope that they could break through the humans' line and create some gaps for their brethren following them.

It was a brave effort, a worthwhile effort. Even so, it still failed, the soldiers of the Battersea Guard keeping their scuta locked together despite the force applied by the Ghoules ramming into their wall, the spears behind them having to do little more than wait for the beasts to run onto their steel.

Most of the Ghoules met their doom with less dignity than those who screamed their defiance as they sprinted toward their deaths. The bulk of the beasts tried to stop their progress in order to avoid the soldiers' steel, but their pace, which proved so important to their success in most other situations, led to their downfall in this instance.

These Ghoules skidded or tumbled down the slope completely out of control, the agility normally associated with these beasts nowhere to be seen. Unable to arrest their forward progress, the Ghoules slammed into the shield wall with their backs or heads as they slid down the slope or cartwheeled through the grass.

Dani and the soldiers with her finished the hurt and often disoriented beasts with a practiced competency, the swords in back barely needed as the spears punctured eyes, throats, and chests.

The Elder met a fate similar to that of his Ghoules. Maria

took particular pleasure in killing the beast with a timely and well-placed spear of light that ripped through the Elder's staff and then right through his gut when he stepped onto the hill's gentle downslope, almost slipping as he worked frantically to halt his advance.

It was that clumsy effort that cost him, the Elder unable to defend himself as he struggled not to follow his Ghoules tumbling down the hill. The last vision he had before he collapsed in the long grass were the remains of three Ghoule packs scattered across the top of the hill, not a single beast still alive.

Jerad watched it all from the safety of the shield wall, both happy and disappointed at the same time. The bait and switch had worked to perfection. He had assumed that if he gave the Ghoules a target they couldn't resist, he could use their innate belligerence against them. And he had been right.

The strategy had worked, although not as well as it should have. He had made a bad decision, and it had cost some of his soldiers their lives. He should have been more cautious and stuck to the original script.

One attack, don't become caught in the fight, then lead the Ghoules to the larger force hidden behind the hill. That's what they had agreed to. Instead, he had decided to extend the skirmish, worried that he wouldn't be able to entice the beasts from behind their barricade if he only came at them once.

When Jerad turned, Dani was standing right in front of him, her expression a thundercloud, though it softened just a bit when she recognized his anger at himself and the remorse written all over his face. Still, she was too worked up to stop herself now. Dani grabbed Jerad by the shoulder straps of his armor and pulled him close, their noses almost touching.

"That was not the plan, Sergeant," Dani hissed quietly, her exasperation and irritation plain, though the Corporal of the Battersea Guard didn't want all the soldiers with them to hear their argument. "You were only supposed to attack the Ghoule fortification one time. That should have been enough to draw the beasts' attention. And then you were supposed to escape back the way you had come and not become involved in a sustained action that ceded control of the fight to the Ghoules. You did not have to take the risks that you did. It was unnecessary and dangerous."

"I know, you're right," admitted Jerad, hoping that his agreeing with her would mitigate her anger. "We stayed too long. I thought that I needed to remain engaged a few minutes more to ensure that they would follow. I didn't want to run away and not have the beasts come after us."

"The risk that you took wasn't worth it," countered Dani. "If they didn't follow you, we could have tried again with some other ploy. You didn't need to place yourself in a position where you couldn't break away. If you had gotten stuck and couldn't get free, there was no way that the companies with me could have reached you in time. You and everyone with you would have been Ghoule food."

"Yes, but with Maria ..."

"No buts," cut in Dani forcefully, using the voice that had become second nature to her when she commanded the Battersea Guard while Tarin and Jerad had gone with the Volkun to repair the Weir. "Stick to the plan. No revisions on the run. I'm not ready for you to die just yet."

"You're right," said Jerad. "I'm sorry. It won't happen again."

Not expecting an apology from the usually flippant and self-deprecating Sergeant, Dani stared into Jerad's eyes. The humor she had grown accustomed to seeing in those blue orbs wasn't there, nor was the exhilaration that she expected to glimpse after what had still proven to be a successful action. She could, however, discern the guilt that festered within him because of the higher than anticipated cost of his decision and the pain that he felt for the lives that had been lost.

Dani nodded then, knowing that there was no reason to belabor the point and beat up on Jerad. He was doing that to himself quite well on his own. Instead, she released her hold on his armor and then punched him hard enough in the arm to make him wince.

"We all make mistakes," she said quietly. "And those mistakes mean people die. There's nothing that we can do about that. It's the nature of our business."

"I know, I just ..."

A hard look from Dani stopped Jerad from saying whatever he was going to say.

"You can't allow these mistakes to keep you from doing what you need to do. These soldiers depend on you, Jerad. They trust you. They know you care about them."

"Even after what just happened? After so many died?"

"Even after that," confirmed Dani softly. "Because they make mistakes too. They understand that you're weighing their lives in every decision that you make. Just make sure that you learn from your mistakes, and you'll hold onto their trust even when things like this occur."

With a final nod to remind him that she was right, Dani walked off to where the wounded were being cared for, Maria already among them and helping the soldiers she could.

As he watched her go, Jerad shook his head, trying to understand how he had come to deserve someone like Dani. Rough on the outside, yes, but with a heart bigger than any he had ever come across before.

He was still irritated with himself. Nevertheless, she was right. He needed to learn from his mistake, and he promised himself that he would never put his soldiers in that same situation again.

But first, he needed to help with the wounded and have Maria check around them to ensure that they had time to recover from this fight before they went looking for the next clash against the Ghoule packs haunting these mountains.

"I UNDERSTAND *that Sergeant Brexston is having a great deal of success on the other side of the Winter Pass,"* said Noorsin Stelekel.

"So I've heard, General Stelekel," replied Declan.

It hadn't taken long for him to grow accustomed to communicating with the Duchess of Murcia through her use of the Talent as they spoke in each other's minds. It made coordinating the Caledonian defense much easier, since Declan and the Blood Company were several leagues to the west in the mountains surrounding the Winter Pass and Jerad and Tarin had several companies of the Battersea Guard to the east.

"And how are things going for you?"

"Better than expected, Duchess Stelekel," said Declan. *"Even the Elders find it difficult to control the beasts when the Ghoules believe that they have easy prey in front of them. It gives us a better chance of dictating the terms of the engagement. So far, we have. To great effect."*

Declan then explained how he had tricked the Ghoules into a rushed attack, having his soldiers build the beginnings of a fortification near one of the trails that the beasts were using in their attempts to work their way around the Caledonian Army that was arrayed in the Winter Pass. The ploy had worked better than Declan had thought it would.

The Ghoules attacked while his soldiers were seemingly working on the breastwork, not even giving any thought to the possibility that more might be in play here than what they saw. Declan's soldiers had dropped their tools and picked up their shields and spears, forming a tight defensive line to face the beasts who rushed at them. Even then, the Ghoules were undaunted, believing that with their numbers they would enjoy an easy victory.

Declan and his gladiators had weathered the initial charge quite well, keeping the beasts back. And then the real fun began. The rest of the Blood Company emerged from the hidden trenches that they had dug farther up the slope, crashing into the Ghoules from behind and the sides, slaughtering the beasts in a matter of minutes.

"Clever," said Noorsin.

"But not enough," said Declan. *"A small win for us. Still, we need more than just some small wins if we're to have any chance of holding against the beasts."*

Holding back the Ghoules was a key step in their larger strategy, Declan knew, and what he and the Blood Company had just accomplished would help with that. But slowing down the beasts wasn't good enough. They needed to stop the Ghoules' advance cold if they were to have any hope of keeping the beasts bottled up in the Winter Pass.

Yet how to do that? Conventional attacks in the gorge bought them some time, though certainly not enough. The Ghoules were too many, and they were too unyielding. The beasts never surrendered. They fought with a viciousness fueled by their rapacious hunger. And they had run only once, and that was because they had no Elders with them to fight against the Magii. That likely wouldn't happen again.

"No, not enough over the long term if we are to have any chance of keeping the Ghoules from the Kingdom."

"There is something that we can consider that might help with that. Granted, no more than a delaying tactic. Of course, the more time that we can earn the better our chances of success."

Declan then told Duchess Stelekel about the tunnels that they had found on their side of the gorge. Those shafts led down from the trails that the Blood Company was protecting into the Winter Pass itself. Ghoules would have a difficult time making their way through most of the tunnels because of their size, the narrowness forcing the beasts to shuffle through rather than walk, only able to move single file, and then having to turn to the side to avoid becoming stuck.

"*You want to raid behind the Ghoule lines,*" said Noorsin, having already thought through what Declan had on his mind.

"*I do, Duchess Stelekel. We can send a few squads through to test the concept, just to see what happens. When my gladiators seek to escape, they should have no problem holding the tunnel because of the size of the Ghoules. No more than one of the beasts can approach at a time. A few well-aimed spear thrusts and the beasts will be helping us get away by blocking the path for us. If nothing else, it will keep the Ghoules wary of what might come at them from behind.*"

"*An excellent proposal, Declan. Please begin as soon as you are ready. Anything we can do to reduce the pressure in the Winter Pass is worth trying.*"

Noorsin certainly appreciated the Master of the Gladiators' creativity, as well as that of the Captain and the Sergeant of the Battersea Guard. Even so, she knew as well that their efforts, no matter how effective they might be, were not long-term solutions. The only real chance for halting the Ghoules' progress rested with the Protector and his desperate plan to cripple the source of the Ghoules' power.

13

THROUGH THE CALDERA

"I wouldn't get too near to that," said Bryen. "You're not going to like it if you do."

"Why not?"

Davin had edged closer to a hole that stuck up about a foot out of the ground from which steam billowed out. He was leaning over and trying to get a better look while still staying clear of the hazy white mist.

He was curious as to what might be happening beneath the ground that caused the dewy haze and the ripples of water that gurgled out and stained the rock a rust color. Since they had entered this part of the Lost Land, which was shrouded in a heavy, stinking fog that revealed its secrets for just a moment at the touch of the wind and then covered them up again just as quickly, he had counted two dozen spouting geysers along the way that sent hissing streams of boiling water into the air with a distressing regularity.

Bryen and his friends were moving through what Viktor had named the Caldera. When the spirit of his uncle described the path that he had taken through the Ghoules' homeland, he had noted that the experience of hiking across the fractured, treacherous countryside was both marvelous and frightening at the same time. Bryen could understand why. As he glimpsed the wonders of his surroundings, he could only agree. As Davin was demonstrating all too frequently, the features of the landscape were dangerously distracting.

Steam billowed out of flues in the ground just like the vents that they had seen as they navigated the trenches that had led them here, but at a much faster rate, as if a massive fire blazed in the earth beneath them. That contributed to the grey murk that was so dense at times that they couldn't see anything that was more than a few feet away until a hot gust of acrid wind blew across the valley.

Puddles of boiling mud bubbled over the rims of their earthy containers. Prismatic pools, a perfect blue azure in the very center, then shifting to an aqua green before fading into a yellowish rust or faded red at the very rim, sat still and undisturbed even by the occasional breeze, a misty steam drifting off the surface.

Interspersed between these multicolored basins were copper-colored pools of water that gave off a rancid, rotten miasma. Farther off in the distance smoking volcanos, most no taller than the knolls of the Northern Spine, spluttered and splashed, long trails of lava snaking down the igneous rock to stream into reddish-brown pools of water, steam blasting into the air as the molten rock flowed into the acidic liquid.

"Because that geyser is about to erupt," said Bryen. "You can tell by the bubbling water that's about to stream out. It splatters out faster right before it's going to release the steam building up within it. I'd suggest stepping back. That water is hot enough to give you a wound worse than that of a Ghoule's claw."

Davin backstepped swiftly, almost slipping, his boot catching the edge of a large rock behind him. He feared that he might be in for a worse fate than getting hit by a stream of scalding water.

Bryen got there just in time. The Protector glided across the rocky ground to catch him by the arm and keep him from falling into reddish-brown water.

The geyser would have been bad, the basin much worse, the acid it contained biting through flesh to the bone in just seconds. They both had seen the evidence, full skeletons and random bones lying at the edge of the pools, and where the remains dipped into the acid, the ends were smooth, as if they had been run across a whetstone.

"How can it get so hot?" asked Davin, who nodded his thanks to his friend, his eyes never leaving the spout as he watched a long stream of boiling water shoot out of the hole more than twenty feet into the air, the burst lasting for several seconds before sputtering out at the end, the large gladiator knowing from observation that the process to make that happen already beginning again.

"It's being heated by the magma that's running just beneath the surface."

"How do you know all this?" asked Davin. "You've never been here. And you said yourself you never read anything about the Lost Land in all the books that Declan got for you because no one knows anything about this place other than the stories that are more myth than reality."

"You're right, I've never been here. Then again, in a way I have been here before. It's exactly as I thought it would be."

"Viktor Keldragan," murmured Davin. He should have known. He'd been so taken by the surprising natural aspects of this strange environment that he wasn't thinking as clearly as he should be. "I guess it doesn't hurt to have a spirit guiding your way."

"Yes, he told me all about this part of the Lost Land," confirmed Bryen. "We discussed it last night while I was on guard duty. Viktor actually seemed pleased to be back here, as if his journey, though fraught with danger as he traveled through this forbidding landscape, was something to be savored and remembered. He provided quite a bit of detail as to what we could expect to encounter, and so far he's been spot-on."

"What else did he reveal to you?" asked Davin.

Davin could understand the Magus' perspective on his trek. No one had ever done as he did, so Viktor should be proud of his accomplishments. If not for him, Caledonia would have disappeared centuries ago. Of course, how much longer the Kingdom would continue to exist was currently up for debate, but that was a worry for another day. They had enough to deal with now as it was.

"As I just mentioned, we're walking across what he called the Caldera because of all the volcanic activity. The smell results from the unique features of this environment, the sulfur so common to this region allowing us to enjoy that wonderful stench of rotten eggs."

"Do we need to worry about any of those volcanos blowing their top?" asked Davin. Although he was curious to see an eruption firsthand, he had no desire to be anywhere near here when that happened.

"Probably," admitted Bryen. "It's a volatile land. Viktor said that when he was here in the Caldera it took him longer than he would have liked to make his way through safely because there were so many Ghoules, for whatever reason a problem thankfully we're not dealing with now. He had to hide and wait for the beasts to pass too many times than he cared to remember. He said that because of that he saw at least a dozen eruptions in about two weeks' time. We've been in the Caldera for almost two days, so either we're overdue or this part of the Lost Land has settled down somewhat compared to a thousand years ago."

"That may be so," countered Davin, "but based on what we're seeing now, it doesn't appear that the Caldera is any more stable than it was back then. We just haven't been caught in an eruption, so maybe a big one is coming, one that would put the eruptions your uncle experienced to shame."

"Perhaps so," agreed Bryen, worried that he had identified a note of excitement about that prospect in his friend's voice. "It's certainly possible. I just don't know."

"So the faster that we get through here, the better," said Davin, his eyes drawn to the plumes of smoke billowing out of the broken peaks. It was a struggle for him to take his eyes from the streams of lava flowing down the sides.

"That would be my advice."

"Then let's pick up the pace," suggested Davin, who began to lengthen his strides. To get his mind off the impending doom that he envisioned for them by being caught in a horrible natural disaster, he turned his attention to another concern.

"Is there any fresh water here?" asked Davin, the gladiator now peering into one of the multicolored pools, although staying well away from the crumbly edge of the basin as he feared what might happen if he dipped in a toe. He assumed that the acid would eat right through the leather of his boots and into his flesh.

"No," said Bryen. "Not until we get through the Caldera. All the pools here are acidic. They'll strip the flesh from your bones in seconds."

"A good reminder," said Davin as he walked past another vibrant pool, taking a few steps farther away from its border just to be safe. "Wait ... the Caldera? I wasn't really paying attention when you said it the first time when we entered this section of the Lost Land, what with all the volcanos surrounding us drawing the eye. You mean ..."

"Yes, an active underground volcano."

"So this whole place could erupt at any time? The very ground beneath us? Not just the volcanos to our sides?"

"Pretty much," said Bryen as he led the group between two geysers, one on each side of the trail, and then once past those obstacles toward one of the larger volcanos that was several hundred yards off in the distance, a dense smoke pouring from the rim.

"Wonderful," grumbled Davin. "Just wonderful."

"Well, you did want an adventure," called Bryen over his shoulder. "If the last few weeks haven't been enough for you, then this should do the trick."

"The next time I tell you that I want an adventure," grumbled Davin, "ignore me."

~

As Bryen and Davin led the way through the steaming, stinking, unwelcoming Caldera, Lycia walking just behind them, Aislinn and Rafia dropped back a bit farther. The two Magii continued to search around them for any threats. Their frustration continued to grow with each failed attempt because they had yet to figure out a way to track the Echidna, the virtually invisible, cagey beast that Bryen had fought off demonstrating a daunting and alarming elusiveness.

"Do you miss him?" Aislinn asked the Magus.

She had been trying to bring Rafia out of her shell during the last few days. Rafia had shown a greater willingness to talk, actually offering a few muted and short responses, so she didn't think the question would put the Magus deeper in the doldrums.

Besides, she needed something else to think about as she struggled to locate the evasive creatures hunting them. The Ghoules were bad enough, but at least she could find them.

The Echidnae were an even more dangerous threat, and no one had any desire to be taken by surprise.

She and Rafia had discussed these beasts, assuming that because of their unique skill and the number of carcasses visible, they were fearsome predators. Because of that, they had both wondered whether the reason there were no Ghoules in the Caldera was because of the Echidnae.

Perhaps these beasts fed on whatever they wanted, whether touched by the Curse or not. Perhaps that's why Ghoules appeared to stay out of this part of the Lost Land. Perhaps it had nothing to do with the terrain and everything to do with what hunted here.

The Ghoules were not fools. Why risk an encounter with a monster you had little chance of killing because you couldn't see it?

"More than I expected," Rafia admitted softly, the twinge of sorrow that had settled within her heart sparking through her as her thoughts, never too far to begin with, turned to Sirius.

"It makes sense, doesn't it," said Aislinn, who continued the conversation carefully, not wanting to push too hard. "You've known him for a very long time."

Aislinn knew the discussion was necessary, because allowing her grief and sorrow to build up within her wouldn't be good for Rafia or them. Aislinn believed that Rafia needed to talk about it so that she could move on. Rafia likely believed that as well. Yet that conversation was like a two-edged sword. On the one hand, Rafia could take the next step as Sirius became more of a memory. On the other hand, taking that next step would make Sirius' death all the more real.

"Yes," Rafia replied, her mind wandering a bit as she recalled some of those moments with Sirius.

In the Shattered Peaks fighting the Ghoule Legions during the First Ghoule War. Spending time on Haven both before and after she was named Keeper. Visiting other Magii across the

Kingdom. Staying at the Aeyrie for meetings of the Order of the Magii, she and Sirius always finding time to steal away in the surrounding forest so that they could enjoy some privacy.

Just missing at the harbor in Roo's Nest a Magus particularly close to her heart who had turned to Dark Magic because of her incessant and irritating need to know more despite the cost of following such a perilous path and believing that she could escape the taint. Clashing over the direction their relationship should take. Fighting over what she realized now were the most inane matters. Yet through it all, even when they were angry with each other, trusting one another with their lives.

"But we'd grown apart the last few centuries," she continued after almost a minute had passed, finally coming back to herself. She had searched for the Echidna again. Still, no luck. "When we first became more than friends, it was something special. Unfortunately, we lost the spark somewhere along the way. Our relationship became comfortable. Something that was always there for us. Something easy. Something safe. And as a result the passion that had been there in the beginning wasn't there anymore."

Rafia slipped away again for a second, her eyes narrowing. Aislinn knew it wasn't because she was using the Talent to search around them. No, she was moving down a different path. An important path. The Keeper of Haven finding a truth she acknowledged rarely.

"Thinking about it now, however, even in the beginning we fought. Sirius seemed to forget or ignore the fact that we clashed quite a bit. Looking back now, it seemed to be a key part of our relationship. We spent as much time arguing with one another as we did caring for one another. I know that's a terrible thing to say as I think back on some of our better moments together, but it's the truth. We were together for a long time, and we probably shouldn't have been."

Rafia shook her head, then smiled. "It was just the easy

thing to do. Why start over when we had invested so much of ourselves into what we had built between us, flawed though it was. I loved him, and he loved me, but not the way you need to love someone in order to have a good, lasting relationship."

For quite some time, Aislinn was at a loss for words, not knowing what to say. She had never expected that Rafia would be so honest and open with her. Finally, she broke the silence that had stretched between them. "If you had been together so long, how did you gain the courage to take a step back when you did? That couldn't have been easy."

"It wasn't," Rafia confirmed with a gentle smile. "Sirius threw a fit when I first suggested it."

"Because he was upset about losing you?"

"That's what I thought initially," said Rafia. "Although as I thought about it more, I realized that his reaction was more complicated than that."

"How so?"

"He didn't like the idea that we would be taking some time apart. That bothered both of us in large part because we were so used to being together. But I think with him there was an added dimension. This sense of failure. That we couldn't continue to make it work. That's what seemed to be the biggest issue for him. If you hadn't noticed during your time training with Sirius, he likes to solve problems. He thought that he could solve any problem, even those with no good solutions."

"And he viewed the problems in your relationship as something to be solved."

"Exactly. That's what helped to make things so difficult between us. If you're spending most of your time in a relationship trying to solve problems, you have very little time for the relationship itself."

"That's a huge hurdle to jump."

"It is," confirmed Rafia.

"Then how did you get past it?"

"I guess that as time passed, we both believed that we had reached a point in our relationship where we felt that we could always reconnect whenever we wanted. We had done so many times in the past because we had been apart so often as we conducted business for the Order, so having that experience under our belts, we both trusted that we could be away from each other for a while and then connect once more without any difficulty." Rafia's voice softened, her eyes turning watery, though she held onto her tears, Aislinn realizing that she was seeing more emotion from the Magus than she ever had before. "In the end, we took each other for granted. We didn't realize that life might get in the way. Or rather death."

"I'm sorry, Rafia," said Aislinn, reaching out and grasping her forearm warmly, giving her a squeeze to demonstrate her support. "Sirius was a good teacher, a good friend, and a good person. I wish he was still here with us."

"So do I," admitted Rafia. "I do miss him. What I would give to fight with him just one more time. To have just one more argument. I'd even let him win."

The Magus was quiet for a time, Aislinn leaving her to her thoughts. She was glad that Rafia had talked at least a little bit about what she was dealing with, and she didn't want to demand too much from her with her emotions still so raw.

"The one thing I would like to suggest to you is what I told you a few nights ago when you were talking with Lycia," offered Rafia, her eyes, just seconds before filled with memories of the past, now focused once again on the present. "Don't wait. If you care for someone, don't wait. Time is too short to waste on inconsequential things."

"And what if what you want isn't what the other person wants?" Aislinn asked, her voice catching a bit in fear.

"Then at least you know and you can move on. I guess I should refine what I'm suggesting. Don't wait and don't waste your time. If what you want isn't what the other person wants, then you owe it to yourself to find what you want."

Rafia then looked at Bryen, who was a good thirty to forty yards to the front with Lycia now striding next to him, Davin having fallen back, obviously intrigued by the unique features of the landscape they journeyed through and less so the conversations between his sister and his friend. "Although I don't think you'll have to worry about that with the Protector. Come on. Let's move a bit faster and catch up. With this stinking fog getting thicker I don't want to risk losing one another."

"ARE YOU WORRIED?"

"About what?" asked Bryen.

"About your Lady Winborne speaking with Rafia?" asked Lycia, the gladiator walking next to Bryen and giving him a gentle push on his shoulder as well as a self-satisfied smirk, taking some pleasure in teasing Bryen. "The Magus has some very strong opinions. Who knows how what she says could affect the Lady Winborne."

"You're right about Rafia," agreed Bryen. "She certainly doesn't pull her punches. And Aislinn's not my Lady."

"Could have fooled me," replied Lycia with an even broader grin.

Bryen wasn't worried about Aislinn and Rafia talking, rather he was worried that they would fall too far behind, as he didn't want to lose anyone. The wispy fog was becoming denser and was limiting their visibility to only a few yards. The mist billowed and churned ominously every time a gust of hot, rank air blasted off one of the volcanos that paralleled their path and swept through the unstable valley, then settled back down into an almost impenetrable haze.

With his thoughts on other matters, even as several pointed responses came to mind, he chose to ignore Lycia's dig about Aislinn, knowing what drove it and also conceding that he owed Lycia the truth. Something that he didn't relish and had been hoping to avoid for a little while longer, yet realizing in that moment that running away from what he assumed would be an unpleasant conversation would simply create more problems between them farther down the road, and he didn't want that.

"We need to talk," said Bryen, a nervous flutter settling in his stomach. In that moment, he would have preferred to be fighting a black dragon on the white sand. It would have been easier than engaging in the conversation that he needed to have with Lycia.

"We do," admitted Lycia, her voice softening, the normal bravado leaking out of her.

For a time, Bryen was quiet. He knew what he had to say, he just didn't know how to say it. Not without hurting Lycia.

"Just speak your mind, Bryen," Lycia finally urged, the silence wearing on her nerves. "I won't stab you for being honest. Besides, it's better to rip a bandage off then leave it there and allow it to turn black and crusty."

Bryen sighed, unable to stop himself from smiling at Lycia's graphic imagery. She was right. They had been honest with one another in the Colosseum -- that's why they were such good friends -- and he wanted that to continue. "I do love you, Lycia."

"But not in the way that you love the Lady of the Southern Marches."

"No, not in that way," he admitted in a deflated voice, taking her advice and not deflecting, ripping the bandage right off.

"I should have told you sooner, I just didn't know how. I was scared and I didn't want to hurt you more than I already had." Bryen sighed in frustration, believing that he was failing miserably in trying to explain himself, but having no choice other than to complete the task he had set for himself.

"It's just that things have changed since I was taken from the Pit," Bryen continued. "I've changed. I don't have any better way to explain it, though I wish I could. You're important to me, you always will be, but so is she." He wished that there was more that he could say to lessen the sting of his words. Nothing came to mind. So he stopped, knowing that anything else that he might add was simply wasted words. "I'm sorry."

"There's nothing to be sorry for," said Lycia softly, needing to take a few seconds before she could get the words out so that her voice didn't break. Her usually challenging, often irascible, energy had drained away from her. She felt sick now that her greatest fear, though suspected for quite some time, finally had been confirmed. "You know, I knew things had changed between us as soon as you returned to the Colosseum to lead the rebellion. It wasn't hard to figure out. I just needed to hear you say it."

"Again, I'm sorry for not being honest with you sooner, and thank you for understanding." Bryen realized that Lycia was letting him off the hook. She could have made this much more difficult for him. She had chosen not to, taking a kinder path. That was something that he appreciated. "How did you know?"

"You don't look at me the way that you look at her."

He nodded, smiling sadly, his stomach curdling, not really knowing what else to say, not wanting to confuse things between them or make them any worse than they already were.

"You need to tell her," Lycia finally urged as they made their way past a huge pool of steaming, acidic water, the blue in the center so bright that it reminded Bryen of the sky on an early spring day when walking the beaches along the Silent Sea. "She deserves to know how you feel. Even with all this hanging over us. Better to decide what you want and tell her so she can decide if she wants that as well."

"You're right," agreed Bryen. "I will. I just need to find the right moment."

"There will never be a right moment," said Lycia. "Don't wait. You don't know what may happen next, so better not to lose the chance when you have it. Tell her. Soon."

Bryen nodded. He realized that what Lycia was telling him was not only good advice, but also could be applied to how she felt about him. A painful remorse flowed through him. He wished that he could be the person that Lycia wanted him to be. He knew, though, that he couldn't. His heart had drawn him to another.

"You've been listening to Rafia," said Bryen, slightly amused but more thankful that Lycia still supported him. She still viewed him as a friend, even though he couldn't give her what she wanted.

"It's good advice," said Lycia, her spark beginning to return as she nudged him again with her shoulder, her voice sharpening. "Don't wait. What we're doing now, the challenges that we face, it's just like when we were in the Pit. You don't know what the next day will hold, so you need to make the most of the days that you have. Promise me that you'll do that."

Before he could reply, Bryen stopped suddenly, Lycia walking a few steps past him before she halted as well, looking back at him with a look of concern. She had seen him do this before, and when he did something bad always happened.

"What is it?" asked Davin in a whisper, the gladiator catching up to Bryen and Lycia. He gripped his spear tightly, his head swiveling in all directions. He knew what it meant when Bryen did this. They were in imminent danger.

Bryen had been using the Talent to scout around them, always keeping that search in the back of his mind even as he talked with Lycia. He wasn't worried about Ghoules. Those beasts were easy to detect. Rather, he was trying to ascertain how to track the Echidnae, a challenge that he had yet to master since he had come across that first beast.

But he believed that he may have found a way to do it. The solution that popped into his mind as his thoughts drifted harkened back to what he had learned with Sirius when he and the Magus had first left Battersea and made for Haven with the goal of learning how to break the Protector's collar.

During that journey, Sirius had taught Bryen how to identify Ghoule packs even when an Elder was trying to mask their location. He had been trying the same approach with respect to the Echidnae, and he thought that he had solved the dilemma.

Rather than focusing on the Echidnae, he concentrated on the unique taint of the Curse emanating from the beasts, which was quite distinctive. Finally, he had latched onto what he was looking for.

It was faint, barely there at all when compared to what he sensed when looking for Ghoules, which certainly made sense since these beasts seemed to have been created to hide in this environment, silent killers for the Ghoule Overlord. Although not so faint that Bryen couldn't identify it.

He would need to show Aislinn and Rafia what he had done so that they could all track the Echidnae. Thankfully, those almost perfectly camouflaged beasts were not currently a direct threat. Although the Echidnae were still following them, the beasts were maintaining their distance for now.

The closest one was about a mile away. Maybe that single beast functioned as a scout, the larger pack of five about a mile behind that monster. None of them were coming any closer, so he wasn't worried about them. Not yet anyway.

His concern was drawn toward a more mundane threat, though still just as deadly. A Ghoule pack was moving directly toward them from the north. Based on what they had learned in the last few days, he had never expected the Ghoules to actually enter the Caldera. Yet here they were, almost upon them.

"Ghoules," said Rafia, she and Aislinn having trotted up the path to join them, identifying the beasts as well during their frequent searches. "Coming from the north directly toward us."

"Do they know that we're here?" asked Lycia.

"I don't think so," said Bryen. "I think they're just on the same path that we are."

"That may be so, but we have nowhere else to go," said Davin, "unless we turn back."

Aislinn glanced around them quickly. Unfortunately, Davin was right. They were on a narrow stretch of ground that was barely a path that bisected two large pits of bubbling mud that stretched out in both directions for hundreds of yards.

"That won't work," said Bryen. Not only because the Ghoules would likely catch them if they tried to go back the way they had come, to say nothing of the time that they would lose, but also because he could sense the Echidna scout coming closer, now no more than a half mile away and approaching at a fast pace. "An Echidna is coming toward us from the other direction. We can't go back."

"Here," Aislinn said, stepping off the trail into a small, semi-circular space that extended into the mud pot on their left. "There's enough room for all of us."

"But they'll see us," protested Davin as they all moved onto the dirt just off the trail that was barely large enough for all of them.

"I'll make sure that they don't," said Rafia. "We've done this before, so remember, no movement and no noise. Either can break the illusion. If the Ghoules catch us here, we truly have nowhere to go, so let's not allow that to happen."

The Magus reached for the Talent, instantly blending the group into the environment, the thick fog drifting through the air helping to strengthen the illusion. And just in time. A dozen Ghoules appeared out of the mist, spears held at the ready, as they loped between the multicolored pools of acid and mud pots.

Bryen and the others didn't make a move or a sound as the beasts started to pass them by, the Ghoules no more than five or six feet away from them. Lycia and Davin had steel in their hands, and Bryen and Aislinn were ready to call on the Talent, if the situation demanded it. Even so, they hoped that Rafia's illusion would hold, and so it did, a few of the beasts even glancing in their direction just out of habit and seeing nothing other than the long expanse of bubbling mud that stretched off toward the volcanos to the west.

It took less than a minute for the Ghoules to stride by. For the Caledonians it felt like hours before the last of the beasts finally trotted past. Davin was about to breathe a sigh of relief, having held his breath the entire time, when he stopped himself. He almost gasped, needing air, catching himself and taking a long, slow, deep breath just before he gave them away.

The Elder, the last in the line of Ghoules, stopped right across from them. The beast, well over seven feet tall, stood there for several seconds, his staff of twisted black ash releasing a continuous, thin stream of Dark Magic. The Ghoule's large head slowly turned as the beast looked around in all directions.

The Elder clearly sensed that something was off, and the beast was trying to determine what it was. He was unconcerned by the fact that his pack continued to move on to the south as he remained standing between the two pools of mud, more interested in finding the cause for his unease.

Bryen was about to reach for the Talent, wanting to be ready if he saw the few fine wisps of Dark Magic begin to spin across the top of the Elder's staff at a faster pace. The slight touch of Rafia's finger on his right hand, the movement so slight that he could barely feel it, stopped him.

She wanted him to wait. She trusted in the illusion that she had created. She wanted him to do so as well.

Bryen had faith in the Magus, so he did as she asked, delaying no matter how much he hated doing so, even when the Elder raised his nostrils and sniffed the air. He had never seen a Ghoule do that before.

Could the beasts track by scent? He didn't know for sure. He didn't think so.

The action still concerned him. Nevertheless, he had promised Rafia. He needed to trust her. So he didn't reach for the Talent even as every fiber in his being told him that he needed to do just that.

He was pleased to see his faith rewarded.

Just as quickly as the Curse began to spin across the top of the Elder's staff, it winked out. The Elder took one last look around before moving off into the fog after his Ghoule pack.

Rafia waited a full minute before releasing her hold on the Talent. "They're well beyond us now."

"Can they do that?" asked Lycia.

"You mean smell us?" asked Rafia.

"Yes, I've never seen an Elder do that before," said Aislinn.

"Honestly, I don't know," replied Rafia. "I've never seen an Elder do that before either, and I've been fighting them for centuries." She shrugged, as if to say what they had possibly discovered was important, though not as critical as continuing on with their mission. "If they can, I'm sure the stench of sulfur is the strongest scent they'll find here. I doubt they'd be able to smell us even if they were standing right next to us."

"You know, when we first came here, I hated the odor of this place," said Davin. "Now it's growing on me."

"It might not be us that distracted the Elder," offered Aislinn.

Rafia nodded. "I like how you're thinking. You believe the Elder can catch the scent of the Curse."

"It would certainly make sense," replied Aislinn. "So you

believe that the Elder somehow caught the scent of the Echidna?"

"It stands to reason."

"It does," cut in Bryen. "But we'll need to continue this conversation later. Come on. We need to get moving. Fast."

He started walking toward the north again, weaving his way between the two pools of gurgling mud, everyone else hustling to catch up, his pace making them all begin to worry again.

"The Ghoules are coming back?" asked Aislinn.

"No," he replied. "The Echidnae are coming toward us from the south."

"From the south?" asked Aislinn.

"Yes," Bryen replied. "You remember the Elder and Ghoule pack you were tracking that simply disappeared right before the Echidna attacked?"

"Yes," replied Aislinn, her mind working furiously as she began to put the puzzle together. "You don't think that ..."

"I do," Bryen replied. "I think the Echidnae slaughtered that Elder and Ghoule pack, and they're about to do it again to the beasts that just went by. I don't think the Elder was sniffing the wind for us. I've never seen Ghoules do that before when we've encountered them, so I agree with you and Rafia. I think you're both right. The Elder is a creature of the Curse and likely has the ability to sense other beasts crafted from Dark Magic. I think the Elder sensed, if only for a brief instant, the Echidnae, then lost the scent. The fact that we were standing there was irrelevant."

"Why would the Echidnae do that?" asked Lycia. To her, it seemed almost to be a form of cannibalism.

"They're hungry, and the Ghoules and Elder are easier game than us," said Rafia.

"That's my guess," said Bryen. "Now let's see if we can put some distance between ourselves and the oncoming Echidnae. I'm not interested in getting caught in the slaughter to come."

14

A NEW FRIEND

"How close can the beasts get before they know we're here?" Tarin asked.

The Ghoules had been pushing hard the last few days, seeking some way to penetrate the Caledonian defenses and, failing that, attempting at least to force them to give ground. The Caledonian Army only had done so grudgingly, falling back to the south less than a mile, keeping their line intact, desperate to stay clear of where the Winter Pass widened behind them, despite the beasts' constant pressure.

Still, the seemingly never-ending battle was wearing down the Caledonians, the Ghoules attacking day and night, searching for a weakness, for some way to break the stalemate. They needed a chance to regroup, to take a breath and rest if only for a day. Tarin hoped that what he and the Battersea Guard were about to do would give them that much-needed respite.

He stood well north of the Caledonian line in the Winter Pass, most of his soldiers lined up in tight squares with their backs against the snowdrifts that extended out into the gorge. The border of the wide, muddy trail that ran down the length of the canyon, a small stream zigzagging through its center, was just a few dozen yards in front of him.

Tarin felt incredibly exposed, and he didn't like that one bit. Even so, this was his idea, his proposal that had put his soldiers here to take this risk. He believed that the potential benefits of success outweighed the danger of discovery, so he had no choice but to be exactly where he was now. No risk, no reward his mentor liked to say, and this was quite a risk.

In Tarin's opinion, if you wanted to be a good leader and earn the trust and respect of your soldiers, you needed to lead by example. The Sergeant who had first got him thinking about joining the Battersea Guard when he was a child, the man who had become his mentor, taking the time to instruct him in the rudiments of using a sword while he was in the Battersea market waiting for his father, had taught him that, among a great many other lessons. Tarin had never forgotten it, along with virtually everything else the old soldier had chosen to share with him.

That's why he stood in the open now, waiting impatiently to see if his ruse would work.

"They can stand right next to us, no more than a few feet away," said Cerillia. "So long as we don't move and don't make a sound, we'll be fine. You have nothing to worry about."

Tarin just nodded, fearing that his nervousness might come out in his voice. She was young, at least to Tarin's eye, although that didn't mean much with a Magus. The woman looked to be in her twenties, not much younger than he was, but for all he knew she could be centuries old, and he certainly wasn't going to ask. She was also well dressed, wearing expensive and impeccably tailored hunting clothes, coming across as a Lady of Caledonia because of her polished manners.

That's why Tarin was having such a hard time reading her, and he prided himself on his ability to size someone up with just a glance. She differed from the other Magii that he had met except for Duchess Stelekel. All the others usually presented themselves as physicks or instructors, seeking to fit in rather than stand out. Cerillia didn't, obviously traveling in circles that the other Magii usually avoided.

What was undeniable was the one feature that Cerillia had that was common to all Magii. The hardness in her eyes that couldn't be missed, making it seem like your deepest thoughts, your deepest secrets, were being examined and evaluated every time she looked at you, and that if she needed to step on you like she would step on a bug in order to achieve a larger objective she would do so without giving it even a second thought.

"And if we do either?" He knew the answer to his question, having done this very same thing before in the Dark Forest while heading to the Sanctuary with the Protector, but he was anxious, and for some reason he liked talking with this Magus. The power that she controlled made him slightly uncomfortable. Still, there was something about her that had captured his attention.

"Then we probably die," said Cerillia with a deadpan expression.

"Uplifting," said Tarin with a touch of dry humor. He was already feeling calmer, confirming what he already knew helping him.

"But true," said Cerillia, the Magus allowing a soft smile to reach her eyes, appreciating the touch of sarcasm. "I thought that you would prefer the truth, Captain. I don't take you to be one who wants to be placated."

"Thank you for the compliment, Magus. You're correct. Good or bad, I only care for the truth."

"Cerillia."

"I'm sorry?" asked Tarin, confused for a moment as he had shifted his attention to the northern end of the Winter Pass. The faint swishing noise that was carried by the gentle gust of wind working its way down the gorge had drawn his focus. It sounded like a cut cornstalk being whipped through the air, and it was growing more prominent with each passing second. He had grown familiar with that dreaded noise. It presaged the arrival of the Ghoules.

"You can call me Cerillia, Captain Tentillin. Not Magus. Just Cerillia."

Tarin looked at Cerillia for just an instant, trying to read her one more time and failing to do so as he was caught by her deep, blue eyes. He didn't want to get distracted, but he was finding that objective difficult to achieve. She was quite beautiful. Then he smiled.

"Cerillia. And please call me Tarin."

His using her name earned him a smile in return. However, the banter between them stopped then, the swishing sound increasing in intensity and drawing their attention back to the fast-approaching Ghoules.

OTHER THAN THE soft sound of their rapid passage disturbing the air around them and the few splashes when they misstepped and their clawed feet pounded into the many puddles that littered the floor of the Winter Pass or splashed into the stream that accompanied them toward the south, the Ghoules sprinted toward the unsuspecting humans with a quiet and deadly purpose.

Their constant attacks of the last few days had gained the Ghoules little more than a mile or so of ground and not the breakthrough that they strove so desperately for. Nibli had ended the fight and pulled the Ghoules back a league, hoping that the humans would think that they were resting before they attacked once again. Instead, Nibli sought to catch the humans when they were most vulnerable, sending as many of his

Ghoules toward the humans as he could with the sun rising in the east.

From what the Ghoules could see as they advanced rapidly down the center of the Winter Pass, it appeared that Nibli's ploy had worked. Their prey was less than a quarter mile to the south, and it was exactly as they were told it would be by the scouts who had snuck down the canyon just hours before.

The humans had built several structures with which to defend themselves. The large ballistae and towering trebuchets were dangerous if you weren't paying attention, though really of little concern. Usually, the Ghoules could get out of the way with plenty of time to spare whenever those devices shot a bolt or hurled a boulder at them. Troublesome, yes, a concern to pay attention to, but not deadly.

What the Ghoules found more challenging to get past were the moveable walls, the humans lashing together logs to form barricades that were at least twenty feet high and twenty or so feet across. The humans used their horses, levers, and pulleys to move and raise these walls quickly, latching them together with steel braces and creating whatever design was necessary based on the terrain so that they could defend themselves, a balustrade running across the top allowing them to look down on the Ghoules and fight from an advantageous position.

This construction had proven to be a much more effective defense than anticipated and more dangerous for the Ghoules than anything else the humans had tried against them. Despite the beasts' incredible agility and their ability to leap into the air twenty feet or more, doing so made them particularly vulnerable to the humans waiting atop the wall.

The soldiers took an irritatingly satisfying pleasure in riddling with spears or arrows any Ghoule foolish enough to try for the top. In consequence, this one invention had helped to slow the Ghoules' advance to a crawl, prolonging the battle and delaying the humans' inevitable defeat.

The Elder at the front of the Ghoule Legion leading their advance had to give Nibli credit for his decision. The humans clearly weren't ready for them, and there was no way that they would be. The Ghoules would be on them in less than a minute.

The beast raised his staff into the air, then twisted his wrist, so that the black ash was parallel to the ground. With that command, he led half the column to the west while another Elder led the other half to the east around a large rocky stack that jutted out of the center of the canyon. The natural obstruction helped to shield them for a few seconds more from the humans who remained focused on the work that they were doing to get their barricade in place, unaware of the threat that sprinted toward them.

When Nibli had told Senjak what was required of him, the Elder had accepted the order without issue, even though he had worried that the humans would see them coming. That the surprise so necessary to their success would be lost. Yet as he rounded the rocky stack and joined once again with the other half of the column, he realized that his concerns had been a waste of time.

The beast grinned broadly, revealing his sharp, saw-toothed teeth. The humans were putting in place the fortification that the Ghoules had found incredibly difficult to conquer, the soldiers in the process of connecting the hundreds of sections to form a larger wall, so intent on their task that they were oblivious to the danger at their backs.

Best of all, the fortification was not yet complete, a dozen or more pieces meant for the center of the line still not in place. The Elder picked up his pace, his Ghoules following suit, the beasts' black eyes blazing with a desperate need.

The Elder believed that the humans were weak, though he could not deny that they had fought with a remarkable ferocity, likely because they understood that not doing so meant a faster death. Now, though, the humans weren't ready, and he was about to catch them at the worst possible time.

If they could destroy the wall, then the Ghoules could slaughter the humans. Finally. And when that task was complete, they would feast.

~

"READY?" Cerillia whispered, a rapacious grin giving her visage a hawklike quality. It was not what Tarin expected as he looked upon the prim and what he took to be very proper Magus.

Tarin nodded. "Ready."

The Captain of the Battersea Guard raised his sword slower than he normally would have, not wanting to break the illusion crafted by the Magus, yet knowing that all the soldiers with him saw the movement, as well as those on the other side of the gorge. The entire time he lifted his arm, he watched as the Ghoules sped by, thankful that the beasts all remained unaware that several companies of soldiers hid from them on both sides of the canyon, all of the beasts focused on the incomplete fortifications to their front, none of them thinking for a moment that a more dangerous threat hid just feet away.

When the last of the Ghoules loped past the rocky stack and began to reform into a single column, he slashed down through the air with his sword, his soldiers roaring a challenge as they advanced from their positions along the snowdrifts on both sides of the Winter Pass, charging into the Ghoules' flanks at the exact same moment that a series of massive explosions ripped through the middle of the confused beasts.

The Magii who had been hiding on top of the stone pillar flung more than a dozen spheres of blazing energy at the beasts, targeting first the Elders who ran in the midst of the large formation. Each strike sent half a dozen beasts flying into the air, all of them torn and broken before they crashed back onto the mucky turf.

Cerillia added her strength to the attack. Unable to see clearly from the side, she threw several blazing orbs into the air, not caring where they landed among the Ghoules. She simply wanted to add to the chaos and remove as many of the beasts from the fight as she could before it really began.

With the Ghoules preoccupied by the Magii's assault, Tarin led the attack from the east and Jerad from the west. The Battersea Guard slammed into the Ghoules from both sides, shields locked, two walls of unstoppable steel knocking many of the beasts from their clawed feet, spears thrusting right over the steel rims into the helpless Ghoules, the soldiers stepping right over or even on the dead beasts, pushing as deep into the mass of disorganized, milling creatures as they could, seeking to tighten the snare and use the resulting turmoil against their foes.

The archers who suddenly appeared on the snowdrifts, having stayed hidden under a thin layer of snow as the beasts approached, helped with that. Leaving the Elders to the Magii, the archers concentrated their assault on the Ghoules who attacked the shield walls, shooting their shafts right over the heads of the spears, hindering the beasts' efforts to put up an effective defense.

Wanting to keep the Ghoules off balance, before the dirt and rocks that had been thrown into the air by the Magii's attack returned to the earth, Rashaan Overkin, Captain of the Murcian Guard, charged out of the gap in the middle of the unfinished wall with several companies of soldiers at his back, nudging his horse in one specific direction.

The Elder leading the Ghoule attack realized in that brief moment before the mounted soldiers plowed into him and the other Ghoules with him in the front rank of their quickly disintegrating column that Nibli's ruse had failed. Rather than surprising his prey, he and his Ghoules instead had fallen victim to the humans' trap.

Somehow the humans had known that they were coming. The humans had been ready. And now his Ghoules were paying for Nibli's error. A mounted soldier, spear extended, was bearing down on him, and he had nowhere to go and no time to employ his Dark Magic.

Overkin fought with his preferred spear, an unadorned weapon that had been passed down through his family for generations. Yet he didn't need to use it until after he had trampled the Elder he had targeted, understanding the danger these purveyors of the Curse presented, and then ridden over several more of the beasts before the charge slowed. The large number of Ghoules now being pressed together from the front and the sides required a more methodical approach, and he was ready for the necessary change in tactics.

The Captain had assumed that they would reach this point. The Murcian line stayed strong and unbroken, the cavalry using their heavy, unwavering horses to push the Ghoules backward at a walk, spears lashing out into mottled green flesh.

The speed of the assault didn't matter. What mattered was ensuring that the Caledonian advance never halted. If that happened, it meant that the Ghoules had found their backbone.

The soldiers forced the Ghoules back the way that they had come. The rocky stack at their backs, the pressure being applied by the Battersea Guard on each side limited their options and their ability to move as the beasts were slowly but relentlessly compressed into a tighter and tighter space that made any attempts by the Ghoules to mount a coordinated defense all but impossible.

As the Battersea Guard and the Murcian Guard continued to advance step by step, the archers on the snowbanks firing down steel-tipped shaft after steel-tipped shaft, and the dozen

Magii standing atop the stack and the dozen more now lining the top of the wall having turned their attention to the Ghoules after eliminating all the Elders who had been a part of the surprise attack, it was only a matter of time before the inevitable end came, although not as the Elder who had led the expedition and now lay dead, trampled into the mud, had assumed that it would.

The clash was over in less than an hour, the remainder of the Ghoule Legion retreating to the north. Several dozen Elders and more than five hundred Ghoules lay dead or dying in the mud and muck thanks to the well-coordinated efforts of several thousand soldiers who knew exactly what they needed to do so that the Ghoules could not use their natural advantages against them.

Once the fight was done, the Murcian Guard and the Battersea Guard left the beasts where they lay, taking their own dead and wounded as they headed back toward the fortifications, the soldiers who had been working on the wall, or rather giving the Ghoules the impression that they were, now moving the missing pieces of the barricade back into place, leaving just one twenty-foot-long section missing in the center to allow the soldiers to stream through.

"Well done, Captain," said Cerillia. She and Tarin had waited until the Magii had climbed down from the rocky stack and the archers had slid down the piles of snow to join the soldiers moving toward the wall before heading in that direction themselves. "I had my doubts just because of the coordination required, but your plan was quite effective. I've never seen such an efficient death trap put into place."

"I'm not sure if that's a compliment or not," said Tarin with a grin, hoping the Magus would sense the sarcasm with which he offered the comment.

He was quite proud of how the battle had played out, although he certainly regretted the number of soldiers who gave their lives or were wounded during the effort to take the Ghoules by surprise. It hadn't been many, yet every soldier killed always left a black stain on his heart. He knew that it was unavoidable, another lesson from his mentor, that in every battle soldiers died no matter what you did to prevent it. Still, it bothered him, and he knew that it always would. He was glad for that. If it ever didn't, then he would know that he had become someone who he didn't want to be.

"By all means, it is a compliment," said Cerillia, having missed the Captain's dry wit. "I mean no offense. I'm simply impressed when a good strategy is applied flawlessly."

He nodded, slightly embarrassed, realizing that the best way to communicate with the Magus was to be direct with her at all times, acknowledging her serious nature.

"My compliments to you as well, Mag ... Cerillia," he corrected, when he saw her arch an eyebrow.

Cerillia smiled, then touched his arm. "Perhaps when we have a moment, we can celebrate our victory properly."

The Magus then gave Tarin a look that he didn't know how to interpret, though it sent a slight thrill through him along with a touch of concern. He chose to ignore the latter and focus on the former, unable to disregard the attraction that he felt toward the woman who had demonstrated such a unique skill in killing Elders and Ghoules.

"I'm sure that I can find the time," replied Tarin after a brief pause.

15

SURPRISE, SURPRISE

The only sound that traveled through the grove, a thick coating of pine needles covering the ground and helping to dampen any noise, was that of the wind. The hot, gusty breeze worked its way between the trees, rustling the branches ever so gently and carrying with it the faint scent of rotten eggs from the Caldera, that foggy, tumultuous land less than a mile north of the tree line. Then the stillness of the night settled around the copse once again, the breeze, which did little to assuage the warmth that seeped to the south, dying away.

Banshee was glad that it did. With her heightened sense of smell, she hated the stench of the Lost Land. The malodorous stink had gotten stuck in her nostrils. Because of that everything around her smelled wrong. Everything tasted wrong, even the small game that she and the other Griffons had been living off of for the last few days.

She didn't want to be here, but she had no choice. She had promised her friend that she would wait for him here at the very edge of the Great Forest until she learned from Bryen where she needed to meet him. And she would accede to his request even though she didn't like it. She knew that Bryen was counting on her.

It was early morning, darkness still heavy on the land, the sun not yet a thought in this gloomy country. Banshee and the other Griffons had just returned from a night of hunting across the long grass that extended back toward the Shattered Peaks. They had been surviving for the most part on rabbits, and even those had been few and far between.

They had gotten lucky last night, catching up to a small herd of caribou that they had found near the western edge of the Trench. The Griffons hadn't seen game that large since they had entered the Lost Land through the Weir, and they were quick to make their kills.

Banshee wanted to sleep. That had been her practice since Bryen had gone north. Resting during the day. Yet she couldn't. She was worried. Bryen usually reached out to her with the Talent every night just to check on her and to let her know where he was. She hadn't heard from him for two days and that bothered her.

Worse, it felt like the connection that she shared with Bryen had been blocked somehow, probably because of the vile residue coating this forsaken land. She couldn't communicate with him. She couldn't sense him with the clarity that she enjoyed normally.

Griffons were attuned to the magic of the world, both the Talent and the Curse, and she could sense the dark cloud of evil forming far to the north, coming from the direction toward which Bryen headed. He could probably feel it too. It wouldn't stop him, however. He would still go to the north.

No matter what might be waiting for him.

No matter the risk.

He had no choice.

That troubled her even more. Not that he was moving deeper into the Lost Land, but that she wasn't there with him.

Griffons rarely interacted with people. When they did, it was usually because of a great need or a connection that had been established between human and animal. With Bryen, it had been both for Banshee. She had helped him before, and during that time of need the connection between them had strengthened. They were friends now.

So what was she to do? Stay here as he asked her to? Allow him to face alone the evil that was gaining strength to the north? Or should she take a different path? One that allowed her to play a larger role in the events that she sensed were about to take place?

She pushed to the side the questions that disturbed her and kept her from her sleep.

She trilled softly, barely louder than the breeze that drifted through the branches once more, bringing with it as always the terrible smell of the Caldera. Her preternatural senses had noticed the shift within the wood to her front.

Subtle. Unrecognizable to most any other animal, but it was enough to capture the attention of the Griffon.

It hadn't been a sound or a movement. It had been no more than a feeling. The evil toward which Bryen journeyed was coming toward her out of the darkness.

Banshee's golden eyes sparkled in the gloom. She looked to her sides. Four other pairs of glowing golden eyes flashed back at her, their massive shapes hidden by the dark of night and the large, twisting tree roots around which the Griffons had settled.

There was no need to communicate. Banshee's companions sensed the change as well. They knew what came toward them through the trees, trying to hide their approach and failing, because they could not hide from the Griffons what they were. Of what they were made.

With a shriek of rage, her paws curled beneath her, Banshee launched herself across the glade, slamming an unsuspecting Ghoule into the long grass, her sharp claws puncturing the beast's chest. With a blindingly fast peck she pierced the Ghoule's throat with her sharp beak to ensure the beast never rose again. Leaving the Ghoule to die, Banshee took to the air, then dove down just a second later, crashing into another beast's back, her sharp claws ripping through the Ghoule's armored shoulders, the creature breathing its last as Banshee crushed the Ghoule's head into the turf and broke its neck.

When Banshee looked up from her latest kill, she saw that all the Griffons were involved in the fight, the massive animals more than a match for the Ghoules, who had finally come up against an opponent who had natural abilities against which they couldn't compete. The Griffons used the darkness to mask their attacks, darting out of the sky to catch a Ghoule unaware, then leaping back into the air, circling around, looking for another opportunity to dive down onto a Ghoule from above.

Banshee was about to lift herself back into the air when she sensed a movement just behind her, the sense of evil emanating from the assassin trying to sneak up on her stronger than any of the other Ghoules in the glade. Timing it just right, Banshee kicked back with a hind paw. She heard a shriek of surprise, a slam, and then a soft gurgle. She whipped around.

The Elder lay back against a tree, four bloody punctures in his chest, his back broken just like the black staff laying across his lap. The beast struggled for the breaths that wouldn't come, hisses of air bubbling out of his wounds.

Banshee snorted in disgust. She knew these beasts. She had fought one while Bryen was riding her back. She understood the danger they presented with the Dark Magic they controlled.

As the Elder expired in front of her, she snorted a second time, this time with satisfaction. One fewer Elder in the world was a good thing.

With a screech that blasted through the Great Forest, Banshee launched herself back into the air, the Griffons not already gliding above the trees joining her. She and her brethren had killed more than a dozen Ghoules in only a few minutes. There was no need to kill the rest that were following behind this pack and risk the appearance of another Elder. The beasts couldn't pursue them anyway. Not at the speed they would be going.

The Ghoule attack confirmed for Banshee what she needed to do now.

If these Ghoules had found her, they would have no trouble locating Bryen and his friends. She and the Griffons with her would fly toward the Cauldron. Toward where she had last sensed Bryen. Toward the source of the evil that contaminated the Lost Land.

She hoped that she would get there in time.

16

KNOCKED OFF BALANCE

"We are the soldiers of Caledonia!" shouted Jurgen Klines. "We stand! We fight! We die! That's who we are! That's what we do! Do it well!"

The Blademaster was more than happy to borrow one of the favorite sayings from the Blood Company and adopt it as his own, certain that Declan wouldn't mind. In fact, his friend probably would be pleased. The Sergeant of the Blood Company's words energized Klines' soldiers, giving them an added burst of strength and purpose, as they fought along the parapet that ran across the top of the movable wall, the barricade stretching for almost a quarter mile from one end of the Winter Pass to the other.

Duchess Stelekel with the Murcian Guard surrounding her fought from the middle of the wall while Duke Winborne held the right flank. The Blademaster was responsible for the left flank. So far, his troops had done well against the Ghoules. The beasts had returned after their defeat of the previous morning and had attacked since before first light, not letting up since, charging time after time against the barricade, uncaring of their own losses and unconcerned by the soldiers waiting for them with bloodied spears and swords on the balustrade.

Some of the beasts succeeded in jumping right onto the top of the parapet. Thankfully, that was a rare occurrence. The soldiers, not surprised by the Ghoules' agility, responded just as fast, using shields and spears to knock them back in the direction from which they had come, refusing to give the beasts purchase.

More often, the Ghoules used their sharp claws to dig into the logs and climb the wooden barricade. At the beginning of the fight, the soldiers had few problems dislodging the beasts, as the Ghoules attempted the maneuver on their own with little coordination. It wasn't until the Elders recognized the utility of such an attack and began to send entire packs up the wall at the same time that the Caledonians started to worry, the Ghoules behind the climbing beasts throwing spears at the soldiers atop the balustrade to give their brethren a better chance of gaining the wall.

The tactic had proven more effective than the Blademaster would have cared to admit. A half dozen times now seven or eight beasts had reached the top as a group and then tried to extend their hold over the parapet, wanting to give the Ghoules below them the chance to join the fight on the wall.

The Ghoules fought viciously to maintain their footing, understanding that the battle would be won if they could capture a segment of the barricade, giving their comrades below a path over the obstruction. Klines' soldiers fought with even more fire, as they knew what would happen if the Ghoules managed to gain control over even just one section of the pieced together wall.

Knocking the Ghoules from their perch was some of the bloodiest fighting of the war to date, but it was absolutely necessary, the entire Caledonian defense hinging on the outcome.

Because of the Caledonians' back-breaking efforts, the Ghoules had yet to enjoy a foothold on the parapet of more than just a few minutes. Even so, the Blademaster was worried. The Elders were sending more packs against the wall with more Ghoules right behind them throwing spears to keep the soldiers focused on defending themselves rather than defending the barrier. If this continued, it was only a matter of time before the beasts gained their objective.

A soldier just a few feet down the line screamed in agony, his shout catching the Blademaster's attention. The man fell backward off the wall, a blackened spear sticking out of his chest. Another soldier followed, the woman choking on her own blood thanks to a neatly placed stab to her throat and tumbling off the parapet, dead before she hit the ground.

Klines knew what was coming next as the soldiers to either side were forced to duck behind the logs, more spears streaking through the air just above the wall where they had been standing. With the spears forcing the soldiers to keep their heads down, several pairs of claws appeared atop the rough-hewn logs, and then the beasts were there, flinging themselves over the top, swinging and stabbing with their long spears, raking leather and flesh with their claws, striving to clear more space along the parapet for the Ghoules coming after them.

The soldiers fought back with a fury born of desperation. Yet despite their heroic efforts, the beasts were too strong, too fast, and too many. In just seconds the Ghoules killed a squad of soldiers and cleared the bodies from the balustrade to make space for the Ghoules behind them that were clawing their way up the barrier.

Klines didn't even think about what he needed to do. He simply acted. Whether it was a good or bad decision would be determined based on whether he lived through the next few minutes.

Sprinting down the rough boards that served as the parapet, he jumped over a wild swing by the Ghoule on the farthest edge of the breach and sliced across the beast's throat with his steel. The Ghoule collapsed to his knees, his claws going to the blood spurting from his neck.

Klines left him, knowing that the wounded beast had only seconds to live, continuing his attack by charging right into the midst of the dozen Ghoules who had already pulled themselves atop the wall. His blade was a grey streak as he cut and slashed, scoring the mottled green flesh of the Ghoule who faced him a half dozen times before the Ghoule even got in a strike of his own, the Blademaster trying to force the beast back into his cohorts, hoping that if he could shrink the space in any way it would make it much more difficult for the Ghoules climbing the wall to find a place on top of the barricade and hinder the efforts of those already there.

The narrowness of the balustrade aided Klines in his endeavor, because only one Ghoule could come against him at a time, maybe two if the beasts were clever. But he had yet to find a clever Ghoule. The beasts appeared to be no more than blunt instruments for the Elders, none of whom had yet to reach the top of the wall thanks to the efforts of the Magii dispersed along the barrier.

Even so, that didn't reduce the risk that he had taken in any way. The Ghoules were dangerous fighters, perfectly designed killing machines. It took all of Klines' wits and experience to keep himself alive as he engaged the Ghoules who were seeking to expand the footing they had gained and that they refused to yield.

Using his sword to push to the side the lunge by the Ghoule he was facing, he grabbed the spear with one hand so that the beast had to fight to pull it back. At the same time, he twisted his wrist and sliced across the beast's thigh in a backward blow.

His steel didn't cut deeply through the natural armor of the beast. Nevertheless, it was enough to draw a hiss from the

Ghoule, not of pain but rather of anger, which was then followed by a grunt of surprise when Klines released his hold on the haft of the spear, the Ghoule's hard tug to regain the use of his weapon throwing him off balance and right over the top of the wall to fall among the beasts clambering for their opportunity to gain the parapet.

Klines grinned malevolently at how easily he had tricked the Ghoule, then ducked beneath the wild swing of the next Ghoule standing on the balustrade, the blow designed to take his head from his shoulders. With the sword safely past him, Klines rose up and in the same motion drove his steel right into the Ghoule's groin.

With a kick to the chest, the Blademaster knocked the wounded beast from the parapet, his blade sliding free with a sickening gurgle, and turned his focus to the next Ghoule in line, the beast facing him now more intrigued than worried upon seeing how quickly the Blademaster had dispatched one of his brethren.

This Ghoule was more thoughtful than the last, not rushing to the attack right at the beginning of the combat. Instead, having observed the Blademaster's skill, the beast feinted a few stabs with his spear, forcing Klines to step back as he parried each thrust.

Klines realized that the beast knew what he was doing with his spear. He didn't need to kill Klines, at least not right at the start. The Ghoule just needed to hold him in place, thereby giving more of the Ghoules scrambling up the wall the opportunity to join him in the fight. Once that happened, Klines would no longer be a threat and he and his brethren could leap into the Caledonian rear.

The Blademaster corrected himself as he allowed his instincts to take over, his blade whipping out in front of him as he tried to pressure the Ghoule into a mistake, not wanting to give the beast the time that he was seeking. His initial estimation had been wrong. Because now he was facing the first Ghoule that he could describe as clever.

Despite the Ghoule's attempts to keep him in place, Klines realized that the beast's thoughtful and best efforts were wasted. The Blademaster had caught the movement out of the corner of his eye and the Ghoule seeking to delay him hadn't. Klines was ready for what was going to happen next. He was certain that this Ghoule and the others on the balustrade weren't.

"Archers, release!" shouted Klines, who ducked a swing by the Ghoule and stayed in his crouch, getting as close to the planks as he could, hugging the rough wood of the parapet.

A series of thwacks echoed in the Blademaster's ears, again and again and again, the noise similar to that of an angry swarm of bees, steel tips biting into Ghoule flesh with a frightening and welcome rapidity. More than a hundred archers had taken up positions just below and a dozen yards from the wall in three rows. As one the first row released their barbed arrows. Then the second. Then the third. The first ready to fire again as soon as the third row sent their shafts into the beasts.

But there was no need. The damage caused by the three flights of arrows at such close range was catastrophic for the Ghoules, each one pierced at least four or five times, many of the beasts slumped across the parapet or pinned against the top of the wall, breathing their last if they hadn't done so already. And for those who were still alive and attempting to fight, feebly, because not a single Ghoule escaped without at least one grievous wound, another surprise was waiting for them.

Feeling the tremble of the wooden planks beneath his feet, Klines rose and stepped out of the way, allowing Benin and his squad of soldiers to slam into the beasts with their shields. The few injured Ghoules who could still fight were eliminated with a brutal efficiency, several other squads following after Benin to close the gap along the top of the wall and push back the Ghoules who still were attempting to climb over despite the Caledonians' deadly counterattack.

Certain that all was as it should be at least for now, Klines finally stepped back, thick black blood dripping from his blade, allowing the soldiers to throw the dead Ghoules back over the wall to fall at the clawed feet of their comrades. It was a hard fight, a dangerous one he had just engaged in. He probably should have given his actions more thought, but he didn't feel as if he had the time to do that. He had needed to act, and he had done so. And in that moment, with his adrenaline surging through his veins, he felt more alive than he had since his duel with Killen Sourban.

He was also proud of how his soldiers had performed against such intense pressure. They had employed the tactics that they had been taught with an unmatched skill. Undeterred by the ferocity of the Ghoules, they had fought with a cold and efficient purpose.

Even so, Klines knew that they needed to shift their approach. This would not be the last of these attacks. The Elders had just confirmed how effective they could be. In fact, the Ghoules were already massing at specific places beneath the barricade, the Elders about to send several more packs up the wall hoping that the weight of numbers would give them the victory they sought. It was a good strategy, because eventually they wouldn't be able to dislodge the beasts from the wall if they gained a foothold and expanded it rapidly.

No, they couldn't wait for what the Ghoules were going to do next. They needed to go on the offensive now, if for no other reason than to knock the Ghoules for a loop. Make the Elders question their strategy. Even if just for a time. The Caledonians had to do something unpredictable and make the beasts think twice about attacking the wall.

"Blademaster!" called Benin, the Sergeant pointing farther down the wall to the east.

Klines feared the worst at his Sergeant's call. Surprisingly, he grinned again, seeing the flag. This was the chance that he had been waiting for. It was what the Caledonians on his flank required right now. Kevan had pushed on his side. Now he was holding his troops in place. It was his turn now.

"Benin!" shouted the Blademaster. "It's time to have a little fun."

The Sergeant appeared right next to him. "Yes, Blademaster. The soldiers wait for you."

The Blademaster and Benin quickly climbed down the ladders affixed to the planks that didn't reach all the way to the ground, dropping the last few feet and then trotting over to where their war horses waited for them at the front of several columns of mounted soldiers. As they pulled themselves up into their saddles, the company of archers who had helped to close the breach climbed up onto the wall, punching the tips of their arrows into the planks so that they could reach them quickly.

With a nod to the Sergeant in charge of the archers, the next part of the battle began, the soldiers atop the wall sending flight after flight of arrows down into the milling Ghoules. The beasts were deadly fighters with their spears and swords, and just as much with their claws, but they didn't carry shields. So their natural reaction was to sprint back from the wall, out of range of the arrows, waiting for the archers to finish their attack before they once again sought to scale the obstacle.

The Caledonians put that time and space to good use as the archers kept the Ghoules a few hundred yards from the wall. Using the ropes, pulleys, and draft horses that had been employed to put the wall in place originally, now they were used to turn two of the walls inward, opening a gap in the barricade.

Raising his sword into the air as he nudged his destrier into motion, the large animal leaping forward, its hooves digging into the mud to propel it through the opening and out over the dead Ghoules littering the ground beyond, Klines let loose another shout.

"We fight for Caledonia!"

A huge roar from the cavalry following him echoed off the mountains that bounded the Winter Pass, Benin riding right next to the Blademaster, raising a battered horn to his lips that he kept for just such occasions and blowing with all his might, the deep blare joining the cries of the screaming soldiers to blast down the gorge.

When the Ghoules first saw the split appear in the wall, they thought that it was a gift, many preparing to brave the arrows for a chance at the opening. Perhaps the humans had made a mistake or they were trying to pull the barricade farther back down the canyon. Then, much to their displeasure, and for some even fear after having faced this dreadful experience one too many times, the mounted column burst from the gap, charging straight toward them.

For just a few seconds, the Ghoules stood still, surprised that the humans would take such a risk after they had almost lost control of the wall. Then, finally, the beasts began to move, slowly at first, then faster as more joined in, racing toward the charging cavalry, not wanting to give the mounted soldiers the chance to get up to speed.

However, by then it was too late. The horses had built up their momentum, the soldiers urging them out into a broader line, three rows this time, ten yards between each one.

The Caledonian cavalry slammed into the Ghoules, who were still little more than a mob, the large war horses trampling and crushing the beasts. The soldiers then turned their mounts in a wide arc, avoiding a prolonged engagement and heading right back through the gap in the walls, the two pieces already closing before all the soldiers had made it back through.

Then, farther down the line, another column of cavalry rode out from between two sections of the wall that had been turned inward, the Ghoules not even seeing it happen, so intent their focus on defending themselves against the soldiers who had first run their destriers through their ranks. This column of Caledonian cavalry did just as the first had done, widening their line and forming into three rows, each one ten yards apart, the soldiers allowing the bulk of their bloody work to be performed by their horses, spears thrusting down and swords slashing out to finish the job before maneuvering right back into the gap through which they had appeared.

And so it went for the next several minutes, gaps appearing in the wall in an indeterminate rhythm just as other openings closed, columns of mounted soldiers surging forth to slam into the disordered Ghoules before retreating back in the direction from which they had come.

After leading the first charge, the Blademaster watched it all from atop the wall, a broad smile breaking through his usually taciturn countenance. He had to give Duchess Stelekel credit. It was her idea to create the movable barricade, having learned of something similar being employed in some forgotten land across the Burnt Ocean. She had adapted the idea for their own use, suggesting how with certain modifications they could move the pieces faster and allow what was obviously a defensive structure to be used in a more offensive manner. To great effect, as the Caledonians had just shown.

The General of the Caledonian Army was a devious woman and a worthy leader.

After what they had just accomplished, he believed that with all his heart, as did all the soldiers fighting with him.

17

MONSTERS IN THE NIGHT

It had taken most of the day to reach the northern boundary of the Caldera, the landscape changing as the sun began to set, the acidic and multicolored pools, mud pots, geysers, and volcanos gradually replaced by low hills that rose at a steep angle toward what appeared to be a small, almost impenetrable mountain range if not for the many broad, fast-moving rivers that flowed to the south between the peaks. Here, though the stench of sulfur remained, the smell was much more restrained, allowing Bryen and his friends to breathe a bit more deeply a less noxious air.

They hiked toward that higher ground to the north by following one of the nameless rivers, having found a small, barely visible game trail that tracked the fast-flowing water and allowed them to avoid the dense vegetation that pushed at them from the side and sought to reclaim the path, large roots with sprouts of green sticking out stretching across the footpath every few feet.

This new environment had a steamy feel, the air hot and humid in the lower reaches, the plants large and leafy, ferns crowding around the spruce, cedar, and hemlock trees that soared into the sky, many of them covered in moss and lichens, long vines snaking down for hundreds of feet to touch the ground.

While taking a short break, the steep climb, heat, and humidity draining them of energy, Lycia leaned down over the edge of the trail, staring at the swift-running water as it rushed by. With the light of the day receding and the shadows lengthening, at first she wasn't certain. Then she saw what she was looking for, her suspicions right on target, wisps of steam rising off the river's surface.

"I would stick with the water we have in our canteens," said Rafia, the Magus crouching down next to her so that she could study the steam for a few seconds, confirming the faint odor of rotten eggs wafting up, before pushing herself back to her feet.

"Acid?"

Rafia nodded. "Just like from the pools in the Caldera, though perhaps not as strong here, more diluted. Still, this is not a very hospitable environment with it resting atop a massive underground volcano. What we just walked through to get here is only the most obvious section of it."

"What happens if it blows?" asked Lycia.

"Catastrophic devastation," answered Rafia. "The landscape ruptured and broken. The volcanos belching out tons of magma to cover the land and clouds of soot and ash spiraling into the sky to block the sun for months before a pile of cinders several feet deep smothers an already grey and burnt environment."

"Nothing would be able to live here. It would mean the end of the Ghoules."

"Correct," agreed Rafia.

"Any clues as to when this might happen?" asked Lycia, in part because she didn't want to be caught in it herself, yet also because she wondered if that was another factor in the

Ghoules' desire to take Caledonia for their own, a way to escape a devastating disaster.

"No idea," replied Rafia, who spun around slowly, looking in all directions.

Lycia assumed that she was using more than just her eyes to search around them, the Magus also employing the Talent. When the Magus looked back down at her with a smile, she guessed that meant that they weren't in any immediate danger, though how one defined immediate danger in the Ghoules' homeland with the Echidnae still tracking them and various Ghoule packs beginning to appear more frequently in their vicinity was up for debate.

"Though it would be best if we weren't here when it happened," added the Magus.

Lycia nodded, wordlessly agreeing with that statement. "Where is it coming from?" the gladiator asked, motioning toward the steam.

"My guess is from the Boiling Lake," replied Rafia.

"Viktor Keldragan's naming conventions for this land may lack creativity, but it does tell you what to expect. I'll give him that much."

Lycia pushed herself to her feet, recalling what Bryen had shared with them from his conversation with his uncle. The spirit of the Magus had explained that once they reached the rim of the Caldera, the land to the north would rise steadily, just as they were experiencing now.

From here on out, they just needed to follow one of the several rivers that led toward its source. Supposedly, the water in the Boiling Lake was so clear that you could see the silty bottom that ran to a depth of almost fifty feet on a cloudless day. But he had also cautioned to stay well clear of the water, the steam rising off the river telling her everything that she needed to know.

Viktor had also explained that you could see the dozens of

hydrothermal vents situated on the bottom of the lake that were just like the geysers of the Caldera. Those vents spurted large amounts of hot, acidic water into the lake, giving the inland sea its name.

Unprotected flesh would be scalded at just the slightest touch. Viktor had likened it to holding your hand in the middle of a blazing campfire for several seconds. Another unpleasant risk. She should have expected nothing less from the Lost Land.

In the middle of that broad expanse rose the Cauldron, the monstrous volcano, supposedly dormant, sticking out of the water several miles from the shore. And on top of that island, the sheer sides of which were more than a mile in height, was the Temple of the Ghoules. Their ultimate destination.

"Come on," said Rafia. "We don't want to get too far behind, and I believe Bryen has found us a good spot to settle in for the night just up ahead."

Lycia followed the Magus up the trail, eyes still on the river, just as much watching her step as the trail narrowed and the vines that ran across its length thickened into obstacles that required her to jump or climb over them, the foliage reminding her in some ways of the twisting roots that made traveling through the Dark Forest such a challenge. The deeper they journeyed into the Lost Land, the more it confirmed for her that this wasn't a place for them.

She was glad that she had come so that she could help Bryen, but she also was looking forward to getting back to Caledonia and an environment with which she was more familiar and comfortable. An environment that wasn't as dangerous as, if not more so, than the beasts hunting them.

In less than an hour, they reached a protected promontory that extended out over the river, what had once likely been a natural bridge, but over time had eroded on the far side, a large section crumbling into the water. The location gave them few options for escape, a weakness they were willing to accept, because it was also a strength, the one important advantage of the selected precipice being the fact that it limited any attacks to one direction.

With darkness having descended, it didn't take them long to settle in for the night. There would be no fire. It would just serve as a beacon for the various beasts hunting them. Aislinn and Bryen took the first watch, so Lycia and Davin lay down on their cloaks to get a few hours of sleep, thankful that the temperature had dropped, if only just a little bit. Rafia rolled herself into her cloak a short distance away.

The two sentries, who had taken up a position where the promontory connected with the trail, both knew that she wasn't sleeping. The Magus barely slept at all since losing Sirius.

For a time, Aislinn and her Protector stared off into the darkness. Eerily there was no noise other than the rushing of the water below them.

Unlike the forests that they were familiar with in Caledonia, even the Deep Wood and the Dark Forest, both gloomy and haunting, revealing on occasion the sounds of a bird or the scrabbling of a small animal, the wood around them appeared to be devoid of life.

There was no discernible movement. Just the occasional gust of wind brushing up against the trees. Once the breeze played through, silence reigned again, the forest becoming a muted black against the sable of the night.

"Does this remind you of anything?" asked Aislinn in a soft voice that Bryen could barely hear even though he was standing right next to her. Neither wanted to disturb the silence any more than they had to, the rush of the river fading into the background as they both strained to listen for anything that might sound out of the ordinary.

"In the Waste," he replied just as quietly with a subdued

smile. "Something was out there with us, just as there is now. It was right before you became a Magus."

"Before we both became Magii." Aislinn smiled to hide her increasing nervousness, having wanted to have this conversation for quite some time. She had been putting it off because of her concern regarding the possibility that it might not go the way she wanted. Now, however, with them approaching the Temple of the Ghoules and the increasing possibility of a second combat for Bryen against the Ghoule Overlord, she felt the need for some certainty, even if that certainty didn't conform to what she most desired. "You know, I've been speaking quite a bit with Rafia about Sirius." Saying her former instructor's name brought a slight catch to her throat.

"How is she doing? I know this isn't easy for her."

"As well as can be expected, I guess."

"I knew that she and Sirius were close," offered Bryen. "I just didn't know how close until I saw how they interacted with one another at Haven."

"That must have been quite an experience." Aislinn could only imagine, having watched the two Magii spend most of their time together squabbling after they arrived in Tintagel.

"It was," Bryen chuckled softly. "They were very good about avoiding the one topic that they really should have discussed."

"Sounds familiar," said Aislinn with a knowing look, seizing on the opportunity that Bryen had given her.

Bryen glanced at her, realizing what he had just done.

Aislinn ignored his worried expression, refusing to let go of this opportunity. "One thing that Rafia has been telling me in talking about the time that she spent with Sirius has really resonated with me."

"What would that be?" Bryen couldn't stop himself from asking even though he had a sense that he already knew the answer after having spoken with Rafia himself, although that conversation had been her idea and not his.

"Don't wait."

"I've been hearing that a lot lately," grumbled Bryen. "What do you mean don't wait?"

"I mean with respect to our relationship," said Aislinn.

Bryen nodded. He had assumed that this conversation would be coming. He just hadn't known when. "What about our relationship?"

Aislinn nudged him with her shoulder. "Are you purposefully trying to make this difficult for me?"

"Me?" Bryen replied softly, his voice betraying that he was indeed being difficult. He didn't have a great deal of experience with conversations such as this one, where you were expected to be open, honest, vulnerable. Ten years in the Pit had made functioning in that manner with another person difficult for him. So his first instinct had been to deflect.

"If we survive this," began Aislinn, "what's next for us? Is there even an us?"

"You want me to court you because you're a Lady of Caledonia?" He was able to get the words out without breaking into a grin, although it was a challenge, and then he grimaced when she punched him sharply in the arm to demonstrate her irritation.

"You are making this difficult for me," objected Aislinn in a whisper, giving him another nudge with her shoulder. "This isn't easy for me either, you know."

"Maybe just a little bit," he admitted with a wink that she caught out of the corner of her eye.

"Will you please take this seriously?"

"I will," he promised, nodding and taking on a more circumspect expression. "I'm sorry."

"We've been spending more time together."

"We have," Bryen agreed.

Aislinn waited a moment before continuing, biting her lip, thankful that the dark hid the blush that was erupting on her cheeks. "We have been engaging in behavior that I was raised to believe was reserved for those wanting to share a life together."

"We have," Bryen agreed once again. "It has been quite enjoyable."

"Bryen," said Aislinn, the tone of her voice suggesting that she was losing patience.

"Sorry," he said quickly, before she hit him again with the fist that she was making.

Aislinn nodded, then sighed. "I was just thinking that we should talk about what comes next for us if we succeed here in the Lost Land. I don't want to be in the same position as Rafia and Sirius were. I want to know where we stand."

Aislinn didn't know what to say beyond that, and Bryen certainly wasn't helping. But she wasn't going to stop now just because her anxiety was making her feel as if she was about the throw up what little she had eaten for dinner.

Don't wait.

That's what Rafia had said, and Aislinn believed that it was excellent advice. It was necessary advice based on where they were going. So she wasn't going to wait. Not with the danger they were facing now. Not with the danger to come.

Locking away her fear, Aislinn stepped up to Bryen and cupped his cheeks with her hands, pulling him to her for a kiss. It was brief, very brief. More like a taste than anything else, Bryen's eyes locking onto hers. But she hoped that her action would do more to push their conversation forward than her jumbled words ever could.

When Bryen didn't react for several seconds, just staring at her, Aislinn feared that she had made a mistake, that taking Rafia's advice, though it had felt right in the moment, was actually wrong. That Aislinn had misinterpreted Bryen's feelings for her despite what had happened in his cell in the gladiators' compound and the moments that they had taken together during the weeks that they had journeyed to the Sanctuary. That she had given their relationship a level of seriousness that he did not.

When those thoughts leaped into her mind, her fears, some real, some imagined, which were never far from the surface, joined them, multiplying her concerns exponentially. Why would Bryen have any interest in her after what her father had done to him? After how she had treated him when he had first arrived in the Southern Marches?

She was a fool to think that he would reciprocate her interest in him. Maybe he was just playing with her.

Before her thoughts and worries could travel down the dark road she had set them upon and from which she feared they would never return, Bryen reached up, put his hand on the back of her neck, and pulled her in close for a second kiss that seemed to last forever. When he finally released her, they were both grinning.

"You need to stop worrying about how I feel about you," whispered Bryen. He could sense what was churning through her. Her emotions playing havoc with her reason. "You have me heart and soul. That will never change. Never."

Aislinn's smile broadened as she listened to his words, thrilled to have finally gained some insight into Bryen's feelings and his intentions toward her. She had been waiting for this for so long. She had feared that what she felt for him was not what he felt for her.

"Even beyond this?" asked Aislinn, unable to control her need for clarity.

"Even beyond this. You'll have a difficult time getting rid of me."

"And what of the future and your desire for a fresh start?"

"There's nothing wrong with a fresh start."

"I know there isn't," agreed Aislinn. "And I know why you

want to begin again. If I was in your position, I would want the same."

"But you're not in my position," nodded Bryen.

"No, I have responsibilities to my father and to the Southern Marches."

"I know," Bryen sighed, "I'm all too aware."

"So if you want to be with me, and I need to be here, how do you decide between the two?"

"Between what I want to do and the demands that I must meet?"

"Yes, exactly that."

Bryen sighed. He had been thinking about this for quite some time. He felt an almost visceral urge to begin again. To start fresh, believing that he couldn't do that in the Kingdom that had enslaved him and his friends. But the thought of leaving Aislinn was like a stab in the heart.

"As I said, you'll have a difficult time getting rid of me," repeated Bryen, understanding that sometimes compromise was needed to gain what was most important to him. "You have me. All of me. Like it or not."

With Bryen's words a rush of excitement crushed the fear that had played through her whenever she thought about her relationship with him. She then reached up toward Bryen once again, pulling his lips to hers. This kiss ended much more quickly than the last.

"They're here," Aislinn said, pulling her lips free from Bryen's.

It was a statement, not a question. Bryen had shared with Aislinn and Rafia how he had learned to track the Echidnae.

She had been practicing throughout the day, allowing the Talent to flow through her, searching around them constantly, maintaining her hold when she latched onto that tiny trace of ancient, distinctive evil that revealed their hunters, continuing to track the beasts even as she did other things with the Talent. Another skill she had learned from Rafia just that afternoon.

"And close," Bryen whispered. "Be ready."

Bryen had been thinking about various ways to fight the Echidnae ever since he had faced the one that had tried to take them by surprise in the Caldera. He had decided that taking on these monsters without being able to see them wasn't a real fight at all. It was a recipe for disaster, the Echidnae enjoying every advantage. So the only way to have a chance against the beasts was to make them play by his rules rather than the other way around.

Bryen thought that he knew how to do just that. Having tracked the Echidnae as they approached through the forest, the beasts slithering out onto the very beginning of the promontory, though still unseen because of their magical camouflage, Bryen opened himself to the Seventh Stone.

It was tricky at first. Even with the monsters so close, no more than a dozen feet away, they were invisible, the darkness helping to hide them, and it was incredibly hard to get a fix on them because of the primeval Dark Magic that had been used to create them.

Yet, even though his first few attempts failed, Bryen didn't give up, searching for the faint hint of evil that would reveal the Echidnae to him. Then he had it. As he had done so many times before to Elders and to the Ghoule Overlord himself, he connected a strand of the Talent to the two Echidnae that were seeking to sneak into their camp.

In seconds, it was done. Using the hollow thread crafted of the Talent, Bryen used the Seventh Stone to drain the beasts of the Curse, taking the Dark Magic within himself and the artifact. As he did so the natural camouflage gifted to the Echidnae by the Curse faded away, displaying the monsters, each one taller than a Ghoule by at least a head.

They were still formidable, deadly adversaries. Now,

however, they could be seen, which meant that they could be killed. Aislinn didn't waste any time, charging straight toward the beast that had been attempting to slide around her along the edge of the precipice so that it could come at the sleeping figures behind her.

Pulling free from its scabbard the sword with the Winborne crest given to her by the Blademaster, she infused the blade with the Talent and leapt at the Echidna, the creature's eyes widening in shock, never expecting its prey to get a fix on its location, not yet realizing that its primary protection was gone.

The monster raised a scaly forearm to block the steel that swept down toward it, at the same time weaving backward as fast as it could. The Echidna received its second shock of just the last few seconds when the glowing metal cut through its armored flesh almost to the bone. The monster reared up to the tip of its tail in pain, hissing in anger.

In that brief moment, Aislinn took in her opponent. It was much as Bryen had described. The Echidna's upper body looked much like that of a Ghoule. The obvious difference was below the waist, which best resembled that of a massive snake, its long, scaly tail giving the monster a sinuous movement and a constant, side to side swaying motion.

Much like a snake, the beast had a whiplike speed, shooting forward, reaching for Aislinn with its claws, then twisting backward before lunging again, trying this time to bite her with its fangs, which she knew thanks to Bryen were filled with a paralyzing toxin. Each time, Aislinn was ready, scoring the beast twice more, leaving long gashes that leaked a thick black blood across the Echidna's other forearm and shoulder.

While Aislinn kept one of the Echidna occupied, Bryen faced off against the other monster. The blades of the Spear of the Magii, infused with the Talent, lit up the darkness, Bryen spinning the weapon so fast as he struck the beast in rapid succession that often it appeared as if he was managing a blazing circle of energy.

At the beginning of the combat, the Echidna dodged out of the way, sliding across the rock on its tail with a remarkable ease.

It wasn't long, however, before the beast quickly grew tired of being on the defensive, its instincts requiring that it attack. The Echidna lunged forward with its claws, each digit as long as a dagger blade, with a speed that a giant scorpion would have envied.

Bryen knocked back each slash with a confident strike of his own, leaving the Echidna bleeding from a dozen wounds in less than a minute. Clearly, the monster was not used to dealing with prey that fought back with any success.

Its mounting frustration was becoming quite obvious, the beast working itself up into a frenzy as it lashed about with an increasing freneticism. Even so, the monster achieved very little as Bryen kept the Echidna near the trail, not allowing it to move any closer to the campsite.

The growing desperation of both beasts played right into the hands of Aislinn and Bryen. They didn't have to kill the beasts. They just needed to keep them from getting any closer, because they knew that they would soon enjoy an advantage for which the two monsters likely were unprepared and would not be able to recover.

Both of the beasts howled in anger, annoyed, confused, when they were forced closer to the edge of the precipice, the river running right below, Lycia and Davin joining the fight without making a sound, other than their steel whistling through the air, both weapons infused with the Talent by Rafia so that they would have little trouble cutting through the Echidnae's armored flesh.

In seconds the contests between the monsters and Bryen and Aislinn shifted from uncertain combats to guaranteed outcomes. Davin and Lycia raced in from the sides, which forced the Echidnae closer together, unable to escape the trap. Davin and Bryen thrust with their spears and Lycia and Aislinn slashed with their swords, pressing closer to the beasts, limiting their space to maneuver more and more and with each step pushing them toward the acidic whitewater raging just below the promontory.

Through it all, Rafia stood behind them, several spheres of energy dancing across her fingers as she waited to assist if there was a need. She realized almost immediately that her help wouldn't be required for this clash.

As the four fighters tightened the noose, the Echidnae fought with a greater vigor, yet with little positive result. By tightening the space around the beasts, Bryen and his friends limited the monsters' options, and more often than not now, the two beasts were getting in each other's way as they tried to defend themselves from the searing steel that cut into their flesh with a horrid and painful regularity.

What the Echidnae had viewed initially as an easy hunt quickly turned disastrous for them, Bryen taking advantage of Davin thrusting his spear into one of the monster's tails, the beast wailing in agony as the Talent within the blade burned through its flesh, the terrible wound limiting its mobility.

With the Echidna held in place by the spearpoint Davin had driven all the way into the ground, Bryen swept the Spear of the Magii across the beast's throat. The monster's body collapsed to the stone as its head dropped into the acidic water that was only ten feet below the ledge.

The other Echidna attempted to slither across the body of its brethren and rush back to the safety of the forest. But it was not to be.

Lycia was too fast, cutting down with one of her swords, the blazing blade slicing completely through the Echidna's tail. The beast toppled to the rock, and before it could shriek in pain, Aislinn was there, driving her blade right between the monster's shoulder blades, the second Echidna collapsing across the remains of the first.

"The rest of the pack?" asked Lycia, her eyes immediately going to the silent forest to their front, worried that more of the snakelike monsters were about to emerge and avenge their fallen brethren.

"They've moved farther away," said Rafia. "This was just a test. The Echidnae wanted to see what we could do. They probably thought that two of their kind would be enough to kill us all, but they never considered the possibility that Bryen could steal their natural camouflage from them."

"So they'll continue to track us," said Lycia.

"Yes, they won't let us go," replied Aislinn.

"No, they won't," confirmed Bryen. "Whether because they obey the Ghoule Overlord or they're just hungry, I don't know. But I have no doubt that the only way to get them off our backs is to kill them all."

Davin nodded, having already reached that conclusion as he stared at one of the dead beasts, flipping over the one with its head still attached so that he could get a better look at it.

"What's the matter?" asked Lycia, not understanding why her brother was staring at the Echidna's visage.

"I thought the Ghoules were difficult to look at, yet these Echidnae truly are ugly creatures."

Bryen stepped next to Davin then, looking down at the dead monster, studying the beast. He then shifted his gaze to Davin.

"I don't know," he said. "Do you remember that gladiator who took a liking to you? The one with the big ears? He was just as broad as Dorlan and more dangerous. And he had that growth on his neck. No one could determine what it was, and everyone was afraid to take a closer look because he wasn't completely there and you never knew what he was going to do.

You remember, him, right? I really do think that he had a crush on you."

"He was much better looking than this beast," protested Davin.

"Was he though?"

18

——————

DEAD EYES

"How far away are they?" asked Rafia, seeking confirmation of her own efforts.

She had been using the Talent to track the Echidnae, the monsters clearly not convinced to stop the chase despite losing two of their pack the night before, and she was having a difficult time keeping tabs on the beasts. The monsters moved with a speed that put the incredibly swift Ghoules to shame, changing direction so fast and so frequently that the touch of darkness that revealed their presence kept flitting about. They were there for just a second, then gone, and then back again.

And so it went, a constant, frustrating struggle to maintain the connection that would give her a hint of warning before the next attack. It was those few seconds that Rafia wanted. She knew that brief moment in time could be the difference between life and death, because they were all certain that there would be another attack.

Aislinn was dealing with the same challenge as Rafia. Her frequent curses, mumbled just under her breath, demonstrated that she was having just as hard a time pinning down the beasts as the Magus was.

"Much closer than we would like," Bryen replied. Even he was finding it difficult to track the Echidnae, working just as hard as the others, the advantage given to him by the Seventh Stone the only reason that he hadn't lost track of the monsters yet. "Half a mile at most. They're starting to come closer than that now. I get the feeling that they're done following us. They'll be on us soon."

"How can you tell?"

"The way that they're moving," replied Bryen. "They know exactly where we are so every so often one or two of the beasts moves farther ahead than the others, cutting the distance to us by no more than a few hundred yards, then they slip back to their pack."

"They're testing us again," said Rafia.

Bryen nodded. "They are. They want to see what we're going to do if anything in response to their movements. They're trying to spook us. Make us do something rash. I doubt they'll have the patience to keep this up for long. Their movements are becoming more agitated."

"How many?"

"It's hard enough just tracking them," protested Bryen.

"I know that," snapped Rafia, not angry with Bryen, but rather with herself for failing to keep an eye on the beasts. She felt like a novice Magus who couldn't accomplish the simplest of assignments.

Bryen ignored the venom in her voice, understanding that it wasn't directed toward him. "Six," he replied finally, allowing several seconds to pass before doing so. He didn't want to be wrong with his count. "Yes, six left in this pack." The beasts were all moving in this direction, though they were not following the same path, zigzagging through the forest that covered the mountain.

"Wait a second. Six in this pack. There is more than one pack?"

"Yes, at least two more packs, though I can't really get a read on their numbers. Those packs are a league away."

"Wonderful," said Rafia sarcastically. "More of the beasts."

"We need to be ready," said Bryen. "We're vulnerable here."

"Don't I know it," grumbled Rafia.

She, just like everyone else in their small party, had been glad to leave the Caldera, knowing that doing so brought them closer to their objective. But the going was more arduous now and more dangerous. The landscape more treacherous.

They were spending more time climbing than hiking as they followed the swift-running water that cut between the mountains toward the Boiling Lake, and the trail that they had been following along the steep cliff that gave them a much-too-close view of the river had for all intents and purposes disappeared. The path was now no more than a ledge barely wide enough to place a single boot without slipping off the edge, made all the more perilous by the vines and brush seeking to reclaim the narrow space.

"If they're finally coming for us in force, they picked the right place for it," muttered Rafia.

After dispatching two of the beasts on the precipice that jutted out over the river they now traced, they had spent a long night on the promontory, waiting for morning, not wanting to continue without the sun. Bryen would have preferred to move as soon as they had killed the Echidnae. Still, he understood the limitations they faced, so he forced himself to ignore that urge.

The trail had been getting more challenging to traverse the higher up they hiked into the mountains and with the acidic river, the noxious smell oftentimes overpowering if they got too close, serving as one boundary as they worked their way along the peak, it was too big a risk to take. One wrong step and one of them would be in the drink.

So they had waited until first light. They didn't have to deal with the Echidnae while they remained on the promontory, the beasts keeping their distance, not coming any closer until now. Bryen wished the monsters hadn't waited. It would have been easier to fight them on the ridge than here.

Bryen couldn't say for sure why the monsters had delayed their attack. The Echidnae stood a good chance of overwhelming him and his friends on the precipice if the beasts had come at them all at once. Even so, he had a guess as to why they had picked this moment to make their move.

While sharing information about his travels in the Lost Land, Viktor Keldragan had noted that the trails along the rivers narrowed and then disappeared entirely the closer they got to the Boiling Lake, just as was happening now. So although they were finding it more difficult to make headway in the forest, they were making good progress.

Once past the mountains -- and from what he could see it looked like there were only two small peaks left before they made it through the gorge, a bright gleam maybe a league to the north suggesting a large body of water waiting for them -- they would reach the Cauldron where the Dead City of the Ghoules, Mertvey Gorod as Viktor had named it, was situated. In the center of that dead metropolis rose the Temple of the Ghoules, the apex of the Ghoule Overlord's power and the likely location of the Curse.

Good for them, not so for the Echidnae, the beasts probably not having any way to pursue them once they got out onto the lake. So the monsters likely felt some urgency to take their prey now. Otherwise, they'd lose the opportunity entirely.

It was the most logical course. If he were hunting prey as the Echidnae were, he would have done the same. He appreciated the monsters' maneuver even though if it proved successful it meant a hard end for him and his friends. In his mind, this was the perfect place for an ambush. They had only one direction to go and their surroundings limited their mobility.

They also couldn't move as fast as they would have preferred. With the forest reclaiming most of the trail running along the river, the steepness of the faint trace of a path along the cliff face forced them to slow down and take their time as they scrambled and climbed along the almost sheer sides of the gorge. Because of the rough terrain, they were spending most of their time cutting their own trail now as they worked their way across the thick vines and vegetation that clung to the ridge.

"Crap!" shouted Davin.

His friend's exclamation broke Bryen's train of thought. He watched in horrified fascination as the gladiator fought to maintain his hold on the scarp, having lost his grip on a vine that had torn free from the rock. That surprise set off a dangerous chain of events, Davin losing his balance as he scrambled to keep his position along the escarpment, his feet, already too large for the small ledge he was standing on, slipping free before he could even shout again.

Beginning to lean away from the precipice, with his free hand, Davin desperately tried to dig his fingers into any crevice that he could find in the cliff that sloped down at a precipitous angle toward the river far below them. There was nothing there for him to work with, the face of the mountain sheer where he was falling away from it.

Before Lycia or Bryen, who were working their way as swiftly as they could across the cliff face on either side of him, could do anything to help him, Davin fell backward through the air, the acidic water of the river beckoning to him.

Only for a split second, thankfully. The deceptively fast and agile gladiator made a last gasp grab with his other hand, shouting in triumph when he curled his fingers around a large vine.

Davin grinned broadly, believing that the worst was over.

He had arrested his fall. He had saved himself from a fate that he wouldn't wish on his worst enemy.

Well, that wasn't entirely true, he admitted to himself. He wouldn't shed a tear if a Ghoule or an Echidna took a bath in the steaming river.

He didn't have the time to congratulate himself for escaping a certain, gruesome death. His eyes widened in fear. His mouth opened, about to utter a curse, when the large vine ripped away from the rock with a sound that resembled cloth tearing, the long creeper now dangling free from the mountainside for more than a hundred feet. Having nowhere else to go, Davin went with the vine as he swung out from the ridge and over the raging whitewater.

Not wanting to think about what would happen if he slipped or the vine tore free from the rock entirely, Davin focused instead on maintaining his grip, reaching up with his other hand to grasp the creeper so that he had just a little more stability. Rather than fighting what was happening to him, the gladiator simply went with it, allowing his momentum to take him out over the water and then bring him back toward the rock face.

Bryen was waiting for him when Davin got there, having made sure that the vine that he was holding onto was firmly secured to the rock when he reached out and grabbed Davin's arm, holding his friend in place when the gladiator, having lifted his legs toward his chest so that he could stop himself with his feet before he slammed into the cliff, came to a stop against the ridge.

"Getting bored?" quipped Bryen. "Just needed to have a little fun?"

"Yes, that's it exactly," replied Davin, gasping for breath as he struggled to bring his racing heart back under control. He closed his eyes and leaned his forehead against the cold stone, glad that his unexpected and unwanted adventure hadn't ended as badly as it could have.

"What were you thinking?" demanded Lycia from his other side, taking him to task for what had just happened, her heart still in her throat, dreading that she was going to lose her brother.

"It's not like I meant to do that," he protested. "I slipped!"

"Don't do it again," she ordered.

"Don't worry." Davin smiled then, letting her anger wash off him as he opened his eyes and lifted his head off the stone, knowing that her reaction resulted because of her fear for him and appreciating her concern. "I won't."

With Davin safely back on what passed for a trail along the cliff face, Bryen ignored the brother and sister, instead shifting his attention to a soft rustling that he heard every so often that was masked at times by the sound of the water rushing between the mountains, the rustling coming from no more than a few dozen yards above him.

"Rafia? Aislinn? Do you sense them?" Bryen had released his hold on the Talent while he was helping Davin, and now that he felt the natural power of the world surging through his veins once more, he was having a hard time recovering the faint touch of darkness that he had been tracking since the night before. The monsters were flitting about too erratically.

"There!" said Aislinn, pointing about twenty yards above them and to the right.

Bryen sensed it now as well, catching the faint scent of evil that revealed the beasts that were hunting them. A cold ball of fear settled in his stomach when he realized why. The Echidnae had just shifted their strategy, choosing speed over deception.

He had been right in terms of what he guessed the hunters would do. Six Echidnae were coming directly toward them now, advancing sinuously down the cliff face, hoping to use the vegetation to hide their movements until right before they attacked Bryen and his friends.

"Above us!" he shouted.

At the same time, he opened himself to the Seventh Stone, using the power within him to send out thin tubes of invisible energy that latched onto the beasts despite their frenetic movements without them even being aware. Then, as he had done before, Bryen used the Stone to drain the monsters of the Dark Magic that allowed them to blend in so perfectly with their surroundings.

Aislinn gasped at the terrifying sight now that Bryen had revealed their attackers. The Echidnae slithered down the rock face, snakelike tails whipping across the vines and rocks, claws extended to rip into their flesh.

MUCH TO BRYEN'S ANNOYANCE, the Echidnae didn't seem to have any problems at all with the steep slope, the beasts' serpentine movement allowing them to slide across the foliage growing atop the stone with little difficulty. Every so often the monsters looped their tails around a protruding rock or a thick vine that hung loose from the cliff to gain some much-needed balance and stability as they launched themselves at their prey with a rabid ferocity.

The Echidnae's mesmerizingly dexterous movements created a host of problems for Bryen and his companions. If it wasn't bad enough that they had to fight monsters even deadlier than Ghoules, they also had to do it with one hand on the hilt of their weapons and the other grasping onto one of the vines that ran down the length of the ridge. All the while they hoped that they wouldn't also have to deal with what Davin had experienced, unexpectedly swinging out over the abyss because a vine broke free or, even worse, falling into the raging river below when their handhold gave way under the stress of their actions.

The Echidnae launched themselves at their prey, their hope for any easy kills dashed thanks to Bryen eliminating their magical camouflage.

Davin fought with a dogged determination, his Talent-infused spear cutting through the air in front of him with the speed of a giant scorpion's stinger. Even so, the Echidna that was attempting to take him from above slithered out of the way of each of his strikes with a disappointingly graceful ease.

Realizing that he needed to change his approach in order to have any chance of surviving this encounter, Davin feinted a jab, then swung his spear as if he were trying to scrape the beast from the rock face with his steel. The adjustment in his tactics had the desired effect, the blade slicing across the Echidna's ribs, eliciting a hiss of shock and pain.

It wasn't a deep wound, though it was enough to enrage the beast as it stared at the black blood that seeped down its abdomen and drenched its tail. Glaring at Davin with an undisguised hatred, the Echidna coiled its tail beneath it, then propelled itself at him, claws longer than several of his daggers reaching for his flesh.

Davin watched all that was occurring as if it were in slow motion, realizing instantly that he had nowhere to go. If he didn't move, he likely died, whether skewered by the Echidna or falling from his place into the whitewater.

He calculated quickly that he had no choice but to take the risk that flashed through his mind as the only option for staying alive. Reaching for the vine that had come loose and now hung right next to him, the one that had taken him out over the river despite his lack of interest in doing just that, he grabbed hold and pushed off against the stone with his feet.

The gladiator drifted away from the attack in the nick of time, the Echidna slamming into the rock face right where

Davin had been just a moment before. Davin grinned then tossed a choice curse at the furious Echidna as he swung back out over the river, relieved that he was safe for a few seconds.

When he slammed into the far side of the gorge, his back taking most of the impact, he realized that he had pushed too hard. Yet even with the wind knocked out of him, Davin had the presence of mind to twist around and dig his feet into a few toeholds that he found in the cliff while releasing his hold on the vine, his free hand gripping a thick root that extended out from a crack in the crag so that he wouldn't fall.

He didn't have time to think about how he might be able to swing back and help his friends. The enraged Echidna that had just missed thrusting its claws into his flesh, desperate for its kill, leaped across the gap, claws outstretched, maw gaping wide to reveal the twin fangs sticking out from each jaw that would have little trouble ripping out a huge chunk of meat from his body.

With no ideas for escape, Davin steadied himself against the cliff face, preparing to defend himself, though his choices were limited. He raised his spear just in time, jamming the end against the stone and catching the surprised beast in the chest, the Echidna's momentum allowing the steel to punch all the way through the sternum to emerge from the creature's back.

The Echidna, black blood dripping from its mouth, stared at Davin in surprise and then at the weapon upon which it had impaled itself, never expecting to come to such an end. Gravity then came into play, the weight of the dying beast too much for Davin, so he dipped the tip of his spear, the Echidna sliding off the steel and into the river.

~

As was her habit, Lycia had begun the fight right next to Davin, only using one sword instead of her preferred two as her other hand tightly gripped a long vine that draped itself off the cliff. Her first instinct was to try to help Davin. But she couldn't. Instead, she had to turn her focus to the Echidna that came for her from above. Her steel was a grey blur as she crouched against the rough stone, her feet well balanced beneath her, so that she had a better angle and less chance of sliding off the ridge while defending against the monster's constant attacks.

So far, so good, Lycia thought, as she employed her sword with an almost inhuman precision to keep the beast's claws from ripping across her face. Yet even with her early success, she was worried.

She didn't know what was going on around her with all of her attention concentrated on this single beast, and she really wasn't in the best position to adjust if the Echidna changed its line of attack, such as coming at her from the side rather than from above. Then again, she really didn't have many other choices, the environment they were fighting in limiting her possibilities and restricting the dynamic of the combat.

Even so, that stray thought brought to mind something Declan had harped on quite a bit while she fought in the Pit. Where a combat took place could play a key role in who came out the victor. As much as possible, you needed to control your environment, even when you didn't think that you could.

With that thought playing through her mind, out of the corner of her eye, she saw Davin push himself off the cliff and out over the water. When the Echidna that had been attacking her brother landed right next to her, she decided to do as Davin had done, not wanting to fight two of the monsters at the same time.

Blocking a lunge from the Echidna above her with a back-handed swipe, the beast trying to pluck her eyes from their sockets with its long claws, she gathered her legs beneath her, then pushed off with her feet, though not with as much strength as her brother did. The vine she had been holding onto tore loose from the force she applied, and then she was swinging out over the river.

The Echidna that had been trying to kill her stared at her with a look of confusion that shifted to anger, furious that she had escaped if only for a short time. With a growl, the Echidna launched itself out into the gap and directly at Lycia. But in its rage, the beast misjudged the width of the space between it and its quarry.

Lycia lifted her legs to her chest as the creature flew beneath her, the Echidna lucky to grab onto the vine with one sharp claw just below her feet the instant before it dove past her and fell into the river. The Echidna howled in triumph, the beast turning its slavering jaws up toward her, hissing with spite as it lifted itself up and tried to bite into her ankle with its fangs.

The monster never had the chance to taste her flesh, Lycia calmly slicing through the vine below her feet with a single swing of her sword. The Echidna shrieked in fury, its black eyes locked onto Lycia, right until the monster splashed into the river and was carried away through the gorge submerged within the whitewater that instantly began eating into its flesh.

Lycia glided back across the river and landed against the rock face with a jolt, the vine twisting at the last moment so that she hit the stone with her hip rather than her feet. Even with the hard knock, she was able to maintain her grip on the creeper and with a quick jab drove her sword through the back of an Echidna that was about to slide one of its razor-sharp claws into Aislinn's neck, the Lady of the Southern Marches engaged with another monster on her other side.

The Echidna arced its back in agony as the steel sliced through its spine, never having the chance to see who killed it as the beast slipped from where it had slithered, following its brethren into the river.

Aislinn sensed the movement behind her, hoping that it

was only Lycia, unable to even take a second to glimpse and confirm, needing to focus her full attention on the Echidna that was so intent on trying to dig its claws into her chest. When she didn't feel venom-filled fangs or talons plunge into her back, she assumed that she was right.

Using the blade gifted to her by the Blademaster, she knocked back a series of attacks by the Echidna, the beast so fast that she could do nothing other than concentrate on her defense. That was fine with her, not wanting to take any unnecessary risks that would send her flying from her perch. She just needed to wait for the right moment.

When she recognized it, Aislinn took advantage of the opportunity. As Lycia did on the promontory, when the Echidna overextended, missing her with a lunge, she sliced down with her Talent-infused blade in a viciously fast strike that cut completely through the creature's tail. The beast howled in pain as it slipped from its roost and tumbled down the rock face into the acidic water rushing between the mountain peaks.

Before she could feel good about her success, however, she realized that she had left herself open to another attack against which she wouldn't be able to defend herself, one of the other Echidnae picking that moment to leap for her. Unable to twist around on the vine in time, she cringed, expecting to feel the beast's claws tear into her.

Just then Bryen appeared, having pulled his vine free from the stone and pushed off from the cliff. He slammed into the beast's gut with his shoulder, knocking the monster off its trajectory and instead sending the Echidna tumbling off the crag.

With the strength of his push off the ledge, Bryen ended up on the other side of the gorge with Davin. His friend returned the earlier favor, grabbing onto Bryen's leather armor before he could swing back out and dangle over the gap.

Bryen looked down briefly, though he lost interest quickly as he watched the terror-stricken Echidna struggle futilely against the powerful current. Instead, he took in the larger fight. He and his friends were still alive, though they wouldn't be for much longer if they didn't find a way to escape these beasts, especially with those other Echidnae packs coming their way.

RAFIA DIDN'T HAVE the chance to see anything else that was going on around her, doing the best that she could to maintain her grip on the vine she had selected while fending off the last Echidna with her long dagger. Cutting and slashing with a will, she succeeded in keeping the beast away from her with her glowing steel.

The Echidna was wary of the bite of her weapon, the several streaks of black blood across its claws and forearms testifying both to her skill and the intensity of her efforts.

Yet despite her success against the beast, this last Echidna was annoyingly persistent, and Rafia was rapidly losing patience. So she decided that a different, more direct approach was needed.

With that thought driving her, she shot a bolt of energy against the rock face where the Echidna had found some purchase before the beast could launch itself at her again. In a small explosion of rock, the vegetation and stone slid away, taking the beast with it.

The Echidna screamed in anger until its shrieks were drowned out, its flesh charring and then flaking off as it was carried back toward the Caldera, the beast doomed to a painful death in the whitewater.

"What are you doing over there?" demanded Rafia. Because

of the skirmish, Davin and Bryen were now on the other side of the gorge.

"We didn't have much choice," Bryen replied. "Can you sense the other Echidnae?"

Bryen had been using the Talent throughout the fight to keep track of where the other two packs of Echidnae were. Even though they had just killed half a dozen of the monsters in just a few minutes, they were still sizzling in the frying pan, a dozen more of the beasts coming for them on both sides of the canyon.

"We can," replied Aislinn. "They'll be here soon. Bryen, above you!"

Aislinn noticed the flash of movement just above Davin and Bryen on the mountainside. She couldn't see anything other than the vegetation shifting in a way that didn't look right to her, her use of the Talent confirming her fears.

In a flash the Dark Magic hiding the beast vanished. The Echidna that had been sneaking up on Bryen and Davin from above had believed that it could get even closer before striking, its prey oblivious to its presence, unable to see it, the monster never thinking that it would be discovered until it had sunk it fangs into its quarry.

That proved to be a poor assumption on its part when Davin drove his spear through the creature's mouth right between its fangs, knocking one out, the steel tip punching through the back of its head. When Davin pulled his spear free, the Echidna slid down the cliff face and disappeared.

"Make for the Boiling Lake," Bryen called across the gap, revealing the other Echidnae that had been following after the one that Davin had killed all along the top of the crag. He had used that moment to employ the Seventh Stone, draining the Curse from the approaching monsters so that they would be visible and he and his friends would stand a fighting chance against them. "We'll meet you there."

Without another word, Bryen and Davin tried to make their escape, sliding as fast as they could along the rock face to where there was a fork in the river, choosing the one on the right.

For just a moment, Lycia, Aislinn, and Rafia thought that they could swing across to help Davin and Bryen. They decided against it when they saw the Echidnae waiting for them there. Instead, they did as Bryen suggested and took the fork on the left, the Echidnae on their side of the gorge no more than a few minutes behind them and closing fast.

"It's too quiet," said Rafia.

The Magus led Aislinn and Lycia down the narrow trail that ran along the cliff. The last mountain before they reached the Boiling Lake was much like the others in this range, covered in thick vegetation and creepers that dropped over the side toward the river below, the face above ascending at a steep angle until it met the summit.

All three were feeling a bit better after their fight with the Echidnae, even though Bryen and Davin were now off on their own. No more of the monsters had appeared on their side of the river yet, and now they were moving slightly downward, which confirmed that they were almost through the peaks.

"We should enjoy it while it lasts," grunted Lycia. "There's no cause to question good fortune."

They were moving at a fast pace. Though exceedingly narrow, the trail was clear here, just a rocky path that hadn't been reclaimed by the forest, although the foliage pressing closer certainly seemed intent on doing so. Every so often, they ran through shadows, rocky outcroppings and boulders reaching out over the trail and hiding the three women from view until they appeared again on the other side, all those precariously perched stones seemingly needing nothing more than just a gentle nudge to send them tumbling into the river below.

"Agreed," said Aislinn. Despite their pace, she and her two companions were energized, the adrenaline surging through them after their clash with the Echidnae helping to propel them forward. She hoped that the inevitable crash didn't come until after they were through the mountains and out on the Boiling Lake, well away from these cursed beasts.

It had bothered Aislinn that they couldn't aid Bryen and Davin, but they had their own dangers to navigate. Besides, the Volkun and the Crimson Giant were more than capable of taking care of themselves while causing chaos and destruction at the same time, those two objectives, at least for them, often one and the same.

"Haven't either of you heard the phrase the calm before the storm?" Rafia asked over her shoulder. "Just because circumstances are in our favor now doesn't mean that they will stay that way."

"One of Declan's many sayings?" asked Aislinn.

"No, I don't think so," said Lycia, who glanced behind them just to make sure none of the monsters were on the trail. She didn't disagree with Rafia. That the Echidnae would be on them again soon. She just didn't want to deal with that reality until it was necessary. "I would have remembered that one."

"Declan hasn't cornered the market on witty sayings," grumbled Rafia, although she admitted to herself that he did have quite a few good ones.

"He does seem to have the perfect maxim for every occasion, though, doesn't he?" asked Aislinn.

"That may be, but I learned that phrase from my parents."

"You should share that saying with Declan," suggested Lycia. "You know how he's always looking for new ones."

"That I do," replied Rafia. "And maybe I will. If we escape

these beasts, because the problem with that saying is that it's usually right."

"Above us!" shouted Aislinn, having used the Talent to track the Echidnae as a pack of the monsters sought to catch up to them. "They're on the cliff face, just a hundred yards behind us."

None of the three bothered to look back over their shoulders, instead watching where they placed their feet as they increased their pace, now sprinting down the trail, more concerned about the beasts behind them than the hazardous conditions of the trail. They could hear the Echidnae now, screaming and hissing, the beasts moving faster than they were. Even with the steeply angled slope, their hunters already were paralleling them just a few dozen yards up on the ridge.

"I hate when I'm right," groaned Rafia, reaching for the Talent as she raced down the trail, tiny spheres of energy appearing just above her fingertips.

She didn't believe that they could escape the beasts. She did think that she could slow them down. With a quick flick of her wrist, the tiny orbs shot up the side of the mountain, floating in the air behind the fleeing women.

After just a few seconds passed, a shriek of surprise and then pain drew Rafia's gaze, the Magus smiling as she took in with just a glance the success of her quick thinking. She never broke stride, however, using the distraction to gain some additional distance on their pursuers, Lycia and Aislinn right on her heels. All the while thanking Bryen for using the Seventh Stone to remove the monsters' magical camouflage.

Four Echidnae, likely the scouts for the larger pack that was still several miles away, were hot on their heels, their serpentine tails powering the monsters toward them. The beast in front of the other three had slithered right through the spheres that she had left in their wake. The energy, drawn to the Curse that was a part of the beast, swirled around it for just a flash, then surged toward the beast and bit into its flesh.

It wasn't enough power to kill an Echidna. At least not right away. However, it was enough to distract the monster. So much so that the beast swatted at the sparks of energy that began to burrow into its flesh, not seeing the rocky knob that stuck out from the cliff face because of its frantic and useless efforts to brush away the painful irritants.

The Echidna slammed into the obstruction at full speed, finding itself knocked off course. Before the Echidna could recover, the beast's tail whipping about in a desperate attempt to catch something that would curb its fall, the monster slid off the cliff face, the beast failing to grasp one of the vines that ran off the edge by just a few inches.

Rafia smiled with a vicious pleasure. One down. Still, there were three more to go. And this wasn't the place to engage in a fight. They needed to find some other option that might give them a better chance of surviving the next few minutes.

Having watched Rafia fling the Talent behind them and then hear one of the monsters disappear over the side, Aislinn decided to try her hand at improving the odds. Skidding to a stop, she focused her attention on a point just a dozen yards in front of two of the onrushing Echidnae.

The monsters undulated down the cliff face at an incredible speed, their tails swishing from side to side through the foliage, the beasts focused on their prey that had stopped so foolishly rather than trying to flee.

"What are you doing?" demanded Lycia, the gladiator stumbling to a halt just in time before she crashed into Aislinn and knocked them both off the trail.

Aislinn didn't bother to respond, maintaining her concentration and sending three small bolts of energy shooting from her palm. The Talent slammed into the cliff face just a dozen yards above them and right in front of the charging Echidnae.

She timed the attack perfectly. The explosion of power hit the beasts with its full force, tearing vegetation and rock from the mountainside and blasting the beasts out over the edge to fall far below.

"Well, if you're going to do that, then I won't complain," conceded Lycia.

"I appreciate your flexibility," replied Aislinn, who turned quickly and ran after Rafia, who hadn't bothered to stop and was now a good fifty yards ahead of them. "Come on. We're not done yet."

Lycia quickly glanced over her shoulder and then above them. Aislinn was right. Their fight was far from over.

Two more of the beasts were close behind, yet these Echidnae had spread out. One of the monsters came at them along the trail, the other along the rock face. Even if Aislinn hit one with the Talent, the other would be on them before she could do anything about it.

There was nothing for it but to run and hope that they could stay ahead of their hunters until they caught up to Rafia. Although the Magus showed no signs of slowing down, maintaining her lead over them as they raced along the trail.

Lycia and Aislinn had gone no more than a dozen yards before the path began to curl around the mountain, heading toward a series of switchbacks far off in the distance that appeared to offer a way down to the forest far below. They doubted that they would make it that far with the two Echidnae behind them and closing fast.

They increased their pace as best as they could manage, wanting to put as much distance as possible between them and their pursuers, knowing at the same time that their attempt was doomed to fail. The beasts were too fast. Reaching that realization at the same moment, rather than feeling sorry for themselves, they shifted their focus to finding a good place to defend themselves.

Sprinting down the trail, the Echidnae swiftly gaining on them, they ran beneath a long, rocky ledge that stuck out over the trail. They were about to head back out into the sunlight when both Aislinn and Lycia gasped in shock, two hands reaching out from the rock face and pulling them through the creepers that ran down the side of the mountain. Those surprisingly strong hands then released their grip and swiftly adjusted the vines that they had disturbed upon entering the cleft so they fell back into place.

"Quiet," whispered Rafia, "and don't move. We're hidden for the moment with the Talent."

Rafia had employed the Talent to map the terrain through which they were fleeing, seeking any aspect of the landscape that might aid them in their attempted escape. She had found what she was looking for farther down the trail, knowing that Aislinn and Lycia would stay on her heels as she made for the hollowed-out crevice in the ridge that was just big enough for all three of them to slip in and stand side by side.

They didn't have to wait long for the power of the mirage to be tested, the screeches of the Echidnae preceding the beasts and echoing down the mountain. Lycia wanted to reach for the swords in the scabbards on her back. Instead, she forced herself to remain still, knowing how fragile the illusion that Rafia created was, even with it being strengthened by the creepers in front of them.

She would have to trust in the Magus, though that was hard to do when every instinct told her to whip out a sword and drive her steel into one of the beasts when she heard the scrape of an Echidna's tail as it slithered down the path, now no more than a few feet away, only the vines separating them. Then a loud thump announced that the Echidna that had been tracking them from above had joined the first on the trail.

The two monsters had slowed, and Lycia could understand why. Their prey had disappeared. From where they were now, the beasts had a clear view down the trail, and there was nothing to see.

Rafia raised her finger to her lips as the Echidnae slithered to a stop right outside their hiding place, the beasts communicating with one another through a series of barks, grunts, and hisses just as the Ghoules did. Useful information, in her opinion, though not very helpful in that moment. Especially if they didn't make it out alive from this cramped space.

Why hadn't the beasts continued on down the trail? There was no way that they could see through the illusion that she had created. Even though they were no longer in sight, there was no reason for the beasts to stop right in front of where they were hiding.

Then she understood when a sickening realization struck her. She was wrong. These beasts were excellent hunters for a reason, and not just because of their ability to blend into their environment. No, these monsters knew how to track, and they had stopped here because the faint scuff marks of their prey's boots on the rocky trail had stopped here as well.

Rafia's eyes tightened, a shiver of cold running down her spine, when she saw a single claw reach between the vines, beginning to pull them back, the hisses of the beasts on the other side of the creepers increasing in intensity. Even with Rafia using the Talent to hide them, the Echidnae knew that they had cornered their quarry.

Before Rafia could act, a burst of energy shot from Aislinn's hand, the blazing white light so hot that it burned right through the vines hiding the crevice and then through the two beasts waiting hungrily on the trail, the Talent leaving behind nothing but a few pieces of charred flesh that fell off the trail and swirling ash that danced in the gusty wind that played along the sides of the mountain.

Rafia looked at Aislinn, who had removed the Echidnae as a threat with a devastating finality.

"Direct and aggressive," said the Magus, nodding her head in approval. "I like that."

Aislinn nodded in return, appreciating the compliment.

The Magus then stepped out from their hiding place. She looked to both sides and then up the slope toward the summit. Rafia held up her hand, asking them to wait as she used the Talent to search around them, taking her time, wanting to make certain, wanting to ensure that she didn't miss anything like the faint hint of corruption she associated with another pack of Echidnae.

"Did you find any more of these nasties?" the Magus asked Aislinn.

"No, not near us, at least not yet. The larger pack is about two miles to the west and coming this way around the mountain. They'll be here in about ten minutes."

Rafia nodded, having confirmed just as much herself. "Then we better get moving." The Magus began to trot down the trail at an easy pace, not feeling the need to rush with the distance they had gained on their pursuers.

The gleaming water beckoned to them from the north, less than a mile away, the switchbacks that they would be coming to soon taking them right down to the beach. By the time the Echidnae made it this far, they should be out on the Boiling Lake.

They had gone no more than a few hundred feet when they stopped again, listening to a series of screeches that echoed off the mountains. More Echidnae, though nothing for them to worry about. Those beasts were on the other side of the river.

When silence fell once again, they picked up their pace, driven on by their worry. Those sounds came from the direction that Bryen and Davin had taken. There was nothing that they could do to help them. All they could do was hope that the two survived what hunted them.

"FASTER, DAVIN!" urged Bryen. "They're gaining on us."

The two gladiators scrambled along the small trail that hung onto the side of the gorge like an afterthought, giving them a much closer view of the river rushing beneath them than either of them would have preferred. After taking the fork, the path had begun to descend slowly, the several switchbacks requiring them to backtrack while the Echidnae chasing after them came down on a straight line, allowing the beasts to catch up to them faster than they would have otherwise.

"I'm going as fast as I can," he called over his shoulder, not bothering to turn around. He didn't need to look to understand that they were in trouble. He could feel the beasts getting closer, the hair on the back of his neck prickling as if they were about to run into a lightning storm.

So close, yet still so far, Bryen thought. He could see the end of the gorge as the mountains dropped off to the lakeshore. He could see the sun glistening off the steaming water of the Boiling Lake no more than a mile away. But Bryen knew they weren't going to reach the safety of the water. That they couldn't keep running, not with the beasts breathing down their necks.

"You ready?" Bryen called to Davin.

"As I'll ever be."

"I thought you were all about the adventure?" shouted Bryen. "You don't sound very excited about what we're going to do next."

Bryen throwing in a touch of humor at a time like this made Davin crack a smile even as the shrieks of the Echidnae and the sounds of the beasts' noisy and rapid passage across the rocks and foliage assaulted their ears.

"I've decided that I've had enough of this adventure," called Davin, "and I must admit, I'm very tired of running."

"Good. In three, two, one …"

Bryen grabbed a vine that hung down right in front of him and then ran off the cliff, his momentum swinging him away from the trail and farther down the side of the mountain, tracking the trail. At the same time, Davin turned and crouched, his spear extended as he dug the end into the dirt of the trail. Thanks to Bryen's use of the Seventh Stone, he had no problem seeing the monsters.

The Echidna right behind him was so surprised by Davin's action that the beast slithered right onto the steel point, piercing the monster in the gut. Davin grunted in satisfaction, then gave his spear a violent twist before ripping the weapon free and allowing the beast to collapse in the dirt and loose shale.

He then turned and took a few steps farther down the trail, another Echidna coming up right behind the first. Feeling as calm as he did when fighting on the white sand, and not feeling the need to rush, he coolly reached out and grasped hold of a vine. Once he had a good grip, he gave the Echidna a wink and ran off the mountainside just as Bryen had done to swing farther down the trail himself.

He had misjudged, however. The Echidna pursuing him was closer than he had thought, and when he looked back he saw the beast preparing to leap after him. With the beast so close to him, he was certain that the Echidna would catch him in the air.

Recognizing his probable fate, Davin realized that he had spoken truthfully just moments before. When he left the Colosseum, he was up for any adventure that would take him away from the white sand. Now, after all that had happened, and what was likely about to happen, he had experienced more than enough adventure for the foreseeable future.

He needed some peace and quiet. At least for a few days. Because he knew as well that he would become bored and would soon begin to yearn for more excitement, which was why the rigors of the Colosseum had affected him less severely than they had so many others.

Cringing at the thought of the Echidna's fangs sinking into his neck, he glanced behind him as he swung through the air, his eyes widening, the monster dropping down toward him, claws reaching for his flesh. Then he felt a gust of air at his back. He grinned and laughed when he heard the collision.

Bryen had noticed the danger that he was in and had come back around on his vine. His friend had timed it perfectly, cutting behind Davin and slamming into the Echidna right after it had launched itself from the path.

Bryen didn't crash into the beast full on. A smart move since the weight and size of the creature might have been enough to knock him from his creeper. Rather, Bryen hit the beast with just enough force to change his trajectory, the Echidna pinwheeling away then slamming headfirst into the cliff below the trail before the beast scraped its way down the ridge and dropped into the river.

Bryen's quick thinking had earned them a brief respite. A very brief respite, because several more Echidnae were almost upon them.

Once Bryen landed back on the trail, he was away again, sprinting down the trail and then launching himself off the path, using the vine to swing farther away from the Echidnae who had been just a few feet away from driving their claws into his back before he took to the air again.

From then on, it became a running and soaring battle, Davin and Bryen using the vines to leapfrog past one another, swinging out over the river to escape the Echidnae as the beasts chased after them. When the beasts got too close or an opportunity presented itself, and inevitably there were several chances to inflict some damage on their pursuers, the beasts not only dangerously persistent and fast, but also ravenously hungry, one of the gladiators would stop and make a stand, seeking to hold the trail against the onrushing monster, while the other gladiator swung back around behind the beast.

This simple approach allowed them to trap the Echidna and attack from two directions at once, although they needed to be incredibly fast with their kill because so many of the monsters were after them. Then Bryen and Davin swung back off the trail before the remaining Echidnae could join the fight.

Their tactic, which proved to be quite effective time and time again, allowed them to remove three more Echidnae from the hunt. Even better, as they continued along the trail they were getting closer to their goal, the shining waters of the lake drawing closer with each breath that they took.

Even so, the combat wasn't over. Far from it.

The Echidnae's failure to kill them and the loss of so many of their brethren had enraged the beasts and driven them into a frenzy, the two remaining creatures hurtling across the cliff face as they attempted to come at them from above. Not having any other options, both Bryen and Davin grabbed onto creepers and leapt off the trail.

Just in time. The closest Echidna slid down the steep slope and landed right where they had been standing just a moment before, almost slipping off the edge because of its hasty fall, using its large tail to latch onto a root sticking out of the rock to prevent that from happening.

The other Echidna jumped out after them, reaching for the vine that Bryen had selected and grasping it with its claws just a dozen feet above his head. The Echidna hissed down at Bryen, its fangs sparkling in the sunlight as it spun itself upside down, twisted its tail around the vine, and then began lowering itself toward Bryen, the beast's claws, reaching out for him, large enough and strong enough to crush his skull if they took hold.

Bryen's initial thought was to cut the vine. Then he cursed himself for a fool. That wouldn't help him in the least, although he assumed dying in the acidic water of the river would be preferable to becoming this beast's next meal. Yet there was little else that came to mind as the Echidna pulled itself down toward him, Bryen holding onto the vine with one hand, his other hand gripping the haft of the Spear of the Magii.

Staring for just a second at the steel within his grasp, an idea finally came to him, and with the monster now just a few feet from him, he hoped that it wouldn't be too late. Bryen pointed the tip of one of the blades toward the beast, sending a bolt of the Talent that was no larger than a needle straight toward the Echidna.

The Echidna's proximity, unsettling though it was for Bryen, was exceedingly helpful in the end as the tiny spike of energy tore right through one of the monster's eyes and then burned through its brain, sizzling through its body before bursting out of its tail.

For a moment, the Echidna remained on the creeper, frozen in place. But as its blazing black eye faded, the beast's strength vanished, and the dead Echidna dropped off the vine.

Bryen ducked as best as he could, the heavy body almost knocking him from the creeper when it fell through the air. Nevertheless, he maintained his grip on the vine, though just barely, the glancing blow across his shoulder sending him spinning around in the air.

He realized that his problems weren't over when he twisted back around toward the trail. He was looking at the far side of the fork again before coming back around toward the path, Bryen having no way to stop the nauseating circular motion. The other Echidna, hissing and spitting its fury, stood there on its tail waiting for him as his momentum brought him ever closer to the beast.

Struggling to maintain his grip on the spinning vine with just one hand, his vision started to blur as a sense of vertigo struck him, his stomach rebelling as he continued to go around in circles. Bryen didn't know what to do next, fearing that after all that he had done to get this far he was going to meet an ignominious end, his final resting place the gullet of an Echidna.

When he was no more than a few feet from the trail, struggling to turn himself around so that he could face the waiting Echidna before it plunged its fangs into him, a grey streak shot past him, just missing his ear by a whisker. When he finally spun back toward the trail, just about to crash into the Echidna and expecting to see the beast reaching for him with its dagger-like claws, he breathed a sigh of relief while also trying to hold down the contents of his stomach.

Davin's spear stuck out of the beast's throat, the point buried deeply in the stone and pinning the Echidna against the ridge. That threat eliminated, Bryen braced himself for hitting the rock wall, taking much of the impact on his shoulder and thigh, then grabbed onto Davin's spear so that he wouldn't fall off the trail, his head still spinning when he finally let go of the vine.

"Nicely done," said Bryen, as Davin landed deftly back on the trail right next to him, releasing his hold on the creeper. "Thank you."

Bryen pulled the spear free, the Echidna slumping to the trail and slowly sliding off the ledge. He then dropped to his knees, eyes closed, taking several deep breaths, trying to contain his nausea. It was no use as Bryen spewed the contents of his stomach over the edge. Feeling better, he used both spears to push himself to his feet, then handed Davin's weapon back to him.

"My pleasure," said Davin, who examined the steel quickly just to make sure that none of Bryen's vomit marred the weapon. Satisfied that only the blood and gore of the Echidna streaked the steel, he turned his focus to what he believed was a more important matter. "It was quite a throw, wasn't it?" Davin grinned at Bryen, obviously pleased by his success.

"It was," Bryen replied, wanting to give his friend the moment that he had earned. "Right on the mark."

"I can't think of ever having seen a better throw," continued Davin.

"As I said, it was quite a throw."

"Better even than when Dorlan flung his spear at that giant lizard, taking the beast right in the mouth?"

"I don't recall seeing that," said Bryen, finally standing straight again, his stomach settling now that it was empty. He shook his head, though just barely, even that slight motion making his head and gut protest. He was not surprised that Davin was stuck on this topic.

Davin and Dorlan had engaged in a friendly competition during their time together in the Pit, the two gladiators having a unique ability to irritate the other and doing so as frequently as possible if for no other reason than to help pass the time. If Bryen backed up Davin's story on this throw, Davin could use it against the gladiator who was larger than most small cottages.

"How could you not remember that?"

"I might not have been paying attention," said Bryen, enjoying the touch of aggravation that had dripped into Davin's voice. He didn't want his friend to get too cocky.

"How could you not have been paying attention to something like that?"

"I was probably thinking about how to stay alive during my next combat," Bryen replied. "Though I do have to say that if Dorlan made that strike as you say, right into the maw of a giant lizard, it really must have been quite a throw."

Davin's eyes widened in alarm, feeling as if the advantage he hoped to gain was slipping away. "Even so, it couldn't have been better than the throw I just made."

"Maybe," said Bryen, understanding that his noncommittal response would aggravate Davin even more.

"How could you even suggest that ..."

Bryen held up his hand, cutting off Davin. They had almost reached the end of the trail, the first switchback leading down to a small wood and then the beach only a few hundred feet farther away. Checking behind them with the Talent, Bryen confirmed that the few remaining Echidnae, though still tracking them, were not getting any closer. At least not yet.

He expanded his search, finding Rafia, Lycia, and Aislinn just on the other side of the mountain. Their friends were making good progress and were just a little farther away from the beach than they were. Best of all, he didn't sense any Echidnae on their side of the river, which meant that the three women had killed however many of the beasts that had been foolish enough to hunt them.

"Come on, let's head for the beach," said Bryen.

"Are we in the clear?" asked Davin as he followed his friend down the twisting and turning trail, anxious to get off the mountain.

"No. There are still a few more back there. They're keeping their distance for now, though, so if we're fast we should be able to steer clear of them."

"You know, I'm glad that Declan isn't here," said Davin, feeling the need for conversation. He wasn't always comfortable with silence.

"Why wouldn't you want him with us?"

"Because if he saw us doing what we were doing with those vines, swinging along the mountainside, he'd probably turn it into some kind of training exercise, and once is enough for me. Fun though it was, I don't ever want to do that again."

"I'm with you on that," agreed Bryen, bile rising in his throat at just the memory of his fight with the Echidna on the vine and what it had felt like to be spun about like a children's top.

Bryen stopped suddenly, staring farther down the trail.

"What is it?" asked Davin. "Another of these beasts?"

Bryen nodded. Even though he had removed the Dark Magic that so perfectly camouflaged the Echidnae, this beast, which must have broken off from the rest of the pack during the fight and wasn't too far below them on the path, wasn't visible, having blended into the thick vegetation with its natural coloring.

"It's about a hundred feet down the trail. Just keep walking, but slowly. Give me a chance to come at it from a different direction."

"You want to use me as bait?" protested Davin, hating the idea.

Bryen shrugged. "Do you know where the beast is?"

"No," Davin replied, realizing that with that admission he had lost the argument before it had even begun.

"Then get moving, but, as I said, slowly."

Davin growled to himself in annoyance, then started walking down the path. Slowly, as Bryen had said, maybe too slowly because of his natural hesitation, hopefully not giving away the fact that he knew what waited for him.

He didn't care. Why had he agreed so readily to Bryen's request?

With each step he took, he strained to see anything to his front that would reveal where the Echidna hid, any flash of movement, any rustle of vines. When he looked behind him, Bryen had disappeared. Now he could only hope that whatever plan his friend had crafted was a good one.

"Down!" shouted Bryen.

Davin responded instinctively, dropping to the rough stone and dirt of the trail as his friend swung by just above him, Spear of the Magii held out to his front.

Bryen drove one of the weapon's blades straight through several vines just above the trail only a few feet away from Davin.

When Davin got back to his feet, he couldn't understand why Bryen had aimed for that particular tangle of vines. Peering more closely, at long last he saw it, the green skin of the Echidna allowing the beast to hide in among the plants and bushes.

The beast had one claw extended toward Davin, though it wouldn't be coming any closer, Bryen having thrust the Spear right through the beast's chest, the Talent infused within the blade burning through the monster. In seconds, it was done, the Echidna nothing more than a pile of ash on the trail.

"That was quite a performance," said Davin. "Better, in fact, than many of your combats in the Pit."

"What do you mean?"

"You've always been a bit frightening," offered Davin. "Dead eyes. A brooding quiet that for some reason always seemed to catch the attention of the women in the stands. Much too skilled with a blade. Those scars probably help you as well, making you seem even more dangerous."

"Thanks, I guess," replied Bryen, not sure where his friend was going with his comments.

"But now your ability with the Talent," tsked Davin. "That takes it to a whole other level."

"If you say so," shrugged Bryen.

"I do. Just one request."

"What's that?"

"Don't use me as bait! I think I soiled my trousers again."

19

LESSON IN POWER

"**D**uke Winborne, are you certain that this is a good idea?" asked Spencer Hedman, a young lord from somewhere north of Roo's Nest. "I ask not because of a lack of trust, but rather because of my knowledge of your skills and abilities."

Kevan couldn't remember from where exactly the popinjay who stood before him was from. It didn't really matter. His thoughts were focused on the niggling worm of concern that ran through his mind that wouldn't go away.

It was good that this Lord and his friends were here. Yet the question plaguing him was much more important than this boy's concerns about the role he would play in the fight against the Ghoules. The question was much more basic than that.

How long would they live?

Lord Hedman had arrived with several other young lords. Kevan knew after perusing them with just a single glance that none of them had yet to be in a battle, much less a skirmish, or even just a clash, whether with the Ghoules or anyone else.

They all wore the finest leather armor, supple and soft without a scratch marring it. The hilts of their blades were fitted with beautiful and priceless jewels. Their horses were of the finest stock.

Yet no matter how hard they tried to hide it, Kevan could tell. They were as green as the first grass of spring.

Even so, that didn't stop them from trying to present themselves as young men and women wise to the ways of war. And their lack of experience wouldn't stop Kevan from throwing them against the Ghoules when the battle began again.

"Too much is at stake," continued Hedman, the self-appointed leader of the small group that had been riding for the past two weeks to reach a point about a third of the way into the Winter Pass. "I have heard good things about Noorsin Stelekel, her knowledge and beauty, her ability as a ruler, though nothing having to do with fighting the Ghoules, I'm sorry to say. I'm not questioning your judgment, or the judgment of the other Dukes who appointed her, but should we really put our faith in the Duchess? Is there not someone with greater martial skill to lead us? Someone with a reputation that precedes him?"

Duke Winborne simply stared at the young lord. Hedman said that he wasn't questioning his judgment, even as he was. His patience never good to begin with, it was already wearing thin. Even so, Kevan chose not to interrupt.

The boy could finish the speech that he so obviously had been preparing ever since he had ridden across Caledonia to get here. Kevan would disabuse him of his prejudices and misconceptions after he talked himself out.

Hedman had ridden hard from the western coast of Caledonia to join the fight against the Ghoules within a day of receiving the summons from Duchess Stelekel. But he, just like so many of the other young lords and ladies with him, wasn't there solely to fight the invaders from the north. The pup had little doubt that he would beat the beasts back, what with the martial skills he had developed in the practice yard.

No, his primary goal was to make a name for himself. If he was to achieve the position in the world that he desired, that was most befitting of his rank, that he so clearly deserved, then he needed to enhance his standing, his reputation, and his wealth. The war against the Ghoules was his best and most immediate opportunity to do just that.

Unfortunately, that arrogant, self-serving perspective didn't allow him to comprehend the dire nature of the circumstances in which the Caledonians found themselves, nor did he seem to care. His thoughts were fixed on his future and not on the futures of all the people in the Kingdom who were at risk.

"That's not to say that I'm belittling her abilities," said Hedman. "I greatly admire the Duchess Stelekel, particularly her efforts to get us this far against the Ghoules, although I had assumed that when I arrived we would be closer to the Weir. Perhaps for our final push against the beasts a change in approach might be most appropriate and allow us to achieve our objective all the faster."

Hedman looked at Duke Winborne with a small smile and a nod. He had learned early in his life that flattery often worked best with those above him in rank, having proven quite effective in his efforts to gain favor in the lands surrounding Roo's Nest. Yet, he couldn't tell how Duke Winborne was receiving what he was saying. It was like talking to a stone, the Duke's grim expression and unforgiving eyes making him nervous.

As Hedman's discomfort increased, Kevan continued to stare at the young lord, his fixed countenance not betraying what he was really thinking. He had yet to say a word, allowing Hedman to do all the talking. He didn't feel the need to help the young, inexperienced Lord, who was digging a hole for himself quite well on his own.

"Is she really the best choice for the challenge that we face in this moment?" asked Hedman, thinking that Duke Winborne permitting him to continue to present his argument meant that what he was saying resonated with the man who, in his opinion, should be leading the Caledonian Army. A man who could, if he chose to, help propel Hedman farther along the path that he was certain would lead to glory, riches, and a name known throughout the Kingdom. "Should we not have someone leading who has a better understanding of and more experience in what it means to fight?"

"Duchess Stelekel is the most qualified person to lead the Caledonian Army," Kevan finally said, growing tired of the young lord's attempts to convince him otherwise. To convince him that he should lead the combined forces of the Kingdom.

Kevan wasn't a fool. Yes, there was a good bit of misogyny driving Hedman's argument, as well as just as much self-interest, both of which he ignored for the time being. There was much that Kevan wanted to say about that, but he held his tongue.

The young lord seemed to believe that if he could convince Kevan to take the reins of power, he could come along for the ride. The boy had misjudged him. Although that wouldn't stop Kevan from putting him to use.

Hedman had a sword and a horse. He could fight. That's what mattered. Whether he lived or died was a secondary concern to Kevan, numbers the key variable for him at the moment.

"In the fight against the Ghoules, young man, rank means nothing. Gender means nothing. Reputation means nothing. Only skill, intelligence, imagination, and an unwavering commitment to do what must be done has any meaning. Duchess Stelekel has that and more."

Hedman took a moment before responding, not sure what to say as he had never considered the possibility that Duke Winborne couldn't be won over by his words. Failing to gain what he wanted through the application of his silver tongue was a rare occurrence and had knocked him off his stride.

"That's an enlightened and somewhat dangerous perspective, Duke Winborne."

"Yes, I guess some with little experience in the real world would think so," Kevan agreed, seeing the veiled slight strike home when Hedman flinched as if he'd been struck across the cheek with a glove. The Duke's voice was amiable, though his eyes sparked with a contempt that made Hedman and the other young lords with him take a step back.

While studying the young Lord, Kevan considered the time that he had spent with his daughter's Protector, the gladiator and now a Magus and the only person with a chance of stopping the Ghoule Overlord. Kevan had learned the hard way, and much to his embarrassment, that nobility had little to do with a title and everything to do with a person's decisions and actions.

If this young Lord and the others with him learned that lesson quickly, they might make it through the next few days. And if they didn't, well, there was only so much he could worry about at one time. He certainly would appreciate their sacrifice.

"Yet I've discovered thanks to some of my more recent experiences that a broader perspective is needed in order to succeed in this world," continued Kevan. "That doing as we've always done is simply the opportunity to repeat our mistakes rather than learn from them and move in a new and better direction."

"Are you certain about this?" asked Hedman, not really listening to what Duke Winborne had just said, instead thinking that perhaps the Duke was simply giving him the opportunity to push a bit harder, the older man enjoying the attention that he was receiving and wanting a little more of it. If so, that was fine with Hedman. He would do what was needed to get what he wanted. Obviously, it couldn't be easy to live within the shadow of a woman. Perhaps the good Duke just wanted one more nudge from him. "Your reputation as a soldier, as a leader, is unmatched, likely never to be equaled, in fact. Should you not put the needs of Caledonia above all others?"

"I am doing just that," replied Kevan, an edge now in his voice. He was done with this conversation and this young Lord who wanted to play at being a soldier. He didn't have any more time to waste on these inexperienced fools. He needed to focus on preparing for the Ghoules' next attack, which, from what the scouts were reporting, would come soon after night fell. The darkness would require the Magii to use the Talent not only to keep the Elders at bay, but also to light the battlefield if they were to have any chance of holding their position. That additional strain on their few Magii would make the approaching fight all the more challenging. "The Duchess of Murcia is the right person to lead the Caledonian Army."

"I don't know if I can abide being commanded by a woman," muttered Herkul Renselar, one of the lords who had met Hedman on the road. He was from the southern shores of the Bay of the Dead. Unlike Hedman, Renselar had no qualms about saying what he truly believed, not feeling the need to dance around the real issue, lacking many of the social niceties that Hedman put into play so frequently and so well.

Kevan stared at Renselar with the same touch of contempt in his eyes. He actually knew this lordling, or at least he knew the family. He was just like all the others who had arrived.

Another boy who thought himself a man looking to make a name for himself. His very high opinion of himself had given Renselar a condescending smirk and an insufferable attitude. Renselar had done very little in life other than live off the reputation of his father, Harold, who before he was struck down by a chronic illness that kept him confined to his bed was one of the most renowned fighters in Caledonia.

Kevan closed his eyes and took a deep breath, seeking to quell his rising irritation. These two and the others with them were about to learn a very hard lesson, assuming any of them survived.

"With that perspective, lad, you're not going to do well when the hard truths of life hit you in the face," said Kevan, sighing, his exhaustion from fighting daily for the last few weeks coming to the forefront. "If you don't want to fight under Duchess Stelekel's command, that won't be a problem."

Hearing that, Renselar perked up, ignoring the first part of what Kevan had said, unsurprised that even if the Duke wouldn't change his mind about Duchess Stelekel, he would at least make a special accommodation for him. His expression soured when Kevan continued with the rest of what he had to say.

"You can leave. Your soldiers will stay here with me, however. I'll add your troops to my own. To win this fight, we don't have time for malcontents. Isn't that right, Blademaster?"

Jurgen Klines walked out of the fading light, having just completed a circuit of the Caledonian line to ensure that all was ready on top of the movable wall. The soldiers well equipped with arrows and spears. The companies of cavalry positioned where they were supposed to be for when the time came to take the offensive or simply attempt to shift the momentum.

"Quite right, Duke Winborne," said Jurgen Klines, flipping a foot-long dagger in his hand. The new arrivals were mesmerized by the action, the rhythm of it, the consistency of the blade spinning through the air, the Blademaster catching the tip between his thumb and forefinger without fail, time and again, the blade never stopping. "We don't have time for egos. They only get in the way of what we need to do here. It's a difficult task to begin with, made all the more difficult if several privileged lords who have never fought in a battle believe that they know all there is to know about defeating the Ghoules."

Hedman's eyes widened at the insult, never having been

offended in such a way and not knowing how to respond when the insult came from reputedly the best swordsman in Caledonia. Renselar actually placed a hand on the hilt of his blade, too young and too foolish to calculate the risk of doing that.

Hedman, Renselar, and the others with them believed that they were more than capable of fighting the Ghoules. In fact, they believed that they were better fighters than most of the soldiers in the Winter Pass. But none of them, except perhaps Renselar, was willing to risk the ire of the Blademaster, a man who every single one of them wanted to emulate, the reputation of Jurgen Klines known and respected far and wide throughout the Kingdom.

No, they didn't want to challenge the Blademaster unless someone else protested, at which point they could add their voices to the mix, feeling more confident through strength in numbers. Yet no one said a thing, silence greeting the Blademaster's very direct and on-point statement. Not even Renselar, who was usually filled with an undeserved bravado.

"I assure you, Blademaster," said Hedman, who, realizing that he needed to swallow his pride to avoid a potentially fatal altercation, placed a hand on Renselar's arm, hoping that his action would calm his oftentimes rash friend. Thankfully, the young lord's sword remained in its sheath. Renselar was a hothead. Hedman had learned that quickly on the way to the Shattered Peaks. Having him challenge the Blademaster to a combat with less than an hour having passed since their arrival was not the entrance that he wanted to make. It certainly wouldn't benefit his reputation. "We know how to fight Ghoules. You have nothing to fear in that regard."

Before the young lords could make a mistake that they would come to regret, Noorsin Stelekel, General of the Caledonian Army, appeared out of the falling darkness, lighting her way with a ball of energy glowing just above her palm. If meeting the Blademaster face to face wasn't intimidating enough, seeing the Duchess of Murcia making use of the Talent was even more frightening.

Hedman and Renselar's eyes widened in alarm, the two taking an involuntary step backwards. They had heard rumors that Duchess Stelekel was a Magus, but had only taken those tales to be just that. Rumors. Until now.

"Well, that's excellent news," said Noorsin, her eyes gleaming brightly from the glow of the energy that still danced atop her palm. "We shall put to use your knowledge and courage immediately. We shall learn from you. Both of you with your soldiers shall lead the vanguard and fight from the very center of our line. What do you think, Blademaster? Are these two young lordlings and their friends up for the task?"

"We shall see," grunted the Blademaster noncommittally, his dagger still flipping through the air with frightening regularity, Klines not even needing to look at the blade as he did it. "Of course, there's only one way to find out." His green eyes sparkling in the light provided by Noorsin's magical sphere, he nodded. "I think that's an excellent idea, Duchess Stelekel. They can show the other soldiers who have fought the Ghoules for the last several weeks their mettle. I'm sure that our veterans can learn something from these brave and skilled lords."

Hedman, Renselar, and the others suddenly realized the position in which they had placed themselves, several of their faces turning slightly green. Worse, they had no way to escape the trap that they had set for themselves without losing face. Trying to do so would only make them appear to be cowards and that they simply couldn't allow. So they stood there in silence, knowing that they had boxed themselves in, trying to figure out how the tables had been turned upon them so quickly and effectively.

"Indeed, Blademaster. Could you see that these young heroes are placed where they should be in our formation?"

"With pleasure, Duchess Stelekel. I shall do that right now."
The Blademaster then led away the speechless lords, the
dagger still effortlessly spinning above his fingers.

After Klines took the new arrivals into the settling night,
Kevan turned to Noorsin with a satisfied grin.

"Did you have fun doing that, Duchess Stelekel?"

"I did indeed. They needed to be put in their place."
Noorsin let go of the Talent, dark descending as her light
winked out. She reached out for Kevan's hand, taking it into
hers. "Now come with me, Duke Winborne. There are some
things that we need to discuss privately before the battle begins
again."

20

BOIL, TOIL, AND TROUBLE

The inland sea that stretched off into the distance for as far as the eye could see was crystal clear, the water appearing to have no color, the brownish grey of the silty bottom visible even at a depth of one hundred feet. The bright blue sky and blazing sun aided the clarity.

Even so, the water was anything but calm, churning violently in a curious, regular rhythm that had nothing to do with the wind that gusted every so often from the west. Rather, steam drifted off the surface and the many hydrothermal vents that rose out of the silt blasted heated, acidic water into the loch, creating dozens of spots, some as small as fifty yards and many as large as several hundred in circumference, where the lake boiled hotter than a pot over a fire.

Around each vent, large waves rolled out in all directions, the watery crests crashing violently into each other with a peculiar frequency that gave the lake's churning a strangely measured tempo. Thus Viktor's decision to name the body of water the Boiling Lake.

Davin and Bryen watched it all for several minutes, almost spellbound by the rhythm. The only sound they heard during

that time was the waves lapping against the shore, unexpectedly gentle compared to what was happening farther out in the
lake. Still, they remained where they were for several minutes
more, cautious, hidden among the trees that bordered the
rocky beach.

They could see the tracks of Ghoules all across the sand in
front of them, most of the imprints recent. Before they took
another step, they wanted to make sure that there were no
surprises coming their way. Because as soon as they walked out
from the copse, they would be visible and vulnerable to any of
the beasts who might be looking for them.

"It's fascinating if you really think about what we're looking
at. The fractures beneath the surface, the vents and the geysers
in the bed of the lake shooting superheated water up toward
the surface to create that churn," whispered Bryen. "If we actually went into the lake, it would probably feel like a hot bath ...
until the acid began to eat through our flesh, of course. So we'll
want to avoid falling in."

"That's all very interesting," said Davin, shaking his head
in bemusement at his friend's interest in the natural science
of the Lost Land. He was curious as well as to what caused
this unique body of water. Although not so curious as to
forget the more immediate concerns pressing upon them,
such as escaping the Echidnae and Ghoules and making it
across the Boiling Lake. Not to mention the Cauldron, the
very center of the Ghoule homeland, which probably had
some unique feature that was more dangerous than what
they were facing now, but he could worry about that later.
"And I appreciate the warning, though after seeing what
happened to the Echidnae who fell into the river, I won't be
going any closer to the water in this cursed landscape than
absolutely necessary. Besides, I forgot to bring my swim
trunks."

"Smart move on your part," said Bryen, cracking a smile

even as his eyes never left the beach, his gaze sweeping up and down the sandy and rocky lakeside.

"I thought so myself," replied Davin, nodding. "Now back to why we're here. How are we supposed to get across? Do you have a plan?"

"You know me," Bryen replied with a grin.

Davin snorted softly with a restrained laughter, staying quiet, not wanting to reveal their position to any wandering beasts. "I do know you. That's what worries me. You're making it up as we go along, aren't you?"

Bryen shrugged. "We don't really have much choice, do we? This is new territory for all of us."

Davin couldn't disagree with his friend, and in all honesty, he was more than happy to make it up as they went along. The flexibility and the need to make decisions with barely a thought appealed to him. Besides, they were the first people to set foot in the Lost Land since Viktor Keldragan. There was little to go on but the recollections of a spirit.

That last thought stayed with Davin. They had entered the Lost Land without any problems, although based on what had happened since then, it seemed that leaving would be more difficult. Much more difficult. He understood that and could work with it, so long as he exited the Lost Land just as Bryen's ancestor did. Alive.

Of course, there were no guarantees in that regard in this bizarre place. Davin should have assumed as much when he came here with Bryen. Nothing was ever easy in life, and if it was, then there was always a catch. He had learned that the hard way first on the streets of Tintagel and then on the white sand.

"I figured as much. What do you have in mind?"

"Follow me," said Bryen, who began to walk between the trees without making a sound, staying on the edge closest to the beach.

"Follow you where?" Davin watched Bryen go, then had no choice but to follow, placing each foot carefully, moving as quietly through the grove as he could. "What can you see that I can't?" Davin assumed that Bryen was using the Talent to take in more of what was around them than just what was currently in their range of view.

They traveled about a hundred yards farther west along the coast when Bryen stopped and crouched down against a tree. Davin joined him a few seconds later. Looking out across the Boiling Lake, he could see the Cauldron rising thousands of feet out of the water. A haze, whether caused by smoke or clouds he didn't know, hid the top of the dormant volcano that rested several miles offshore. Having spent too much time in the Lost Land already, he assumed the former. Smoke or steam from what simmered beneath the island.

Bryen nodded toward the beach about fifty yards farther down the rocky shore.

"That's what we need."

Davin peered over Bryen's shoulder and saw the first thing that had made him smile since he had entered the Lost Land. A small boatyard had been built at the edge of the water. Several skiffs, all in various states of construction or repair, sat on large blocks of wood.

Each skiff was about forty feet long and ten feet wide with a mast that could manage a single square sail. The hull curved nicely so that the vessel would glide through the choppy water. The most unique feature were the sides, which were built at least six feet above the deck, Bryen assuming that construction quirk a way to protect anyone aboard the vessel from the caustic water that splashed and sprayed across the surface of the lake with a remarkable predictability.

He noticed as well that those curved hulls were covered, or were in the process of being covered, in a thin metal that appeared to be lighter and more pliable than steel. He assumed that innovation protected the wooden keel from the acidity of the water, which likely could burn through the hull just as fast as it could through flesh.

"Farther down the beach past the workshop," said Davin, pointing to a spot right where the water met the shore. "That should do the trick."

Bryen nodded. "That it should."

One of the skiffs with a hull fully covered in metal had been pulled out of the water recently. Unlike many of the vessels currently sitting on blocks, this one had a sail.

Both he and Davin saw the water still dripping off the hull, the acid contained within it staining the metal a rusty ochre, a pattern of small pockmarks visible, the corrosive liquid eating into the shield. So the metal was a temporary protection. They would need to be careful and fast, getting across to the Cauldron as swiftly as they could. There was no way to tell how long the thin barrier would protect them, and he had no desire to test the temperature of the water.

"Any of the beasts around?"

"Do you mean Ghoules or Echidnae?" asked Bryen.

"Are you just trying to be difficult?" asked Davin with a hint of exasperation. "Either or both. Any possible dangers that could slit me open from groin to gut."

"Not really," replied Bryen, smiling at Davin's lack of enthusiasm for his response. "And it's more like second nature. Being difficult irritates Declan to no end. Sometimes I couldn't resist."

"I know," replied Davin. "I got to see a lot of that. It's fun to watch unless you're the one dealing with it, so I now have far greater sympathy for Declan."

Bryen grinned, though he kept his eyes on the beach and the small shipyard. He didn't see any Ghoules, even though he knew that they were close. Dozens of tracks crossed the sand and a large fire burned in the forge.

As he took a closer look, it seemed that the beasts were less concerned with their shipbuilding and more focused on filling their bellies. He couldn't tell what was twirling on the spit over the flames, but that was probably for the best because from this distance it resembled something that he didn't want to think about.

Bryen reached for the Talent and searched around them once again just to make certain. The Echidnae were still up on the mountain, not yet having come down toward the beach. The Ghoules who should have been on the beach were by the trail that he and Davin had taken, either looking for them or maybe worried that the Echidnae might be coming down to feed, drawn there by the monsters' screeches.

"No immediate dangers," said Bryen. "The Ghoules are several hundred yards up the beach by where we came into the grove. I wouldn't expect them to stay there for long, so we'll need to be quick."

Davin nodded, having assumed as much. "Where are Lycia, Aislinn, and Rafia?"

"Right behind us by only a few minutes. They're coming down a different trail, so they should be able to avoid the beasts."

"No Ghoules waiting for them?"

"No, they've got a clear path."

"Then let's get to it," suggested Davin.

Davin and Bryen sprinted out from the grove and down the shore, making straight for the skiff that had just recently been pulled up onto the beach. They began pushing the vessel back into the water, careful to keep their hands clear of the trickling water that ran down the hull. Despite the craft's size and weight, they had a fairly easy time of it, the sense of urgency playing through their minds giving them a useful burst of adrenaline.

"Do you know how to sail?" asked Davin as the first waves of the lake touched the stern.

"Why do you think I'd know how to sail? I was in the Pit for ten years."

"You were also in the Southern Marches," grunted Davin, the two gladiators almost done with their task, the midsection in the water, the bow about to be. "Battersea is on the coast. I thought that maybe you got out onto the Silent Sea with Aislinn. Seems like sailing was something you'd do there with a pretty lady whenever you had a chance, especially on the coast."

Bryen didn't need to see Davin's face, which was blocked from his view because they were pushing on different sides of the keel, to know that his friend was grinning. He chose to ignore Davin's insinuations.

"The Silent Sea isn't so silent," explained Bryen as they finally got the skiff into the water, leaving just a few feet of the bow on the beach so that they could push off quickly. "So no, we didn't. Besides, we were focused on other matters."

"What matters might those be?" asked Davin when he looked back around the bow, his raised eyebrows contradicting his innocent expression.

"How to stay alive with assassins and Tetric a constant danger," Bryen replied in a sharp tone, clearly not interested in Davin's attempt at humor.

"Fair enough," said the gladiator. "Then how were you expecting to sail this to the Cauldron?"

"I was going to use the Talent if my one other option didn't work out."

Davin nodded. "Will using the Talent give us away to any Elders if they're nearby?"

"Probably," Bryen replied, "which is why using the Talent is my second option."

"What's your first option?"

"You'll find out soon enough," replied Bryen, who turned back toward the small forest lining the shore, his body tensing, the gladiator bending his knees and standing on his toes, the Spear of the Magii now held loosely in his hands. "We've got company."

Davin followed his friend's gaze and then grunted with annoyance. Four Ghoules raced out of the woods, howling in rage as they brandished their spears, their clawed feet digging deeply into the sand and flinging it behind them. Whatever had caught their interest on the other side of the wood hadn't held it for very long.

"There's our other option," said Bryen, nodding to a spot just behind the Ghoules, as he and Davin, weapons at the ready, strode forward a dozen yards to meet the Ghoule charge, wanting to gain more space to maneuver and avoid getting stuck right up against the lakeshore.

When Davin caught the shadow of movement behind the charging Ghoules, he understood what his friend had in mind. He had been partially correct in his assumption, and he never should have doubted Bryen, because even when he said he didn't, he always had a plan. It had been foolish to think otherwise, Declan's methodical approach to life obviously having become ingrained within the Protector.

The Ghoules sprinting across the beach, spears raised, hissing and screaming in anticipation of the kills to come, likely thinking that they'd be able to add more meat to their fire, never considered the possibility that they themselves might be in danger from a source other than the Echidnae that threatened to come down from the mountains.

That lack of foresight proved costly when Aislinn and Lycia, Rafia trailing them by just a few steps, burst out of the wood on an angle that would allow them to close the distance to the beasts without the Ghoules becoming aware of them unless they turned around. And in that moment, their ravenous hunger driving them forward, the Ghoules only had eyes for Bryen and Davin.

Once she got in range, with her glowing sword Aislinn cut across the back of the knee of the Ghoule trailing behind the others, sending him tumbling to the sand in shock, the beast not able to comprehend yet how he had fallen. Lycia did the same with one of her swords, hamstringing the Ghoule that was just a few steps behind the other two, the beast crashing face first into the beach, the sand stuck in his craw muffling his scream of agony.

Lycia and Aislinn left the two beasts writhing on the ground and maintained their pursuit of the other two. Rafia was more than happy to complete their work for them, using her Talent-infused long daggers to finish the beasts with two precise stabs into the back of their necks.

The two Ghoules who had gotten a lead on their brethren continued their charge, focused solely on the two humans standing by the water, so filled with bloodlust and hunger that they didn't even realize that they had lost two of their pack.

Davin was the first to face one of the Ghoules, using his adversary's momentum against him by stepping to the side and letting the Ghoule slip by him, his blackened spear shooting past Davin's ribs by several inches. At the same time, with a hard shoulder, Davin knocked the beast off balance to fall onto his back in the sand. Before the beast could rise, Lycia was there, driving the tips of both swords through the Ghoule's throat.

The last Ghoule took no notice of his partner's rapid demise, caring only about the human who stood before him who appeared to be entirely unconcerned by his rush as he slowly twirled a double-bladed spear from hand to hand. The Ghoule should have considered a more cautious advance, but the lack of fear on the part of the human didn't register with the beast, a lethal mistake.

The Ghoule had decided on a very basic strategy, and he meant to stick with it. Either stab the human in the chest with his spear or, failing that, simply crash into him and use his greater weight and strength to crush the human into the beach.

Sensing that there was little subtlety to the Ghoule's attack, Bryen waited until the very last second when the Ghoule was committed to his rush and wouldn't be able to adjust his strategy in time. Not wanting to meet the charge of the massive Ghoule head-on, understanding that there was only one likely fatal result if he remained standing where he was, Bryen dodged nimbly to the right, sliding across the sand beneath the Ghoule's thrust and kicking out with his left leg as he did so, catching the back of the Ghoule's left leg with his own.

His legs tangled together, the beast slammed face first onto the beach, stunned, not understanding what had just happened. Before comprehension could dawn, Bryen was already up and standing above the beast. He slammed his blazing spear into the creature's spine and gave the blade a sharp twist for good measure. The Ghoule howled in agony, though the sound was muffled by the mouthfuls of sand stuffed into his maw, the beast twitching a few times before his last breath left him.

Just then, Aislinn ran up, gleaming sword at the ready. As Bryen pulled free the Spear of the Magii, she realized that he had everything well in hand.

"I was coming to help you."

To Bryen, she sounded a little put out that he hadn't waited to finish the beast until she had arrived.

"I know, but we don't have much time. More Ghoules are coming this way through the wood, and I need you to do something for me."

"What would that be?" Her raised eyebrow brought a grin to Bryen's stern visage.

"Humor at a time like this." He motioned toward the craft waiting for them at the edge of the water. "Take us out onto the lake."

They trotted over to the skiff. Davin was there by his side in just a few seconds. Aislinn climbed aboard, careful to stay clear of the gentle waves, then offered her hand to Lycia and Rafia as they pulled themselves over the unusually high side of the craft. Davin and Bryen then gave the skiff a final shove, pulling themselves up and over the side at the same time, taking care to keep their boots well above the steaming water beneath them.

"A gift, my Lady of the Southern Marches," said Bryen, stretching out his hand to encompass the entire vessel.

"You're too kind," she replied, moving to the mast, tightening and loosening several different ropes as she went until she had the sail exactly as she wanted. Then she returned the way she had come, Davin and Rafia scrambling out of the way as Aislinn reached for the single rudder set in the vessel's stern, which was positioned on a large block so that she could see above the protective sides and steer the vessel.

"They're coming!" warned Lycia, who had remained at the aft of the skiff, swords drawn, ready for the next round of their combat.

The remainder of the Ghoule pack stationed on the beach and charged with working the forge emerged from the small forest. At first, the beasts could only stare, taking in the carnage on the sand. Their shock burning away thanks to their anger, the Ghoules lifted their smoldering black eyes, taking in the skiff just off the beach and moving out onto the lake. With a roar, the Ghoules charged through the sand, their sights set on the five humans.

Aislinn ignored everything going on around her, barely hearing the Ghoules' shout or Lycia yelling at her that they needed to go faster.

Instead, she remained calm and under control, working the tiller, concentrating on the one task that could get them to safety. She shouted in triumph when she found what she was looking for, the sail filling, catching the wind that began to propel the vessel across the lake at a fast clip.

"Excellent timing," murmured Bryen, who stood next to her, though he remained facing back toward the beach, his gaze never leaving the Ghoules. He didn't think that the beasts would give up easily, not after losing one of their vessels and four of their comrades.

"I do what I can," replied Aislinn, who had a steady hand on the tiller, keeping the wind in the sail as she began to take a curling path toward the Cauldron, the volcanic island still no more than a dark haze off in the distance.

"Thank the stars that you can sail," noted Davin.

"My father taught me," Aislinn replied. "He used to take me out onto the Silent Sea when I was younger. He made sure that I knew how to handle any kind of vessel that was smaller than a cargo ship."

"I'm glad to hear it," Davin replied. "Because Bryen is useless when it comes to sailing. If you hadn't arrived with Lycia and Rafia when you did, we'd probably be the ones on the spit in the Ghoules' forge."

"So we've finally found something at which my Protector doesn't excel," Aislinn said with some amusement, tacking slightly to the northeast in search of better wind, struggling to do so, the roiling surface complicating her efforts.

"Indeed we have," said Davin. "It's about time too."

"Your Protector?" asked Bryen with a raised eyebrow.

"Yes, my Protector."

"I thought you didn't like using that term."

Aislinn gave Bryen a dazzling smile, catching the rare spark of humor behind his often emotionless, cold eyes. She remembered how she had reacted when Bryen had first been thrust upon her by her father.

She had been furious. She had hated her father for encumbering her in such a way, for not trusting in her ability to take care of herself.

Because she could do nothing once her father's decision had been made, she had transferred her anger to Bryen. At least at the beginning. The circumstances between her and her Protector had changed over time in ways that only broadened her smile.

"It's grown on me."

"Is THERE anything you can do that would give us more speed?" asked Bryen.

"Not unless you can make the wind blow stronger and directly toward the island," Aislinn growled in aggravation. Thinking about it, Bryen probably could, but attempting it for the first time while sailing across an acidic lake didn't sound like the best idea.

It hadn't taken long for the Ghoules on the beach to get another skiff into the water, raising a sail faster than any of the Caledonians thought was possible. Since then, Aislinn had spent just as much time trying to stay ahead of the pursuing beasts as getting the craft to the Cauldron.

The wind was irritatingly fickle on the Boiling Lake. Strong gusts shooting across the water lasted for several minutes, helping them to keep their lead, and then just as swiftly disappearing, leaving them dead in the churning water. The next few minutes would pass agonizingly slowly as the Ghoules gained on them before Aislinn found another burst of wind that would allow them to stay clear of the beasts at least for a little while longer.

"The Ghoules are almost upon us," warned Davin.

"I'm well aware of that," Aislinn said with more venom than she intended.

She didn't need to look behind them to know that the Ghoules had cut their lead to almost nothing. The beasts' increasingly loud hisses and barks coming from just a dozen yards off the stern told her everything that she needed to know.

"Is there anything that we can do to help?" asked Bryen, sensing her annoyance.

Aislinn shook her head in frustration. "No, the Ghoules know this lake better than I do. They know the winds and they know which of these boiling pots to avoid, and they're using that knowledge against us." She looked to the port side. The Ghoules had found another gust and were right next to them now, only a few yards separating the two crafts. She knew what was going to happen next.

"That may be," said Bryen. "But you've gotten us this far. I have no doubt that you can get us to the Cauldron."

Aislinn shook her head in aggravation, though at herself, not Bryen. She needed to stop feeling sorry for herself and make sure their craft stayed on course. She had every intention of repaying her Protector's faith in her. "I'll keep looking for the wind."

"And in the meantime?"

"Prepare to be boarded!" she shouted.

Bryen, Lycia, and Davin all turned as one to the port side. Within seconds the skiff carrying the Ghoules crunched against their stolen vessel, cracks appearing in the sides of both ships. Two Ghoules stood on the elevated railing, claws digging into the wood to hold them in place, waiting exactly for that moment of impact. Bending at the knees, the Ghoules jumped through the air, landing heavily though dexterously on the deck of the scow.

The instant that the beasts' clawed feet hit the wood, Aislinn found a gust of wind that filled the sails, tacking to the east to run with it, speed rather than direction more important to her now. She knew that they couldn't afford to have any more

Ghoules boarding their skiff, so she spent just as much time trying to milk as much out of the wind as she could, managing the tiller with a deft touch, attempting to prevent the other Ghoules who had perched themselves along the rail of the craft just off their port side from jumping across and joining the two beasts who had already bridged the divide.

A bit of bad luck struck only a few seconds later. To maintain her speed, Aislinn had no choice other than to turn to the west once again. That brought her skiff right up against the Ghoules' vessel, the hulls of the crafts scraping together, several pieces of thin metal flaking away from the keels of both crafts.

With nowhere else to go, and few other options available to her, Aislinn began to use her skiff as a weapon, repeatedly slamming her craft against the starboard side of the Ghoules' vessel so that the beasts had something else to worry about, such as keeping their own scow afloat, rather than trying to send more beasts over into her own craft.

Although Aislinn's efforts proved effective, the beasts perched on the railing unable to leap the gap, instead needing to concentrate on maintaining their own balance in order to avoid falling into the lake, there was still the not-so-small matter of the two Ghoules who had already made it across, the beasts howling in triumph as their clawed feet dug into the deck, allowing them to advance unhindered toward Aislinn as she guided the skiff through the water. That sense of victory dissipated quickly.

Davin and Lycia leapt at the beasts, desperate to keep them from the helm. The brother and sister wove a web of steel to their front, Davin with his spear, Lycia with her twin blades. Their quick action, reminiscent of their time together in the Pit, forced the beasts back toward the bow of the vessel.

Bryen was impressed with the fluidity of the twins' defense. They didn't need to say anything. Davin and Lycia knew exactly what the other was going to do before he or she did it.

Because of that unique and valuable understanding between them, Bryen was certain that his friends would eliminate the Ghoules as soon as there was a good opportunity to do so. And with Rafia standing next to Aislinn, the Magus able to offer their skipper some additional protection as she steered the skiff, he could do what he believed needed to be done.

"Protect Aislinn," Bryen said to Rafia.

"What?" Rafia asked incredulously. "Where do you think you're going?"

"Don't worry. I'll be back soon."

Ignoring Rafia's protests, Bryen stepped up onto the railing and crouched down, grasping the polished wood with both hands, the skiff bucking like a wild bronco and threatening to throw him off into the churning water. He realized that if he missed the mark, he would die, painfully. Still, he believed that the risk was worth it.

They had to escape the Ghoules, and he believed that he could help with that. Just as much, however, they needed to get off the lake as fast as they could. Even with the metal shielding on the bottom of the hull, when he looked over the railing, the sides of the skiffs that were racing through the water were smoking, the acid slowly but surely burning through the barrier and into the hull, which had been damaged in several places because of the frequent collisions.

When he felt the skiff leap almost ten feet out of the water, rising up and over a large wave right at the edge of where two boiling pots met, he pushed off the wood railing with all his might. For just a second, as he soared through the air between the two vessels, he feared that he had misjudged. That he was simply jumping toward a horrible fate.

Thankfully, just as Bryen hoped more than expected, the Ghoules' skiff turned toward him, the beasts unwilling to allow their prey to escape. That maneuver permitted him to land on the deck near the stern of the vessel rather than in the caustic waves. When his boots hit the wood, he stumbled as the skiff fell into a trough. He rolled with the motion and was instantly on his feet, the Spear of the Magii in his hands, staring across at two very large Ghoules who stood between him and his primary objective.

He ignored the six other Ghoules on the craft for now. They wouldn't be a problem until he got past the two Ghoules blocking his way, the tight quarters on board the skiff working against the beasts. And though he wouldn't have minded killing every last one of the beasts, he hadn't risked boarding the vessel for that. He had something else in mind for bringing the Ghoules' hunt to an end.

Before either of the shocked Ghoules thought to attack, Bryen killed the one closest to him, slashing across the beast's throat with a compact stroke of his Spear that was really no more than a flick of his wrists. He then turned to face the dying beast's companion. The Ghoule, enraged at how easily Bryen had killed his comrade, lumbered toward him across the deck.

Bryen's combat with the charging Ghoule served another unexpected though useful purpose. It distracted the other Ghoules on board the vessel, the beasts momentarily less concerned now with joining the two Ghoules who had leapt onto the stolen skiff and more interested in getting at the human who had the temerity to board their vessel. They howled in rage, having to wait their turn, the Ghoule's broad back preventing any of the other beasts from joining in the fun.

For several seconds, Bryen warded off a series of lunges, the Ghoule trying to drive his spear through his flesh and end the fight before it really even began. No such luck for the Ghoule, however.

Bryen bided his time, knowing from experience that the beast would make a mistake, and when the Ghoule did he could take his chance. He didn't have long to wait.

The Ghoule overextended on a thrust that permitted Bryen

to spin to the side and cut across the beast's ribs with his blade. The Ghoule stumbled, the slash both long and deep. That gave Bryen the real opportunity that he had been looking for, and he rushed forward to make the most of it.

Pushing past the wounded Ghoule, who slumped against the side of the vessel, trying and failing to keep his guts from spilling out of the wound, a stream of black blood leaking out onto the deck along with the beast's intestines, Bryen cut down with his spear. The Talent-infused steel smashed down into the tiller, cutting through the arm of the Ghoule steering the vessel, the beast stumbling back in shock and pain to fall back into his brethren, delaying them even further from getting into the fight. Thankful for that little bit of luck, Bryen slashed down with his Spear one more time just to make sure that he destroyed the tiller completely.

Nodding in satisfaction as he examined his handiwork, Bryen grinned. He was certain that the Ghoules wouldn't be able to steer the skiff anymore. One less thing to worry about. He didn't grin for very long, though, as he considered his next challenge. Getting off the drifting vessel that had already begun to turn away from the direction Aislinn was steering. Complicating that already difficult challenge, he also needed to avoid some very angry Ghoules.

Bryen danced back as one of the beasts forced his way past the others, lunging for him with his steel. He pivoted to the side just in time, the Ghoule slamming his spear into the wood instead of Bryen's flesh, the sharp tip catching fast.

As the Ghoule pulled back on the spear, trying to free it, his massive shoulders bunching at the effort, Bryen glimpsed Aislinn swerving the skiff in toward him. He decided to take another possibly fatal risk, because this might be his only chance.

Bryen pushed in on the indentation halfway down the haft of the Spear of the Magii, breaking the weapon into its two component swords. He then sheathed the blades in a smooth motion in the scabbards across his back.

Taking two quick steps, he jumped onto the Ghoule spear that was still stuck in the side of the skiff with his right foot and then with his left launched himself off the astounded Ghoule's head. For several seconds, Bryen soared through the air, sensing the Ghoule reaching for him from behind, knowing that it would be a near thing and hoping that the beast's daggerlike fingers didn't dig into his back.

Much to his relief, Davin caught him, grasping his forearm as his right foot hit the railing. He fought desperately for his balance, his friend pulling him over the side before he fell back into the lake. Bryen nodded his thanks, pleased not only to be back aboard the right vessel, but also to see that the twins had killed the two Ghoules, pushing their bodies up against the bow.

"Bryen, don't you ever do that again!" ordered Aislinn, her anger plain as she gripped the tiller strongly and turned the skiff to the north on a course that would lead directly to the Cauldron, the wind currently in their favor and pushing them through the waves at a steady pace.

"I was just trying to make sure that we could get away," Bryen tried to explain. "Otherwise we'd be fighting these Ghoules all the way to the Cauldron. With Davin and Lycia keeping the two who boarded us busy, I thought I would take a chance at ending their pursuit entirely."

"It was more of a risk than you needed to take," cut in Rafia, who could see that Aislinn had a lot more to say to Bryen, but deciding that it would have to wait. The Lady of the Southern Marches needed to concentrate on navigating.

Despite her irritation at Bryen's decision to place himself in such a risky situation, the Magus watched with some satisfaction as the Ghoules' skiff veered away, the vessel beginning to take on water as one side dipped down, only inches off the water. Then another stroke of bad luck hit the Ghoules, the skiff slamming down into a trough. With no functioning rudder, the vessel stayed there, a large wave crashing down onto the beasts, the Ghoules screeching in pain as the caustic water burned through their armored flesh.

Rafia looked away from the Ghoules, the beasts' skiff dead in the water and them soon to join it, focusing her sharp gaze on Bryen and seeking to impart a lesson with a voice that made him think of Sirius.

"Sometimes the best solution is the most direct one," the Magus lectured. "There's a time for finesse and there's a time for strength. Now's the time for strength."

"You're talking about more than just what happened now, aren't you?" asked Bryen.

"Yes, I am." Rafia's eyes gleamed, pleased that he was so quick to pick up on her meaning, a small smile creeping onto her stern visage. "Have I told you how much I like you?"

"Many times," Bryen replied, still trying to determine if the Magus was praising him or criticizing him for what he had just done. He pushed that thought out of his mind. It didn't really matter now. What was done was done.

"When we get to the Cauldron, when you get to the Temple of the Ghoules, the time for finesse will have come to an end, because in that moment the only thing that will matter is strength."

Bryen nodded. "You have nothing to fear in that regard."

"Good," said Rafia. "I didn't think I did." Rafia nodded toward the Cauldron, still a good distance away. "Do you think you can get us there faster? I feel like a duck just waiting to be gobbled up by a shark out here."

During their escape from the Ghoules she had seen several other skiffs out on the water, thankfully all of them moving away from them and not close enough to see what was really going on. None had demonstrated any interest in them as a result. But there was no guarantee that their luck would hold in that regard.

"Do you think it's safe to risk?"

"I think it's a risk worth taking," replied Rafia. "Let's see what you can do."

Bryen nodded. She was right. The sooner they got off the water, the better. Especially with these fickle winds slowing them down, forcing them to change direction regularly, increasing the chances that some of the other Ghoule skiffs might come their way.

"I spoke too soon!" shouted Rafia, who was almost blown back into the helm, Bryen sending a gale-force wind into the sail that propelled the skiff across the waves at a breakneck pace. "Forget what I said for the moment. More precision than power until we make landfall."

"Sorry," Bryen said, although he didn't sound very conciliatory to the Magus. He decreased the amount of energy he was applying, the mast creaking loudly and threatening to snap off at the base, the cloth beginning to tear free. Aislinn and the twins gave him dirty looks once they regained their seats. "I just got a little ahead of myself."

"You did that on purpose, didn't you?" accused Rafia. "Just to make a point."

"I'm hurt that you would think that."

Bryen's contrite expression of innocence made the Magus smile and then laugh. In that moment, she couldn't help but think of his parents, two of her former students who had displayed much the same temperament and the willingness to push boundaries whenever it suited them.

"You know, I really do like you, Protector. Even when I don't. Now try to get us to the Cauldron without sinking us."

21

BEHIND THE FALL

"Any ideas on how to reach the top?" asked Davin.

"Several," Bryen replied, "although most of them are not very appealing."

When they beached the skiff, they had pulled it up the rocky shore, hiding it as best as they could among the large boulders that had fallen from the soaring precipice above them. The Caledonians then walked along the narrow beach that circled the dormant volcano, staying close to the cliffs to avoid the corrosive water and to use the many sea stacks that jutted out from the shore as cover, not wanting to be seen by the occasional Ghoule skiff that sailed between the Cauldron and the mainland.

They had thought initially to scale the mile-high heights. It wasn't long before they admitted reluctantly that without the right equipment it would be impossible to climb the sheer face. Now they were looking for some way that would allow them to reach the top that wouldn't bring them face to face with Ghoules.

Although there were only a few tracks of clawed feet in the sand, the marks were fresh, which meant every second they remained on the beach increased their chances of being discovered. That sobering reality pushed them to keep moving and find a solution to their latest challenge quickly.

Despite the dilemma they faced, if nothing else, their luck seemed to be holding. None of the Ghoules who might have been on the beach or on the rim of the Cauldron had glimpsed their fight with the Ghoules on the water. The use of the Talent also apparently did not capture the attention of any Elders who might be in the vicinity. At least they hoped that had been the case.

"Your uncle didn't share with you how to reach the top?"

"He did," Bryen said.

"When were you going to tell us?" asked Davin, motioning with his hand for everyone to get behind a sea stack that had been battered by the wind and the water, the lone, worn-down sentinel standing several hundred feet tall. They remained there, hidden in the rocky mount's shadow, until a lone skiff sailed away from the Cauldron and out on the lake, slowly sliding from view as it headed for the far shore.

"I didn't want to get your hopes up. He was here more than a thousand years ago. How he made it to the top may not be an option any longer." Bryen shrugged his shoulders to suggest that he was doing the best that he could with the information that he had. "Just a little farther down the shore and then we'll know if how he did it will also work for us. If not, we'll have to figure something else out."

"What are you looking for?" asked Aislinn, who walked on Bryen's other side. It was hard to miss how her Protector spent more time gazing out upon the inland sea than at the cliffs that towered above them.

"The Ghoules coming this way on their skiffs."

They had yet to see anything that would offer them any hope of having an easy way to reach the summit of the Cauldron. No trail cut through the igneous rock. No caves in the base to hint at a hidden passageway. The only unique feature along the shore that they had seen from the lake but had only heard so far as they continued to circle the island to the east along the beach was the first of the dozen waterfalls that fell off the rim of the Cauldron a mile above them and fed the Boiling Lake.

"Why?"

"I want to see where they go. It's the best way to confirm the viability of the path my uncle suggested."

Bryen and the others continued to move carefully along the shore until they finally reached a point that allowed them to look up at a waterfall that was at least a mile wide, staying well away to avoid the splash, the noise created by the tons of water slamming into the lake every second so great that they could barely hear themselves think, the ground shaking because of the power of the constant flow.

Finding a niche large enough for all of them to hide among the boulders that littered the coast, they pulled a few more rocks around them to create a better hideaway. Then they settled down to wait, all of them assigned a different direction to watch. Bryen and Aislinn focused on the waterfall itself, in particular where it appeared to meet the cliff on the near side.

It didn't take long for Bryen to gain the chance to test the knowledge imparted to him by Viktor Keldragan. After less than an hour had passed, a lone skiff glided through the waves toward the Cauldron, a pack of Ghoules visible above the high walls of the vessel.

The beast who was steering the craft made directly for the waterfall. Right before the craft sailed beneath the torrential cascade of water, the skiff turned to the port side and disappeared into a small gap in the cliff face that wasn't visible from where Bryen and his friends were hiding.

"So this is how your uncle made it to the top," said Aislinn, impressed by how the Ghoules had slipped through the hidden opening. They would never have been able to identify the gap if they hadn't seen the Ghoules use it themselves.

"It is," Bryen replied. "He said he went through a passageway that led up behind a waterfall. It seems that we'll be able to take the same approach so long as there aren't any Ghoules in the way."

~

"Everyone ready?" asked Davin.

The gladiator hated waiting, so the last few hours in their hidden alcove watching the sun sink below the horizon had been an exquisitely painful form of torture for him. Even though he was impatient, Davin, just like the others, had no desire to tempt fate and brave the path that Bryen believed was behind the waterfall in the light of day. The dark of night would help to mask their movements and increase their chances of evading any lurking Ghoules. He had managed to control his impulse to get moving by tracking the skiffs of Ghoules that sailed in and out of the hidden harbor, wanting to get a sense of what might be waiting for them.

"Wait a moment," whispered Rafia.

Another skiff of Ghoules had just appeared, coming around the bend of the Cauldron from the other side and gliding across the lake, heading straight for the waterfall. Davin bent his knees and lifted up onto his toes, thinking that they might have to eliminate the beasts. But the Ghoules kept going, guiding the skiff through the barely visible gap in the stone, not even bothering to look at the beach.

"There are no Elders with them," said Bryen.

"Then let's give the beasts some time," suggested Rafia. "We'll follow them. I just don't want to be too close. I doubt any other Ghoules will be coming after them until morning. Sailing the lake at night would be too dangerous even for them."

Davin dropped back down, both glad and disappointed that he didn't have to fight the beasts who had just arrived. Glad because he had no real desire to take on an entire Ghoule pack if it could be avoided. Disappointed because it meant settling back in the alcove they had created for another almost interminable wait.

More than an hour passed before Bryen finally rose, appearing to be no more than a shadow among the rocks, Davin chomping at the bit to get going.

"We should be able to head up now," he explained. "There are no crafts coming this way, and the Ghoules who just landed are about halfway up the escarpment."

The rest of his party emerged from their hiding place, working out any kinks before following Bryen along the cliffs toward the slit in the stone that was right next to the waterfall.

Having used the Talent to scout around them to confirm that they were alone, Bryen walked confidently across the beach, then stepped through the gap in the rock, a small trail wide enough for them to walk single file running along the base of the cliffs and around a small harbor in which three skiffs were moored. Walking carefully so as not to slip into the steaming water, Bryen made his way around the curling coastline, the others staying right behind him.

He didn't stop until he came to where the very edge of the waterfall rained down into the lake. Right where Viktor said it would be. A stone ledge just above them created a large space that kept them safe from the acidic water falling from the rim of the dormant volcano.

Using the Talent to craft a small ball of energy, Bryen flung the light ten feet in front of him, the shining orb staying in place. The light revealed the beginnings of a tunnel that was broad enough and tall enough for several Ghoules to walk through shoulder to shoulder.

Placing his faith in what his uncle had told him, Bryen

walked into the shaft of carved stone, the sphere of light preceding him.

～

"Careful," said Lycia. "We're not in a rush."

She had reached out to catch Davin's arm as he stumbled on a large rock that protruded from the path.

"I'm getting tired of dodging Ghoules," her brother grumbled. "I'd rather just fight them now. It's easier than hiding."

"We won't have to fight them if you take your time and stay quiet," urged Lycia.

They had spent the past few hours sneaking through the tunnels that wound their way through the base of the Cauldron all the way to the top. Several times, they stepped off the path out of necessity to hide in recesses to avoid the handful of Ghoules who were moving up or down the main trail. Rafia used the Talent to blend them into the darkness once she was certain that there were no Elders about.

Having finally reached the summit, they emerged out of a cut on the rim of the Cauldron, a full moon lighting their way. They didn't feel the need to hurry, knowing that there were no Ghoules coming behind them. Besides, they wanted to give Aislinn the time that she needed to use the Talent to ensure that there were no Ghoules near them on the crest. It only took her a few seconds to confirm that the closest beasts were farther north by the city.

"We can go now?" asked Rafia, now just as impatient as Davin to be on her way.

"We can," Aislinn affirmed.

Yet none of them moved out of the cut immediately. The brightness of the moon gave them a clear view of what stretched out before them, and they needed a few minutes to take it all in.

22

———

DEFENDING AGAINST THE BREAK

"We are ready," said an Elder to the leader of the Ghoule Legions, having reached the top of the stone pillar that stood in the center of the Winter Pass, the same outcropping from which the day before the Magii rained down death and destruction on the Ghoules. "We are hungry."

"For flesh and blood?"

"Always," the Elder hissed, "and for revenge."

"Good," said Nibli, the Ghoule Overlord's general staring out across what would be the battlefield for the third straight day. "We will gain that and more today."

Nibli had come south during the night bringing with him the last of the Ghoule Legions to cross into Caledonia. His Ghoules had done well since they had advanced from the Weir, pushing the humans back to where they were now, the tip of the dagger-shaped Winter Pass just a little more than a league beyond them.

His Ghoules had made good progress. Even so, despite their success, they had not yet achieved the breakthrough demanded by their Master that would give them a clear path to the Kingdom.

That didn't mean the battles of the last few days hadn't proven useful to their cause. Nibli's Legions had slowly cut away companies of soldiers from the Caledonian Army and destroyed several large sections of the mobile walls that faced him now, an obstruction that had proven to be more of a problem than he imagined that it would be. A clever creation, he had to admit, but it wouldn't hold his Ghoules back for much longer.

Nibli thought that he could bring the humans close to collapse if the right amount of pressure was applied in the right place. His Ghoules' constant attacks had worn them down, weakened them. Reduced their numbers to the point where they would have no chance of holding back the more than four thousand Ghoules who had accompanied him down the Winter Pass. Confident in that knowledge, he had decided to implement a new tactic, one that he was certain would allow him to achieve his primary objective of crushing the humans and gaining favor in the eyes of the Ghoule Overlord.

"You know what to do, Issen," said Nibli.

The Elder nodded, then began climbing down the tall stack of rocks, his sharp claws making the drop down a quick and easy endeavor. When Nibli saw him reach the ground and sprint off toward the Ghoules massing just a few hundred yards in front of the wall, an evil grin split his maw. Nibli turned back toward the human fortification and called on the Curse, the Dark Magic spinning around the top of his twisted staff in thin black threads, accelerating and expanding as he allowed more of the power to fill him.

After he had called forth the tremendous burst of power that he believed would be necessary, Nibli pointed the head of his staff toward the makeshift barricade directly to his front. A stream of sable energy shot from his staff, sizzling through the air, blasting apart one section of the wall, sending the soldiers standing atop the parapet flying through the air along with thousands upon thousands of needle-sharp slivers of wood that shredded the humans caught within the radius of the explosion.

The Magii lining the wall had been taken by surprise, unable to defend against his attack, crafting imperfect, incomplete shields from the Talent that they never got in place in time or were not strong enough to maintain against his onslaught.

That only made sense.

He was the chosen of the Ghoule Overlord, after all. He controlled more of the Curse than any of the hated Magii could possibly imagine. They were fools to think that they could actually challenge him, and those who just did had lost their lives because of their stupidity.

Before the pulp and dirt had settled, fractured wood still crashing to the ground, the Ghoule Legions massed beneath the stone pillar surged forward, howling as one, the noise echoing off the sides of the gorge, the beasts driven forward by the sharp commands of the eager Elders who ran behind them and even more so by their rapacious hunger.

Nibli's grin broadened as he thrust his staff into the sky and added his voice to the cries of his Ghoules, pleased as more streaks of Dark Magic shot toward the Caledonian wall. Most of the attacks did little damage, the Magii stationed there ready now and capable of defending against his Elders' attacks. As had just been demonstrated, however, they were not capable of defending against him, not unless they banded together, and they couldn't do that now that they were fighting for their lives against his Elders.

He had decided to ignore the wings of the Caledonian Army for this attack, choosing instead to concentrate this latest assault on the very center of the now shattered defensive line. He was tired of attempting to use deception to achieve their goals. It was time to play to the Ghoules' strength, and the greatest of those was brute force.

If his Ghoules penetrated the wall here, they could flank the humans on both the east and west and then crush them against the sides of the Winter Pass. Once that was done, his Legions could flood the Breakwater Plateau and the lands beyond with barely any opposition.

With that objective fixed firmly in mind, Nibli meant to help his Ghoules do that now that his Elders, almost all of whom were concentrated behind the attacking force, had drawn the attention of every Magii on the wall. In just seconds, dozens of combats between the Curse and the Talent erupted in a space that was only a few hundred yards wide.

With the Magii fully occupied, and seeing that the Caledonians were frantically trying to close the gap that he had created in the barrier by shifting the mobile walls on both sides of the hole, though struggling to do so because of the fractured timber and steel that was in the way, Nibli directed several more streams of the Curse toward sections of the wooden barrier next to the one he had already destroyed, the Magii not in a position to oppose him.

He laughed as he did so, relishing the devastation that he caused, the screams of fear and pain from the soldiers as they were caught in the blasts, killed either by the Curse or the splintering wood and collapsing walls, energizing him. He felt a thrill run through him that could only be compared to his first bite of human flesh.

And then his Ghoules were there, sprinting toward the gap, just yards away from the massive pile of detritus. Nibli stopped his own attack then, nodding to himself in pleasure. His few minutes of effort had proven fruitful, leaving the center of the wall a shattered and smoking mess just as his beasts began to climb over the wreckage.

As he watched the battle escalate in intensity, he realized

that this was going to be a harder fight than he had anticipated. Even though he had smashed their main defense and created a gap several dozen yards wide, still his prey fought, not fleeing as he thought that they would.

Instead, the humans gave ground grudgingly. It was a doomed effort, Nibli believed. The Caledonians would never be able to recover from the shock and power of his assault, his Ghoules too many for them to hold back and too ferocious.

The next few seconds confirmed his beliefs, his Ghoules surging over or through the wreckage of the wall and then slamming into the cavalry massed behind the broken structure with an unbridled brutality. That had been the key part of his strategy. Breaking through the mobile barrier was the first step. The second, getting in among the mounted soldiers before they could charge, was just as, if not more, important.

And now, after weeks of fighting, his Ghoules had done it. They were through.

Thanks to him. Thanks to the power gifted to him by the Ghoule Overlord.

Nibli sent a few more streams of the Curse arcing over the wall to fall among the soldiers yet to engage with his steadily advancing Ghoules, then turned to climb down from the rocky stack and rejoin the battle.

The end was near.

The humans might disagree with him, but there was no doubt in his mind. The Caledonian Army would fall today, and with his Ghoules so close to the tip of the Winter Pass, there would be nothing to stop his Legions from overrunning the Kingdom.

∼

"SOLDIERS OF CALEDONIA!" roared Kevan. "We ride for our Kingdom! We ride for our General!"

Kevan nudged his horse slightly to the right with his knees, the superbly trained animal responding immediately to his command. Noorsin rode right next to him along with several other Magii. Spreading out to both sides of them were six cavalry companies the Duke of the Southern Marches had pulled from the right flank as soon as he recognized the danger posed by the Ghoule attack at the center of their line.

He led those companies back around the Caledonian host on a wide arc, the mounted soldiers now lined up opposite the swarming mass of Ghoules. The beasts were just seconds away from breaking through the hard-pressed cavalry that had been stationed behind the breach in the wall and were now fighting for their lives, the Ghoules applying their greater strength and agility against the Caledonians who had been pressed together like so many fish in a barrel and couldn't bring the power and strength of their war horses to bear against their attackers.

"For the General!" roared the hundreds of soldiers in reply.

As one, the Caledonians, spears lowered, urged their horses to a gallop, the animals' hooves churning through the mud.

Kevan and his reserve arrived just in time, slamming into the Ghoules just as the first few beasts maneuvered through the hard-pressed soldiers and looked down toward the southern end of the Winter Pass with little to stop them. Adding the weight of their horses and the force of their charge to the admirable efforts of the already engaged soldiers, they succeeded, at least for a few heartbeats, in slowing the Ghoules' advance.

Yet despite that initial shock, the beasts continued to pour through the large gap in the shattered wall, adding their might and ferocity to that of their brethren.

The small advantage that Kevan had gained through his timely attack disappeared much faster than he would have preferred. He and his soldiers now faced the same problem as the soldiers positioned right behind the breach, having no choice but to remain engaged with the Ghoules who had climbed through the debris with little opportunity to maneuver. The fighting was so close and so intense that Kevan felt as if there was nothing else in the world but blood and sweat, screams and curses, steel and claw.

Because of the intensity of the melee, Noorsin and the other Magii with her were unable to assist the soldiers, having to shift their attention to the Elders who were now coming through the gap in the wall and firing shards of the Curse into the milling soldiers and Ghoules, not caring what they struck, seeking only to eliminate the mass of bodies so that the Legions still waiting on the other side of the breach could push through and then past the Caledonian Army.

"Any other ideas?" asked Noorsin, who crafted a shield from the Talent to protect her right side, the hardened energy stopping a Ghoule from driving his spear between her ribs, the steel scraping harmlessly across the barrier.

Before the beast could lunge at her again, she sent a streak of energy back the other way, the Talent blasting through the beast's chest and then into the back of the Ghoule behind it, both Ghoules crumpling to the ground and instantly lost in the surging sea of motion the desperate fight had become. Noorsin nodded in satisfaction. Two for the price of one. A good bargain in her opinion.

"Me? No," grimaced Kevan as he slashed with his sword, slicing across a Ghoule's arm and taking several of the beast's clawed fingers with the cut. The Ghoule reared back in shock and pain, that instant of hesitation giving the soldier squaring off against the now wounded Ghoule the opportunity to thrust his spear right into the beast's groin, the Ghoule collapsing into the mud and quickly disappearing among the steel-shod hooves of the war horses that moved up and down the battlefield according to the tempo of the fight like the surf on the coast of the Southern Marches. "But I believe the Blademaster has something in mind."

Just a few seconds later, the mass of soldiers and Ghoules who were linked together by blood and death shuddered and lurched.

The Blademaster had arrived.

With Duke Winborne trying to contain the flood of Ghoules by using his hastily brought together companies as a cork, Jurgen Klines now tried to put that cork back in the bottle. The Blademaster brought forward on the left flank six companies of soldiers formed into testudos, shields to the front, spears poking forward over the rim of the steel scuta, swords right behind, while on the right flank Benin led six more companies in the same formation.

Rather than employing the shock of a cavalry charge, the Blademaster instead wanted to apply a constant pressure that would force the Ghoules back the way they had come, hoping that his and Benin's testudos and the soldiers with Duke Winborne weren't overwhelmed during the process.

Because that was a distinct possibility. At least initially, however, the additional pressure worked, bottling up the Ghoules and preventing them from broadening the breach. Yet how long that pressure would remain in place was anyone's guess.

Through cleverness and an almost suicidal courage, the Caledonians achieved a stalemate. Still, that wasn't good enough. They had not discovered how to force the beasts back onto the other side of the fractured wall.

Through it all, Kevan stayed as close to Noorsin as he could, the Duchess of Murcia resembling one of the Warrior Queens of old, controlling her horse with her legs as she shot bolts of energy from her hands and formed shields made of the Talent to protect the soldiers around her, doing all that she could to eliminate the Elders who had joined the larger fight, and barring that, keeping the servants of the Ghoule Overlord from harming her troops.

Sensing the sizzle in the air, Noorsin ducked and urged her horse a few steps to the right, which took longer than she would have liked because of the press of soldiers and Ghoules around her. A stream of the Curse barely missed her, instead ripping into several fighters behind her, turning their bodies to ash.

This latest assault pulled her eyes to the top of the broken wall. An Elder stood there, a massive cloud of Dark Magic spinning above his head.

Even from a distance of a hundred yards Noorsin could feel the power within the beast, and she guessed that in the absence of the Ghoule Overlord this was the Elder leading the Ghoule Legions. This had to be the one who had caused the breach. Not wanting to give the beast another chance to attack, Noorsin released a dozen bolts of the Talent, the blazing energy streaking over the heads of the Ghoules and soldiers to her front and slamming against the shield that the Elder crafted just an instant before her attack struck.

The way the Elder nonchalantly used the Curse to build his barrier, as if he was doing nothing more than humoring her by deigning to engage in a combat, filled Noorsin with a burning rage that she hadn't experienced since her fight against Tetric in the Broken Citadel. Determined to show this beast that she was more than he could handle, Noorsin sent a steady flow of daggers constructed of light toward the Elder.

The beast kept his shield in place, preventing her attack from striking home, not even bothering to counter, clearly enjoying the Magus' mounting frustrations.

And so it continued for almost a minute, Noorsin's inability to puncture the Elder's shield becoming more infuriating with each passing second, made even more so when it appeared as if the Elder was laughing at her. The beast was amused. He was simply playing with her!

That was something she couldn't abide, her rage becoming white hot. Yet instead of allowing her anger to guide her decisions, she sought to calm herself. It was because she was able to maintain her composure that she remembered something that Sirius had taught her when she was an apprentice.

Now it was her turn to laugh. Throwing the daggers of light once again, this time she added a special twist compliments of her former mentor, directing the energy so that it curved around the beast's shield.

Noorsin shouted in triumph when she heard the shriek of surprise and agony from atop the shattered logs carry over the din of the battle, the overconfident Elder knocked backward off the broken wall. She had done it! She didn't think that she had killed the beast, but at least she had removed him from this clash.

Yet despite her success, this one good result wouldn't be enough to win the battle. Even with Kevan's quick thinking and the efforts of the Blademaster and his soldiers, the Ghoules with the help of their Elders were still forcing her troops back, inch by inch, expanding the breach.

The Caledonians were pushing from three sides to close the gap, and they still couldn't get the traction that they needed. She likened it to trying to turn off a broken spigot. No matter how you turned it, the water just kept flowing.

And then her worst fears were confirmed. They were about to be caught in a vise. She saw another Ghoule Legion begin to climb over the broken wall while several packs caught in the milling mass of fighters broke free, fighting their way past the soldiers brought forward by Kevan. There was nothing to stop those beasts from sweeping around behind the Caledonians or making for the Breakwater Plateau.

Yet even with that terrible knowledge, Noorsin smiled grimly. They were in dire straits, true; however, all was not lost.

She could feel it now, the ground beginning to shake, the puddles of water dotting the ground rippling, as thousands of hooves pounded against the ground.

~

"FOR THE SOUTHERN MARCHES!" roared Tarin Tentillin, his sword pointed toward the hundreds of Ghoules who had fought their way through several companies of Caledonian cavalry.

Jerad and Dani rode with the Captain, having helped him bring almost the entire Battersea Guard around on a broad arc from the left flank, doing much as Duke Winborne had done on the right, but with a great many more soldiers at their backs. If Tarin was to have any chance at closing the gate the Ghoules had opened, he wanted to use the biggest hammer he could find.

The men and women from the Southern Marches were now at a full charge, two long lines of cavalry, the first separated from the second by ten yards. Their war horses strained at their reins, taking in the energy, excitement, and even touch of desperation that radiated from their riders.

Right behind Tarin came what he hoped would prove to be the deciding factor in the battle. He had pulled Cerillia and several other Magii from the walls to go with him, knowing that the flanks had no meaning if they couldn't stop the Ghoules from breaking through their center.

"Target the space five yards in front of us when we hit the Ghoules if you can!" shouted Tarin so that he could be heard over the thunderous hammering of the horses' hooves into the muddy ground. "Then in five-yard increments from there."

Tarin wanted to ride through the beasts and not get caught

in the mix as had happened to Duke Winborne. If they could avoid that fate, then they had a chance at pushing back the Ghoules. And if they failed, the fate of the Caledonian Army and the entire Kingdom was sealed. Cerillia understood that.

"Consider it done," she replied, her gaze never leaving the Ghoules who were preparing to meet their charge.

Cerillia and the handful of Magii did exactly as Tarin requested, sending spears formed from the Talent looping over the first few ranks of Ghoules to blast into the beasts crushed together behind them. The Magus appreciated the value of the tactic as she and her peers maintained their onslaught, their efforts creating gaps among the Ghoules challenging them. Those spaces allowed the Battersea Guard to charge right through and then over the beasts, the risk of getting caught up with the Ghoules minimized.

In turn, Tarin was impressed by the precision demonstrated by Cerillia and the other Magii as the Talent crashed down time after time exactly where he needed it to strike. Relishing the opportunity, he and the Battersea Guard pushed forward with an uncompromising will toward Duke Winborne.

Tarin had almost achieved his objective, the Battersea Guard containing the beasts and then adding to the pressure that the Blademaster was applying to both flanks, when disaster struck. The Captain had just wounded a Ghoule with a precise slash of his sword across the beast's hip, the Ghoule attempting to evade his charge by jumping over his horse but mistiming his leap. That beast no longer an immediate threat, Tarin nudged his war horse toward a Ghoule who had just succeeded in pulling one of his soldiers from her saddle.

He was about to slash down at the beast's neck before the Ghoule could bring his spear up when he realized too late that he had made a fatal mistake. That wounded Ghoule wasn't as badly wounded as he thought, coming at him from the side, spear about to slam into his ribs, neither Jerad nor Dani close enough to help him.

Tarin was in the process of resigning himself to the inevitable when a bolt of light sped right behind him, the heat singeing the hair on the back of his neck. The sizzling energy struck the charging Ghoule right in the face, the beast collapsing to the ground in agony as the Talent melted the flesh from his skull with a white-hot intensity.

Taking a deep breath to calm his nerves, Tarin looked behind him. Cerillia rode up, a hawkish grin on her face, obviously pleased by her success.

He nodded his thanks and then turned his horse back to the battle, wanting the men and women of the Southern Marches to continue to push against the beasts. As he urged his mount back to a gallop, sword slashing down to the left and right whenever a still-standing Ghoule reached for him, he made a note to himself that if he survived this fight he needed to thank her for saving his life.

As Tarin and his troops continued to force their way deeper into the mass of combatants, the savage battle in front of the breach continued for several more minutes. Neither side was willing to budge, too much blood and flesh had already been paid by monster and men.

Although the Ghoules enjoyed a great deal of initial success when Nibli gave them a path through the barricade, they faltered in one key regard. They failed to stop the charge of the Battersea Guard, and that proved to be the difference in this particular fight.

The soldiers from the Southern Marches refused to be denied. Once they connected with Duke Winborne and Duchess Stelekel, they proved to be unstoppable, the momentum shifting drastically as they forced the Ghoules back toward and then through the breach in the barricade. When the last Ghoule finally climbed back the way he had come, the soldiers of Caledonia reclaimed the broken sections in the wall and thousands of voices shouted in triumph for their hard-earned, bloody victory.

Yet though the Caledonians had recaptured what had been theirs at a terrible price, the Ghoules didn't flee after their defeat. They only went so far as the stone pillar that rose a few hundred yards from the Caledonian defensive line.

The Ghoules were not broken, only beaten, and they could take some solace for their efforts.

They remained less than a league from the entrance to the Winter Pass. More than one thousand feet of the movable walls had been destroyed, negating the utility of the construction as a barrier. And the Caledonian Army, though successful in its efforts today, was bruised, battered, and greatly weakened. Ten companies' worth of soldiers were killed or wounded in the fight to expel the Ghoules from their lines.

As a result, though Noorsin was relieved as she surveyed the damage to the wall and the carnage surrounding it, she also was worried. They had stopped the Ghoules for now. But she understood that even with their bloody success, there had been too many desperate moments in the fight that had almost cost them everything.

They were losing the war, their end assured if they weren't able to change the dynamics of the conflict. And from where she was standing she didn't really see any way to make that happen.

A cold fear slowly burrowed into her heart as she offered what help and comfort she could to the wounded. She realized that the next Ghoule attack would break them, and then the beasts would run free in her homeland.

23

THE DEAD CITY

"I t's called Mertvey Gorod," explained Bryen, relaying the information his uncle had shared with him. "In the Ghoule language, it translates to The Dead City. Once it was a thriving metropolis. No more, however. Why, I don't know. Viktor didn't know. He hypothesized that the city and its people began to die with the coming of the Curse. The only part of the city that's still used is the Temple of the Ghoules, which you can see rising in the city center just over there. That's where the Ghoule Overlord and the Curse reside, of that I'm certain, and based on the tremendous amount of Dark Magic that I can sense being used there, I'm assuming that the Curse is taking a new host even as we speak."

When Bryen and his friends exited the passageway and moved away from the rim of the Cauldron, they realized that the island was aptly named. Rolling grassland and a few small forests gradually led down through the massive crater toward the huge, abandoned city that rivaled Tintagel in size.

The small party reached the outskirts of Mertvey Gorod by midday, traveling through the fractures in the land to stay out of sight. The cracked and brittle landscape offered a glimpse of where the lava had flowed the last time the now dormant volcano had erupted.

They never came into contact with the few Ghoule packs wandering atop the crater. Aislinn tracked the beasts with the Talent and led Bryen and the others away from danger a half dozen times before they finally stopped in a copse on a small hill that allowed them to look down onto the empty homes and buildings that marked the boundary of the center of Ghoule power.

Mertvey Gorod was a city of squares and rectangles. Most of the buildings were one-story communal structures that stretched over entire blocks. Wide streets and canals that had dried up long ago, steep, arched bridges spanning the gaps, separated those long blocks. Off in the distance toward the city center they could just make out a huge square that wrapped itself around the Temple of the Ghoules, the truncated pyramid rising several hundred feet into the air and dominating the metropolis.

"So this place isn't inhabited?" asked Lycia, peeking out from between the trees. Nothing moved in the streets other than dirt and plants sticking up through the cracks in the stone caught by the wind. Nothing emerged from the entrances to the buildings. Nothing made a noise. In Lycia's opinion, definitely a Dead City. "It looks that way, I admit. But are you certain? You know how I don't like surprises."

"From what Viktor told me, most of it isn't," said Bryen. "Except for around the Temple."

"But you can't tell for sure?"

"No," Bryen replied reluctantly. "What we see is what we get. There might be some surprises waiting for us, but we can't tell. Aislinn, Rafia, and I have all tried to search Mertvey Gorod with the Talent. We can only sense a persistent layer of the Curse covering the city. That film of evil is so strong that it's preventing us from identifying Ghoules or anything else that might be lurking within. All I can suggest is be smart and be careful."

"Fair enough," said Davin. "Your uncle has been right on point so far. We should get going. If the best time to go after the Ghoule Overlord is before he's been made flesh again, then let's get to it. I'd prefer to do it when the sun is still in the sky."

The gladiator pushed himself up from where he was sitting against a tree, about to walk down the hill toward the city. They had been hiding within the grove for more than an hour, and his natural impatience was getting the better of him again. He was tired of waiting. He wanted to bring this adventure to a close. He could sense that they were reaching the conclusion of their quest, and the anticipation of how it all might end was almost driving him to distraction.

"Just a moment," Bryen said in a sharp whisper. "There's more to entering Mertvey Gorod than just walking into the city."

"What do you mean?" asked Rafia.

"It's something that Viktor explained to me. He said that when he came here, when he made his way across the Cauldron, he knew that he hadn't been spotted. Even with all the Ghoules on the plateau, he was sure of it. However, as soon as he crossed the boundary into Mertvey Gorod, he was hunted. The monsters that defend this city knew that he was here the second he stepped across the metropolis' border. Even his use of the Talent to mask his progress didn't work. The Ghoule Overlord's creatures came right for him."

"Did he have any ideas as to why that happened?" asked Aislinn. "Some kind of triggers or traps crafted from the Curse?"

"That's it exactly. Viktor believed that the Curse, because it lies heavily on the city, alerts the guardians to anyone or anything crossing the boundary who is not touched by the Curse."

"What was it that came for him?" asked Lycia, not wanting to ask the question but feeling the need to do so, even as she dreaded the answer.

"Slayers."

Bryen's response elicited several groans and a few frustrated looks. They were more than familiar with the Ghoule Overlord's assassins, having battled the beasts in the Dark Forest and then all the way across the Breakwater Plateau. None of them had enjoyed the experience.

"I hate Slayers," grumbled Davin. "Nasty bastards and never easy to kill."

"This from the Slayer of Slayers," said Lycia, giving her brother a companionable nudge to his shoulder, trying to ease the tension building within all of them. "You really are tired of this journey if you don't want to use this opportunity to burnish your reputation."

They all smiled at that, even Davin.

"I don't know if it's still a legitimate concern that there are Slayers still tied to the city, but I think we need to assume that what happened with Viktor will happen with us."

"How many Slayers?" asked Davin.

"Viktor said that when he was escaping the city, Seventh Stone and black diamond in hand, six were after him. Maybe more."

"That's a lot of Slayers," grumbled Lycia. No one was willing to dispute that belief. Three of the beasts almost had been more than the Blood Company could handle even with the help of several Magii.

"Then we need to be ready for that," agreed Aislinn.

"I think there's one approach that we can take that will reduce the risk of at least some of us running into Slayers," said Rafia.

"What would that be?" asked Davin.

"We split up."

"I'm sorry I asked the question," he grumbled again, already having a sense of where the Magus was going with her proposal. "How does splitting up help us get to the Temple?"

"It doesn't help us do anything," confirmed Rafia. "It does help Bryen get there, and right now the only thing that matters is that Bryen make it to the top of the Temple of the Ghoules so that he can challenge the Ghoule Overlord before he becomes whole again. If he doesn't destroy the Curse, then everything we've accomplished so far will mean nothing."

"No pressure," Lycia murmured to Bryen.

"There never is," Bryen replied with a smile, appreciating Lycia's latest attempt to lighten the mood.

"What would you suggest?" asked Lycia, turning serious again.

She hated Slayers just as much as everyone else. But the Magus was right. They had come here to help Bryen complete his mission. Anything they needed to do that would assist with that, no matter how dangerous, was worth considering.

"That we split into two groups. Aislinn with Bryen. You two with me."

"Why?" asked Aislinn.

"Because what Bryen said about Viktor coming here gave me an idea. Thanks to the Seventh Stone, Bryen holds the Curse within himself. So, if what I know of Dark Magic is correct, he should be able to pass through the city without incident. He won't trigger a response from the Slayers."

"That makes sense," said Aislinn, "but that wouldn't apply to me. How could I go with Bryen and still not bring the Slayers down on us?"

"The Protector's collar."

Out of habit, Bryen's hand immediately went to the cool silver circling his neck. When the magic still ran through the collar, it had bound him to Aislinn. They had broken that connection before making for the Sanctuary, so he didn't understand how the collar would help them now. He was about to voice his concern when Rafia continued with her explanation.

"Yes, the bond provided by the Protector's collar that bound Bryen to Aislinn is no more. The connection between the two, though, remains. Aislinn has not been touched by the Curse, yet she is still connected to Bryen. So I believe that if she remains close to Bryen as they make their way through the city, and by that I mean right next to him, then she will enjoy the same protection that Bryen will. He should be able to reach the Temple of the Ghoules without being waylaid by any creatures looking for intruders. The Curse within him will get him there safely, and Aislinn can use the Talent to assist him when he gets there."

"Which means ..." began Lycia.

"Which means that we're bait," complained Davin, his voice taking on a tired tone of resignation. "Again? Seriously?"

"Yes," confirmed Rafia with barely a touch of sympathy. She knew the risk involved with what she was proposing. Even so, she saw no other way to get Bryen where he needed to be without running into some monsters that they would all like to avoid. "Because if I'm wrong and Bryen and Aislinn are pursued nonetheless, our being bait will still give Bryen a better chance of doing what he needs to do. It will divide the attention of any Slayers guarding this place."

Davin bounced on his toes for a moment then shook his head in frustration. "All right. All right. I know you're right, I just don't like it."

"Neither do I," said Lycia. "Are you certain that it's not better that we all stay together? If Bryen and Aislinn run into any trouble, our blades and your use of the Talent can help them."

"No, better that we split up," said Rafia in a voice that brooked no additional discussion. "As I said, even if I'm wrong, it will mean that we're dividing the Slayers' attention, which also works to our advantage."

Bryen nodded, not liking although still agreeing with Rafia's conclusions. "Are we good?" he asked, giving everyone some time to think about what they were going to do. He stared at Aislinn, waiting for a nod from her before moving on to Rafia and then Davin and Lycia until he had caught the eyes of everyone with him. He then nodded himself. They were in agreement. "One last piece of advice. Stay out of the buildings and the shadows. If there are Slayers here, that's where they'll be waiting for us."

"Always giving us good news," Davin said sarcastically. Then he reached out and clasped arms with Bryen, his eyes hardening.

The Crimson Giant of the Colosseum had returned, Davin viewing their entering the center of Ghoule power as the same as striding out onto the white sand of the Pit. He then walked to the very edge of the trees, staring down at the abandoned buildings, seeking any hint of what might be waiting for them yet identifying nothing out of the ordinary. Nothing that suggested why he was nervous, other than the fact that perhaps he was anxious because there was nothing to be seen.

Davin shook his head in frustration again. He needed to clear his mind. Better to get moving. Better to get doing. This waiting was driving him crazy.

"I'll see you on the other side," said Lycia, clasping Aislinn's arm. She then smiled, which was a rare occurrence for the Crimson Devil.

"I'll see you on the other side," Aislinn replied. "I'll keep him safe or die trying."

"I know you will," replied Lycia, finally releasing her arm. "Sister."

Before they stepped from the trees and down into a cut in

the ground that would allow them to reach the edge of the city without being seen, Rafia pulled Bryen aside for a moment.

"He's here?" she asked Bryen. "You're certain?"

"He's here," Bryen confirmed. "Whether in the flesh or still just in the spirit, I can't say. But the Ghoule Overlord is on top of the Temple. I'm sure of it. If we're going to challenge the Curse, now is the time."

They both looked in that direction, and even from where they were at the border of Mertvey Gorod, they could see the swirl of darkness leaking out from the top of the truncated pyramid.

"We agreed that this risk needed to be taken," said Rafia. "That we needed to come here. That you were the only one with any hope of killing the Ghoule Overlord and destroying the Curse."

"We did," Bryen said. He could understand the Magus' concern.

The Ghoule Overlord could use the Seventh Stone to destroy the Weir that Bryen had created with the help of the Ten Magii. If the Ghoule Overlord became flesh again and killed Bryen here, he could take the Seventh Stone and then unleash his Legions upon Caledonia. Even worse from Rafia's perspective was the possibility that the Curse could make Bryen its own, forcing him to become its new vessel, imposing an even worse fate on the Kingdom. With the Curse manipulating the Seventh Stone through Bryen, the Dark Magic of the Lost Land would reign supreme.

Bryen needed to be ready for what would be required if he believed that the Ghoule Overlord or the Curse itself was about to defeat him. If Bryen wasn't able to kill the physical manifestation of the Curse in the Ghoule Overlord or eradicate the Curse itself, then he needed to be ready to destroy himself and the Seventh Stone before his nemesis took control of the artifact, just as the Ten Magii did after they were contaminated while building the Weir a thousand years before.

"We also agreed that if this goes down the wrong road," began Rafia, choosing her words carefully, "that if it appears that our efforts are for naught, that the Ghoule Overlord is too strong ..."

"Then you need to destroy me with the Talent if I can't do it myself. Yes, I understand. That hasn't changed."

Rafia nodded. She still found it remarkable, how the Protector could speak of his own death with barely any emotion. She could only assume it was because of the years that he had spent on the white sand.

"We can't allow the Ghoule Overlord to gain control of the Seventh Stone, yet we need its power to have any chance at all of defeating him," she continued. "Ironic, don't you think? We are taking a huge risk."

"Quite the dilemma," Bryen agreed with just the hint of a raised eyebrow. "But there's little reward without the risk."

"Are you still prepared for the likely result?"

Although Rafia and Bryen had discussed how to battle the Ghoule Overlord, neither was certain that their strategy would work, neither liking their odds from the very beginning though having no choice but to try because none of the other approaches they had considered were any more appealing.

"Everyone dies," Bryen replied quietly. "Not everyone dies with honor."

"One of Declan's sayings?" asked Rafia.

Bryen nodded. "One of his favorites."

Rafia smiled warmly. "You're a brave young man." The Magus then gave him a brief kiss on the cheek. Aislinn, Davin, and Lycia watched the private conversation, none of them understanding what they might be talking about, although they could guess. "You know ... I would like to see Declan again.

There's something about that man that makes me feel truly alive."

"I think he'd like to see you again as well."

"You think so?" Rafia asked, Bryen's comment broadening her smile.

She had wanted to believe what Declan had told her, but in her experience, men rarely revealed their true emotions. Of course, her perspective might be jaded because of her long history with Sirius. So perhaps what Declan said really was what he meant.

"You couldn't tell?" Bryen asked with a soft laugh. "His normal scowl when he looks at you becomes only a tiny grimace. I figured in time he might even smile."

"He did smile," Rafia replied, "I think."

"Then you're well on your way."

"High praise," the Magus said with a laugh. "I'd like to take on that challenge. I have several ideas already on how I could make him smile quite frequently."

With Rafia's last comment, Bryen nodded and began walking toward Aislinn. There was only so much that he wanted to know, and he feared that Rafia was about to share something with him that he'd never be able to get out of his head. "All right, we're done. We're moving down a path that I don't want to be on."

"What?" Rafia asked playfully. "I don't understand what you mean."

Bryen chose not to engage further, clasping arms with Lycia and Davin, then motioning for Aislinn to lead the way.

It was time to take their chances in Mertvey Gorod, the Dead City of the Ghoules.

24

CENTER OF ATTENTION

"Just so you're aware, I'm not enjoying this even for a second," Davin breathed softly, spear held loosely between his hands, head pivoting from one side to the other and then back again, seeking the hint of any movement. Any sign that would give them warning of an imminent attack.

"I thought you were all about the adventure?" challenged Lycia, though she spoke just as quietly, each hand gripping the hilt of a sword, the gladiator staring into the shadows cloaking the buildings for several seconds before continuing on, knowing that despite her efforts, if a Slayer was hiding in the dark, there was little chance that she would be able to identify it before the monster came at her. They moved down the center of the broad boulevard, wanting to ensure that they had plenty of room to maneuver just in case Viktor Keldragan was correct about what might be lurking within the city proper.

"I was," Davin admitted. "Until we entered the Lost Land and had to deal not only with Ghoules but also boiling mud and acidic water and Echidnae. It was after the Echidnae that I lost my appetite for this journey."

He and his sister were both on edge. The anticipation was

building just as it did when they waited to see what kind of beast was about to be unleashed upon them in the Pit.

The two gladiators and the Magus wound their way slowly around the outer neighborhoods of the Dead City, having chosen the outer ring because of its width. There wasn't a sound to be heard. Not even a gust of wind, the once steady breeze dying. Still, there was a faint sulfurous stench to enjoy, the malodorous odor clinging to the back of their throats.

They wanted to cough to see if they could get rid of the nasty taste. They didn't. They feared what might happen if they made such a loud noise in this silent metropolis.

"Anything?" asked Lycia.

"I can't identify any specific threat. The taint of evil wrapped around this city won't allow for it. It all gets mixed together." Rafia had been searching with the Talent as soon as they had stepped into the confines of Mertvey Gorod. All she succeeded in doing so far was frustrate herself.

"Look out!" shouted Lycia, who lunged forward and shoved Davin out of the way with her shoulder, at the same time bringing her swords up and crossing them above her head in the nick of time, blocking the razor-sharp claws of the towering Slayer that had leapt out from a darkened doorway without making a sound.

Then Lycia was spinning and rolling away, seeking to evade the unstoppable strength of the monster pressing down on her blades, the Slayer's claws coming uncomfortably close to her face. She knew after fighting these monsters that she couldn't allow the Slayer to keep her in one place for too long. Otherwise, she'd be nothing more than dead meat, the monster too fast, too strong, and too aggressive.

Back on her feet, Lycia jumped to the side, the Slayer's tail, covered by bony scales that were just as sharp as her blades, whipping out and missing her by no more than a whisker, the serrated appendage slamming into the street, destroying several of the large stone tiles with the power of that one strike. The onslaught continued for several seconds. Claw. Tail. Claw. Then tail again. And so it went, Lycia having no option other than to stay clear of the determined beast.

Lycia danced away from every strike and lunge, not allowing the Slayer to corner her against one of the abandoned buildings, understanding what would happen if she did. At the same time, she was careful to keep out of the shadows, fearful that another of the killers might be waiting for her there.

When Davin regained his feet, careful not to drop his spear when Lycia shoved him out of the path of the Slayer, his first thought was to help his sister. He realized in an instant that he couldn't, instead spinning around and using his spear to block a slash from another of the Ghoule Overlord's assassins, the beast bursting out of the darkened doorway of the building behind him faster than the black dragons emerging from their nests in the Trench.

From that point forward, Davin didn't bother to think. He moved based solely on his instincts, his spear seemingly having a life of its own as he spun the length of steel this way and that, parrying the Slayer's claws as they swept toward him from every possible angle with a speed that he could barely register. His time in the Pit and under Declan's strict tutelage served him well as he glided nimbly around the street, staying one step ahead of the increasingly agitated monster.

To help the gladiators in their combats, Rafia immediately infused their weapons with the Talent, knowing that it was the only way to ensure that they could cut through the Slayers' natural armor and inflict any significant damage upon the beasts. She could do no more than that unfortunately, as just seconds later she faced her own challenge.

Two more Slayers appeared at each end of the street. Rafia stared at the beasts shrewdly, the Slayers not yet having moved. She understood that the beasts could sense what she was. The power that she wielded. Because of that, they were cautious. Not charging toward her since they had lost the element of surprise.

She had to give the monsters credit. Smart and clever. The Slayers had set a nice trap and they were going to make the most of it, not feeling the need to rush since they had cornered their prey.

Yet they could curb their natural aggression for only so long, their craving for flesh and blood pushing them forward now. The Slayers communicated to one another with a series of barks and hisses that reminded Rafia of the Ghoule language. She assumed that the beasts had agreed on a plan, because the monsters both stalked toward her at the same time with measured steps, their clawed feet clicking on the stone tiles of the street.

A small smile broke the Magus' grim expression. The monsters might be smarter than she thought. Still, that wouldn't matter. Now wasn't the time to hold back. Just as she had told Bryen, now was the time for strength. Precision had little meaning in this situation, only power could help.

Turning sideways, she raised her arms, sending several bolts of energy streaking from her palms down the street in both directions. The monsters had expected the attack, dodging out the way with surprising ease, one of the Slayers even scurrying up a wall before flipping itself backward off the overhang to land not too far away from her.

Rafia cursed as she sent several more bolts of energy toward the Slayers, the beasts unconcerned by her use of the Talent, zigzagging toward her with relative ease, her frustration growing as the two monsters deftly evaded each attack. When the Slayers were no more than a dozen feet from the two gladiators who were still engaged in their combats, Rafia realized that she had no choice. Davin and Lycia didn't stand a chance if they were required to take on more than one Slayer at a time.

Right before the Slayers launched themselves into the melee, Rafia crafted barriers of energy right in front of the beasts. The two monsters slammed their massive claws against the shimmering energy in anger, denied at least for a time the kills they so desired, unable to advance any further down the street.

Rafia remained where she was, Davin fighting the Slayer to her right, Lycia battling the other one to her left. Until the gladiators won their duels, she could do nothing else but focus on keeping her shields in place so that these two hungry beasts couldn't interfere with the twins' combats.

Lycia continued to move with an elegant grace that was lost on the Slayer that pursued her with a vengeful singlemindedness, the monster refusing to let her break free as his claws and tail slashed toward her with a frightening rapidity. Its actions became even more frantic as the monster failed time after time to slice into her flesh, its mounting frustration beginning to take hold.

That gave Lycia the chance that she had been waiting for. Side-stepping the monster's lunge, she sliced right through its tail with one of her blazing swords just as the appendage whipped over the monster's shoulder toward her face.

The Slayer howled from a mixture of pain and rage, then abruptly the sound died in the monster's throat, Lycia's other gleaming sword sticking through its mouth and out the back of its head.

Tearing her sword free as the Slayer fell to the street, she turned, glad though not surprised that Davin was holding his own against the other Slayer. Nevertheless, the monster was enjoying some success against the Crimson Giant, having backed her brother up against the wall despite his efforts to prevent that very thing from happening.

Davin caught her eye right after he used the haft of his

spear to knock away a claw aimed for his throat. Then he nodded.

Davin twisted his grip on the steel and lunged with his spear, realizing that his attack would leave him frightfully open to a potentially devastating counterstrike. The Slayer realized it as well, pulling back its claw to take advantage of the opportunity.

Before the monster could lunge for Davin's heart, Lycia was there, driving both of her blades through the Slayer's lower back, then for good measure slicing off this monster's tail as well when she tore her glowing blades free.

Rafia watched the two combats out of the corner of her eye, keeping most of her attention focused on the barriers that stymied the Slayers wanting to join the fight. She had expected no less from the two accomplished gladiators, and now it was her chance to make an impression on these monsters.

Yet before she could do so, two more Slayers appeared out of the shadows, standing above them on the roofs on each side of the street.

The Magus growled in aggravation. She had been angry when the clash began, she was even more infuriated now. These monsters were too clever by half, these two beasts above her preparing to leap down onto the unsuspecting gladiators.

It was then that Rafia decided that she had to agree with Davin. They hadn't been in the city long, and already she was tired of being the bait. She lost what little patience she had left. It was time to shift the dynamic.

Releasing her hold on the shields that had kept her focused on the ends of the street, the two Slayers that had been pounding uselessly on the barriers stumbled when the obstacles disappeared. Rafia used those few precious seconds to raise her arms so that they were parallel to the ground. With a grin of pleasure that revealed her vengeful side, she whipped them toward the broken stone of the street, a series of lightning bolts sizzling down from a clear blue sky, each one targeting one of the Slayers.

Davin and Lycia ducked as Lycia's lightning bolts ripped apart both ends of the street, the power of Rafia's attack launching shattered stones and bricks hundreds of feet into the air, the ceilings giving way as the buildings on both sides fell in on themselves.

When the cloud of dust and pulverized stone finally cleared, Davin and Lycia pushed themselves up off the ground, unhurt. Rafia stood calmly with an expression of satisfaction exactly where she had been before, surveying the damage that she had caused.

"Remind me never to make you angry," said Davin.

He was impressed. The buildings were gone, now nothing more than huge piles of rubble, and where the Slayers had been trying to break through her shields, long gashes that had to be at least twenty feet wide and just as deep marred the street.

"Thorough," nodded Lycia. "Exceedingly thorough. I like that."

"I do my best," said Rafia with a smile that quickly faded. The piles of rubble on each side of her were beginning to move, cracked and broken bricks and mortar slowly shifting. "But apparently my best wasn't good enough."

"What do we do?" asked Davin as the clawed hand of one of the Slayers worked its way through the detritus.

"Run!" the Magus shouted.

25

BAD TIMING

"So far so good," said Aislinn.

"Yes, but for how much longer?" wondered Bryen, his eyes moving slowly from the left to the right and then back again. He even glanced behind them every few seconds, just wanting to be certain that they weren't about to be attacked.

"You're just full of optimism," joked Aislinn.

Her head also was on a swivel, her eyes never fixing on one place for more than a few seconds, just like Bryen, even as she said it.

"More like realism," he countered, giving the Lady of the Southern Marches a wink and a grin.

When they began working their way through the city, they had started along the edge, taking one of the streets that curled around the outside of the metropolis toward the east. After less than a half hour, having seen and heard nothing that would give them any cause for concern, the city quieter than an abandoned graveyard in the middle of a dark forest, and more importantly no hidden monsters sprinting out of the shadows with their claws reaching for them, they decided that there was no point in taking their time. Better to move swiftly as the wisps of black continued to dominate the summit of the Temple of the Ghoules.

They picked one of the main boulevards that ran straight to the square. Walking shoulder to shoulder right down the middle of the street, their eyes rarely left the unsettling darkness of the large entryways that led into the abandoned buildings. They made good time. Bryen and Aislinn were close to the center of Mertvey Gorod now, the truncated pyramid growing larger with each step they took.

Perhaps Rafia was right and the Curse within him offered some protection or at least the ability to blend into the Dark Magic infusing the city, the Curse covering his skin with a squalid muck similar to that of Mertvey Gorod. Of course, Rafia, Davin, and Lycia's mad dash through the metropolis probably didn't hurt their efforts either.

Just moments before they had heard several explosions on the far side of the city. They had assumed that was Rafia's handiwork, the Magus obviously not afraid to announce her presence in the heart of the Ghoule Overlord's stronghold.

Maintaining their steady pace, it wasn't much longer before they made it to the huge square surrounding the Temple of the Ghoules, the plaza twice as large as the one surrounding the Colosseum. For several minutes, Bryen and Aislinn stood there, waiting, watching, listening.

They scanned the square and the buildings fronting it. They examined the Temple that was several hundred yards distant, seeing more clearly the thick black mist at the very top swirling around the columns that buttressed the dome. They looked for anything that would suggest an imminent threat. They found nothing.

No movement. No noise. Just a chilling quiet and a frightening sense of unease.

Even with both of them using the Talent, they still found nothing to worry them. The overarching sense of corruption that oozed through the very bones of the city prevented them from locating the tell-tale signs of a Ghoule or a Slayer or any other beast touched with the Curse.

Shrugging their shoulders in unison since there was no good reason to continue to delay, Bryen and Aislinn stepped out onto the square and walked toward the Temple.

Still, nothing happened. No movement. No noise.

After having crossed most of the plaza, their confidence growing, the worn steps of the pyramid just a hundred yards away, their faces fell. A large shadow materialized out of what appeared to be a tunnel cut into the base of the Temple.

Aislinn and Bryen stopped and stared. Aislinn pulled the sword from the scabbard across her back. She then infused the blade with the Talent just as Bryen did the same to the twin blades of the Spear of the Magii.

It appeared that their luck had just run out.

"Rafia said that now was the time for strength," Bryen said, looking over at Aislinn and giving her a big grin.

"There's no reason to think otherwise," agreed Aislinn.

They nodded to each other, agreeing on the path that needed to be taken without having spoken a word. Then they walked toward the Slayer, the beast remaining where it had first appeared, guarding the steps leading to the top of the Temple.

When they were no more than a dozen yards away, Bryen and Aislinn broke into a silent sprint, charging the monster, blades blazing brightly as they prepared to strike.

The Slayer, shocked that its prey actually would think to attack it, took a small step back, never having been in this position before. Then it corrected itself, the monster raising a spiked forearm to block the glowing steel slicing toward its chest.

Rather than continue with her cutting motion, Aislinn stepped back and pivoted, swinging backwards with her sword, finding just as much success with the second slash of her Talent-infused blade as she did with her first.

Aislinn had used the Slayer's moment of uncertainty to her advantage, slashing across the Slayer's forearm, the beast hissing in pain as the blazing steel cut through its armored flesh and spikes. She then followed with a slice that cut through the monster's right knee to the bone.

Not wanting to give the Slayer the chance to recover, she continued her attack, wary of the long tail that hovered just above the monster's shoulder, undeterred by the fact that Bryen was no longer with her.

Right before Aislinn attacked the Slayer, Bryen spun back around, cutting through the air with the Spear of the Magii from right to left, shoulder to shin, just as a second Slayer, which had sprinted across the square toward them from the direction that they had come, tried to drive its claws into his back.

The Slayer's eyes widened in disbelief when it raised the stump of its right arm toward its eyes so that it could get a better look at the grave injury inflicted upon it.

Howling in agony, it glided backward, tail snapping over its shoulder, the monster trying to prevent another attack.

Bryen refused to allow the Slayer to disengage. Ducking beneath the sharp bones of the monster's tail, he cut across the beast's belly with a slash that left a long gash across its midsection, a thick black blood leaking out. Bryen then cut down from left to right, slicing off the tip of the Slayer's tail, which earned him a screech of anger and then a hiss of pain. He brought the blade right back up through the same space, the blazing steel slicing right across the Slayer's jugular to stifle the monster's scream.

It was only then that Bryen stepped back, now staring directly at the Slayer's blood-red eyes. He ignored the blood streaming down the monster's front from the horrid wound across its throat joining with the blood from the slash across its belly, the beast's innards already beginning to bulge out of its midsection. Bryen considered the need for one final blow, then decided against it, the hatred in the Slayer's eyes fading as its life drained out onto the stone of the square. The monster's knees buckled as the Ghoule Overlord's assassin crashed onto its back, its gore spreading around it.

Scanning the plaza quickly, satisfied that no more Slayers would be attacking them from the direction of the city, Bryen turned back toward Aislinn as the sounds of steel striking armored flesh rang out across the square. He wasn't worried about her. He knew that Aislinn was more than capable of handling a monster like this one. The sight that greeted him affirmed that belief.

The Slayer was a bloody mess. Its tail was gone. At least a dozen wounds crisscrossed the monster's body. Blood streamed down its chest. The Slayer could only stand on its left leg, its right useless and only connected to its body below the knee by a few loose strands of tendon and muscle.

The monster tried one last attack, perhaps thinking that it might get lucky, that its persecutor might be overconfident or make a mistake. That proved to be a foolish and unjustified hope.

Aislinn easily eluded the lunge and then drove her shining steel right between the Slayer's ribs. Rather than pull it free, she left it there, the Slayer's high-pitched scream intensifying, setting Bryen's teeth on edge. Aislinn used the Talent infused within her sword to burn through the wounded Slayer's body from the inside out.

It didn't take long for the job to be done, the Slayer's flesh and muscle charring, its bones becoming brittle, all of it flaking away. When Aislinn finally withdrew her sword, what was left of the Slayer fell to the stone and then burst apart into a cloud of ash.

"A little angry?" asked Bryen after witnessing how Aislinn had finished the assassin.

"Maybe just a little bit. I was just trying to be thorough."

"Very impressive."

"I've had good instructors," said Aislinn, her voice hard, just like her expression.

Bryen smiled at the compliment, then looked around the square one more time. It appeared that these would be the only two Slayers that they would face. For now.

Rafia, Davin, and Lycia must have drawn the larger share of attention. So he extended his arm toward the steps leading to the top of the Temple of the Ghoules, the Dark Magic continuing to swirl angrily above them.

"Shall we?"

Aislinn nodded and took the lead as they climbed up the steep, worn steps, their calf muscles beginning to burn as they worked their way to the top, needing to lean in toward the carved rock because of the steep angle, one hand always on the steps in front of them to help them keep their balance. When they were just a few feet from the crest, they stopped and ducked down, staying hidden beneath the last few steps.

They peeked over the ledge at the same time, taking in the four oversized Ghoules standing guard around a massive altar upon which lay a fifth Ghoule, this one even larger than the others. Held in place by strands of Dark Magic, the Ghoule's body arced off the stone in an irregular rhythm in response to the swirling mass of the Curse that spun above it. Strands of the Dark Magic broke free from the cloud of evil, whipping around the pillars before shooting down to strike the captive Ghoule, puncturing its flesh, the Curse slowly but inexorably flowing into the selected host.

Now was the time. Everything that Bryen had worked for since leaving Tintagel, everything that he and his friends had sacrificed was to get him to this point. Now was the time to justify the faith and belief that so many others had placed in him.

"Ready?" Bryen asked, staring into Aislinn's eyes, trying to give her a smile, though only managing a weak grin as his thoughts shifted to the task that he had to finish. If he failed, then it meant the end of Caledonia. Not to mention his own death and those of all the people he cared about.

Interpreting in just a flash everything that she saw in Bryen's eyes, she reached out and grasped his arm. "I love you."

"I know," he said a bit distractedly.

"I know!" she repeated in a loud whisper. "I'm telling you how I feel, revealing my heart to you, and that's all you have to say! I know!"

"I love you too," replied Bryen, turning back to her, surprised by her heated response. "I thought we already knew how we felt about each other even though we hadn't said the words yet."

"It's customary to say it, to acknowledge it at a time like this," Aislinn explained.

"Why must those words be said now? We'll have time later when this is all over."

"How do you know there will be a later? We're trying to kill the Ghoule Overlord and destroy the Curse, an evil that's existed for thousands of years. That's why I thought it was appropriate to share how I felt about you."

"I know there will be a later because you're at my side now, and so long as you're at my side there will always be a later," replied Bryen softly, smiling warmly, hoping that his confidence and belief came through in his voice.

Aislinn's lips scrunched up into a knowing grin, then she reached for his leather armor and pulled him close for a kiss.

"Let's kill this monster," Aislinn said as she pulled away, her eyes hardening.

26

***

REACHING THE TOP

"There! To the left!"

Davin and Rafia were right on Lycia's heels as they sprinted down the middle of the main boulevard toward the massive square that opened up before them. The shrieks echoing through the streets behind them gave them an extra burst of speed. They knew what those screams meant. The hunt had begun once again.

When they entered the square, Davin slowed his pace, letting Lycia and Rafia race ahead of him. It had gone quiet just a few minutes before. He trotted backward for a time, his eyes searching for any movement within the huge plaza or the buildings that formed its border. Just when he thought they might be in the clear a howl ripped through the usual silence of the Dead City.

He hadn't seen any more of the Slayers since he, Lycia, and Rafia had scrambled over the wreckage of one of the buildings that Rafia had destroyed. They had slid down into a dry canal and followed the channel until they came to the widest street they had seen yet. Climbing out of the canal, they had followed the boulevard to where they were now.

So far, it had been the easiest part of their time in Mertvey Gorod. But he wasn't a fool. The howls and shrieks were the giveaway. He had no doubt that the Slayers were coming for them.

Finally reaching the steps at the bottom of the pyramid, Davin looked up briefly. Rafia and Lycia were just ahead of him, twenty feet up. With nothing else to do, he started working his way up the narrow and worn stairs, having glimpsed the Dark Magic swirling menacingly above the crest.

How many sane people would be running toward the Curse rather than away from it? he wondered. Davin shook his head both in dismay and amusement. He was really getting tired of the Lost Land and this fight.

Rafia kept her head down as she crawled more than climbed up the steps, her hands reaching for the worn bricks in front of her as she struggled against the steep angle. She was more than halfway up when she caught the movement above her.

Bryen had just pushed himself over the edge and stepped onto the top of the monolith, Aislinn right beside him. Rafia wanted to be there for the Protector. She wanted to help him. And, even though she felt a twinge of disgust at the thought that trailed through her mind, she needed to be there just in case he made a mistake.

She was confident that Bryen would succeed. After having come to know him, having watched him and learned about him and from him, she believed that he was a force of nature in his own right, and that there was no one else better suited for completing the dreadful assignment that had fallen to him. Even so, she couldn't rely just on what she believed.

"Hoping doesn't make it real." She smiled at that, hearing one of Sirius' favorite sayings play through her mind in his deep, raspy voice. Her old friend was right. Hope for the best, plan for the worst, and be ready to do your worst if there was a need.

Putting her head down, she started up the steps again, pulling herself closer to the top. She was almost to the crest when a shout made her stop and turn.

"Rafia, they're here!"

The Magus wasn't surprised by what she saw. Davin and Lycia were just a few steps below her on the pyramid, backing slowly up the steps, one hand reaching behind them for the fragmenting rock so that they didn't fall, weapons in their free hands.

Three of the Slayers had survived her assault. The monsters, covered in a thin layer of dust and grime, stood at the base of the Temple, their blood-red eyes shining with a ravenous hunger that matched the hate that had blossomed there. For the first time, the monsters had failed to take their prey.

The Slayers didn't stay there for long, the monsters leaping thirty feet up the pyramid, their clawed feet digging large gashes into the crumbling stone as they propelled themselves up the steps at an almost unbelievable rate.

"To the top," ordered Rafia. "You two, help Bryen." She could see the black strands of the Curse and guess at what awaited the Protector and Aislinn when they appeared beneath the dome. "I will take care of these beasts."

The two gladiators looked at each other for just a second, hearing the sounds of a fight just beginning above them, steel meeting steel. With a nod to one another, Davin and Lycia obeyed the Magus, rushing up the steps.

As the three Slayers raced toward her, their howls sending an involuntary shudder through her, Rafia reached for as much of the Talent as she could, steeling herself for the combat to come. She was more than confident in her abilities, having proven her skills with the Talent and the blade time after time.

Yet she was willing to admit to herself that three Slayers might be a larger bite than she could chew. With that thought in mind, long strands of energy spilled from her palms, those threads drifting down the pyramid to both sides of her, connecting as they did so, forming webs of energy that shimmered in the bright sunlight.

The Magus nodded to herself, pleased with her construction. That would narrow the path the Slayers could take up the steps, the beasts already having to move more toward the center of the steps as they came into contact with a few of the strands, the Talent slicing through their armored flesh as if it wasn't even there, funneling the monsters toward her.

That done, Rafia pulled her long daggers from the sheaths on her thighs, infusing them with the natural power of the world.

Now she was ready, glowing blades in hand.

Let the Slayers come. Let them find out how difficult it would be to kill this Magus.

27

COMBAT ON THE ALTAR

Just seconds after Bryen and Aislinn appeared on the crest, the churning evil, the spirit of the Ghoule Overlord, the very embodiment of the Curse in the Lost Land, began to transform, taking shape, the rough figure of the Ghoule Overlord appearing before them, the shaped energy staring at them with a pair of haunting hollow eyes.

Much to Bryen's surprise, the billowy form of the Ghoule Overlord extended an arm and beckoned him forward, urging him on, as if he was expecting him.

Bryen's eyes narrowed, understanding why. He was taking a risk by coming here, putting not only himself but all of Caledonia at peril.

That couldn't be avoided. Not if he was to finish the task he began in the Sanctuary.

Bryen would do all that he could to ensure that his nemesis didn't gain what he so desperately wanted. That the Ghoule Overlord would come to regret his hubris. He had already taken the Curse's host. Now he would destroy the Curse itself.

Instead of stepping forward to engage in the combat that he had been hurtling toward since he killed the Ghoule Overlord,

Bryen instead chose to hold his ground, the four Ghoules stationed at the corners of the massive altar gliding away from their positions. The massive beasts formed a line in front of Bryen and Aislinn, spears held at the ready.

It seemed that there was one more obstacle that they needed to overcome. Perhaps the Curse wasn't as confident as it appeared, not wanting to challenge him until he had become flesh once more.

He and Aislinn stood there for a moment, staring at the beasts. These Ghoules were larger than any of the others they had faced. The spark of cunning visible in the back of their deep black eyes suggested that they had an intelligence that was lacking from the rest of their brethren. He could see it and he could sense it. The combats to come would not be easy.

"Are you ready?" Bryen asked, his tone neither hot nor cold, just devoid of any emotion, his focus needle-sharp. Once again, just as he had done hundreds of times in the Pit, he had closed out everything around him. The distractions, the fears and insecurities, the hopes and dreams. He had compressed his reality to just the single task he had yet to complete. He had become the Volkun.

Aislinn nodded. "It's no different than a combat on the white sand. Kill or be killed."

It was Bryen's turn to nod. "Kill or be killed," he agreed. Then he looked at Aislinn, giving her an uncharacteristic wink for a situation such as this. "Let's make sure we're the only ones doing the killing."

With that the Volkun and the Vedra charged toward the Ghoules. Aislinn slashed her shining sword through the air so fast that it appeared to be no more than a streak of light. Bryen spun his blazing Spear of the Magii in a pattern that resembled a sizzling figure eight.

After just a few minutes of pressing the Ghoules, Bryen and Aislinn twisting and turning around one another with an almost inhuman speed as they sought the smallest of openings that would allow them to eliminate one of the beasts to improve their odds, Bryen realized that he had been right. These beasts were more than the Ghoules they had fought to reach this point. Their reactions to his and Aislinn's assaults were lightning fast, and they fought with a focus and economy of motion that was truly impressive. He had rarely seen the like on the white sand or anywhere else.

Nevertheless, that wouldn't be enough to keep Bryen from his goal. He believed that he and Aislinn would find a way past these guardians. Although they had yet to remove one of the creatures from the fight, they had wounded several of the beasts. Nothing more than a few shallow scrapes across their flesh, but that would change. Their early success was enough to suggest that eventually the Ghoules would fall.

And even as the beasts worked together to defend against his and Aislinn's tenacious attack, Bryen could see in their eyes that they knew what the inevitable result would be. That the beasts were only playing for time.

Clearly, that realization didn't faze the Ghoules in the least. They understood their role and their likely fate if they failed. They had been bred for a singular purpose, and they would meet the demands of that purpose. In consequence, they maintained their position, keeping Bryen and Aislinn always to their front, always with the goal of preventing them from interfering with the crucial and abominable process taking place beneath the dome.

As the minutes passed and steel met steel, sparks flying at every touch, one Ghoule after another stepped back, hissing in pain as the Talent-infused blades cut through their armored flesh. Despite their increasingly serious wounds, the Ghoules rushed right back into the fight. The question became not if Bryen and Aislinn would defeat the Ghoules or when, but whether they would do so before the Ghoule Overlord became flesh again.

That was the key issue. Because the longer the Ghoules could hold them in place, the greater the chance that the Ghoule Overlord regained his full strength and power. If that occurred before Bryen could challenge the Curse itself, then he was fairly certain how the combat would conclude, and it wasn't a result that he cared to ponder.

Realizing that a different approach was needed if they were to have any hope of getting past these Ghoules before the Curse became whole once more, Bryen began to open himself to the power of the Seventh Stone, needing that unending reservoir to aid his efforts. Before he could do that, however, he felt the air shifting behind him.

He twisted his body to the side just as Davin thrust his spear through the space in which he had been standing. The glowing steel took the surprised Ghoule facing off against Bryen right through the hip.

The massive beast stumbled back and bellowed in pain. Pushing himself up off the stone, ignoring the savage wound and the thick black blood streaming down his thigh, the Ghoule howled in rage, then charged back into the fight, undeterred by the obvious limp that was slowing him down, the beast dragging his injured leg behind him, having eyes only for the human who had hurt him so badly.

Davin grinned devilishly, pleased to gain such a reaction from the beast. With a deft sidestep, he curled away from the Ghoule who lunged for him. The beast realized too late that he was in danger of losing his balance, in the same motion Davin sweeping the Ghoule's unsteady clawed feet out from under him and sending the wounded Ghoule crashing to the stone.

That one moment of wavering discipline was all that it took for the Ghoules' defensive line to falter, given a final nudge in that direction when Lycia joined the fight. What had once been a strong, coordinated defense quickly devolved into four individual combats with the Ghoule facing off against Davin struggling to stay in the fight.

The gladiators and the Lady of the Southern Marches glided across the stone, giving the Ghoules all that they could handle. Spears lunging and slicing, swords slashing and cutting. The movements so fast yet so precise that they appeared to be almost fluid, one form flowing right into the next, the choreography of the attack revealing an almost unheard-of level of dexterity and coordination.

It wasn't long before the momentum shifted. Each of the Ghoules now suffered from a variety of serious wounds. The Ghoule challenging Davin was the worst off as the beast struggled to remain on his clawed feet with both hips punctured and copious amounts of black blood staining the stone beneath him.

Even more critical, the positioning of the eight combatants had shifted. Bryen and his friends were now closest to the altar, the Ghoules nearer to the steps.

"This is your chance," said Aislinn through gritted teeth as she knocked away the long spear thrust at her thigh, responding with a backhanded slash that would have taken the beast's head off if it connected, instead slicing across the ducking Ghoule's shoulder and drawing a hiss of pain as it cut through the natural armor and then into the flesh.

"I can't leave you and the others," replied Bryen, who stood strong against his Ghoule, his feet gliding up and back as he danced with the beast, the Spear of the Magii cutting forward and back, left and right, with just the flick of his wrists.

"We can hold them," Aislinn said. "You need to go. Only you can do what needs to be done, and this might be your only chance to break away."

"But I ..."

"She's right," cut in Lycia, her twin blades having already

scored the Ghoule opposing her a half dozen times, the beast stepping back for a moment to examine the latest wound, a nasty gash that had taken off most of his right ear as well as a good slice of his cheek to the bone. "We can hold here."

"Go!" shouted Aislinn. "Don't waste what we're giving you."

Bryen fought the urge to stay and fight, wanting to help his friends. He realized, however, that wasn't his fate on this day. A different responsibility called to him.

Turning and leaving Aislinn and the twins to keep the Ghoules off him, he strode unopposed toward the altar and the beckoning, misty form of the Ghoule Overlord.

"You've made my task much easier," hissed the spirit of the Ghoule Overlord, the misty figure of the Master of the Curse staring down at him from above the altar, the threads of black still pulsing, filling the selected host with the Dark Magic of the Lost Land. "I thank you for that. Instead of having to hunt you, you've come to me."

"You've got it wrong," Bryen replied. "I'm here because I'm hunting you."

The hazy Ghoule Overlord laughed at that, the raspy cackle echoing off the top of the dome. "Are you? You believe you have the strength to challenge me? Then prove it. Kill me, Protector. Kill me if you can."

The spirit of the Ghoule Overlord blasted down toward him in the blink of an eye, the flowing strands of darkness wrapping him in the Curse. Bryen responded instinctively, shielding himself with the Talent, though not before thousands of pinpricks of pain erupted across his body at the slightest of touches by the undulating Dark Magic.

The Curse swirled around him, enclosing him in a black haze that built layer upon layer upon itself, blocking him off from the outside world. In just a few heartbeats there was nothing but darkness. No light. No sound. No movement. Only a pitch black. But there was pressure, the Curse pressing down upon him, trying to force him toward the stone even as it scratched against Bryen's shield, seeking a way through.

Understanding that he needed to do something to counter the intense force being applied, Bryen spun the Spear of the Magii above him. Slowly at first, that simple movement requiring all of his strength to combat the bonds of Dark Magic wrapped around him. Then faster and faster as he built up his momentum, trying to break free, the blazing blades cutting through the corrupted mist, burning away some of the Ghoule Overlord's very spirit with every touch.

The shadowy figure of the Curse shied away from Bryen's weapon, whipping around at an almost impossible speed, trying to evade the deadly steel. Bryen barely noticed the howls of torment that echoed in his ears as he redoubled his efforts, refusing to allow the Dark Magic to evade him, slicing away the evil of the Curse piece by piece from the billowing cloud, every strand cut free by the Talent fading away to nothing.

With a cry of rage and a burst of speed, the Curse of the Lost Land finally freed itself from the blazing streaks of light that ripped through its essence, at the same time releasing Bryen from its grip. The miasma of evil reformed above the host strapped to the altar with misty black ropes, hovering there for a moment before shifting back into the form of the Ghoule Overlord, the figure's hollow eyes staring down at Bryen with an unquenchable hatred.

"You think that you can defeat me with that Giant-crafted weapon?" roared the Ghoule Overlord.

After a few seconds passed, Bryen nodded as if he were actually considering the Ghoule Overlord's question. "I know I can. Why else would you run from me?"

"You do not have the power to defeat me, Protector, even

with the Spear of the Magii," hissed the Curse, barely able to contain the fury surging within it. "You're a fool to think otherwise."

"Maybe," Bryen replied. "But that doesn't mean I'm not going to keep trying."

Reaching for the Talent, Bryen twirled the Spear of the Magii in front of him so fast that it resembled a blazing circle. Before the Ghoule Overlord could dodge out of the way, Bryen released from the points of the blades the power that had been building up within him, the Spear of the Magii amplifying the energy that he manipulated, the two streams of pure light forming into one as it streaked toward the swirling cloud of corruption.

The Talent and the Curse met with a concussive boom that shook the very foundations of the pyramid, the bright white light from the Spear slamming into the spinning shield of darkness that formed in front of the spirit of the Ghoule Overlord right before the energy struck.

For several seconds the two powers contested with one another, evenly matched. But as Bryen pulled on more and more of the Talent, the streams of energy shooting from the Spear of the Magii blazing brilliantly, that balance shifted, and not in favor of the Curse.

The Talent pushed against the Curse's shield, forcing it back toward the hazy figure of the Ghoule Overlord. Soon Bryen couldn't tell the difference between the swirling black of the shield or that of the Curse itself.

He was almost there. Bryen knew it. He could feel it. So close to achieving his goal. He just needed a final push to break through the Ghoule Overlord's resistance.

Opening himself to the Seventh Stone, Bryen felt the unending power contained within the artifact flow through him. Energized, refreshed, Bryen added this new source to the Talent he was already employing, the two streams of energy shooting from the blades of the Spear of the Magii at an impossibly fast rate, glaringly bright as the Seventh Stone added its strength to his efforts.

The massive pulse of pure energy struck the Ghoule Overlord's shield with a resounding crack. The reverberation caused the pyramid to shake violently, the pillars holding the dome swaying from side to side, small pieces of carved rock breaking free and crashing down onto the summit. And then a blinding flash and thunderous blast erupted from just above the altar, forcing Bryen to pivot away.

When the flash finally receded, Bryen turned back. For just a moment, he smiled. The swirling cloud of darkness was gone.

He had done it!

He had destroyed the spirit of the Ghoule Overlord. He had destroyed the Dark Magic of the Lost Land.

The Curse was no more.

His jubilation lasted only seconds. With a sinking feeling, Bryen realized that he had been too late. Despite doing everything that he could, Bryen had failed.

Because at that very moment, the Ghoule lying on the altar pushed himself up, the twisted black staff with the glowing black diamond set within its top remade and held tightly in his claws.

The Curse survived.

The Ghoule Overlord had been reborn.

"I WAS RIGHT."

"Right about what, Davin?" grunted Aislinn distractedly, her eyes locked on the Ghoule standing across from her.

"I was right to call you the Vedra. You're almost as fast as Bryen."

"Could we focus on the task at hand?" grumbled Lycia, the

Crimson Devil twisting to the side as she avoided the tip of a Ghoule's spear, then swinging first with the sword in her right hand, then with the one in her left, catching the Ghoule who attacked her with one blade across his shin, the beast stumbling back in agony as the steel cut to the bone, and then cutting off a clawed digit from the other Ghoule who thought to sneak up on her from the same side while she was engaged with the now limping beast.

"I am focusing on the task at hand," countered Davin, some heat in his voice as he blocked a lunge from another of the Ghoule Overlord's guards with the haft of his spear and in the same motion knocked the beast's weapon down into the stone. With the Ghoule bent at the waist, Davin brought his shoulder up under the beast's chin, sending the Ghoule flying back through the air, the winded beast landing heavily on his back.

"My mistake," said Lycia.

She wanted to drive her swords into the slightly dazed beast before he regained his feet. She couldn't. The Ghoule she had just wounded had come right back at her in a hobbling lurch, her swords crossing above her head as the beast swung down with his steel hoping to split her skull. She twisted away and slashed through the space she had been occupying with the blade in her right hand, just missing the beast, cutting through his leather armor instead, the Ghoule already having moved away.

As soon as Bryen turned to face the Ghoule Overlord, Aislinn, Davin, and Lycia had formed their own defensive line, doing all that they could to hold off the four Ghoules who were now desperate to come to the aid of their Master. Although the beasts were skilled in the use of their spears, they failed to do anything more than inflict a few minor wounds on the two gladiators and Magus, all of whom had enjoyed the benefit of training with the Volkun and were applying what they had learned in the Pit quite effectively, much to the frustration of the Ghoules.

"From your other side!" shouted Aislinn.

Lycia turned quickly, blocking with the blade in her left hand a lunge from another Ghoule. She then slashed down with the steel in her right hand to cut across the beast's thigh, the Ghoule careening backward, hissing in anger. She nodded her thanks to Aislinn as the beast snarled in rage, his surprise attack thwarted.

"How is Bryen doing?" asked Davin, unable to turn away from the Ghoules, the beasts' incessant attacks barely giving them the chance to breathe.

Even when one of the Ghoules withdrew, usually to recover from an unexpected and painful wound, there were always three in front of them. So they had no chance to assist Bryen. His friend's combat with the Ghoule Overlord was his own, just as Bryen preferred it.

Even so, Davin was worried. He had heard and felt the two blasts behind him, a rush of air and heat against his back, none of them yet able to determine what had happened after the explosions.

"He's still alive," said Aislinn, not bothering to turn around.

Davin and Lycia knew that she spoke the truth because of her connection with her Protector, so they both breathed a little easier.

"That's good to hear," said Lycia, her twin swords slicing through the few feet separating them from the Ghoules, keeping the beasts at bay.

"So we continue to hold," said Davin.

"We continue to hold," replied Aislinn, her shining steel slicing across the ribs of one of the Ghoules. She had tried to drive her blade through the beast's gut, but her adversary had turned too quickly. Still, she was pleased. It wasn't a fatal strike, although the amount of blood staining the Ghoule's armor and leaking down to his thighs confirmed that the wound would slow the beast. "Until the Ghoules are dead or we are."

~

"You are too late, Protector," said the newly reborn Ghoule Overlord, the beast striding confidently toward Bryen, the long, twisted staff of black ash thunking against the stone with every step, a swirl of evil drifting off the shining black diamond set in the cap. "You had your chance to kill me. You failed. Now you will pay for your weakness. I am the Master of the Curse, and I will take what is mine. I will take you."

A shard of darkness shot from the black diamond, aimed right for Bryen's chest. He barely moved, simply twisting his hands to use the Spear of the Magii to knock away the Dark Magic.

The Ghoule Overlord wasn't done, however, sending shard after shard at Bryen. Despite the severity of the attack, Bryen refused to retreat, not wanting to get mixed in with the clash his friends were currently engaged in not too far behind him.

He stood his ground, batting away bolt after bolt with his shining blades. The attack was so intense that he had no opportunity to counterattack, only able to concentrate on his defense. That needed to change if he was to have any chance of staying alive and free of the Ghoule Overlord.

With that thought driving him, Bryen tilted his spear just a few degrees. This time, the shard of darkness, flying straight and true, aimed right at his chest like all the others, went right back in the direction from which it had come because of the angle of his swing.

The Ghoule Overlord had nothing to fear from the shard, the Dark Magic simply glancing off him. It did throw the monster off his stride, however. That moment of hesitation allowed Bryen to seize the momentum, sending several daggers of light streaking toward the beast.

Forced to halt his assault, the Ghoule Overlord grinned, parrying the slivers thrown at him with relative ease. If this was the best that the Protector could do, the boy would be his soon. The Seventh Stone would be his soon. Then a series of explosions ripped into the stone right in front of his clawed feet, the rock and dust blasting up into the air and forcing the Ghoule Overlord to turn away and take several steps back as he coughed his way through the gritty fog.

Once clear of the grainy haze, he spun back around, raising his staff with both claws just in time, catching the Spear of the Magii before it could slice into his flesh where his neck met his collarbone, though the shining blade did take a sizable chunk out of the black ash. From there the combat continued, Bryen finally having gotten in close with the Ghoule Overlord and staying there so that the beast didn't have the opportunity to use the Curse against him.

Recognizing the danger of allowing the Ghoule Overlord to take the initiative, as much as possible Bryen tried to keep his nemesis on the defensive, his twin blades singing through the air, forcing the beast around the slab. Yet that proved to be no small challenge, the Ghoule Overlord's martial skills a match for those of the Volkun's.

The Spear of the Magii slammed into the Overlord's staff with a staccato repetitiveness, each strike sounding like a distant rumble of thunder, splinters and long slivers of wood dropping to the stone. The two combatants glided around the altar at an almost impossible speed, Bryen refusing to allow the Ghoule Overlord to disengage, vaulting over the slab or sliding across it several times so that his adversary couldn't break away, doing all that he could to keep the beast focused on his attacks.

"Very impressive, Protector," grated the Ghoule Overlord. Finally he had gained some distance, but it had required the massive beast to vault himself backwards over the stone slab to stand on the other side. "But this ends now. The Ghoules will extend their rule. Caledonia first with more lands to follow. And I will take what belongs to me. I will take what I need to do that."

"You offer nothing but words," said Bryen, walking slowly around the slab, the Ghoule Overlord tracking his movements and keeping the altar between them. "Perhaps a little less talking and a bit more doing."

"Enjoy what little time you have left, Protector," replied the Ghoule Overlord. "Soon you will be mine. Heart. Spirit. Flesh. Soon I will be you."

Bryen realized that so far during the combat there had been little separating him from his opponent. They were of a similar strength and skill. As he stalked the Ghoule Overlord around the slab, a snippet of advice from Declan came to mind that had proven effective in the Colosseum. He needed to change the rules of the game if he was going to have any chance of winning. That meant that he needed to take a risk.

That thought guiding him, he opened himself to the Seventh Stone. The artifact had an almost limitless capacity to store energy, whether the Talent or the Curse. He had drained Elders of their Dark Magic. He had drained the Golem of its very essence. Why couldn't he do the same with the Ghoule Overlord?

With that objective in mind, Bryen flung a hollow strand of the Talent toward the Ghoule Overlord, the thread latching on. Momentarily startled by Bryen's action, before the Ghoule Overlord knew what was going on, Bryen pulled on the Dark Magic of his adversary. The thin tube filled with the Curse, pulsing a deep black, Bryen increasing the speed of the pull with each passing second.

Sensing that the barrier that he had constructed within himself remained whole, keeping him free from the corruption of the Curse, he quickened the pace of the flow even more, the Curse surging into the Seventh Stone at an increasingly rapid rate. As he did so, Bryen felt a burst of hope rush through him. He could feel the power of the Ghoule Overlord fading away.

Satisfied that he had done everything correctly, Bryen opened the valve even wider, taking in what felt like a tidal wave of Dark Magic. He had no fear about doing so, remaining free of the taint. The Seventh Stone absorbed all of the cursed power greedily, thirsty for more.

Yet when Bryen looked across the altar and saw the Ghoule Overlord grinning at him, sharp, serrated teeth flashing in the light, apparently unconcerned by what was happening, a flicker of worry lodged itself in the back of his brain.

"You think that you're stronger than me, Protector? Even with the Seventh Stone you cannot challenge me. You should know that by now. You cannot destroy me! But I can destroy you!"

With an evil gleam in his eyes, rather than trying to break the link to the Seventh Stone, to reclaim the Dark Magic being extracted from him, the Ghoule Overlord opened himself to the pull, luxuriating in it, accelerating and expanding the flow, sending an almost uncontrollable torrent of the Curse through the connection that Bryen had created, the Dark Magic flooding into the Protector, inundating him.

Even with the Spear of the Magii in his hands, as the Curse smashed into him like the monstrous waves of the Silent Sea crashing against the rocky coast of the Southern Marches, he could tell that he was losing control. He could feel the Dark Magic contained within him straining to break through the barrier that he had crafted within himself.

He had to stop the flow, to cut off the ever-broadening stream. He couldn't manage the vast amount of the Curse that the Ghoule Overlord blasted into him.

Now! Before the Curse drowned him.

But he couldn't. He couldn't do anything at all as the deluge crashed over him.

He had no control over the energy surging into him, the conflicting powers warring within him.

And then he realized that his greatest fear was about to come true.

The barrier that he had constructed so painstakingly to hold back the Curse shattered, the Dark Magic that he had thought he had contained flooding into him.

SHE WAS QUITE pleased with herself.

Rafia had suffered a few scrapes and minor wounds during her clash on the steps, though nothing serious. She couldn't say the same for the Slayers.

Rafia had used the Talent to narrow the field of battle on the approach to the Temple summit so that only one Slayer could attack her at a time. As she fought the lead Slayer, using her daggers to keep the beast below her, she became more irritated, the two Slayers behind the first trying to attack her with their tails shooting over the shoulder of her opponent.

After blocking a lunge by the Slayer standing right in front of her, one of her daggers taking two clawed fingers from the beast's hand as he pulled his claw back, she sliced across the beast's forearm with her other dagger, her blazing steel cutting to the bone. The Slayer reared back, more in shock than in pain, almost knocking the two beasts behind it back down the steps.

She paid little attention to that, instead stretching out her arms so that they were parallel to the stone. Rather than thrusting them down toward the pitted rock to call upon the lightning that she liked to use so frequently when battling Elders, this time she brought her hands together as if she were clapping. That movement pulled the webs made of the Talent that she had placed on each side of the pyramid's steps together.

The Slayers didn't stand a chance when the strands of energy met. Their howls and shrieks continued for a few seconds, then ended abruptly.

The monsters stood there still as statues, the hate in their blood-red eyes dampened and then tamped out completely as their bodies collapsed into dozens of perfectly cut pieces, their armored flesh butchered when the razor-sharp threads of the Talent sliced through them.

But when Rafia stepped onto the summit of the truncated pyramid exactly when the Ghoule Overlord laughed and blasted a torrent of the Curse into Bryen, her expression shifted to one of horror, her fear roiling her stomach. She realized what Bryen was trying to do. She could see that the Ghoule Overlord did as well and the monster was making the most of it.

The Protector had made a mistake. A terrible mistake. One from which he could never recover.

He had underestimated the strength and insidiousness of the Curse.

A deep regret rushed through her. He had tried. She had no doubt of that. But it wasn't enough.

She realized what she needed to do. She had promised him, and she would keep that promise no matter how much it hurt her to do so.

She didn't mind killing the Slayers. In fact, she quite enjoyed ridding the world of beasts that should never have been created in the first place.

She did mind killing Bryen, even though she didn't have a choice.

Bryen was losing the combat, the Ghoule Overlord over-whelming him with a torrent of the Curse. He could possibly mount a counterattack, she wouldn't put it past him to try knowing how tough the Protector was. Yet as she watched the struggle, that possibility didn't appear likely. The Curse was too much for him.

Growling in frustration, she realized that she couldn't take that risk.

At least if she killed Bryen now and destroyed the host of the Seventh Stone before the Ghoule Overlord could take the artifact, the beast would not be able to bring his Ghoules into Caledonia. The Weir that Bryen constructed would see to that. The Kingdom would be safe, assuming the Caledonian Army could rid the Winter Pass of the Ghoule Legions.

Even though the threat of the Ghoule Overlord would remain, that was a much better result than the Ghoule Overlord claiming the Seventh Stone.

She liked the Protector. Liked him a lot. He was a good young man. But he had become more than a risk. He had become a liability. The interests of the Kingdom had to come before his own.

Bryen knew that. They had spoken about it. And even as her heart was breaking for a second time in just the last few weeks, she took in as much of the Talent as she could. Steeling herself for what she needed to do, ignoring the Ghoule Overlord, she fired a stream of energy straight at Bryen.

Her eyes widened in shock when the Talent slammed into a barrier of energy that flickered into place just a split-second before her attack struck the Protector, a dome of shimmering light now encircling Bryen and the Ghoule Overlord.

Her eyes widened even more when she realized what had happened, because the Talent used to construct the shield hadn't come from Bryen.

Bryen had fallen to his knees, shoulders slumped, arms hanging loosely at his sides as the intense pressure of the Dark Magic bore down upon him, both within and without. The Spear of the Magii had dropped from his grip and lay on the stone, the steel no longer shining, the Talent gone.

Bryen had no strength. No energy. Nothing.

He couldn't even lift his head.

The Ghoule Overlord's Curse had proven to be too much for him. Too powerful. Too demanding. Too crafty.

He was dying, slowly, agonizingly, his soul ripped from his body and replaced by the Curse. The pain was more than he could bear, and he could do nothing about it. He couldn't even scream in response to his misery as the Ghoule Overlord's Dark Magic made his entire body shiver and shake in torment.

He had tried. He had done everything that he could. But he had failed.

He had failed himself. He had failed his friends.

Everything that he had fought for had come to this.

He just wanted it to end. The suffering. The pain. The guilt.

Then Declan's words, which had become so much a part of who he was, drifted through his mind.

"Everyone dies. Not everyone dies with honor."

That thought blasted through his pain, stiffening his resolve.

If he was going to die, it would be on his terms. Not those of the Ghoule Overlord.

He sought the calm, the focus, that had been so essential to his success in the Pit. He couldn't grasp it, staying just beyond his reach.

He tried again, but still no success.

Not knowing what else to do, he did as Declan had taught him, concentrating solely on his heartbeat, the steady rhythm growing louder in his ears. Until slowly, so agonizingly slowly, there was nothing else. Just the steady beating of his heart.

Finally believing that he had gained some small measure of control, he pushed back against the influx of the Curse with what tiny bits of fading strength that he could muster. It was like trying to roll a massive boulder up a hill with just a finger. Nothing happened.

His doubts threatened to crush him as he reached for any of the Talent that still might remain within him. It wasn't until he was about to give up that he found a hidden reserve within himself, an unknown and unused strength, that connected him with a tiny stream of the Talent.

Rather than feeling a surge of elation at his success, he only experienced a burst of renewed purpose. With that tiny stream of the Talent, he needed to do one thing. Cut off the flow of the Curse surging into him.

An impossible task, most likely. Before he could be consumed by his doubts and fears, Declan's words once more pounded within his brain.

"Everyone dies. Not everyone dies with honor."

He tried. He put whatever strength he had left into the effort. No luck. No success.

He was too weak.

He needed more of the Talent, so much more to have any chance of saving himself, but it was all gone.

Every time he attempted to constrict the flow, he only succeeded in compressing the stream a minute amount, the effect so small that it wasn't even noticeable. The change lasted for just a second at most before the torrent of the Curse flooded the barrier he sought to construct, once again forcing its way into him unimpeded.

As he fought feebly against the tainted flood, each defeat solidifying a sense of inevitability mixed with terror within him, a terrible reality stared back at Bryen. The Ghoule Overlord wasn't trying to kill him with the Curse. No, that would be too easy. The beast had a more specialized purpose in mind as he sent the Curse burrowing deep into him. The Ghoule Overlord, sending wave upon wave of corrupted filth into Bryen, wanted to turn him to his purposes, to join with him, to make him both the host of the Seventh Stone and the Curse.

That only strengthened Bryen's resolve to do anything he could to prevent that from happening. Declan's words continued to play through his mind in a continuous loop.

"Everyone dies. Not everyone dies with honor."

Because even as he failed time after time to stanch the flow of the Curse, Bryen sensed the beast's mounting frustration. Because the Ghoule Overlord was failing as well.

What the Ghoule Overlord was doing wasn't working. Yes, the Curse was consuming Bryen, slowly and inexorably. But the Seventh Stone was resisting the beast. The artifact had become so deeply embedded within Bryen that he and the Seventh Stone were now inseparable. They were one and the same in spirit and flesh, in power and purpose. And the Seventh Stone refused to be made a tool of the Curse.

Cursing with anger as he slowly came to understand the unexpected and unwanted resistance that he encountered, the Ghoule Overlord intensified his efforts.

The Ghoule Overlord's clawed hand shot out and wrapped itself tightly around Bryen's head.

Bryen's resistance crumbled as the Dark Magic surged into him at an even faster pace, an unstoppable tsunami flooding every aspect of his existence, body and soul.

To make the Protector into his own image, not only did the Ghoule Overlord need to crush the essence of the Protector, but he also had to do the same to the Seventh Stone.

Once he subjugated the artifact, then the Ghoule Overlord could use the Seventh Stone as he chose. The Protector would be a slave once more, answering to the demands of the Curse. Because when the Ghoule Overlord and the Protector became one, the Ghoule Overlord and the Seventh Stone also would become one.

With the Curse pounding into him at a mind-numbing beat, Bryen sensed what was occurring. The cost he was about to pay. He was losing himself. Who he was.

His memories were fading, replaced by the images, structures, and beliefs held by the Ghoule Overlord so that the beast could remake him.

The Ghoule Overlord was using him. The Ghoule Overlord was becoming him.

It was when that terrifying realization hit that Viktor Keldragan appeared right next to Bryen in his ghostly form, kneeling down, placing a misty hand on his nephew's shoulder.

"You are a Keldragan. We are fighters. We always have been. We always will be. Fight. Fight now! Don't give in to the Curse!"

Bryen wanted to obey the Magus, he was desperate to, but it was too hard.

He was struggling just to form a rational thought that was his own, no longer certain that what passed through his mind belonged to him or the Ghoule Overlord. He stood on the edge of the abyss and as soon as he fell off, the Curse would consume him.

Then, he would be nothing more than a creature of the Curse, nothing more than another tool for the Ghoule Overlord.

He couldn't imagine a worse end. He preferred death, yet there was nothing that he could do. He was gratified that Rafia and Aislinn had promised to end his life if this were his fate, but now he worried that it may be too late.

Bryen thought to use the Talent to destroy himself, just as the Ten Magii did. He believed that it was the only way that he could escape that terrible fate. Distressingly, he had no ability to do it now, no strength, the Talent nothing more than a distant memory. The power of the natural world had been taken from him.

"Take the Spear of the Magii!" commanded Viktor, sensing that his nephew was close to the end, fading, his essence never to return. "You can do it. You must!"

Bryen tried to obey Viktor's command, finding the struggle more difficult than any combat in the Pit. Even as his consciousness began to drift away, his uncle's words stuck with him.

Slowly, so slowly that he never thought he would succeed, Bryen tried to reach for the weapon lying on the stone just a foot in front of him. He willed his hand to move. To take up the Giant-crafted Spear.

Nothing. His own body refused to obey him.

The effort was too much for him. The Spear was too far away. He couldn't do it. He had no strength left. His will was almost gone.

The corrupt energy of the Curse was draining him of everything that made him who he was, changing him into what the Ghoule Overlord wanted him to be. He could feel himself, feel who he was, disappearing, and with it his desire to resist.

He needed to grasp the Spear. He had to!

Yet he had nothing left.

What could he do?

Then another of Declan's lessons drifted through his mind.

"Sometimes your greatest strength is the ability to give in to your greatest weakness."

Bryen hadn't understood what Declan had meant when the Master of the Gladiators told him that on the white sand. He thought he did now.

Having no other options, Bryen stopped resisting. He did something that was almost unimaginable to him.

He let go. He gave in to his accelerating weakness, allowing the last of his energy to drain away, realizing that sometimes, just as Declan had tried to teach him, continuing the struggle required giving in.

Unable to keep himself on his knees as the last of his strength left him, he slumped forward on the stone. As he did so, his right arm went with him, his thumb and forefinger touching the cold steel haft of the Spear of the Magii.

"Well done, lad," said Viktor, the spirit remaining by his side. "The Curse is in you, taking you, and even though you can't feel it, the Talent is in you still. As is the Seventh Stone. Neither the Talent nor the Seventh Stone can ever be taken from you. Now bring the three together. Connect the Seventh Stone, the Talent, and the Spear of the Magii."

"How?" Bryen whispered, barely able to get the words out.

"Look at the haft. Read the inscription. Then you will know what to do."

Bryen was so weak that he couldn't even nod. Still, he had just enough strength to turn his head and look down at the steel as Viktor instructed. He had never really thought about the words until now.

When the darkness surrounds, the light will prevail.

He wasn't certain what the words meant.

Clear, but vague.

Simple, but complex.

Still focused on the words, he sensed the darkness roiling within him, consuming him, taking him, making him its own. But even as the Curse smothered him, still a spark of light remained, protected by the Seventh Stone.

And that's what he needed now, that single spark of light.

When the darkness surrounds, the light will prevail.

Doing as his uncle instructed, he reached for that minute stream of the Talent, the thread so small that it was barely visible.

Bryen felt a tiny surge of exhilaration. He had done just enough.

That thread of the Talent connected to the Seventh Stone, awakening the artifact, making that spark flicker just a little bit brighter, the Spear of the Magii glowing dimly to confirm Bryen's belief.

Thrilled even by that small success, Bryen focused now on the connection he had with the Seventh Stone, the reservoir of the Talent that had always been contained within it, but that Bryen had only used when absolutely necessary. Feeling some of his strength return as the spark burst into a flame, he reached for that pool of energy now, his only hope.

It was like trying to pick up a needle that had fallen on the floor in a pitch-dark room. Just when he thought he had it, it slipped from his grasp. Still, he kept trying, the seconds passing by, his efforts agonizingly slow as he failed time after time. Until finally he felt it.

The Talent contained within the Seventh Stone blasted into him like a bolt of lightning, burning away some of the Curse, giving him just a little more strength, reminding him of who he was.

Now he just needed to make that final connection. He needed to send that deep reservoir of the Talent into the Spear of the Magii.

Bryen had feared that the energy would be too much for him, especially in his weakened state. He realized that he shouldn't have been concerned. The Seventh Stone was guiding him now, and the Spear of the Magii, blazing brightly as the power of the natural world flowed into the weapon, was just as much a part of him as the artifact.

When that final link clicked into place, the Talent, the Seventh Stone, and the Spear of the Magii all working together, Bryen felt a warmth blossom throughout his body, his strength returning in a rush. Then that warmth strengthened, becoming a scalding heat, scouring his body clean of the Curse that had threatened to engulf him.

That burst of energy pushed Bryen away from the edge of the abyss, giving him a new life, a new energy, over which the Ghoule Overlord could exercise no control.

The Talent was his once again. He was free of the Dark Magic, the hold of the Curse gone.

He knew who he was. He knew what he needed to do.

Using the Talent, Bryen released a blast of energy that he centered on himself.

The blinding flash of white light radiated out from him, sending the Ghoule Overlord flying through the air, the beast slamming down on top of the altar, the force of the blow cracking the long slab, the stone breaking down the middle as the two pieces collapsed in on each other.

Feeling reborn, Bryen pushed himself to his feet, the Spear of the Magii gripped tightly in his hands. He stared at the Ghoule Overlord through the eyes of the Volkun, frigid, emotionless.

The beast struggled to extricate himself from the shattered slab, the Master of the Curse cradling the claw that had gripped Bryen's head. The flesh was burnt and charred, the long, withered fingers bent as if they'd been shoved into a burning flame, the Ghoule Overlord unable to withstand the blistering power of the Talent.

"You're right, it is time to end this," Bryen said, his voice cold, hard, determined. The voice of the greatest gladiator to ever stalk the white sand. "The final combat begins now."

Aislinn, Lycia, and Davin continued to hold their positions, their fiery blades forming a steel line across which the Ghoules could not cross, preventing them from aiding their Master. Yet even with that success, they were becoming increasingly frustrated. They wanted to help Bryen, sensing his need, feeling the powers clashing behind them, but they could do nothing other than concentrate on the Ghoules who continued to press them, seeking a way past.

The tide turned quickly when Rafia joined the fight.

When the Magus realized that she could do nothing to help or harm Bryen, the shield around him preventing it, her heart almost broke. Unable to pull her eyes away from Bryen's losing struggle, she watched him slowly slip over the edge, and she powerless to prevent it.

Why the Ten Magii would protect Bryen and then allow him to be drowned by the Curse, she couldn't imagine.

Yet there had to be a purpose behind what they had done, didn't there? They wouldn't sacrifice him without a fight.

Rafia's sorrow turned to hope when the bright light of the Talent formed around him soon after Bryen slumped to the stone. The energy was so blinding that she had to look away, her gaze only turning back in that direction after hearing the blast. Her fear for Bryen shifted into a feral grin, as she took a great deal of pleasure watching the Ghoule Overlord fly through the air and crash into the altar.

Her hope renewed, the Ten Magii somehow giving Bryen what he needed to continue the combat, she focused now on where she could have an immediate and beneficial impact.

One of the Ghoules that Aislinn was defending against had managed to slip behind her while she was combating another of the beasts. She had just parried a lunge by the Ghoule facing her, preparing to meet the next, having no chance to block the spear the Ghoule on her other side aimed for her back.

Rafia got there just before the steel cut into Aislinn's flesh, slashing down with one of her blazing daggers, slicing right through the spear, the sharp point bouncing harmlessly on the stone. She turned to face the Ghoule, the beast looking at his weapon in shock, never having thought that such a thing could happen.

Now understanding who he opposed, the Ghoule growled in anger, throwing the broken spear at her and lunging for Rafia with his claws.

Aislinn had sensed the danger behind her, though she could do nothing about it. Spear to the front, spear to the back, she chose to stand against her first attacker, catching movement out of the corner of her eye near the steps leading to the crest. She hoped that her guess was right, that Rafia had joined the combat, since the Ghoule's steel didn't pierce her back.

Trusting her instincts, she concentrated on the beast who stood to her front. Because in that instant, the Ghoule made a mistake. He got a bit too close to her.

Finally getting the break that she wanted, Aislinn took advantage of it, parrying another of the beast's jabs with his spear, then pulling a dagger from the sheath on her thigh and driving it into the Ghoule's ribs before the beast could step back. At the same time she infused the blade with the Talent.

The Ghoule didn't stand a chance after that, having no way to defend himself against the energy that ripped through his body, burning through his flesh from the inside out.

Grateful to have eliminated one of the Ghoule Overlord's guards, she turned to help Lycia, who fought right beside her. Aislinn realized instantly that the combat had already been decided. The Ghoule, suffering from more than a dozen wounds, the worst a slice across the side of his neck that was spurting blood, was dead but hadn't figured it out yet.

The Ghoule staggered, the blood loss too much for the beast. That's when Lycia struck a final time, once more slashing across the Ghoule's throat to widen her initial cut, the beast's head tilting to the side at an unnatural angle as her steel sliced almost completely through his vertebrae.

When the Ghoule finally slumped to the stone, Lycia spun around, wanting to help her brother. Instead, she discovered that Davin didn't need her assistance. The Ghoule facing the

Crimson Giant crashed onto his back, a large puncture wound from her brother's spear where one of the beast's eyes had been.

Lycia looked in the other direction, not surprised to see that Aislinn had eliminated her opponent as well. Even less so when she observed Rafia finishing the last Ghoule who had stood against them, driving both daggers into the back of the beast's neck, then twisting to snap the Ghoule's spinal cord just to make sure.

"Are you sure he's dead?" Davin asked, both impressed and slightly frightened by the number of wounds Rafia had inflicted upon the beast and how ferociously she had finished him.

"He should be," the Magus replied matter of factly, pushing herself up from one knee and standing next to Aislinn, Davin, and Lycia as they all turned to observe the combat between Bryen and the Ghoule Overlord.

Rafia was thrilled to see the Protector striding toward the Master of the Curse surrounded by a blazing light, the Spear of the Magii spinning slowly from one hand to the next. Whatever the Ten Magii had done, clearly it had worked.

They all wanted to help him, to join the fight. But it could be no more than an unfulfilled desire. The shield was now centered around the broken slab and extended all the way to the pillars holding up the dome, the spirits of the Ten Magii standing between the columns like silent sentinels.

Watching. Waiting. Hoping.

"Can he do it?" asked Rafia.

Davin nodded, a surge of confidence making him smile, as he replied before Aislinn or Lycia could.

"He's the Volkun. It's like he's back where he began. Back in the Pit. No one can defeat him on the white sand. The Ghoule Overlord doesn't stand a chance."

"You still belong to me, Protector! You will always belong to me!"

Bryen ignored the Ghoule Overlord. He had learned after fighting for a decade on the white sand that if your opponent wanted to run off at the mouth, best to let him. Let your adversary distract himself, not you.

You needed to stay focused at all times. One lapse in concentration could mean your death.

The beast had been spouting curses and threats ever since Bryen had cleansed himself of the Curse. With the Ghoule Overlord's burnt claw curled into a grotesque position, the beast tried time after time to break away from him, all to no avail.

Bryen refused to give his nemesis any time to regroup, pushing the Ghoule Overlord, taking advantage of the fact that the monster struggled to defend against his lightning quick attacks with just one claw. Adding even more weight to the Ghoule Overlord's heavy burden, every time Bryen struck the beast's staff with the Spear of the Magii, the blazing blades whittled away another sliver or chunk of wood.

"Once I make you mine, I will kill your woman! Then your friends!"

The Ghoule Overlord pivoted to the left, one of the Protector's shining steel blades missing his arm by no more than a whisker. Bryen watched as the beast tried to break away, needing some way to elude the prey that had become the hunter. Yet he couldn't do it, the Protector twisting his grip on the haft of his weapon and bringing the other blade slicing toward his ribs.

The Ghoule Overlord got his staff in position just in time, blocking the strike, cringing as the blade cut deeply into the black ash, the steel almost slicing clean through, the bottom half now tilted crookedly away from the top. Enraged by what was happening, he continued his verbal onslaught.

"She will be first, I promise you that. You will be me and I will be you when you watch as I bite into her flesh."

Bryen ignored the words, maintaining the calm that had settled around him. The Ghoule Overlord was demonstrating a distinct lack of creativity with his threats, not even registering compared to what he heard while in the Colosseum.

From his experience on the white sand, Bryen knew that now was not the time for emotion. Now was the time for cold logic. Fluid motion. Fast and decisive decisions. And a very sharp, thirsty blade.

Besides, words had no role in the present. Words had no impact unless given agency.

There was nothing in the world for him now but motion and intuition, gliding across the crest and around the broken slab with a remarkable grace. Never allowing the Ghoule Overlord to do anything but wonder from which direction the next attack would come.

The Spear of the Magii whistled through the air so swiftly that it appeared as if the glowing steel blades actually were streaks of light. And with every slash and cut, he chopped off another piece of the Ghoule Overlord's staff, his adversary's usual fluidity of motion replaced by a stumbling shuffle, the beast finding it more and more difficult to defend himself when also dealing with such a serious and painful injury.

Finally, after several more minutes of forcing the Ghoule Overlord around the cracked slab, the beast staggering time and again into the shield crafted by the Ten Magii, Bryen thought that he had the chance that he had been working toward.

The Ghoule Overlord had tired of retreating, this time trying to hold his ground, swinging his staff one-handed for Bryen's head.

The Protector ducked, then twisted around, hoping to drive his Spear through the beast's gut with a backward lunge. Bryen realized too late that it had been nothing more than a feint, the Ghoule Overlord nowhere to be seen.

Bryen spun back around, wary, Spear of the Magii held at the ready, thinking that the beast was trying the same trick on him that he had used against Sirius in the Sanctuary. But when he looked behind him, rather than the splintered staff being thrust into his chest, there was nothing there.

Surprised, he took several steps back, slowly turning around, using the Talent to search around him, looking for any hint as to where the Ghoule Overlord could be.

He sensed it before he saw it, the energy sizzling in the air. A portal of black mist appeared just ten feet away from him, though on the other side of the cracked altar, the wounded Ghoule Overlord stepping out of the gloom, long staff of black ash, damaged but not broken, held tightly in his one good claw, Dark Magic swirling across the top of the black diamond.

"You fight well, Protector. Of course, we knew that already. Your time in the Pit was well spent. Even so, you forget one thing."

Bryen began to walk around the stone slab toward his adversary, confident though still cautious, seeking to continue the combat. The Ghoule Overlord moved away from him, not allowing him to get any closer.

"What would that be?" Bryen asked in the Ghoule language.

"That with respect to the Talent, you are just a babe. But I … I am the source of the Curse in the Lost Land. I am the Curse!"

With that final pronouncement, a flood of Dark Magic burst from the black diamond, surging toward Bryen, enveloping him in a cocoon of darkness, the bright sunlight disappearing, replaced by a misty black that pricked his flesh at every touch.

Bryen pulled on the Talent immediately, shielding himself,

halting the painful stabs before the Curse could drown him as it had almost done once before.

Although Bryen succeeded in protecting himself, he had nowhere to go. More and more of the Ghoule Overlord's Dark Magic swirled around him, trapping him. Turning everything around him to night, the only light coming from the thin barrier of the Talent in which he had wrapped himself.

That tempestuous dark mass then began to press down on him, trying to flatten him against the stone, less interested in piercing his shield, more interested in shattering it with the intense pressure building against the thin barrier.

Such an approach had almost worked once before, so Bryen assumed that the Ghoule Overlord thought it would do so again, putting him at the mercy of the Curse.

The force was so great that Bryen fell to his knees. Then he needed to place his hands on the stone, the Spear of the Magii still clutched between his fingers, trying desperately to resist the Curse as it pushed down on his back. It felt like he was caught right on the coast of the Southern Marches where water met shore, one massive wave after another crashing down upon him.

Bryen couldn't move. He could barely take a breath. The pressure was too great, crushing him to the stone, as breaker after breaker slammed down on top of him, his legs and arms shaking violently from the effort it was taking to not be forced into a prostrate position on the summit.

Yet even with the punishment that the Ghoule Overlord was doling out, Bryen could think, and his mind worked furiously for a solution as his body threatened to break.

No longer able to keep his head up, having no choice but to look down, Bryen stared at the haft of the Spear of the Magii, reading for a third time the words cut into the steel.

When the darkness surrounds the light will prevail.

Those words had already proved incredibly helpful once, so why not again?

The last time he had done this, just minutes before in fact, the Ghoule Overlord had almost turned him with the Curse, the Dark Magic within him breaking free and joining with that being driven into him.

Could he take such a risk now? Should he? Would it save him or would it prove to be his undoing?

Then Bryen realized that he had been so focused on killing the Ghoule Overlord, that he had forgotten a key fact. The Spear, working in conjunction with the power of the Seventh Stone, had removed all traces of the Curse from him. At the moment, the Seventh Stone only contained the Talent. He didn't have to worry about the Curse. Not from within, only from without.

His fear burned away by that realization, Bryen opened himself to the Seventh Stone, pulling in as much of the Talent as he could, until he was almost bursting with the natural magic of the world, white sparks shooting out from his skin, his hair sticking up straight, his eyes blazing with energy. He added that almost limitless power to his shield, strengthening it, solidifying it, not only protecting himself, but also using it to eat into the Curse, destroying it particle by particle every time the two energies came into contact.

The Curse pulled back from him then, attempting to withdraw, desperate to evade the pursuing Talent. Taking advantage of the change in circumstances, Bryen pushed himself back to his feet, the Spear of the Magii in his hands, the pressure that had threatened to crush him removed. Stretching his back, cracking his neck, he breathed in deeply, that feeling of asphyxiation thankfully, wonderfully gone.

He was tired of all the demands that had been made upon him. He was tired of this combat. He was tired of the Ghoule Overlord and the threat that he represented.

He was tired of it all.

It truly was time to end this.

As the Talent continued to spark off him, biting into the Curse, his thoughts inevitably turned once again to the Ghoule Overlord's staff. Right before this fight had begun, the revitalized beast had pushed himself off the altar with the staff of black ash held within his claws. The staff hadn't been there until the process was complete, until the Ghoule Overlord had taken his new host.

Bryen remembered when he had broken the staff when he destroyed the Curse's shell in the Sanctuary. Then, the black diamond had transformed into a mist, racing back to the Lost Land. Coming right back here.

Another puzzle piece fit into place when next he recalled the conversation he had with the Elder Ghoule before the Battle of the Horseshoe when the beasts were following him through the Crumbling Cliffs in the Southern Marches. Right before Bryen killed the Elder, the beast had said that he was, "The only one who can help our Overlord. The only one who can stop our Overlord."

Bryen didn't know what to make of it then, though it was beginning to make sense to him now.

The black diamond was the key. It was the source and repository of the Ghoule Overlord's power, of the very Curse in the Lost Land, functioning in a similar fashion as the Seventh Stone.

Bryen had taken the flesh from the Curse, allowing the spirit to escape. To kill the Ghoule Overlord, both spirit and flesh, Bryen needed to gain control of the black diamond. He needed to make the black diamond his own so that the Curse couldn't escape again and simply take another shell from which to work its evil.

Because if he could gain control over the black diamond,

then he could gain control over the source of the Ghoule Overlord's power. He could gain control over the Curse itself.

It was time to end this combat. And now Bryen knew just how to do it.

With a massive pulse of the Talent, thousands of daggers of white light blasted out from Bryen and tore through the cloud of darkness, destroying the Ghoule Overlord's creation. With that, the entire tenor of the duel changed.

Bryen stood there atop the crest of the Temple, in the very center of the Ghoule Overlord's domain with the Talent surging around him, sparking and flashing, becoming an unstoppable force, as he destroyed the swirling clouds of the Curse with an unrelenting resolve.

The Ghoule Overlord stepped back, shocked that the Protector had freed himself. When he gazed across the cracked altar, the Protector's eyes were pure white, so much of the Talent surging within him, radiating from him, that being this close to so much of the natural energy of the world made the Ghoule Overlord's skin prickle in pain.

Then just as quickly as the Protector emerged from within the Dark Magic that for a time had contained him, he was gone.

The Ghoule Overlord's eyes widened even more, staring in shock and fear at the space just ten feet away where the Protector had stood just a heartbeat before.

In a blinding flash that forced the beast to look away, the Protector reappeared right in front of the Ghoule Overlord, no more than a few feet separating them. Before the Ghoule Overlord's eyes had cleared of the spots clouding them, before he could even move a muscle, he felt a searing pain burn through his body, one of the blazing blades of the Spear of the Magii sliding into his chest, the Talent surging out from the weapon and racing through his insides.

"I may not have a great deal of experience with the Talent,"

Bryen said quietly, holding the Spear of the Magii in place, thereby keeping the Ghoule Overlord fixed in front of him, "but you forgot something. Something critically important." Bryen stepped in even closer to the beast, giving the Spear a twist and earning a grunt of pain in response, his eyes, every pore on his body, vibrating with the natural power of the world. "I am the Seventh Stone."

A pulse of energy raced down the haft of the Spear, then flooded into the Ghoule Overlord, accelerating the process that Bryen had already begun, the Talent ripping through the monster's insides and turning the beast's body to ash.

Knowing that the end was near, with his free hand, Bryen reached out and took hold of the beast's staff of black ash, the shock of the Talent and the Curse meeting once again creating a concussive boom that rocked the pillars set atop the truncated pyramid, the dome shaking dangerously.

With a final look of despair, the Ghoule Overlord realized what was happening and that he was powerless to stop it. Dark Magic rippled atop the black diamond, but he was unable to draw on the Curse, his control over the power dying just as he was.

Bryen was ready when the Ghoule Overlord's body disintegrated into a cloud of cinders. At that very same moment, the black diamond dissolved into a swirling mist just as it had done in the Sanctuary.

Yet now it had nowhere to go. The Curse was already home, at the center of its power. So instead of seeking to escape, the Curse immediately went in search of a new host, a more powerful host, one that it had already tried and failed to take for its own. The evil of the Lost Land blasted right toward Bryen, hoping to take him when he least expected it.

The Curse miscalculated badly. In just those last few minutes, circumstances had changed drastically.

Bryen was the master of the Seventh Stone now.

The Curse battered hopelessly against the impenetrable

shield Bryen constructed of the Talent. It was an effort doomed to fail, yet the Curse had no choice, no other option. It had nowhere else to go, no other possible hosts, because the barrier of energy the Ten Magii had created around the pillars and beneath the dome kept it confined to the area around the broken slab.

The Curse had to take the Protector. The Protector was its only hope.

But it couldn't.

For the first time since the Curse had come to the Lost Land, it realized that it had met its match.

A high-pitched keening burst from the Curse as it sped around the columns, bouncing off the Talent that imprisoned it, unable to break free, no longer bothering to try to take Bryen, the Protector's shield too strong.

Bryen watched dispassionately as the Curse flew wildly above him, and it was then that he realized that all along the Dark Magic had wanted him to become its new host. The Curse had wanted him as soon as it realized that Bryen had become the Seventh Stone.

The Curse had understood from the very beginning the value of taking the Protector, of making the Protector its own. Because if the Curse had succeeded, its own power could have been bolstered by that of the Seventh Stone. If the Ghoule Overlord had caught him, who Bryen was would have died, but his power would have remained for the Curse to appropriate.

But it was too late now. Maybe when Bryen was less knowledgeable about how to use the Seventh Stone, maybe before he had learned how to make the most of the power offered to him by the Spear of the Magii. Not now.

When Bryen grasped that he had tamed the Curse, Viktor once again appeared at his side, offering advice in his ghostly form.

"You know what you need to do next. Use the Spear as your focal point, and we will guide you."

Bryen nodded, ready to bring the combat to its logical and necessary conclusion. Reaching out with the Spear, he touched one of the blades to the shrieking Dark Magic. In that instant everything within the protective dome stopped. That single moment in time froze, the Curse linked to the Spear of the Magii, held in place, unable to move, only a pitiful wail erupting from the bound Dark Magic.

The pathetic lament transformed into a shriek of anger followed by a cry of fear as Bryen worked with the Talent, the spirits of the Ten Magii now standing at his side, aiding him, sharing their power and their strength, helping him to compress the Curse, pushing it back into the form that it had taken before it had tried to escape. Finally, after a tense few minutes, the hazy mist that was the Curse disappeared, the black diamond resting on the rock at Bryen's feet.

He stared down at the glowing artifact, the pulsing black almost frightening in its intensity.

The Ghoule Overlord was dead. The Curse was contained. But he couldn't destroy it. He could only imprison it.

So what to do with it now?

A thought came to mind that made him smile for the first time since he had stepped onto the summit of the Temple of the Ghoules.

He still had one more task to complete. Assuming that he could get there in time.

WHEN THE SHIELD of energy surrounding the columns flickered for several seconds and then vanished, Rafia, Aislinn, Lycia, and Davin were relieved that only Bryen stood near the collapsed altar. They had to squint to see him as the massive amount of power that surged around him made it too bright to look at him directly.

The Ten Magii, visible between the columns during Bryen's combat with the Ghoule Overlord, had faded away when Bryen released his hold on the Talent, their essences returning to the Seventh Stone.

"It's done?" asked Rafia.

"It's done," Bryen confirmed with the grin that she had first seen when she met him on the Haven pier. "I'm glad you didn't kill me."

"It wasn't for a lack of trying. Something was protecting you."

"Someones."

"The Ten Magii."

Bryen nodded, knowing that the Magus would want every last detail of what had occurred beneath the dome. He would be happy to share, just not now. "We need to go."

The ground was beginning to rumble. Gently at first, increasing in potency as each second passed. He could guess at what was coming next.

"What's happening?" asked Davin, the broken pieces of stone that had fallen from the pillars and the dome beginning to shake, the smaller pieces dancing across the crest as the trembling worsened.

"The Cauldron," Bryen replied, almost apologetically. "It's about to blow."

Looking out over Mertvey Gorod, the sound of the earth rumbling became deafening. Bryen watched as the long stone structures began to sway more and more violently, then crumble altogether. Gaping chasms appeared in the ground as a thousand years of pent-up steam blasted hundreds of feet into the sky, huge streams of magma rapidly pouring out and spreading through the Dead City.

The Temple of the Ghoules shifted abruptly as the western

side of the pyramid sheared off, the ground beneath the structure on that side giving way to an immense pool of lava that rapidly bubbled to the surface. Bryen and his friends stumbled a few feet in that direction before regaining their balance, but it was becoming increasingly difficult to stay on their feet. The shaking intensified and the magma continued to spread, eating into the stone, reclaiming it, the wounded pyramid leaning slowly but surely down toward the massive pool of fiery magma.

"It's about to what?" exclaimed Davin. "How could this be happening? You said this was a dormant volcano. Dormant volcanos don't erupt!"

"It was dormant," Bryen replied as he and the others crawled closer to the eastern edge of the crest, the pyramid tilting at an even sharper angle toward the burning ground, flames now licking up that side of the Temple, the stone melting and joining with the magma. "But dormant volcanos aren't dead. They're just dormant. Until they're not."

"Yes, unfortunately, it seems that we breathed new life into this one," confirmed Rafia.

"I really hate this adventure, you know that?" protested Davin. He had never seen a caldera erupt before. He just would have preferred if he had been watching from the outside rather than from within it.

"We know," said Lycia.

With a sudden lurch, the angle steepened, more blocks of stone falling off into the magma as the weakening foundation of the Temple slowly lost the battle to support the weight of the edifice. Having reached the stairs farthest from the side that was sinking, they were all now leaning toward the east so they didn't slide off the crumbling pyramid.

They wouldn't be able to do that for much longer, however. The Temple of the Ghoules was collapsing. Much sooner rather than later.

"Any ideas?" asked Aislinn, who had leaned down and grasped the top of a step, giving Rafia her hand before the Magus slid off the rapidly descending crest and into the bubbling lava that was now only a dozen yards away and approaching rapidly.

"At first I thought of crafting a portal."

"Then why don't you?" demanded Aislinn, the lava licking at the top of the crumbling summit.

"Because help is almost here," Bryen replied, who somehow found the wherewithal to smile when it seemed that their deaths were certain.

Just then they heard a shriek blast through the sky, a massive, winged shadow streaking down toward them.

28

THE END COMES

"Anything from Magus Rafia?"

Kevan had asked the question every day for weeks, always getting the same answer. He never really expected a different response. Still, he couldn't stop himself from asking.

"No," Noorsin replied softly. "I doubt she can get word to us from the other side of the Weir."

"We should have heard something by now," grumbled Kevan.

"We will," said Noorsin, reaching over to grasp his arm warmly, trying to give him some slight reassurance. She understood why he was concerned, his daughter having crossed into the Lost Land with the goal of destroying the Curse. Kevan impressed her for having the courage to let Aislinn go, or rather for not protesting too strongly. She wished that she could do more to help assuage his worry. But there was little that she could say, and she had a larger and more immediate worry with which to contend. "Remember, the only person more focused than you on protecting her is her Protector, and she is with Bryen."

"Yes, but that assumes nothing has happened to the Protector."

"I wouldn't worry too much about that," the Blademaster said with a quiet confidence. "There seems to be little in this world that can kill the Volkun."

The sun was rising above the Shattered Peaks, a bright line forming along the bottom of the Winter Pass and that would steadily shift to the west, burning away the shadow draped across the canyon. Noorsin, Kevan, and the Blademaster sat on their horses in the center of the Caledonian line, watching the advance of the Ghoule Legions, the beasts trotting out of the north at a steady pace, their bloody intent clear.

A shield wall stretched across the narrow gap, the breadth of the Winter Pass here only several thousand yards, replacing the mobile wall, much of that construction destroyed during the last battle and no longer of use. Carefully spaced gaps separated the companies of soldiers all along the line with the cavalry waiting just a few hundred yards back.

Once the command was given, the mounted soldiers would gallop through the channels, seeking to disrupt the Ghoule attack. They understood that as soon as they were beyond the shield wall, the soldiers forming the defensive line would close the breaches. They would be on their own. They wouldn't be coming back through the lines. Not unless they defeated the Ghoules Legions, and they knew the likelihood of that.

The Blademaster hated the cards that they had been dealt, but it was a reality from which they couldn't escape. All they could do was fight their way through it for as long as they could manage.

Kill or be killed. One of Declan's favorite sayings unavoidably ran through the Blademaster's mind. At the moment, that aphorism appeared to be right on target.

He had assumed after the first few clashes with the Ghoules, the beasts slowly and steadily driving the Caledonian

Army back to the south, that this was how it would come to an end. One final battle to decide the fate of the Kingdom.

That's what the Caledonians faced today. Klines grumbled softly to himself. He liked being right, though in this instance his prediction rankled.

The Ghoules had pushed the Caledonians back to the very tip of the Winter Pass, the beginning of the Breakwater Plateau at their backs. The Blademaster and all the soldiers arrayed with him understood the consequences of not holding their line. They knew what waited for them. Still, they stood strong. Out of bravery, yes, though necessity played a role as well.

Declan was right, the Blademaster thought. Kill or be killed.

It was the only choice that they had. He smiled sadly at that. If nothing else, their task today was quite simple.

THE TWO FRIENDS had agreed that if this was the day that they were destined to die, they would accept their fate with good grace. They would attempt to leave this world in a manner that would bring honor to their Duchies and the soldiers fighting with and for them.

With that theme dominating their thoughts, the instant the Ghoule Legions surged toward the Caledonian line, Duke Sten-nivere on the western side of the Winter Pass and Duke Roosarian on the eastern side charged through the gaps between the squares, company after company of cavalry crashing into the Ghoules in a clatter of steel, muscle, flesh, and bone. Hoping to throw the beasts off stride. Maybe even slow the advance, and if they could maintain the momentum of their attack, perhaps even force the beasts back to the north.

The Dukes were pleased with the success of their first charge, riding right through the front rank of Ghoules, the beasts so eager to get at them that they sprinted ahead of the rest of the Legions. That lack of discipline on the part of the Ghoules gave Stennivere and Roosarian the chance to swing back around and charge a second time before the beasts closed with the shield wall.

Each attack had a devastating impact on the beasts, the soldiers trampling the Ghoules too slow to get out of the way, then wreaking havoc with spear and sword, unavoidably striking flesh with every stab and swing. The Dukes wanted to build on that success, ordering their soldiers to loop around and charge a third time, hopefully driving even deeper into the Legions and, if not forcing the beasts to retreat, at least sowing the seeds of uncertainty.

But all good things must come to an end. It was too late. Although the Caledonian cavalry decimated the first few rows of Ghoules, leaving broken and battered beasts strewn about in the mire, rather than seeking to escape, which would be the normal reaction of most any other adversary, the Ghoules instead surged forward, uncaring of the casualties they'd suffered, quickly surrounding the mounted soldiers and pressing in on their flanks.

The Caledonian cavalry couldn't break free. There were too many of the Ghoules and too few soldiers. Worse, Stennivere and Roosarian had lost their most important advantage. Their mobility.

Stuck in place, the Ghoules launching themselves at the mounted soldiers with little concern for their own safety, the Dukes bowed to reality and shifted their formation to several large squares. That adjustment, which took more time than either Duke would have liked and not without a great loss of life, gave them a better chance to defend themselves. Still, they were several hundred yards in front of the main body of the Caledonian Army with no chance of receiving the aid they so desperately needed.

They were fighting for their lives, the Ghoules swarming

around them, seeking any breach that would allow them to get in among the soldiers. And though the Caledonians held strong, the Ghoules finding the squares to be incredibly difficult nuts to crack, those squares inevitably shrank as the beasts dragged soldiers from their saddles, forcing the Caledonians to pack themselves even more tightly together.

Several Magii had ridden out with Duke Stennivere and Duke Roosarian, their goal simple yet difficult. Occupy the Elders so that they couldn't attack the soldiers with the Curse. During those first two charges they enjoyed a great deal of success. When they were encircled, Suzane, Usil, Telly, and all the other Magii with them did everything that they could to help the soldiers find a way to break free from the seething mass of beasts.

Yet it wasn't long before the bulk of their efforts were turned in a different direction, the Magii seeking to prevent the Dark Magic of the Elders from wreaking havoc on the squares, shields crafted of the Talent popping into place to protect against the Curse flying across the battlefield and then disappearing just as quickly, only to appear somewhere else within the roiling mass of soldiers and Ghoules as the Elders shifted the focus of their attacks.

Hoping for the best, though planning for the worst, the Blademaster and Duke Winborne had anticipated just such an eventuality, and they were ready for the change in circumstances. To draw the Ghoules' attention, they released flying wedges on each flank, the soldiers charging out from the shield wall, pushing as deep into the Ghoule Legions as they could, returning to their original positions before risking their flanks.

It was a valiant effort, and it did help to keep the Ghoules off balance, the beasts unable to concentrate on both the cavalry and the infantry at the same time. Despite their success, however, the soldiers forming the shield wall had little chance of reaching the surrounded cavalry, having to return to the

Caledonian line each time they ventured out sooner than they would have liked, fearful of being caught out by the beasts.

As the Blademaster and Duke Winborne urged their soldiers on to even greater exploits, the Caledonians achieved a stalemate with the Ghoules.

Even so, they both knew that their current strivings wouldn't be enough. Eventually the balance they achieved would shift, and not in their favor.

With every passing minute the Ghoules winnowed down the Caledonian Army, more soldiers pulled from the line and from their saddles. The beasts were close to taking control of the battle, and when that happened, the end would not be too far off.

Noorsin and most of the Magii concentrated on defending against attacks by the Elder Ghoules. Even so, the Duchess of Murcia hated the idea of only playing defense with the Talent. So following the strategy that had proven so effective during the last few days, she ordered Cerillia, Irelda, and Cinjin to take the fight to the Elders with their small squads of Magii skilled at killing the beasts versed in the Curse.

The fewer practitioners of the Ghoule Overlord's Dark Magic there were, the better the Caledonians' chances of surviving what they all knew was the deciding battle for the Kingdom.

So far, as the fight raged along the breadth of the Winter Pass, the Magii charged with hunting for Elders had found no lack of targets.

Cerillia and the two Magii with her had already eliminated a fist of Elders, each time taking the servant of the Ghoule Overlord by surprise, usually when the beast was trying to break through another Magus' shield. As fate would have it,

Cerillia's search for prey led her back to Tarin Tentillin, the Captain of the Battersea Guard having what she viewed as an almost uncontrollable need to put himself in danger.

She didn't understand why the Captain continually did this, though she could certainly use it to her advantage, as his lack of fear often led to opportunities that she wouldn't have otherwise.

Cerillia watched as Tarin kept his soldiers moving, driving forward to push back the Ghoules, then retreating for a brief time before advancing once again. The Battersea Guard moved up and down the Caledonian line as a cavalry, helping where needed, preventing any breaches from occurring in the shield wall and, if they did, filling the gap until it could be closed.

Cerillia might not understand the man himself, but she did understand and approve of his logic and strategy. He was smart not to get stuck in a static position. Once that happened, he would cede the momentum to the Ghoules, allowing them to attack at will. With Tarin's approach, the beasts were spending more time and energy preparing for the next attack by the soldiers of the Southern Marches than thinking about attacking.

The Captain's tactics also meant that this was an excellent area to hunt for Elders, several of the servants of the Ghoule Overlord seeking to end the Battersea Guard's dogged resistance, which was hampering the Ghoules' attempts to advance.

Leaving the Magii responsible for protecting the soldiers to their task, Cerillia bided her time, waiting for the perfect opportunity. Or at least a good opportunity, as she wasn't the most patient person, and the urge to attack intensified as the Ghoules pressed harder against the Caledonian line.

When she saw her chance, Cerillia struck faster than a cobra, sending a streak of the Talent over the heads of the soldiers that slammed into an Elder from the side, the beast pushing forward through the mass of Ghoules in search of an unobstructed shot at the shield wall. The Elder wasn't even aware that he had been hit until the Talent burned a hole through his chest, the beast quickly lost in the surging mass of bodies.

"Excellent shot," said Tarin, his sword covered in black blood, the Captain having just led another advance of the Battersea Guard, extending the shield wall to the north to catch the beasts off guard, then retreating before the Ghoules could counterattack. The tactic proved to be particularly effective because the rapid withdrawal often left the Ghoules slightly confused. The archers stationed as the last rank in the line were more than happy to make use of that hesitation, filling the empty space that opened between the Caledonians and the Ghoules with steel-tipped shafts. "Perhaps you could make a try for those beasts just a little farther down the line."

Cerillia looked to where Tarin pointed, identifying three Elders with spheres of Dark Magic spinning atop their staffs, no other Magii in sight. The beasts were intent on widening a breach where the shield wall had weakened, several soldiers in the front rank falling victim to the Ghoules, their replacements struggling to assume their positions. A hole there would allow the Ghoules to pour through, putting the Battersea Guard's entire defense at risk.

"Think nothing of it," replied Cerillia, for just a moment trying to figure out how the Captain, who was always in the thick of the fighting, managed to keep his hair and mustache in perfect order while his armor was dented and battered, scratched and scarred, and covered in Ghoule blood.

Pushing her mental wanderings to the side, the Magus threw a handful of blazing daggers toward the trio of Elders.

Every one of the daggers struck home, the Elders collapsing to the mucky ground and disappearing beneath the clawed feet of the Ghoules or the horses' steel-shod hooves, the battle flowing up and down as Captain Tentillin ordered his soldiers to advance once again, the men and women of the Southern Marches answering his cry with a roar that filled Cerillia with a burst of confidence.

Using that moment to survey the battlefield, she realized that she and the other Magii were doing well, holding off the Elders' attacks and reducing the number of beasts practiced in the Curse at a steady rate.

Still, she understood that it was a numbers game, just as with the Caledonian soldiers and the Ghoule Legions.

There were a great many more Elders than there were Magii. For every Elder killed, two more stepped into the breach. When a Magus died, there was no one to take his or her place.

Eventually the numbers, poor to begin with, would turn against them completely.

THE GHOULES FOUGHT with their customary savagery, never flagging as they slammed again and again against the humans' shield wall, trying to create that one breach that they needed to push past the humans and break out onto the Breakwater Plateau.

Nibli stood at the back of the Ghoule Legions on a small rise in the land that allowed him to look down at the battle rippling back and forth across the Winter Pass. His Ghoules were close to the victory he yearned for, so close that he could taste it. That one fact offered him some small solace and relief from the terrible, throbbing pain that began in his claws and pulsed throughout the rest of his body.

Thanks to the Magus who struck him with the Talent, his claws were twisted and burnt, the flesh crispy and oozing, scorch marks running all the way up his arms and past his elbows. His wounds infuriated him, distracting him from what he needed to do.

The woman had surprised him instead of facing him with the courage that he deserved. Because of her cowardice, he could barely hold his staff, the pain almost too much for him, making it difficult to manage the Curse.

Nibli wanted his revenge. He craved it. He needed it. And he was certain that he would get it.

Soon.

Nibli sensed the fight shifting in his favor despite the ferocity of the humans' defense. They would not be able to stand against him for much longer. His Elders were too strong for the Magii. His Ghoules were too strong for the humans.

The tide was turning. The reign of the Ghoules would begin soon. The humans would be theirs.

That thought brought a sneer and a barked laugh that sent another jolt of pain through him, the laugh transforming into a grimace.

Nibli was about to release the last of his Legions. It would be the Ghoules' final push. The several thousand fighters waiting behind him, desperate to join the fight, would provide that last bit of pressure needed to pierce the humans' shield wall, and then the end would come.

The instant before Nibli issued the command that would doom his enemies, the Elder's senses prickled at the whisper of an almost boundless power drawing near, an uncomfortable foreboding filling him with concern. The General of the Ghoule Legions turned slowly, detecting the disturbance behind them. He felt a crackle of energy in the air, yet he didn't understand what it could be.

His eyes widened in astonishment and a hint of fear when he observed the sparks and streaks of power take shape.

Right behind his waiting Legions, a huge portal of spinning white mist burst into existence and then extended for several hundred yards across the Winter Pass.

Nibli couldn't move, his clawed feet stuck in place, the shock of what he saw too much for him.

He had been expecting his Master. Not this. Never this.

He watched in growing horror as a company of humans marched through the gateway, a few soaring through on the backs of creatures he had only glimpsed on the remotest pinnacles of the Shattered Peaks.

The Ghoules with him turned first in disbelief and then in apprehension, trying to comprehend what was happening, attempting to adjust to this new and unexpected threat as the soldiers advanced toward them at a brisk step, shields locked in front, spears right behind.

Normally Nibli would give little thought to a company of soldiers in his rear, his Ghoules more than capable of managing the hazard. Yet, now he found that his confidence had fled. For the first time since he crossed through the Weir into the lands of men, he felt a touch of fear, watching in horror as streams of energy shot down into his Ghoules from above.

"WE ARE THE BLOOD COMPANY!" shouted Declan, his stentorian voice resonating off the cliffs bordering the battlefield so that all those fighting in the muck could hear, the Sergeant marching right behind the first rank of gladiators, Davin and Lycia next to him. "We stand! We fight! We die!"

"That is what we do!" answered the gladiators, their voices strong, confident. "And we do it well!"

The Blood Company marched through the portal of white mist at a steady pace, accelerating to a sprint as soon as they were through the gate. Bryen had gathered Declan and the gladiators from the mountains to the west when he returned from the Lost Land, having a very specific purpose in mind for his friends.

Declan was glad that he did. He and the gladiators were hungry for a good fight having already cleared the trails bounding the Winter Pass.

Admittedly, it wasn't a very large force that attacked the Ghoules from behind, not even a full company. A hundred warriors in all. But the men and women of the Pit, aided by the three Magii, who, while riding on the backs of their Griffons, used the Talent to blast lanes through the Ghoule ranks, were a force to be reckoned with.

The Blood Company slammed into the wavering and disorganized Ghoules with the savagery of a black dragon, pushing forward, always forward, pursuing the bolts of energy that sent dozens of Ghoules flying through the air, their bodies burnt and broken. Filling the breach the Magii created for them, they expanded the gap with shield, sword, and spear, striving toward the Caledonian line, seeking to leave a trail of death and destruction in their wake as they split the Ghoule host in two.

THE BLADEMASTER WIPED his forearm across his sweaty and bloody brow. He had forsaken his horse because of the press of bodies and now fought on foot with the rest of the Royal Guard. His soldiers fought valiantly, with a courage that couldn't be matched, his troops caught in the middle of some of the hardest and bloodiest fighting of the war and more than holding their own.

Still, he was frustrated just as his soldiers were. They wanted to advance. They didn't want to fight this last battle from the back foot.

He understood the circumstances he and the rest of the Caledonian Army faced. Maintaining a strong defense was the only real option for keeping up the fight, even as that strategy proved to be a losing proposition as the sun moved higher in the sky. Still, he refused to accept his fate.

He held out hope that their fortunes would change. That they could take the fight to the Ghoules rather than ceding the momentum to the beasts.

Just as that desire crossed his mind, massive explosions rocked the rear of the Ghoule Legions, the powerful strikes making the ground tremble, dirt, rock, and broken bodies flying up into the air.

For just a few seconds, the Ghoules opposing him and his soldiers halted their attacks, looking to their rear, unsettled by the earth-shaking blasts.

Jurgen Klines twisted his lips into a cold smile. It was time to make use of the gift he had just received.

"Sergeant Benin!"

"Yes, Blademaster." The Sergeant replied instantly, the soldier never far from the Blademaster's side, his armor and sword covered in black blood, his beard braided to resemble the war axe he held in his hand in perfect condition despite his bloody and harsh struggle of the last few hours.

"The Royal Guard will advance as a unit."

"Our objective, Blademaster?" His Captain's unexpected but greatly welcomed command brought a sparkle to the large Sergeant's eyes. Retreating made him more obstreperous than usual. If he was going to die this day, he wanted it to be while he was fighting in among the Ghoule Legions.

"I wish to speak to the Sergeant of the Blood Company. He is on the other side of the Ghoule host."

Benin grinned, blood streaming down his face from a slice across his forehead, the veteran soldier ignoring the wound. "Yes, Blademaster!"

Benin shouted with the volume of an experienced Sergeant, his booming voice carrying up and down the line.

"Soldiers of the Royal Guard, shift to wedge formation!"

The soldiers responded immediately, taking advantage of the Ghoules' distraction caused by the explosions to the north that ripped through the Ghoule Legions and steadily progressed toward them. Making the necessary adjustments in their alignment, and pleased to do so, the soldiers stood ready.

They understood the importance of today's battle. The necessity of defending. They understood as well that defending wouldn't give them the victory that they needed. The new formation suggested that they were finally getting the chance to do what they wanted to do.

Attack.

"The Royal Guard will advance to the Blood Company!"

A roaring crescendo of voices echoed along the walls of the Winter Pass, the Royal Guard moving as one as they advanced at a steady pace into the Ghoule Legions, their objective several hundred yards to their front and through a mass of confused and indecisive Ghoules.

JERAD PULLED LIGHTLY on his reins, turning his horse toward the north as he ripped his spear free from the shoulder of a Ghoule who had rushed him from his blind side. He had been fighting another of the towering beasts, slamming into the Ghoule with his war horse to knock the beast off balance, then driving his spear into the Ghoule's spine. As had happened to him before, for some inexplicable reason the steel tip had gotten stuck in the vertebra, the collapsing Ghoule threatening to take Jerad's spear to the muck with him.

After several sharp tugs he managed to pull his weapon free just in time, sensing the danger coming at him from behind. He spun his mount around as fast as he could, trying to bring his spear with him so that the charging Ghoule could run right onto the point.

But it wasn't to be. He knew it in his heart. His time had come.

Jerad wasn't fast enough, his spear missing the Ghoule's throat and instead puncturing the beast's muscle just below his collarbone. A painful wound, though certainly not one that would disable a hungry and now very angry Ghoule.

The beast roared in fury, reaching for the spear with his free claw to pull it out. Once that was done, the Ghoule would come for Jerad, who had little chance of drawing his sword in time.

Jerad saw his death in the Ghoule's eyes, disappointed, though understanding that the luck of the battlefield didn't always play in your favor. Even so, that conclusion didn't stop him from trying to pull his sword from the scabbard across his back.

Too little, too late, he realized. The Ghoule removed Jerad's spear with ease and lunged for him again with his blackened steel. Jerad cringed, anticipating the feel of the sharp point piercing his flesh.

Strangely, the Ghoule stopped abruptly, held in place, spear just inches from Jared's chest.

Then he understood why, a sharp spearpoint punching through the beast's neck.

"Why do you put yourself in danger like that?" demanded Dani as she ripped her spear free from the Ghoule's throat, allowing the beast to slump to the ground. "You need to spend more time leading rather than fighting."

"I shouldn't be afraid to do anything I ask you or the other Guards to do," he replied testily, thankful that Dani had saved his life ... again ... and feeling the sting of her words.

"You truly are a fool."

"Why do you say that?" Jerad shouted back, not sure if he should be insulted because he detected a note of concern in her voice.

"No one here doubts your courage. We know you'll always

be with us in a scrap. But you're in command now. The Captain relies on you. We rely on you. We need you to lead more than we need you to fight. Getting yourself killed to demonstrate your bravery won't help any of us. Do you understand?"

"I'm just trying to…"

"Do you understand?" Dani repeated, her voice hard. She nudged her horse next to his and grabbed him by the straps of his leather armor with her free hand, pulling him close, almost taking him off his horse. "If you get yourself killed because you want to play the hero, I will never forgive you. So do you understand?"

"I was just …"

"It's a yes or no question," Dani cut in, her eyes blazing with anger. "Answer it."

"Yes."

"Good."

Jerad shook his head in frustration.

Dani's grin returned. "Now come on. The Protector has returned, and I don't want to miss the fun."

THE MOMENTUM of the battle was balanced on a razor's edge. The arrival of the Blood Company provided a much-needed shock to the fight, the Caledonians seizing the chance to take the initiative, striving to push the Ghoules back toward the north and away from the Breakwater Plateau that beckoned just a few hundred yards behind the shield wall.

Yet even as the Caledonians cut deeply into the Ghoule Legions, the beasts' backbones stiffened. The Blood Company, though it was still pushing forward, seeking to join the Royal Guard and split the Ghoule host in half, was finding each step harder to come by. The gladiators from the Pit had descended once again into a world of blood and gore, slicing, slashing, and lunging with an almost inhuman precision, numb to all that occurred around them, focused solely on breaking the Ghoules, the beasts fighting viciously, giving ground reluctantly.

"Any time now, lad!" shouted Declan.

Bryen nodded as he swooped down right over the combat, Banshee screaming a challenge as her rider sent spear after spear of light out in front of the gladiators, the blasts clearing a track through the massed beasts as they advanced.

Banshee curled back around the Blood Company, Bryen holding the Spear of the Magii in one hand, the blades blindingly bright with the Talent, as he surveyed the destruction he had caused. In just minutes, the Blood Company had cut through the Ghoule ranks with an unrestrained savagery, forcing their way several hundred yards into the Legions.

The Royal Guard was now doing the same, pushing from the other direction, endeavoring to meet the Blood Company in the middle. That was worrisome enough for the Ghoules. Worse, the Battersea Guard was sweeping from the east to the west in front of the Caledonian shield wall, attempting to work its way through the Ghoules and release the cavalry companies still caught within the milling mass of beasts.

All in all, even as their numbers continued to dwindle, the Caledonians had made excellent progress in a very short period of time. Still, Bryen knew that wasn't enough. Declan was right. It was either now or never.

"Take your time," shouted Rafia, the Magus bringing her Griffon close to Banshee, Aislinn coming in on his other side. The Griffons beat their wings at a steady pace so that they remained right next to Banshee as she hovered a hundred feet above the Blood Company.

"And be careful!" ordered Aislinn.

Bryen had explained to Aislinn and Rafia what had happened with respect to the Talent, the Curse, and the

Seventh Stone during his combat on top of the Temple of the Ghoules, understanding how close he had come to losing himself to the Dark Magic of the Lost Land. He took both their admonitions to heart, not wanting to repeat that harrowing experience at the worst possible time.

Opening himself to the Seventh Stone, he allowed the almost limitless supply of the Talent to wash through him, relishing the fiery spark provided by the natural magic of the world. He immediately shifted his focus to the Spear of the Magii, using his weapon as the focal point for what he was about to do next, comprehending now the true value of the Giant-crafted weapon.

With the Spear fully infused with the Talent, the weapon shining as brightly as the still rising sun, Bryen extended the tip of the topmost blade toward the Ghoules swarming beneath him. To begin, he reached out gently with the Seventh Stone, Aislinn's request that sounded more like a warning playing through his mind.

He sensed it at his first tentative touch. A massive pool of darkness. The Curse. The Dark Magic gifted to the Elders. Hundreds of the beasts still alive, still able to manipulate the evil power given to them by the Ghoule Overlord.

That done, Bryen narrowed his focus until he could identify each individual Elder, visualizing the specific points of darkness that flickered across the Winter Pass. As a test, he began with just a few, targeting the Elders engaged with the Blood Company, sending out several hollow threads of the Talent.

The beasts were so consumed with trying to shatter the advancing column, the cords connected without the Elders even knowing. Satisfied that all was as it should be, Bryen began to pull on the Curse within the beasts. Slowly at first, taking in just a little at a time, making sure that all was working as he wanted, because he still had one more step to incorporate within the process.

With the Dark Magic coming through the tubes crafted of the Talent and then into the Spear of the Magii, next he created a link between the bottommost blade to the black diamond that he carried in a small pouch on his hip.

Bryen shouted in triumph, an unusual display of emotion for him. The Curse that he was siphoning from the Elders flowed unrestricted through the Spear, which functioned as a breaker so that he could take in as much of the Curse as he felt comfortable doing with little concern of becoming corrupted, and then back into the most precious artifact of the Lost Land. What had been the source of the Ghoule Overlord's power and the beast's Master as well.

His early success increased his confidence. Now for the final step.

Bryen could work through each Elder individually or in small groups. But rather than drag this out and increase the chances of something going wrong, he chose the most efficient and rapid approach.

The black diamond could pull on all of the corrupted beasts at once. There was no cause to limit it. That goal in mind, he used the Seventh Stone to command the black diamond to take back the tainted power that it had bestowed upon the Elders.

The Curse within the black diamond balked at first, the Dark Magic not wanting to cede control to the Protector. The Curse contained within the tainted artifact even made a final feeble attempt to take Bryen again.

It was wasted effort.

Bryen crushed the attempt with the power of the Seventh Stone. He was too strong now. He was the Seventh Stone and the Seventh Stone was him. There was no distinction between the two. There never would be.

The Curse within the black diamond had no choice but to do as Bryen ordered, the pulsing artifact opening itself to the stream offered to it through the Spear of the Magii. And then, the black diamond reverted to its base nature. Grasping, greedy, the Curse pulled harder, thirsty to reclaim the power it had bestowed upon the Ghoules.

Bryen's approach was both simple and effective, removing the Curse from the Elders and returning it to its original source. But he was doing so much more than that, which became obvious to the Elders as soon as they felt the first painful touch of the incessant, unstoppable pull of the black diamond.

Recognizing the terrifying reality of the peril, the Elders forgot the Magii, the practitioners of the Talent no longer important, and the humans fighting around them. Instead, they searched for the source of this lethal new threat, the Curse draining away from them and with it their strength and their very being.

Following the trail, they located the human with the blazing spear riding on the Griffon, the human who was attacking them in a way that they never thought possible.

The Elders tried to fight the pull, and when they couldn't do that, unable to counter the demand being made upon them by the Curse, they tried to kill the human before the human killed them.

Shards of Dark Magic shot from their staffs, filling the sky with bursts of black energy, yet all to no avail. Aislinn and Rafia protected Bryen as he continued his work, the Dark Magic striking harmlessly against the impenetrable shields of blazing energy that formed around him.

Nibli watched his Elders' useless efforts with a sense of terrified fascination. He knew exactly what the human was doing. He was impressed and horrified at the same time. His Elders stood no chance against the power being employed against them, because it was their own power. It was the Curse itself demanding the return of its insidious gift.

His Elders weakened with each passing second, none of

them having the strength to fight their way past the two Magii guarding the bearer of the black diamond. Nibli could see the hundreds of threads of Dark Magic that connected his Elders to the blazing spear, the Dark Magic surging through the air, returning to the artifact.

Then the first Elder fell dead to the ground, followed by the next. One more. Then three collapsed. A dozen. Twenty more. Their very essences ripped free with the Curse and leaving behind nothing but mummified shells.

Nibli needed to stop the human. Somehow. Before nothing remained of his Elders. But he realized in a moment that combined an uncommon clarity with a frantic horror that there was nothing that he could do.

He recognized the bearer of the black diamond now. The human they had hunted for so long. The Protector who had become the Seventh Stone.

If the Seventh Stone was here and had gained control over the black diamond, that could mean only one thing.

The Ghoule Overlord was dead.

The Curse now served the Protector.

That was the last thought that Nibli ever had. He felt the pull of the black diamond now, the power of the Ghoule artifact reaching for him, calling to the Curse that was so much a part of him, drawing the Curse from him, slowly at first, then faster and faster, not giving him a chance to fight back, until his very being went with it. His eyes closing, Nibli, the Ghoule Overlord's general, slumped to the ground, his body a withered husk.

With Nibli's passing, it was done. Bryen broke the connection between the Seventh Stone and the black diamond, the Ghoule artifact steadily pulsing a deep black, the jewel containing all of the Dark Magic that had once ruled in the Lost Land, that had transformed the people who had lived there into the Ghoules, that had made the beasts into a tool for its own purposes.

The Curse of the Lost Land was free no more. Bryen had caged it.

Even so, several thousand Ghoules still remained in the Winter Pass. A formidable host.

Yet the beasts now fought at a distinct disadvantage, because without their Elders, the Ghoules had no way to stand against the Talent.

The Magii, having watched in wonder as Bryen manipulated the black diamond, didn't waste a second now that the Elders had fallen. Streams of energy, blazing daggers and spears, lightning striking down from a clear sky, slammed into the Ghoule Legions, sending a ripple of fear through the beasts.

The Magii accelerated their attack, refusing to let up, the strength of their assault forcing the Ghoules to take a step back to the north. Bolstered by the success of the Magii, the Caledonians redoubled their efforts, continuing to advance, sending another distressing ripple through the Legions.

Not strong enough to stand against the push, the Ghoules took another step to the north. Then a few more. And still the Talent battered the helpless beasts, the Ghoules unable to bear the brunt of the Magii's attack, the white-hot energy burning through flesh and bone.

The Caledonians rushed into the gaps created every time the natural power of the world struck, intensifying the pressure, the Ghoule host shuddering. Almost as one the thousands of beasts took another few steps toward the north, away from the Magii's deadly onslaught. Then several more steps until the beasts no longer tried to stand against the Caledonians, the momentum shifting as if a dam had crumbled.

Sensing the change, Duchess Stelekel, Duke Winborne, and

the Blademaster ordered their soldiers forward, the Caledonians smashing into the disorganized and disheartened beasts.

No longer able to hold back the storm, the beasts did something that the Caledonians had never seen nor ever expected. The Ghoules of the Lost Land, the monsters of myth made flesh, fled.

The Ghoule invasion of Caledonia had come to an end.

The hunters had become the hunted.

29

———

A FRESH START

Night had fallen in the Winter Pass, a quiet finally settling after a full day of battle, although the fighting still continued farther up the canyon. When the Elders fell, and the Ghoule Legions broke, the pursuit had begun.

It wasn't a mad rush. Noorsin coordinated the hunt with the various Guards that made up the Caledonian Army, assigning each one specific tasks and areas of responsibility. The Caledonians would be hunting the beasts for quite some time, the goal now to keep them bottled up in the Shattered Peaks, the Magii helping to finish the Ghoules if the usually harsh winter that was only a few months away didn't get them first.

Neither Aislinn nor Bryen had any doubts that the work would take years. Although the Caledonians had proven victorious in what some were already calling the Second Ghoule War, the challenge of digging the beasts out of the mountains would continue.

Yet that concern was not top of mind as they stared down at the daggerlike gap, Banshee curled up behind them, the Griffon having taken them to a mountain summit where they could escape the rush of events below them at least for a few hours.

"What did you do with the black diamond?"

"I couldn't destroy it," Bryen replied, his arm around Aislinn's shoulders, pulling her close. "Even with the Seventh Stone and the Spear of the Magii, I couldn't do it."

"So you still have it?"

"For now."

"What are you going to do with it?" Aislinn asked again.

"Probably put it somewhere safe."

"There's somewhere safe for an artifact like that one?"

"Maybe," Bryen replied uncertainly though hopefully. "I need to talk with Rafia first."

"Will you tell me where once you figure it out?" asked Aislinn with a familiar nudge.

"Perhaps."

Aislinn nudged Bryen even harder, almost knocking him on his side and eliciting a laugh from him.

"You don't like not knowing what you don't know," said Bryen, using a phrase that he had learned from Noorsin Stelekel that had become a staple of his vocabulary.

"You're right, I don't," Aislinn admitted, deciding to raise the topic that was top of mind for her. She knew what she wanted, and she needed to know what he wanted, even as she worried that what he wanted wasn't what she wanted. "So what are you going to do? You rebuilt the Weir, and because of that the Ghoules won't be able to invade again. The Ghoules who fled will be hunted and killed, and the Magii will make sure the beasts can't escape the Shattered Peaks. You've given everything Caledonia has asked of you. The Kingdom no longer has any hold on you. You're free."

That last part wasn't entirely true, thought Bryen, although he didn't say anything to correct Aislinn. He was free. No longer a slave. No longer beholden to a Kingdom that had treated him poorly.

A Caledonian did, however, have a hold on him, and because of that he wasn't sure how she would react when he told her what he had planned.

He knew how he felt about the Lady Winborne, and he believed that he knew how Aislinn felt about him. But he also understood how seriously she took her responsibilities, and he didn't feel as if he could or should get in the way of that. After all, she was the heir to the Southern Marches.

He would always be her Protector, even though she didn't need him to be, but now he needed to do something for himself.

Aislinn watched the emotions play across his face, and then it came to her as she remembered their earlier conversations.

"The Caledonian Territories," she murmured. "I should have known."

Bryen nodded with a gentle smile. "I've done what was required of me here. Even after all that, after all that's happened, it still doesn't feel like it's my home."

"You want a fresh start."

"Yes. Where I don't have a history. Where people don't know me as the Volkun. Where I can build a new life. Where I can do what I want to do."

"That makes sense," Aislinn admitted, a ball of fear settling in her stomach, making her feel slightly queasy, worried about her place in that future.

Bryen sensed what was going on in Aislinn's mind, the fear, the uncertainty. To cut it off before it took hold, Bryen smiled, then turned toward her, reaching for her, pulling her into his arms.

For just a second, Aislinn thought that he was about to kiss her. Instead he leaned in close, his lips just brushing hers before pulling back.

"I do want to go to the Caledonian Territories, but I don't want to go alone. I don't want to go without you."

"Is that a request?" Aislinn asked with a broad smile, her initial fear fading away, replaced by a pleasure that felt much like the Talent surging through her, warming her from head to toe.

"It's a proposal," replied Bryen.

Aislinn leaned into Bryen, giving him a soft kiss.

"So a new adventure?"

"Only if you'll join me."

Aislinn pulled back at that, understanding the sacrifice he was willing to make for her. She appreciated the gesture, but it wasn't necessary. She had thought about this quite a lot after their last conversation. She understood what her Protector needed, what they needed. Then she nodded.

"Yes, I think it's time for a new adventure."

"To the Territories?" Bryen asked, his relief almost palpable.

"To the Territories."

THE END

Keep reading for the first two chapters of *Death on the Burnt Ocean*, Book I of my new series *The Tales of the Territories*.

BONUS MATERIAL

If you really enjoyed this story, I need you to do me a HUGE favor – please follow me on Amazon and BookBub. And if you have a few minutes, consider writing a review.

Keep reading for the first two chapters of *Death on the Burnt Ocean*, Book 1 of my new series *The Tales of the Territories*. Available at PeterWachtBooks.com or Amazon.

PETER WACHT

DEATH
ON THE
BURNT
OCEAN

1

THE
TALES OF THE TERRITORIES

Death on the Burnt Ocean
By Peter Wacht

Book 1 of The Tales of the Territories

This book is a work of fiction. Names, characters, places, and incidents are the product of the author's imagination or are used fictitiously. Any resemblance to actual events, locales, or persons, living or dead, is coincidental.

Copyright 2023 © by Peter Wacht

Cover design by Ebooklaunch.com

All rights reserved. In accordance with the U.S. Copyright Act of 1976, the scanning, uploading, and electronic sharing of any part of this book without the permission of the publisher constitute unlawful piracy and theft of the author's intellectual property.

Published in the United States by Kestrel Media Group LLC.

ISBN: 978-1-950236-32-9

eBook ISBN: 978-1-950236-33-6

Library of Congress Control Number: 2022923775

 Created with Vellum

SETTING THE STAGE

The Tales of the Territories continue the adventures of Bryen Keldragan and Aislinn Winborne as they travel across the Burnt Ocean to the Territories, what will eventually become the Kingdoms of *The Sylvan Chronicles*.

The events occur more than one thousand years before the happenings in *The Sylvan Chronicles* and take place in the lands far to the west of Caledonia that have been opened for colonization thanks to territorial grants from the deceased King Corinthus Beleron. There they will take on new challenges, make new friends and enemies, and continue to battle those who have turned to the Curse.

In the Territories, sometimes called New Caledonia, as in the other realms, the ability to use the Talent sets apart the person gifted with this unique skill. But being able to use the Talent is only part of the dynamic. For if a Magus chooses to follow a darker path, the Talent becomes the Curse.

Both *The Sylvan Chronicles* and *The Tales of Caledonia* are a part of the larger world of *The Realms of the Talent and the Curse*.

CHAPTER ONE
A DISAPPOINTING HUNT

"Can't you run faster than that, soldier!" The man standing guard at the entrance to the tower, a very large hammer held in his hand, had to bend down to fit through the doorway without banging his head. He was glad to be free of the confining space as he stepped out onto the grass. He didn't like being locked away from the outside and the fresh air. It made him edgy. "You need to lay off the ale, Bertie. It's all going to your gut."

Bertie huffed and puffed his way up the slope, the once musclebound figure, now going a bit soft around the edges, no more than a shadow in the descending grey mist. For just a second, the man by the door, the hilt of his sword peeking out above his shoulder, thought that Bertie was carrying three large sacks across his broad shoulders. It wasn't until the soldier turned farmer was less than a dozen yards away that the large figure in the doorway grinned, finally able to pick out what Bertie was hauling.

"You try carrying three children up that wretched slope, Duff," muttered Bertie. He struggled to catch his breath as he let down the two daughters who had been slipping from their perches as he sprinted up the hill. He kept the youngest, a boy no more than two years old with his hands twisted tightly in his father's hair, on his shoulders as he ducked inside. "Is Winnie here?"

"She is," Duff replied, giving Bertie a friendly slap across his back for his effort as the man passed by him, glad that he had made it. "Almost everyone else from the village is here as well."

"Not all?" asked Bertie. He turned back through the entryway, the son on his shoulders pulling with greater vigor on his hair, obviously frightened as the thin wisps of white began to darken to a thicker grey. Bertie carefully extricated what few strands he had left on his head from his son's tight grasp. It wouldn't be long now, so they would need to be quick. "Do we need to go back out?"

Duff smiled, nodding his thanks for Bertie's generous, likely suicidal, offer. Bertie was a brave man. Duff had seen it with his own eyes more times than he could count. The soldier in Bertie never really left, just as had been the case for him and so many others in the village. But there was a key difference between them now.

Bertie had a young family. Duff didn't. If anyone went back out into the encroaching fog, it would be him. Only him.

"We should be all right," replied Duff, giving Bertie a gentle nudge so that he would follow his children into the tower. "Why don't you go find Winnie and see what kind of trouble those twins of yours have already gotten into."

Bertie snorted at that. "You've got that right. Nothing but headaches from sunup to sundown. That's why I spend so much time in the fields."

Duff chuckled, hearing the love in his former corporal's voice. With Bertie and his family now safely within the stone broch, Duff turned his gaze back to the valley that stretched out below him. The valley that was disappearing slowly before his eyes beneath a smothering blanket of thick fog.

No, it wouldn't be long now, Duff mused. He chafed at the

circumstances he and the other Highlanders had to deal with, yet they had no choice. Another night hiding in the fortified tower. An occurrence that was becoming all too frequent. How long they would be locked away was anyone's guess.

Just the thought of it was making him itch. This was no way to live. He had journeyed across the Burnt Ocean from Caledonia for the freedom and opportunity that could be had in the Territories. Not to be shut away cowering in fear whenever the fog descended.

He studied the encroaching grey mist as he had done so many times before. It looked no different than the fog he had played hide and seek in as a child while growing up near Roo's Nest. But it was.

Because this fog didn't come off the ocean. Although the Sea of Mist was just a few leagues to the east, this gloom drifted down from the north, no doubt having started out in the Wyld. It then followed the coast through the Northern Peaks, all the way across the Northern Steppe, finally settling here into the northeastern Highlands.

It was an unnatural gloom. Heavy, deadening, and with a much too light touch of dewy moisture compared to what you would expect from a mist coming off the sea. The sun couldn't brighten the haze once it fixed in place, and with that suffocating fog came a sense of palpable evil lurking within, an evil with very sharp claws.

Duff wasn't a superstitious man by nature, not after all that he had seen fighting in Caledonia and beyond his Kingdom's borders. There was little that frightened him, and almost nothing that could take him by surprise, because he had seen it all before.

At first he had scoffed at the stories that he had heard from farther north when the fog had first appeared more than a year before. More like nightmares, actually, likely told by those knee deep in their cups.

He began to believe when that fog made its way into the Highlands with a startling regularity. The fog that some had begun to call the Murk, claiming that it was actually an extension of the terrifying gloom that covered the wild land far to the northeast.

He knew for certain that the tales were true when he glimpsed the hazy figures for himself, those nightmares becoming flesh and blood. Tall and lanky, the monsters in the mist were no more than vague shapes. No one in the Highlands had ever gotten a good look at one. And if they had, it had been right before they had become one of the creature's many victims, and they certainly weren't in a position to reveal their attackers' secrets.

Although not well seen, these monsters were well known. These beasts radiated a sense of menace. A sense that they cared little for life. That they cared only for taking it.

The Wraiths. So named by a trader who had made the long journey from the Wyld and explained that's what those poor souls living in the coastal cities just south of the Murk called them. The monsters that hunted in the fog. The monsters that couldn't be seen unless they wanted to be seen. The monsters that couldn't be heard. The monsters that couldn't be killed.

They were silent assassins, the remains of their bloody work visible once the gloom drifted back to the north. No one caught out in the open when the fog settled over the land had yet survived. The only way to avoid a gruesome and terrifying end was to find a strong, defensible shelter before the thick grey tendrils blinded you.

A shelter like the broch that Duff stood in front of. When the Murk had first appeared, a delegation of Highlanders led by Duff had gone to see the Governor of the Territory. Appointed through a grant given by then King Corinthus Beleron, Torsten Sharperson, a younger brother of the Duke of Sharston, had listened to their entreaties with a smile on his face. He had spoken the appropriate words of support. He had offered his condolences for the people murdered by whatever creatures came with the fog.

The callow lord had assured the people for whom he was responsible, and from whom he collected taxes, that he would study the threat and do what was needed to protect against this new, unforeseen danger. That study apparently was still ongoing, as Duff and the others had seen or heard nothing more from their supposed lord since, or at least that's what the tax collectors said because the Highland Guard was nowhere to be found and the greedy bastards appeared with greater frequency than the Murk and they sought more than just a pound of flesh.

It had been a wasted effort, Duff knew. Governor Sharperson was little more than a thief in a lord's clothing.

Duff stopped himself, his mind always going down a road better left untraveled when he considered how badly the Governor had failed his people. Besides, he was giving thieves a bad name. Most of the thieves he knew at least had some sense of honor, a set of rules they played by.

Torsten Sharperson made up his own rules as he went along, changing them whenever the whim or necessity took him. In reality, he was no different than any of the other nobles granted Territories by Corinthus Beleron.

These lords and ladies who played as Governors in New Caledonia operated by one simple rule. What's mine is mine, and what's yours should be mine.

Just thinking about the Highland Governor's response, or rather the lack thereof, made Duff's blood boil. Several dozen people murdered in just the past year by these Wraiths, and nothing done about it. Not a single thing.

"Are they here yet?"

Duff turned toward the worried, crinkled face of Martin, the blacksmith who lived at the edge of the village and served the surrounding region. He had gathered his family and gotten to the fortified tower at the first signs of the fog, the bell atop the broch ringing loudly and echoing off the surrounding peaks to warn those living in the valley of the rapidly approaching threat. Worriedly, Martin had yet to see any sign of his sister or her family, who lived farther up the slopes to the northeast, their goats and sheep enjoying the grass at the higher elevation.

"No, not yet. But I'm sure they'll be here soon. They always make it."

Martin nodded, taking a deep breath to calm himself. He, too, was a former soldier in the Royal Guard. The idea of a fight never fazed him. He would take on any man or beast without a thought to protect his family. Even though he knew just as Duff did that you couldn't fight the monsters that stalked the fog. Not with any hope of surviving.

In the Murk, for all intents and purposes you were blind, unable to see more than a few feet in any direction in the billowing grey. The Wraiths could hear you. The Wraiths could see you. But you couldn't see them and often you didn't hear them until their steel or claws slid into your flesh. Because the Wraiths moved as if they were a part of the fog while you stumbled about.

The Wraiths were meant to be there. The Highlanders weren't.

If Martin had to enter the fog to look for his sister and her family, he would without a second thought. But he wouldn't be marching toward a combat. He would be going to his death. There was no good way to defend yourself if you couldn't see what you were fighting.

The Highlanders had learned that quickly, and they had taken what action they could to protect themselves even faster. Not caring to wait for help from a Governor who seemed to have little interest in helping them if he couldn't help himself at the same time, they modeled their defense on a series of small fortresses that Duff had seen while serving near the Trench, building more than a dozen brochs in the northeastern High-lands, each roundhouse tower situated in the center of the larger Highland communities.

Each broch had a single entrance with a several-foot-thick oak door wrapped in steel, hinges on the inside with slots for three steel bars to be set in place once the door was locked. The antechamber narrowed to half the size of the doorway the farther you walked in so that a broad man had to turn to the side to walk through, an essential modification to ensure the safety of those taking refuge in the tower.

If somehow the creatures of the Murk broke through the door, one soldier could easily hold the narrow gap. To make the passage even more lethal, slits in the wall on each side allowed for spears and pikes to be thrust through, making the entryway a death trap.

Once past the entrance, a spiral staircase wound its way between the inner and outer walls, connecting the galleries on each level that served as temporary shelters and storerooms. Each broch was eighty feet in diameter and one hundred feet in height, the walls always ten feet thick. Halfway up the towers there were narrow slits for archers, the spaces so small that not even a child could climb through them.

On top of the tower was a large byre, the fire used to signal other brochs before the Murk consumed the flames. More important was the massive bell that could be heard for leagues around and was the first warning that the creatures lurking in the mist approached.

There was also space for archers to fire and a pile of large rocks that could be dropped from the parapet. Useful defenses against more conventional foes. Not so the Wraiths.

Few Highlanders remained atop the parapet when the fog came in, the creatures having an unnatural ability to scale the stone with their clawed feet and hands. When the bell sounded the inhabitants of the broch usually closed the thick shutters and ensured that the door that let out onto the roof, designed just like the main entrance below, was bolted and guarded.

Then they waited. For however long it took. The main entrance wouldn't be opened again until the fog cleared.

"Sally!" yelled Martin. "Hurry!"

The blacksmith had caught the faint movement in the thickening fog, his sister appearing out of the grey. She ran up the slope as fast as she could while holding onto the hands of two of her children, almost dragging them behind her across the large green that surrounded the tower because they were struggling to keep up with their mother. Martin ran out and picked up both children, hustling them through the door.

Benyen, her husband, came right behind her, a small child under each arm like he was carrying sacks of wheat. The boy and girl were laughing and giggling, obviously enjoying the ride, not seeing their father's ashen face and the spark of fear behind his eyes.

"They're already out there," he whispered.

"How could you tell?" asked Duff. Because of their ability to move without being seen and without making a sound, the Wraiths usually couldn't be identified in the Murk unless they wanted to be. When they wanted you to know that they were watching. That they were waiting to kill you.

"I could feel them," Benyen replied.

Duff nodded, not questioning his friend's explanation. He was a former tracker in the Royal Guard. He had explained to Duff once while they shared an ale in the only tavern in this small village that much of what he did as a tracker wasn't based on what he saw or heard, but rather on what he felt.

Admittedly, they were both quite sloshed at the time, but Duff had never been a tracker, so he was in no position to dispute his friend's answer. And he had yet to come up against an instance when Benyen's feeling hadn't been right on target, both in Caledonia and here in the Highlands.

"Where's Mari?" asked Sally, standing in the doorway, fear and desperation coloring her voice for her oldest daughter.

"I thought she was here with you," said Benyen. "You didn't bring her from the house?"

"I thought she was with you," countered Sally, a look of terror spreading across her face.

"Where was she before the bell rang?" asked Duff.

"She was tending to the goats along the ridge to the northeast," said Benyen.

A sick feeling settled in the pit of Duff's stomach. That was the direction from which the fog had come. From the direction it always came. The retired sergeant cursed silently.

"You all get inside. I'll get her."

"I'll go with you," said Benyen. "I can ..."

"You can move faster than I can and more quietly," continued Duff, taking in his friend's slim frame that seemed to allow him to move with a speed and grace that he had only seen one other time, several years before.

Duff hadn't wanted to attend the gladiatorial games in Tintagel. If truth be told, he had seen enough blood and gore for a lifetime and had no desire to see any more.

Even so, he didn't want to explain that to his friends. They were quite intent on taking in the spectacle, so in the end he acquiesced to their demand.

Strangely, when it was done, he had valued the experience. Not for the unnecessary violence and slaughter. No, that had sickened him. Rather it had given him the chance to watch the Volkun fight. The Wolf. The greatest gladiator in the land, and much to his surprise a young man at least a decade younger than he was who exhibited the seasoning and savvy of a hardened soldier.

It was an experience that he would never forget, and it had

confirmed for him that it was time for him to move on, to leave Caledonia and the army and make a new life for himself. Someplace where he could avoid the fighting that, although he excelled at it, he had come to dread. The fighting that unfortunately seemed to have followed him across the Burnt Ocean to his new home in the Highlands.

"But I don't have a family," Duff finished with a strong hand on Benyen's shoulder. "You do."

"She's my oldest daughter, Duff. I can't leave her out there."

Duff gripped Benyen's shoulder a bit more strongly, hoping that his bruising grip infused a sense of confidence within his friend, making sure that he caught Benyen's eyes and kept them on his own. "You're not leaving her. I'm going to get her."

Benyen stared at his former sergeant for several seconds. He had known Duff ever since he had joined the Royal Guard. Usually his sergeant had a smile on his face. When there wasn't, then you knew that there was going to be trouble. And you never wanted to get into trouble with Duff.

Duff wasn't smiling now. His hard expression just made the man more frightening than he already was, inadvertently aided by the wound that he had taken across his scalp that extended from the back of his head around the left side to just beneath his jaw. The hair had never grown back where he had been sliced open, so Duff kept his head shaved.

Thanks to the Magus who healed him, the wound was just a very thin, white scar rather than a jagged patch of flesh. It still proved to be unsettling to look at, however, Benyen always wondering how his friend had survived such an injury. Duff had told him once that it was because he had such a hard head. After getting to know Duff, Benyen had believed him.

It was because of that wound that Benyen finally nodded, then stepped back. Duff was the toughest man he knew. He would bring Mari safely to the broch or he would die trying.

Duff returned the nod, then stepped out into the billowing fog.

"Tommie!"

"Yes, Sergeant!" replied a slim woman wearing spectacles. She, too, had served in the Royal Guard with Duff along with many of the other men and women in this Highland settlement. Archer by trade, some said that she could hit an ant at one hundred yards. After watching her in a skirmish against a band of brigands, no one was willing to challenge that assumption.

"Is that the last?"

Tommie looked at the paper she carried, running through the list of the families quickly. "Yes, Sergeant. That's the last."

Duff nodded, then started walking down the slope toward the northeast, calling over his shoulder, "Lock it up."

"But Sergeant ..."

Tommie never had a chance to complete her protest, the fog swallowing Duff after he had taken only a dozen steps. Growling in irritation, Tommie stepped back and then called to Benyen and Martin for help. Together, the three of them pushed the heavy steel door in place, locking it, then settling the three bars in the brackets across the oak and steel.

Turning away and heading up the spiral staircase that led toward the balustrade, Tommie wanted to check the door that led to the roof to make sure that it was just as tightly sealed. As she did so, she wished Duff well and hoped that she would see her sergeant again.

Even so, Tommie was a practical woman. She refused to allow her hopes to get too high. Few ever survived the Murk, especially on their own. To be caught in the fog was a death sentence.

Likely even for Duff. A man who should have been dead, but apparently couldn't be killed.

~

Why didn't I follow my brother when I had the chance, Duff wondered as he slowly, ever so slowly, navigated down a steep, narrow path that led to the long grass along the cliffs that Benyen's goats preferred. He could barely see where he was walking, moving more by memory and touch than sight as the grey mist swirled around him.

His brother had received a grant from the King to settle the Western Isle, which was just off the coast of the Ferranagh Territory and on the other side of the continent. Maybe that's why he hadn't made it out there yet.

It had been a long trip across the Burnt Ocean. Duff had gotten tired of the storms that seemed to strike every other day, sending the merchant vessel dipping into the troughs and then surging over powerful crests, much to his displeasure his stomach mimicking the motion of the ship. That and those massive wakes that he had spied from the crow's nest, thankfully those creatures swimming through the sea not interested in his ship, because if they had been he knew the likely result.

Because of all that, when he landed in Ballinasloe, he had no desire to get back on the water. Instead, he had decided to visit with several of his former soldiers who had settled in the northeastern Highlands. He had thought that he would only be in this rugged, beautiful land for a few weeks at most, the urge to leave Caledonia, the desire to see more of the Territories, pushing him farther west.

Yet in just a few days that desire to move on had gone quiet. He had been in the Highlands for almost five years now.

He liked it here. He liked being with his friends. And he couldn't bring himself to leave in part because of the Murk.

When that cursed fog rolled in, and with it the terrors that it hid, he couldn't make himself go even though it was the smart thing to do. Of course, Duff had never been accused of being too smart. He had been accused of being too stubborn, of failing to give his superiors the respect that they believed they deserved, of offering unwanted opinions, of refusing to accept orders from fools ... and of several other faults that he tended to ignore or forget when doing so was convenient. But he had never been accused of being too smart.

And he had never been accused of running from a fight. In consequence, he was still here with his friends, making a good living as a hunter and trapper, and helping out whenever they needed it, whether with the flocks or the crops.

Or wayward children caught out in the fog.

He stopped again, just as he stopped every few steps, spending more time listening than moving, seeking any sign, no matter how small, that a Wraith might be near. Because the Wraiths were always near when the Murk came.

About to begin his downward journey again, Duff heard a scrape maybe ten feet to his left. The noise sent a shiver down his spine. He kept one foot above the ground, not wanting to give himself away. Not wanting to cede the advantage of surprise just yet.

He had his sword strapped to his back and several large knives on each thigh. He liked to be prepared for anything. But his weapon of choice was the large hammer that the fingers of his right hand gripped almost delicately. The thick wooden handle tapered to the steel head, a weapon and implement that many a blacksmith could barely lift much less swing with any effectiveness. In his hands, however, the steel felt right. As if it was meant to be there and was simply an extension of his arm.

A faint shadow coming down the gentle slope drifted toward him. He could see nothing from the knees up. He pulled back his arm, ready to strike, his focus solely on the threat that approached. His shallow breaths thundered in his ears. A cold sweat ran down his back. Then a soft bleat released the tension that had been building up within him, and he had to fight not to laugh with relief.

A goat trod carefully down the rocks, rubbing against his leg in welcome as he passed. Duff closed his eyes in thanks for just a second. At least he knew that he was close. With this fog, in addition to worrying about the Wraiths, he feared that he might walk right off a ledge. Wanting to avoid that possibility, he allowed the goat to precede him, showing him the way, and hoping that the animal's movement would mask his own approach.

Duff continued along the trail. Slowly. Carefully. Vigilant with each step. Doing all that he could to ensure that he didn't make a sound.

Once, he thought he saw a large shape coming toward him from his right side. That froze him in place. But he couldn't even be sure that he had seen what he had thought he had seen, the figure passing through the fog so swiftly.

Then another shadow appeared, this one feeling more substantial. The tall shadow remained there above him on the crest of the hill. Not moving. Not making a sound.

Watching.

Waiting.

Hunting.

Duff wasn't certain that the shadow was a Wraith. Nevertheless, he couldn't be certain that it wasn't, and he had no desire to find out. He remained where he was even as his knees began to ache, then throb, the wear and tear of decades of military service catching up to him at the absolute worst time. He ignored the pain, knowing that it was nothing compared to what it would feel like to have a Wraith's knife slice across his throat.

Now he knew what it felt like to be hunted, and he would be the first to admit that he hated the feeling. He wasn't afraid to fight a Wraith. It's just that if he was going to combat one of these monsters, he wanted to be able to see the creature so that he could have at least some possibility of success.

In the Murk, all the advantages played to the Wraiths. If he were found, he was nothing more than a sitting duck to be slaughtered at a Wraith's convenience.

With those negative thoughts taking up residence in his mind, he stayed perfectly still, barely breathing, his eyes fixated on the shadow in the mist that was no more than a dozen feet away. As the minutes passed agonizingly slowly, he realized that he'd have little chance of getting a blow in with his hammer.

If the shape in the fog was indeed a creature of the Murk, then the Wraith would be on him before he could even take a step with his rickety knees. His best chance was to grab a dagger from a sheath on his thigh and hope that the Wraith slipped coming down the slope and fell on him. That certainly wasn't a good way to win a combat, but it might be the only way in his current circumstances.

Several minutes more passed before his patience was finally rewarded. The figure in the fog either moved away, disappeared, or was never there to begin with.

Duff didn't care. The only reason he had been able to see the shape in the first place was because he was near the coast and a strong breeze off the Sea of Mist had thinned out the usually dense mist. Still, he waited several more minutes before finally pushing himself forward, his aching knees screaming in protest.

He ignored the pain, working out the stiffness as he continued farther down the trail, step by slow step. Every so often another soft bleat sounded to either side, confirming that Duff was moving in the right direction. As he stopped every few feet, the mist caressing him as he listened for anything that might suggest that a Wraith was near, his thoughts turned to how to find Mari in the fog. He should have given that a great deal more thought before he left the safety of the broch.

Her father had been an excellent soldier. A good fighter. Smart. Creative. Disciplined. Always prepared. The last suggested to Duff that Benyen probably had taught all his children what to do if they were ever caught out in the fog.

Bringing a mental map of Benyen's property along the cliffs to mind, Duff thought of the most likely place where he would have taught his children to go. Somewhere Benyen would have a camouflaged shelter or a place to hide.

Then he had it. Benyen had shown him just a few months before while they were clearing a patch of ground so that he could expand his garden. There was a cut along the cliff that led down to a small cave. If you didn't know what you were looking for, you would walk right past the trail to get there.

Duff continued down the path in that direction, moving no faster than his grandmother, who had two bad hips, would have, stopping and listening for a minute or more after taking only two or three steps. It was a slow process, nerve-wracking, but so far, so good. No more menacing shapes appeared in the fog, and in just a few minutes the cut between two large boulders, one resting right in front of the other, appeared in front of him.

He waited several minutes before disappearing between the rocks, worried that a Wraith might be watching him. The monsters in the mist were smart. They were also cunning. He didn't want to lead one of the creatures toward Mari if she was hiding here.

Yet, it seemed that his caution was unnecessary. No sound. No movement. There was nothing to suggest that he had anything to worry about.

Duff continued down the narrow trail, walking very carefully, not wanting to make a noise with all of the loose rock beneath his feet. When he finally reached the end of the path, the dark mouth of the cave opening before him, he stopped sooner than he wanted to.

Something wasn't right. He could feel it immediately. There was a presence ahead of him that shouldn't be there.

An unexpected though welcome flash of sunlight that broke through the fog and lit the first few feet of the entrance to the cave confirmed it for him.

For just the blink of an eye, before the fog blocked the sun once again, Duff caught sight of a tall figure standing just a few feet inside the grotto. The incredibly brief glimpse still gave him a good look at the creatures who were terrorizing the Highlands when the Murk came in from the north, or at least as good as he was going to get with the Wraith's back turned.

Unnaturally tall and thin, the Wraith wore what Duff took to be a whitish grey leather armor, its unprotected flesh shifting between shades of white and grey. He understood now how the creatures hid so well in the fog. Their natural coloring allowed them to blend in perfectly.

What really drew his eye were the weapons that the Wraith held between his exceedingly long clawed fingers. He had never seen anything like it before, a three-foot-long rod with a grip in the center, half-crescent blades on each end curling in opposite directions. It was as if two long daggers had been melded together at the handle.

Nasty pieces of work and certainly to be avoided. Then Duff realized that he wouldn't be able to. The Wraith had taken another step deeper into the cave.

Thankfully, the Wraith hadn't sensed that Duff was only a few feet behind him, the creature's attention focused on the back of the hollow. That could mean only one thing.

When the Wraith took another silent step deeper into the darkness, Duff struck.

On silent feet of his own, he rushed toward the Wraith, swinging his hammer with destructive accuracy, the metal head crushing the creature's right knee. The debilitating injury did nothing more than elicit a hiss of pain from the Wraith, the creature tottering because of the blow though not falling to the ground. At the same time the injured Wraith swung his twin-bladed weapon behind him, hoping to catch Duff unprepared.

The Sergeant suspected that the Wraith would make such a move. It's what he would have done in his place. That's why he was able to avoid the steel.

He was ready, knocking the blind swing away with his hammer. Before the Wraith could turn fully, Duff pulled a dagger from the sheath on his thigh and drove it into the back of the creature's other knee. He had thought about trying for the Wraith's lower back, then decided against it, not knowing if such a strike would kill the creature because of his armor. Therefore, in his opinion, better to disable the Wraith, which finally collapsed to his knees on the rocky ground.

Duff swung one more time with his hammer, not wanting to miss such a good opportunity. The metal struck true, slamming into the Wraith's head and sending him to the dirt.

"Mari!" Duff hissed as quietly as he could.

In just a heartbeat, she was there right in front of him, Benyen's oldest daughter, all of ten years old, ready to defend herself with a dagger in her hand.

"Are you all right?" Duff whispered, kneeling down and hugging the young girl to him.

"Yes, Uncle Duff," she mumbled into his shoulder, her voice calm. She appeared to be less upset about being out in the fog than he was.

"Good. Then let's go."

Duff pushed himself to his feet, his knees protesting the entire time. He was about to head back outside the cave, Mari's hand in his own, when a tall, strangely thin figure that was barely more than a shadow coalesced out of the grey haze.

The Wraith stood in the entrance to the cave, Duff having a hard time picking out the creature, the fog having thickened during his fight with the now wounded, hopefully dead, creature. He did see the Wraith blocking their way turn his head to his left, taking in the crumpled form of his brethren.

"Mari, get behind me," Duff ordered gently.

Mari complied quickly, her eyes widening in terror as the Wraith took a few more steps into the cave, stopping no more than a spear's length away from Duff.

Duff crouched, one foot in front of the other, hammer raised above his shoulder. He wasn't a fool. He couldn't be a fool to have survived for so long as a soldier.

No, he was a realist. He knew just how fast and deadly a Wraith could be. Therefore, he had no illusions as to how this combat would end. He could only hope that he could create an opening so that Mari might be able to slip away.

"You will die here."

Duff stared at the Wraith, stunned. Though some of the words were difficult to understand because of the peculiar accent, Duff was able to comprehend the monster.

"Yes, that's a very strong possibility," Duff replied as calmly as he could, although his heart was beating so fast that he thought he was going to pass out.

"You do not fear death," said the Wraith, nodding as if he had just made a great discovery, still having made no move to come forward farther into the cave.

Apparently, the creature wanted to have a conversation. Duff was more than happy to accommodate him, enjoying whatever time he had left in this world while he searched for a solution to his dilemma.

"I don't," replied Duff, who then clarified. "I don't want to die, but I don't fear it."

The Wraith nodded again, although Duff couldn't tell for sure with the fog swirling around the figure. "The other humans I have killed have always begged before I cut their throats."

"I won't beg."

"Do you really want to try your hand against me? You took my comrade through deception. You will not do the same with me. Better just to accept your fate."

"Looks like I don't have much choice," Duff responded with a shrug. "Better to fight than to surrender. You might kill me, but it will be on my terms, not yours."

In the silence that followed, the Wraith appeared to consider what Duff had said, then shook his head as if he had reached an important decision. "Then I will kill you quickly. You have courage. You deserve a swift death."

Duff didn't know what to make of that comment. Should he be flattered? Should he thank the monster? He didn't have the chance to contemplate it further.

The Wraith burst forward, his movement so fast that Duff could barely track it. Still, he got his hammer square to his body, blocking the Wraith's slash. Duff thought that he was doing well until the blade in the Wraith's other hand sliced across his shoulder.

Gritting his teeth against the pain, Duff pivoted away from the bloody steel, swinging his hammer toward the Wraith's unprotected side. The creature leapt over the hammer with a remarkable dexterity and immediately rushed forward again, Duff having some difficulty keeping up with the Wraith's attacks. The retired sergeant survived the onslaught by blocking or avoiding the most dangerous attacks and ignoring the dozen bloody slices that welled up with a deep red on his arms and across his chest.

The wounds were shallow. He would live. For now.

"You will die, human," said the Wraith, stepping back,

making sure that he continued to block the entrance to the cave, not wanting either of his prey to have the chance to bolt like a hare.

"You're probably right," said Duff, seemingly unconcerned by the possibility.

Before he could get out the rest of what he wanted to say, a streak of steel shot right by his head. Mari's throw wasn't perfect, but it was good enough, the dagger spinning through the air and slicing across the side of the Wraith's throat.

Not enough to kill the beast, the cut no worse than what Duff might do if he were trying to shave without a mirror. Even so, it was enough to distract the creature, and it was the unanticipated though very much appreciated chance that he couldn't afford to lose.

Duff jumped forward, smashing his hammer into the Wraith's hip, hearing the bones crack as he did so. For good measure, he drove his dagger in between the creature's lower ribs, just to give the collapsing Wraith something else to worry about.

Then he reached behind him, grasped Mari's hand, and ran out into the fog, hoping that no more of the Wraiths waited for them along the cliffs.

Duff and Mari ran as fast as they could, which wasn't very fast, more like a trot, the fog thick and threatening, slowing them down, Duff's bad knees not helping. Duff didn't mind. They needed to be careful. Putting some distance between them and the two Wraiths was good. Silence and another place to hole up even better.

Duff was trying to recall every aspect of Benyen's property, having visited more times than he could remember. The house was too large and had too many windows for it to be of any use.

It was also in the direction they had come from. The barn had too many entrances. He couldn't defend them all. The pens were too open.

Mari started pulling him toward the east. "Where are we going?"

"Just follow me."

Duff had little choice as no good solution came to mind. Besides, she was the one who had gotten them past the second Wraith. As they made their way through the fog, he convinced her to slow down. Mari, anxious, wanted to move as fast as she could, desperate to get out of the open. Duff stopped her every few steps, worrying about what might be around them, what they might miss or give away if they moved too swiftly.

It made for slower going. But better slow than to be taken by another of the creatures in the fog.

It wasn't long before they walked through a copse, Mari leading them with her unerring sense of direction to a small cottage built into a cliff that was really no more than a shed, the structure falling in on itself. That didn't bother Duff in the least.

The roof still appeared to be solid, not thatch but wood beams packed tightly together and filled with dirt, thick grass growing on top of it. The stone walls were still strong. Best of all, there were no windows and much of the doorway was blocked by a large pile of rubble.

"How did you find this place?" asked Duff as they scrambled over the stones that rose to his chest.

"I like to explore," Mari replied, sitting against the back wall, leaning her head against the cold stone as if this was nothing more than a regular day for her.

"Were you exploring today? Is that why you missed the bell?"

"Maybe," Mari replied reluctantly.

Duff nodded. "We'll keep that between us. How does that sound?"

"Thanks."

Duff peered out from the doorway, looking for any hint of movement in the fog. Nothing. What he wouldn't give for a storm right about now. It would drive out the fog and the Wraiths with it.

"Your father teach you how to throw a dagger?"

Mari nodded, then grinned. "Said I was a natural."

"He was right. If you weren't, we'd both be dead."

Duff glanced to the left. Of course, there was still a good chance that they both still could die.

Four shapes had appeared, positioning themselves in a semicircle around the cottage, the figures drifting in and out of the swirling fog. As one, the four stepped forward, or rather two stepped forward. The two in the center hobbled.

Duff shook his head in amazement. The two Wraiths he had encountered in the cave already were back on their feet. Clearly, their injuries were severe. The first Wraith he had taken down with blows to both knees could barely stand. The second leaned to the left side, trying to keep his weight off his shattered right hip, one clawed hand pressing against the wound in his side. Yet there he was.

He couldn't see the Wraiths' faces, but he didn't need to. He could feel the hate radiating from them.

The Wraiths wanted another chance at him and Mari. So be it. This time, however, the Wraiths would have to come for them while they were in a more defensible position, and that would give him an advantage that he hadn't enjoyed before.

Duff prepared himself for the charge. It didn't come from the direction that he had expected.

The Wraith to his far left glided through the fog, blades in each hand. Duff acted without even thinking, swinging his hammer and hitting a rock that was on top of the pile that blocked the doorway. The stone shot through air, batted with a shocking accuracy and striking the Wraith in the forehead. The creature crumpled to the ground, not moving for several seconds before it slowly tried to push itself up, then slumped back to the dirt, groaning, unable to get his bearings.

"Did you plan on doing that?" whispered Mari, who peeked around the pile of rocks, a broad grin splitting her usually serious countenance.

"Would you believe me if I said yes?"

"No, I wouldn't."

"Good for you," said Duff. "Just as sharp as the blade with which you're so skilled."

Duff shifted his attention to the right. The Wraith who had been standing there was gone. The heavy thumps on the roof and the dirt that sifted down between the beams revealed the creature's location.

For almost a minute, the Wraith walked and jumped above them, seeking a way in. Then he appeared in front of the cottage again, having jumped down without making a sound. Despite the age of the cabin, the roof was still in excellent shape. Lucky for them, thought Duff.

With no other options, Duff assumed that the Wraiths would attack through the doorway. He might kill one of them. Maybe two of the monsters if he was lucky. But not all three who still stood. And not if the one who was struggling to regain his feet rejoined the fight.

"You have any more throwing knives, Mari?" Duff asked.

"I just had the one," she replied. "My dad said I was too dangerous with them. Better I just have one at a time."

Duff nodded. After seeing her accuracy, that made good sense. Although if they survived this combat he planned on talking with Benyen about that. This young lady should be carrying as many knives as she could.

Desperate times called for desperate measures. He pulled

two daggers from the sheaths on his thigh. They were the smallest he carried and a bit longer than what Mari probably was used to. Even so, he was certain that she would make good use of them. She was a natural after all. He handed them to her without taking his eyes from the Wraiths.

"You have earned yourself the right to live, human," said the Wraith Duff had spoken with before he had injured the creature's hip. Imagining the pain that he must be feeling, Duff didn't know how the Wraith could still be on his clawed feet.

"That's very kind of you," he replied from behind the pile of rubble. "Thank you."

Mari looked at him as if he were playing the fool. Duff shrugged. The Wraiths might be trying to kill them, but there was no reason to be impolite.

"Enjoy the time that you have left, human. We will be back for you. We will not forget you. Count on it."

Silence fell over the small clearing then, the fog billowing as if it were being stirred by a giant hand, Duff staring out into the mist, hoping to glimpse any movement. Yet there was nothing to be seen. The Wraiths had disappeared into the mist.

Even so, Duff didn't sleep that night, staying back within the doorframe, his eyes seeking to pierce both the darkness and the fog, drawn to the slightest sound, the slightest movement. He didn't breathe easy until the sun began to rise, the warm reddish glow revealing that the fog was moving back toward the north.

Even then, he and Mari remained within the cottage until every wisp of greyish white had drifted away.

They were lucky to be alive.

He smiled when the warmth of the rising sun hit him. A saying from his former Sergeant in the Royal Guard ran through his mind: "You make your own luck, because no one else is going to make it for you."

Declan had so many sayings that Duff could never remember them all. But there was always some truth to them.

For a brief moment, he wondered how that crabby bastard who was difficult to like but impossible not to love was doing. The man had made it his mission in life to ensure that every one of the soldiers he commanded did exactly as he instructed exactly how he wanted it done. Duff wouldn't be alive now if not for the discipline and precision Declan demanded.

And once again, Declan had been right. He and Mari had made their own luck against the Wraiths, and they were still alive because of it.

CHAPTER TWO
A NEW START

"Was there ever a time when you thought that this would be possible?" asked Aislinn Winborne.

She rode on the back of Astuta. The Griffon had befriended her after rescuing her from the collapsing Temple of the Ghoules, the link between the two growing during the last few months thanks to their many flights together. Although the Caledonians had decimated the Ghoule Legions in the Winter Pass, there were still a large number of the creatures to be dealt with in the Shattered Peaks, and she much preferred that work to what was required of her as the Lady of the Southern Marches.

"What do you mean?" Bryen Keldragan asked.

Aislinn's eyes narrowed, one eyebrow rising. Her Protector seemed to have an almost uncontrollable desire and ability to make the simplest things more difficult than they needed to be, just like this conversation.

"You know exactly what I mean," she countered, her eyes gleaming.

"I don't know that I do. Do you mean with respect to Caledonia? The Ghoules? The Weir?"

"Bryen ..."

There was a touch of friendly menace in Aislinn's voice, which meant that he was beginning to aggravate her. A skill at which he excelled, though one that he had learned should be used judiciously and at the right time. And clearly, based on the look that Aislinn was giving him, now was not the right time.

"Sorry, force of habit." He smiled at Aislinn, then turned his gaze back to the Weir, one hand gripping tightly to Banshee's feathers, the other stroking her golden neck as they glided along the boundary of the magical barrier. He was using the Talent and the Seventh Stone to check the Weir's structure, making sure that the weave was just as strong as it had been when he had put it in place a few months before.

"Maybe you should come up with a less irritating habit."

"As you command, my Lady."

Aislinn couldn't stop herself from smiling, although she chose not to return the playful banter. They had spent the last few weeks preparing for their journey with little time to talk of anything else.

"So was there a time when you thought that this would be possible?" she repeated.

Bryen continued to examine his creation -- well, not his entirely, the Ten Magii assisting him of course -- checking the weave, looking for any hitch that would suggest a weakness. He had spoken with Viktor Keldragan, the spirit of his uncle, only the night before, who assured him that he had nothing to fear. Still, he had wanted to inspect it for himself. Just to be certain.

"You mean that we'd be able to do what we're about to do?" he responded, clearly distracted.

"Yes," Aislinn replied. "Even after all that you and I had a hand in during the last few months, that we'd be able to make a fresh start."

The list of meaningful events really was quite extensive as it ran through her mind. Ending the reign of Marden Beleron and freeing the gladiators. Reaching the Sanctuary and reconstructing the Weir. Entering the Lost Land, killing the Ghoule Overlord, and gaining control over the Curse. Stopping the Ghoules' second invasion before the beasts could reach the Breakwater Plateau and flood the Kingdom.

"I was hopeful," Bryen admitted as he continued to examine the Weir. "But not confident, not if I'm being completely honest. I thought the odds would catch up to us eventually. They still might."

Bryen had a lingering fear that he'd made a mistake when working with the Ten Magii to rebuild the Weir. That the magical construction was all going to unravel and allow the Ghoules remaining in the Lost Land to invade, which was why they were here now, flying above the Shattered Peaks to the west. He needed to be certain of his work.

But he realized that it was wasted effort and wasted worry. Viktor was correct. The Weir was exactly what the Magus said it was. A new creation. Stronger than the last. Never to weaken. Never to fail.

"You have nothing to worry about. What you did, it will never be undone. The power will never fade thanks to the Seventh Stone."

"How did you know that I was worried about that?" asked Bryen, Aislinn seeming to have read his mind.

"Just a feeling."

"You think you know me pretty well," he said with a smile that also mixed in a gentle challenge.

"I do know you pretty well. Sometimes better than you know yourself."

"Because of the collar?" he asked, touching the silver metal that he still wore around his neck.

"At first, yes. But not now. Now I know you because I know you."

Her smile said everything that needed to be said as they turned away from the shimmering, almost translucent barrier that flashed when the sunlight struck it, Banshee heading to the south, Astuta right on her wing, having almost reached their destination.

A few more minutes passed before dozens of flattened stone peaks sticking out of a billowing fog came into view. Only a quarter of each sandstone pillar was visible, and for some not even that much, the stacks rising out of the floor of the Trench, the canyon a mile wide and just as deep.

Banshee and Astuta glided halfway into the Trench, then landed atop the stone pillar from which a blazing energy shot up into the air, down into the fog, and to the east and west for as far as the eye could see. Both Griffons shrieked a challenge. They sensed the black dragons that lurked far below them, living in nests dug out of the sides of the canyon and the stone pillars.

Despite their deadly nature, those creatures were of little concern to the Griffons, the black dragons rarely leaving their lairs. Rather, the Griffons kept watch for the Wyverns. Smaller versions of the black dragons, these animals were known to fly through the fog and then shoot back down, careful to never risk getting too close to the Griffons, although more than happy to taunt them from afar, perhaps even tempt them to come closer to where the larger number of Wyverns might have a better chance of earning a kill.

This was the first time that either Bryen or Aislinn had returned to the Sanctuary since that fateful day when Bryen had crushed the dreams of the Ghoule Overlord. Of course, he would be the first to admit that he could never have accomplished that task without the help of so many others.

After sliding off the backs of the Griffons, both he and Aislinn used the Talent to search for any threats that might be near. That done, neither moved for several minutes. They simply stood there, taking in the quiet. A strange serenity draped over the summit upon which the most important battle in the last thousand years of Caledonian history had taken place.

They then walked slowly across the stone surface that gleamed in the sunlight just like the stone used to construct the Aeyrie. The almost clear white rock was marred in more places than they could count by a large scattering of stains, many a reddish brown that had dried over time. Just as many if not more were a deep black, the dried blood mixing closest to the ten columns that surrounded the depression cut into the center of the sandstone pillar, the color reminiscent of the rust-colored pools of acid common in the Lost Land.

Neither felt the need to rush as they did their best to step around the reminders of that deadly fight. Their thoughts inevitably drifted back to all that they had to do to get Bryen to this summit so that he could rebuild the Weir and stop the Ghoule Overlord. The many clashes with the Ghoules, the Elders, and the black dragons. And, of course, all the people they had lost along the way, the friends who had sacrificed themselves for the greater good.

Walking through the entrance to the Sanctuary, Bryen's eyes flickered over the columns closest to the steps, reading the names of the Magii carved into the stone. Oraan Kvo. Clarissa Dumay. Mikayla Benewyn. Viktor Keldragan.

They and the other Ten Magii had given their lives after crafting the first Weir, and their spirits had aided Bryen in making the second. They were still with him thanks to the Seventh Stone.

Walking down the steps into the excavated oval, Bryen and Aislinn stopped for a few seconds, taking in the six pedestals upon which six of the Seven Stones rested, held in place by barely visible threads of gold wire. The center pedestal, reserved for the Seventh Stone, was empty, just as it should be.

The stream of energy that erupted from the Stones blasted into sky at a steady, unbreakable flow, the incredible power, which also permeated the hollow, making the hairs on their arms and the backs of their necks stand on end.

Bryen walked over to the center pedestal, taking the same position he had when he had worked with the Ten Magii to craft the Weir. Then he waited, Aislinn watching him from the base of the steps.

The power for the Weir continued to flow at a constant, unstoppable rate, the barrier itself remaining strong, glassy in appearance although solid, the shimmering whitish grey never fading, never flickering.

Finally, Bryen nodded, the tension that had been troubling him draining away. Both Viktor and Aislinn were correct. When he had last entered the Sanctuary, he had disrupted the flow because the Seventh Stone had joined with him. Now, his presence had no impact whatsoever.

He smiled. One less thing for him to worry about. He could leave Caledonia knowing that he had done all that he could to ensure the safety of the Kingdom against the Ghoules. Knowing as well that he could leave his past here and start fresh in the Territories.

"You know, he was proud of you," said Aislinn. "He might not have told you, knowing him he probably didn't, but he was."

"I know," said Bryen ambiguously. He still wasn't sure how he felt about the Magus because of their complicated past, still trying to come to grips with who Sirius truly was and the role that he had played in Bryen's life during the short time that he had known him. "I think that more than anything he was just pleased that we succeeded in stopping the Ghoules. That was his primary goal as soon as he assumed his position as Master of the Magii. In the end, he achieved it."

"You're right," Aislinn agreed, who walked up to him and

took one of his hands in her own. "He did care about you, though. He didn't always show it, in fact he probably didn't know how, but he did."

"I know." Bryen couldn't bring himself to admit that he had cared about Sirius as well, not really having any desire to delve deeper into those emotions. At least not now.

He was willing to admit to himself that he missed the old Magus, wishing he was still here with them. He had never really taken the time to process Sirius' death, always moving on to the next challenge until finally reaching the point where he now had the opportunity to contemplate the impact that Sirius had on him, both the good and the bad.

The Magus had done a lot for him. He had expected even more from Bryen, demanded it, in fact.

Sirius had stood ready to kill him if he had made the single mistake that would have allowed the Curse to corrupt him.

And when it proved necessary, when Bryen's life hung in the balance, the Ghoules pressing the Blood Company and Bryen struggling to craft the Weir, Sirius had stood against the Ghoule Overlord even though he knew that he was going to die, giving Bryen the extra minutes that he needed, sacrificing himself for his grandson.

"He was the hardest tutor I ever had," said Aislinn. "He was the cranky, irascible uncle I never had. He pushed me. Every day."

"I know, I was there for a part of it."

"There were times when I hated him." She could sense that Bryen was experiencing many of the same emotions that she was, and she hoped that talking about it would help him.

"Me too," Bryen replied in a soft voice.

"I loved him too."

"I don't know if I would go that far," murmured Bryen with a shy grin.

"Everything he did, he did for a reason."

"I can't dispute that."

"I know, you don't have to say it. He pushed me because of my skill as a Magus. He did the same to you because of what happened with the Seventh Stone. He wanted us both to succeed. For us."

"I know. But it wasn't just for us."

Aislinn nodded, unable to disagree. "For him as well. Sirius always had a larger goal. A larger purpose. Our success was his success. But there's nothing wrong with that."

"You're right. I just wish he had been more honest with us from the beginning. It would have made things easier."

"True," nodded Aislinn, her fingers gently rubbing Bryen's hand. "That would have been asking quite a lot from him, though. He was who he was."

"You're using my own words against me again," Bryen said with a smile.

"I am," Aislinn admitted. "Do you hate him?"

"No, I just feel sorry for him. For me as well. A part of me kind of wanted to spend more time with him once all this was done. There were some things that we needed to talk about. It would have helped both of us if we did. Now it's too late."

"I don't know that he'd be able to teach you much more about the Talent."

"Not with respect to the Talent." Sirius had been his grandfather. He would have liked to know the answers to dozens of questions he had about his family and himself. Viktor had provided those few details during their conversations that he could, but there was a thousand year gap that the dead Magus now tied to the Seventh Stone couldn't fill. Not wanting to dampen what had been a good day so far, Bryen shifted to a different topic, remembering too late that this issue had been a thorn in Aislinn's side since she had first told her father her decision. "Did your father try to convince you to stay again?"

"It was a very muted attempt this time," admitted Aislinn.

She had been thankful for that, not wanting to get into another argument with him. She had grown tired of her father's efforts to change her mind, subdued though they were most of the time, a few episodes more animated. "It would have been a much more difficult conversation if not for Noorsin's gentle guidance."

Her father had been badgering her ever since she had told him that she'd be accompanying Bryen, raising repeatedly her duties as the Lady of the Southern Marches, the responsibilities she needed to fulfill to her people and her Duchy. Then, inevitably, his argument for her staying shifted to how much he needed her in the Southern Marches followed by a host of other excuses to keep her in Caledonia.

She knew that he did it not only because of his sense of duty, but also because of his love for her. His fear for her safety. She had humored him as much as she could, at the same time deflecting each argument with a stronger argument of her own for her going to the Territories.

That hadn't stopped him from trying, though the energy of each attempt he made faded as her father began to understand why she needed to do this. Why she couldn't not do this.

He didn't want to hold her back. He was just afraid for her. Even more so, he was afraid for himself. Of what life would be like with her gone, if only for a time.

"You expected him to keep trying to keep me here, didn't you," said Aislinn, raising her sparkling eyes to his, the cold grey sending a delightful shiver through her.

"I did. I thought that his willingness to commission a ship that would take the Blood Company to the Territories was the fastest way for him to get me out of his hair."

"My father is sorry for what happened," Aislinn said, though she wasn't trying to defend her father. Everything had worked out in the end, better than she could have imagined, all because of her father's decision to make Bryen her Protector.

That still didn't excuse what he had done, however. That rash decision could never be forgotten and Bryen would never forgive him that.

"I remember the apology."

"You could be right," said Aislinn, having thought much the same herself, which was why she hadn't told her father that she would be going to the Territories until construction of the ship was well underway. "Or he could be trying to make amends."

"Do you really think so?" Bryen's tone suggested that he was quite skeptical.

Aislinn smiled. "I don't know. I do know that you still make him uncomfortable."

"That's his problem, not mine."

"I'm not suggesting otherwise."

"Are you sure you want to go?" Bryen asked, afraid to do so but needing to know, his worries, some real, some imagined, gaining too much traction in his head. They had not spoken about it since she had told him that she had accepted his offer, and that had been months past. "You know what you're leaving behind."

"I do know what I'm leaving behind," responded Aislinn, her voice hard now, challenging. Contained within that tone was the Magus who was almost as strong as Bryen in the Talent, the Vedra of the Pit.

"I do know what I'm leaving behind," she repeated, taking her hands from Bryen's and pulling on the shoulder straps of his leather armor so that they were nose to nose. "I also know what I'm gaining by going with you."

She then leaned forward, her lips brushing against Bryen's. Tentatively at first, then with more ardor, neither able to control the passion between them that was never far from the surface.

THE END OF CHAPTER TWO

To keep reading, go to PeterWachtBooks.com or Amazon.

LOOKING FOR MORE …

This short story is a prelude to the events in my new series *The Tales of the Territories* and is FREE to readers who receive my newsletter.

Learn more at PeterWachtBooks.com.

www.ingramcontent.com/pod-product-compliance
Lightning Source LLC
Chambersburg PA
CBHW070233200726

48293CB00005B/1597